BLINDLY ACQUITTED

PARANORMAL PRISON SERIES

KATIE MAY

EXPRESSO PUBLISHING, LLC

I'm honestly running out of people to dedicate my books to. So...to Kelsey from Chicago. I don't actually know a Kelsey from Chicago, but if you are her, then hi! This one is dedicated to you. I think this means we're best friends now.

CONTENTS

FOREWORD

This is a paranormal prison reverse harem romance and a sequel to Blindly Indicted. You should not read this book if you haven't read Blindly Indicted first. It is not suitable for anyone under the age of 18.

These men...

They're bloodthirsty psychopaths. They literally kill people with smiles on their faces. If that offends you in any way, then this book might not be for you. It contains strong language, scene of graphic violence, sexual situations, and flashbacks of assault.

Please take care of yourself. I would love for you to read my book, but if flashbacks of abuse and sexual assault are triggering for you, I would recommend putting this down. Your health and safety come first.

RECAP OF BLINDLY INDICTED

Here's a brief, *brief* recap of Blindly Indicted for those of you who need a tiny refresher! If you don't need one, skip to chapter one and enjoy!

Nina Doe has been kept in a mysterious compound her entire life until she escapes. She's blind but is able to see through the eyes of others. She is picked up by the supernatural police and is accused of killing an important council member, Raphael Turner. She is placed in Nightmare Penitentiary in a maze underneath the main prison known as the Labyrinth.

While there, she meets Kai (known as Blade to the inmates) who is her childhood best friend from the Compound. She also meets twin demons, Abel and Cain, a wolf shifter named Bronson, and a mage named Damien. She also becomes mated to the leader of a rival gang, Rion.

Obviously, all of the psychopaths fall in love with Nina, and she falls in love with them.

She ends up getting removed from the prison by another councilwoman, Alyssa Timmer. Alyssa reveals that she is the leader of the Compound and Nina's biological mom. She confesses that she has been experimenting on supernaturals to make them super soldiers and that Nina is a tribrid, a combination of angel, demon, and human genetics. Her father was human, her mother an angel, and they added demon DNA scientifically. While the experiment effectively turned Nina into a tribrid, it also took away her eyesight.

Alyssa also admits that Raphael Turner, the man that Nina was accused of killing, worked for the Compound as well and that when Nina fought off her attackers and escaped, Raphael's DNA ended up on Nina (which led to her being convicted) and that Alyssa was actually the one to kill him. Nina uses her powers to kill Alyssa and is taken into custody by the supernatural police once more, where she is sentenced to life in prison.

Back in the Labyrinth, she reunites with her guys and they propose to her.

She beat Nina up in the ring before being killed by Braelyn.

- **Alyssa Timmer** - a councilwoman and Nina's biological mom who ran the Compound. She is now dead. She killed Raphael Turner.

- **Raphael Turner** - the man Nina was originally accused of killing. He was a councilman and a member of the Compound. He was killed by Alyssa after Nina escaped.

- **Lionel Green** - a slimy councilman who used to pay Cain and Abel for sex before they escaped.

- **Narian Teres** - the leader of the assassin guild Damien worked for before he was sent to prison.

CHAPTER 1

NINA

The throne room has become not only my kingdom but my home. As we stand in the center of the room, my back to his chest, I allow the sensations and feelings he evokes within me to flood my system, my long lashes fluttering shut.

This…

Standing in his arms…

In *any* of their arms…

It's where I belong.

I don't need a kingdom built on blood, sweat, and tears. A kingdom shrouded in darkness and sin. A throne built from bones and stitched together with fear.

I just need them.

He brushes at the back of my neck before trailing his fingers down my arm. When he reaches my hand, he intertwines his fingers with mine, squeezing once.

As always, flames spark in my veins at the menial touch and liquid heat pools in my stomach.

"Guess who?" His husky voice curls around me until I'm practically drowning in it.

"The mailman?" I ask immediately, conjuring up images of the comedy Rion made me watch the other day. Well, he watched it, and I merely looked through his eyes. It was a hilarious story about a wife who was cheating on her husband with the—you guessed it—mailman.

"Ha. Ha. Ha. Very funny, Bambi." Abel releases me, and instantly, my body cries at the loss of connection. I turn in the direction of my sunshine twin and burrow my face in his neck. I breathe in his sweet scent as a low chuckle reverberates through his chest. He drops his hand to my lower back, the heat from his skin searing me through my white dress. "There is no way a mailman can get down here."

"Not true!" Rion pipes in from somewhere...above me? He must be lying on the rafters again. "Booty Snap used to work for the postal service before he ended up here."

"There's someone named Booty Snap?" I ask softly, cocking my head to the side. "Does he have a good... err...booty?"

Abel growls and pulls me back against his chest once more. I allow my head to rest snugly on his shoulder, grazing the skin of his neck with my teeth.

"Don't talk about another man's booty," he warns darkly, and Rion, above me, breaks into raucous laughter.

When his laughter finally begins to subside, he manages to stutter out, "Y-You said booty."

I don't need working eyes to know that Abel will be rolling his.

"Why are you here, Shifter?" the demon asks as he peppers languid kisses up and down my neck. Lightning shoots through me as I melt against him.

"I thought you were supposed to be training Nina, *not* kissing her," Rion points out helpfully, his voice sounding from directly in front of me. I don't even jump at his sudden arrival. I've become used to Rion's ninja ways.

"But I like kissing," I say with a giggle as I enthusiastically press my lips to the base of Abel's throat. His pulse skips a beat as a low groan escapes him.

"I like kissing too." Rion takes a step closer until they're caging me in—an impenetrable wall of solid, well-defined muscle. "But only if I'm kissing you, Buttercup. And your titties. Can I say titties? Or do you prefer mangos? Squash? Gah, not squash. Abort mission! I will not be kissing any squash, thank you very much. I will kiss Damien though, but that's only because we're totally a ship. Dion for the win! We masturbated together, so that practically makes us husband and husband." Rion's monologue is cut off by a rather girly squeal, and I immediately push my awareness into Abel's mind.

It's a gift I've had since I was a young child. Though my eyes may be blind, I'm able to see more clearly than any other person I know. I can literally *enter* another person's head and use their eyes...and their other senses, though I'm not as skilled at that yet.

Damien has his knife held to Rion's throat as the eccentric shifter releases peals of hearty laughter. As always, the two are as different as night and day.

Rion is only a few years older than me, and his tan skin reminds me of burnt porcelain, his arms sleeved in intricate tattoos. The most recent one, applied only a couple of weeks ago and still red-rimmed, depicts an unfurling yellow flower with exactly six petals.

A buttercup.

His straight brown brows shadow even darker eyes, as dark as obsidian. His brown hair is buzzed on both sides with artful waves at the top.

Damien, on the other hand, looks as if he stepped off of a magazine cover. His dark hair is slicked away from his aristocratically handsome face. Everything about this man is perfectly proportionate—from his high cheekbones to chiseled jawline to smooth brows currently furrowed in annoyance. He wears a crisp black suit that clings to his lean frame, emphasizing the muscles he keeps hidden. He's smooth, elegant, and so incredibly handsome that my mind goes numb and my thoughts turn sluggish. He's a powerful mage with the ability to conjure basic elements and use healing magic. He is also able to procure rare items for those of us inside the prison, such as new clothes, speciality foods, and games…though I don't believe he uses his magic to get them. As a skilled assassin, he has numerous contacts throughout the world who help him smuggle stuff inside.

"Damien," I say with a smile, and he turns his head slightly to pierce me with his brilliant sea-blue gaze. Immediately, he slides the knife back down his sleeve and strides towards me, easily removing me from Abel's embrace and into his own.

"Angel," he breathes in a voice he only reserves for me. To the rest of the world, he appears desensitized, almost impassive, but I see the man brimming with passion underneath. Nothing but warmth emanates from his eyes, slowly melting the ice encased around his heart. He considers himself frigid, incapable of love and affection, but he proves to me every day how wrong that notion is. "Excuse me for a second, my love. I need to go gut Rion."

"Rude," Rion huffs, crossing his arms over his chest. "If you wanted me out of my clothes, all you had to do was ask, not threaten me with murder." When Damien freezes, his eyes frosting over, and Rion's smirk grows, I know I need to de-escalate the situation before Damien quite literally decides to kill my shifter mate. Rion loves pushing his buttons—but only when I'm around to be a buffer.

Pushing myself onto my tiptoes, I press my lips to the

corner of Damien's mouth. Instantly, he relaxes, arms banding around me and evoking an irrevocable sense of safety and security. "No murder."

Damien sighs disgruntledly but concedes. With another smile, I kiss his lips again and dance backwards, pulling out of Abel's head and embracing my customary darkness. I've learned to accept the monsters that lurk in the darkest corners. Heck, I've even learned to *love* them. It's not the dark I'm afraid of. Not anymore.

"Are you here to check on us?" I tease, jumping on the balls of my feet and holding my hands up like a prized fighter. "See if we're actually training? Kicking butt?"

"You can kick my butt anytime," Rion says suggestively, earning him another whack from Damien.

When we discovered the truth about my heritage—that Councilwoman Alyssa was actually my biological mother and that I was part angel, part demon, *and* part human—my guys insisted that I needed to train. Fortunately, I have two demons of my own to teach me how to wield my darker side. Damien has helped me with my angel lineage, despite being a mage himself. Now, his nickname for me takes on an entirely different meaning. Even Braelyn, Rion's second in command and one of my closest female friends, has been helping with my training.

"Today, you're going to go inside Rion's head and not only use his senses, but hear his thoughts as well." Damien speaks candidly, almost nonchalantly, as if he has no doubt in his mind that I'll be able to achieve the impossible.

I'm able to speak telepathically to my men, but so far, I haven't been able to hear any of the thoughts they don't wish to share with me. I'm not even sure if I want to invade their privacy like that. There are some things that deserve to be secret.

My hesitation must be evident, for Damien sighs once more. I hear the familiar clack of his polished loafers against the cement floor before he comes to a stop in front of me, the heat from his body almost palpable. He places his hand beneath my chin and guides my face up towards his.

"You need to learn how to hone your powers," he says curtly. "You're unlike anything we've ever seen before."

"Shit, man, you can't just say that to a girl," Abel groans from somewhere behind him.

"You're different," Damien continues, ignoring Abel's interruption. "And that makes you a target."

"I'm…different?" I whisper, rubbing at my arms. At first, my differences lay with my sight, or lack thereof. It's unnerving to know that there are even more things that set me apart from the others.

"Fucking hell," Abel gripes beneath his breath. And then, voice muffled, he adds, "Compliment her. Quickly."

"And you have nice hair," Damien finishes, as if that one compliment can take the sting out of his previous words.

"There's nothing wrong with being different," Rion breaks in. "I'm different. Actually, my mom says I'm so different that we had to do ten different paternity tests to determine who my true father was. Spoiler alert—he called himself the human bungee cord."

"Please, Angel." Damien's voice is soft—too soft for the others to hear. It's a voice meant solely for me. "I can't sleep knowing that you could be in danger."

I release a ragged breath, shoulders physically deflating like a storm has swept the tension away in one fatal wave. "If Rion agrees." The last thing I want to do is take away his free will. If Rion doesn't want me sifting through his private thoughts, then I won't. It's as simple as that. I love him enough to respect his decision.

Of course, I shouldn't have been worried.

"I've been wanting you in my head for months now," Rion says excitedly. "I've been fantasizing about this moment. Penetrate me, Buttercup. Penetrate me nice and deep."

"Am I the only normal one here?" Abel murmurs as flames immediately engulf both of my cheeks. Thanks to the men, I've been better at understanding…err…sexual innuendos. They never fail to make me blush scarlet, though.

"If you're sure…" I trail off warily, stomach twisting into dozens of tight, intricate knots, before I close my eyes and focus on the awarenesses around me. Each one is a brilliant portal of light, and all I have to do is tug on the one I want. Damien's can only be described as cold, a frozen tundra one can become lost in. Abel's reminds me distinctly of sunshine, while Rion's is a combination of the two, evoking feelings of joy from deep within me. It's his I travel to, until I'm able to see through his eyes.

His gaze is trained firmly on me, as if there's nowhere else he can even look. It's unnerving to be the sole focus of his gaze, but also empowering. Through his vision, I can see my thick black hair cascading loosely down my back in soft waves. Damien has procured a white dress for me that cinches around my waist before spilling down to my calves. All of the men have a strange fascination with me in white dresses. And to be honest, I like the way the color contrasts with my onyx hair. I've never cared about my looks before, but I find that I want to look beautiful for these men.

Despite that, I could be wearing a burlap sack and they'd still look at me as if I'm an ethereal goddess.

Taking another deep breath, I focus on his senses.

What does he hear?

What does he smell?

What does he feel?

Abel's incessant chattering reaches me, followed immediately by Damien's curt, "Shut the fuck up before I kill you." I can hear Rion's heartbeat as if it were my own, each consecutive pound rushing through me.

The familiar scents of mildew and mold assault my senses, though I shouldn't expect anything else from the Labyrinth, especially in the fight ring where we're currently residing. Damien was able to barter for vanilla-scented candles for our personal quarters, though, after I mentioned they were my favorite scent.

Finally, I'm aware of the soft material of Rion's shirt caressing his broad chest and stomach. I'm also aware of a piercing pain in his lower region, almost as if all the blood has rushed to his...

Through his eyes, I watch my cheeks turn crimson once more at the realization that Rion is turned on.

Focus, Nina! I tell myself sternly as I dig deeper, drilling a hole into Rion's essence and soul. Bright lights engulf my awareness as I'm swept away in the riptide that is Rion's mind. Image after image bombard me, each one a depiction of me in some shape or form. The first time we made love. Our first kiss. Last night, when I slept in his bed and he held me to him.

His voice reaches me, seeming to come from the end of a tunnel. It caresses my mind, each lick as soft as a moth's wing.

She's so beautiful. So, so beautiful. How did I get so lucky? Fuck, I love her. I love her so damn much. Why is she blushing? She's so adorable when she blushes. I want her to blush every second of every day. Maybe I'll just paint her cheeks red. Is that weird? That's weird. Don't be weird, Rion, we talked about this. Normal is the new normal. Wait. I don't think that's how the saying goes. Maybe I should ask Abel? Nah. I'll ask Damien. It always pisses him off when I ask stupid questions. Oh! If he kills me, can Nina kiss it better? Maybe I'll let him cut off my cock just to get her lips down there...and you're doing it again. Thinking crazy. Remember? Normal. N. O. R. M—Oh! Shiny! I love that ring on her finger. Our ring. She's ours, and I'll kill anyone who tries to take her from us.

I pull myself into my own body with a gasp, my head spinning at the sheer amazement of what I just did. I heard Rion's thoughts! A giddy laugh escapes my lips unbidden as I gleefully clap my hands together.

"I did it!" I whoop enthusiastically. In a span of seconds, I'm across the room and jumping into Rion's arms. He releases a startled grunt as I tackle him to the ground, planting kisses on his cheeks and forehead. "I did it!" I repeat, pushing up onto my elbows above him. He tenderly brushes at a long strand of my black hair, placing it behind my ear.

"So you know," he whispers, voice surprisingly somber.

"Know what?"

"Know how much I love you."

My heart stutters once before flatlining as I behold the beautiful, kindred soul beneath me. From the very beginning, when I thought he was nothing but a cat named Mr. Scruffles, he managed to slay me with the expertise of a seasoned killer. I recognize a bit of myself in him—a bit of the loneliness that no longer clings to me like a second skin. We've not only found love but a family, one that I'm so incredibly grateful for. Piece by piece, these men have slowly mended the shattered shards the Compound left behind, making me feel whole.

"I love you too," I say with a jovial smile. My smile is so big, my cheeks hurt, but when he pulls me into a hug, the impending dread consumes me and my smile fades.

Fear momentarily stills my lungs, making breathing

impossible. From experience, every good thing is immediately followed by something horrendously bad. Life gives... but it also takes away.

And what exactly does fate plan to destroy this time around?

CHAPTER 2

KAI

I made my throne out of bones, woven together by the tears and blood of my enemies. Not literally, of course —I'm not Damien—but metaphorically. Everything I have in life, every power I possess in this godforsaken prison, comes from hard work. Dedication.

Murder.

I don't like to use that term. *Murder.* It conjures images of a blade slicing open a pale neck until blood wells or a body sprawled on a guillotine, waiting for the blade to drop. I don't do that. At least not anymore.

As I sit on the high-back chair, my mind drifts to Nina, as it often does whenever I have a moment to myself. Her beautiful face consumes my every thought, and I can't stop the dopey smile from cleaving my face in two. Before any of my subjects can catch a glimpse, I mask it into one of careful indifference.

I stare down my nose at Marcus, a vampire whose lips are currently curled into a sneer. Beside him, restrained by two of my men, is Rowan, a shifter.

Bronson, my chief enforcer, stands directly beside me, his hands clasped behind his back and a fierce expression on his face. He's the largest man in this prison by far, his entire body hewn from stone. The blond scruff on his jaw combined with his tousled hair gives him an intimidating appearance, like a wolf seconds away from pouncing. Not a bad analogy, considering the fact he's a shadow wolf.

Cain stands on the other side of me, his trademark scowl firmly in place. It never ceases to amaze me how different he is from his cheerful twin, Abel. They've both endured similar hardships, but while Abel's has made him embrace life with gusto and wild abandonment, Cain's has turned him bitter. Only Nina is capable of cracking the tough outer shell he wears around himself like armor.

Tensions between the two groups have been...strained. And that's putting it fucking mildly. It's hard to eradicate years upon years of hatred and bigotry. For as long as I can remember, my gang and Rion's have been at each other's throats, quite literally. We killed their people for sport, and they, ours. But we only recently decided to disband the gangs and come together in happy fucking harmony.

"What's the meaning of all of this?" I drawl lazily as I stare between the two men. Marcus's bleached blond hair is streaked with blood from a wound on his head. His eyes are solid red, his pupils nowhere to be seen, as if blood has eaten away at the darkness. Rowan, similarly, is sporting numerous bruises, his face mottled and scarred. When my men ran into the throne room, explaining that two of my subjects had gotten into a brutal fight, I'd been enraged. Fighting should only happen in the ring.

We're not fucking animals, despite the warden's claim otherwise.

"This fucking asshole disrespected me," Marcus snarls,

fangs elongating and dripping with salvia. He looks feral, and a surge of satisfaction courses through me. It may be fucked up—hell, I'm pretty sure it's all kinds of fucked up—but I love seeing the monsters in this prison lose their control. But like any pet owner, I'm willing to put them down if they step out of line. If they bite too quickly.

And that's my favorite fucking job in the world.

"Marcus, Marcus, Marcus." I click my tongue as I slowly rise to my feet. "You need to use your words. How did our dear friend, Rowan, disrespect you?"

Normally, Rion would be here with me to handle these petty disputes, but he was adamant that he stalk Nina. I believe his exact words were, "If I don't stalk her, someone else might, and then I'll have to cut off his balls and feed them to myself."

Crazy fucker.

As I step closer to the feuding men, I'm slightly disappointed when they don't cower away in terror. Fuck. Am I losing my touch? That won't do. I have a prison to run and a woman to protect. I can only accomplish both when I'm evoking fear in my enemies.

I'm not evil. At least I don't think I am. I don't necessarily enjoy inflicting pain on others. Sure, I like killing evil men in need of a firm hand…a firm hand wrapped around their throats and squeezing until the life drains from their eyes.

But I'm not Damien. I don't get hard from the kill like that crazy fucker does. For the longest time, only stabbing his knife into someone's stomach got him erect. It was all kinds of fucked up.

I do what needs to be done to protect my home, which happens to be the basement of a supernatural prison. We call it the Labyrinth. The hallways are constantly shifting and changing, making escape impossible. I heard a rumor that a guard got stuck down here when he couldn't remember the way out. He was quickly torn apart by the monsters he locked away.

"I didn't disrespect nobody," the shifter, Rowan, exclaims in a heavy Southern drawl.

"You fucked my girl!" Marcus screams, spit flying.

Once more, I tsk my tongue, shaking my head in disapproval. "Is that true, Rowan? Very disrespectful." My smile grows when his face pales and he actually staggers back a step.

"Marcus told me that he wants to fuck Nina," Rowan blurts, side-eyeing the vampire. Marcus freezes, face draining of color, as Bronson begins to growl, low and threatening. I wasn't even aware he'd transformed into his wolf. "That's not true!" he yells.

"Cain." I nod towards the sex demon, who steps closer, face bereft of expression.

"Tell me...do you think of fucking Nina?" he whispers, pushing his power into those words. As always, my cock hardens instantly, and I have a vivid image of taking Nina against the wall as I pound into her sweet, perfect pussy.

Marcus is sweating, eyes wide with panic as he attempts to fight off the compulsion. But he can't fight against us. No one can. "I...I..."

Cain sends another burst of pure lust, and I just barely hold in my groan. Rowan, on the other hand, is not as skilled as I am and begins palming his erect cock through his pants.

"I...I...I dream of fucking that sweet ass," Marcus blurts, practically salivating. "If I could get her alone for even a second, I would take what I want from her, whether she wants it too or not. I would fuck her until she's screaming and crying, begging for release. I would play with those perfect breasts that I've fantasized about for months. I would make her mine."

Red consumes the entirety of my vision, and my breathing saws in and out. How dare he? The thought of anyone hurting, even touching, Nina sends me spiraling down a direction I don't know I can escape from.

Before I can react, before I can punish this man for his horrible words, his eyes widen in panic and horror. He desperately touches his stomach where a blade is now protruding from his skin.

Without preamble, he collapses to the ground in a pool of his own blood.

Damien stands above the pathetic excuse for a man, a satisfied smile on his face as he removes his blade from Marcus's back.

"Did you hear what he said?" Cain hisses, hands balled into fists. His skin is darkening like fissures of lava are expanding the length of his body. Tiny horns sprout from his head as he wrestles for control.

Damien blinks innocently. "What did he say?"

"You didn't...hear what...um...he said?" Rowan stutters, backing away from the deranged serial killer and assassin. Smart move.

"He just bothered me." Damien shrugs nonchalantly as he begins to hum softly beneath his breath. With one final look at the crazy man, Rowan runs from the throne room like his ass is on fire. Again, smart move.

I exchange a wary glance with Bronson, still in his wolf form. If Damien knew this vampire was talking about raping Nina, his death wouldn't have been quick. Oh no. It would've been immensely painful—hours of unrelenting torture until he begged for death. And, honestly? I would've helped.

There are not a lot of things that I hate, but rapists are one of them. And people who threaten Nina.

Forcing myself to regain control of my turbulent

emotions, I nod towards Cain and Damien. "Get rid of the body."

Without needing further instruction, Damien makes quick work of dragging the bloody bag of shit towards the back room, where he'll drop it down a makeshift laundry shoot we created years ago. Instead of a laundry room, however, the body will land directly in an incinerator. Cain gets on his hands and knees and quickly scrubs down the cement tiles until they're practically shining. Normally, we have people who do this for us, but not one of us wants to risk our girl walking in on something she shouldn't see.

Perfect timing, for seconds later, Nina rushes into the room with Rion and Abel.

As always, my throat turns dry when I feast my eyes upon the sheer perfection that is Nina Doe, the woman who will soon be my wife.

I drop my gaze to the brilliant ring flashing on her finger, my lips tilting upwards.

"Cain! Kai! Bronson!" she says with a bright smile, stopping first at the sex demon, who is closest. The harshness of his features immediately soften when he sets eyes on her. In that moment, he's not a killer or even a monster—he's hers.

"Trouble, what are you doing here?" he asks softly as he kisses her. She melts against him, and my smile widens. At one point, the sight of the two of them together would've made me unbearably jealous. But now, I realize that she's exactly what my brothers need. She deserves all the fucking love in the world. And our love? Our love is explosive.

"I wanted to see how you guys were doing, of course," she explains with another cheerful giggle. We try to keep her as far away from this shit as possible, despite the fact she's the unofficial queen of the Labyrinth. Still, I can't deny that her presence soothes something inside of me, something jagged and hard.

Bronson whines, demanding her attention, and she drops to her knees beside the immense beast. Most people would be terrified of Bronson's wolf form. He's nearly as tall as Nina, with red, piercing eyes, pitch-black fur, and abnormally sharp teeth. But instead of seeing him as a monster, Nina sees him as...as Bronson. As the giant of a man who cares for her more than anything else in the world. A man who wants nothing but a family of his own, a family with Nina.

After hugging the terrifying wolf senseless, Nina stumbles to her feet, using Bronson's head to steady herself, and turns her blind gaze onto me.

"Kai," she whispers dreamily as she rushes forward, jumping into my arms. I tighten my grip on her, knowing that only here, only in my arms, no harm will ever come to her. If I could, I would tie her to me and never let her leave.

"Hey, baby," I whisper, kissing her nose, both of her cheeks, and then her lips.

"Are you hungry?" she asks anxiously as she runs her fingers through my shoulder-length hair. I just barely hold in the moan that wants to escape. Fuck, it feels so good when she does that. Too good. "You guys didn't eat today." She lifts her head from my neck to address the room as a whole, and I very reluctantly set her on her feet.

We left before she awoke to oversee the prison. Abel was assigned to watch over her until this afternoon, when we could all get together and treat our girl to a home cooked meal. Well, a Braelyn-cooked meal.

"Did *you* eat?" Bronson growls sharply, and I turn just as he buttons up his pants. Abel, almost absently, hands him his flannel shirt, and he shrugs it over his shoulders, leaving it unbuttoned.

"Fuck, did you forget to feed her, Abel?" I turn towards

the trickster demon, fire spewing from my eyes. He holds his hands up immediately, like a prisoner approaching a cop.

"Of course he fed me!" Nina slaps my chest with another giggle. "I'm not a pet."

"No, you're Nina. The love of my existence," I say immediately, and I relish the adorable blush that climbs up her neck and to her cheeks.

The door to the backroom opens and closes, and Damien steps out, wiping blood from his dagger. As always, he's immaculately dressed in a form-fitting suit and crisp white shirt, not a speck of blood on him. I don't have the faintest idea how he's able to make every kill so…clean. I'm actually a little jealous.

His eyes gravitate immediately towards Nina, surveying her body for injuries, as if she got hurt in the ten minutes he's been away. I can't begrudge him, since I often do the exact same thing. Seemingly satisfied there's not a hair out of place, he nods seriously and rests against the wall, arms crossed and blade hanging languidly from his fingers.

The door to the throne room is wrenched open suddenly, and a red-faced man stumbles in.

"We're done for today," I growl immediately, glaring at the shrewd, unassuming man. I recognize him as Ben, a warlock who works in the kitchens. He was a chef before he was arrested for the murder of his wife's secret lover.

"I need to talk to you guys." He bows his head subserviently as his eyes flicker from me to Nina. "My king. My queen."

"He's so adorable," Rion coos, bending at his waist to stare into the man's eyes. "Can we keep him as a human pet? I've never kept a human pet before. I promise I'll take good care of him. Feed him. Give him water. Scoop out his poop. Please, Buttercup? Please?" He bounces excitedly from foot to foot, pure insanity reflecting from his gaze, but Nina simply rolls her eyes.

"Rion, my love, you can't keep humans as pets."

If anyone else were to say that to him, he would stab him or her before that person could even catch their bearings. Only Nina is allowed to call him out on his insanity.

"Please. I need to talk to you." Ben's voice wobbles as Nina gracefully walks forward, eyes concerned.

"What's the matter?"

"Baby," I warn, stepping towards her.

I see the blade only a second later. Releasing a roar of fury, I tackle Nina to the ground just as the blade catches the side of my stomach. The rest of the men lunge at Ben as I huddle protectively over a wide-eyed, trembling Nina.

"What...?" she asks breathlessly as I hiss through my teeth.

I don't have to look to know that Ben is being dragged away to Damien's torture chamber.

Someone tried to *kill* Nina. If I had gotten there a second later...

"Are you okay? Are you hurt?" I ask desperately, pulling myself onto my elbows to survey her body. If he hurt her...

"I'm fine. What's going on?" Her voice trembles with fear, and I hate that. I fucking hate that. She should never be scared when she's with me.

"Bambi!" Abel practically throws me to the side, and he and Cain crowd around a pale-faced Nina. I clench my teeth against the pain as I stare at the blood staining my gray shirt. Fuck, that hurts like a bitch.

Nina releases a sudden intake of breath, and it's only then that I realize she's in my head currently, using my eyes to see.

"Kai, what happened?" she crawls towards me, and Abel and Cain follow behind her.

"I'm okay, baby. I'm okay." I gather her in my arms,

ignoring the pull of my skin, and hold her close to my rapidly beating heart.

Someone tried to *kill her*. There's no doubt in my mind that that blade was meant for her.

I'll set this entire fucking prison on fire if that's what's necessary to keep Nina safe. Because without her, my kingdom means nothing.

CHAPTER 3

NINA

I'm…numb. That's the only word I can think of to use. I honestly don't know how I'm supposed to feel. Someone tried to *kill* me. If Kai hadn't pushed me out of the way…

A shiver cascades through my body as I wrap my arms around my midsection.

"Trouble, are you okay?" Cain asks with a gentleness belying the harshness that twists his features. Through Kai's eyes, I see my dark twin's face contort into something primal and animalistic, his lips compressed in a thin line. When he turns towards me, his features immediately soften like ice melting on an abnormally hot summer day.

"I'm…I'm fine," I manage to stutter out at last. Is it cold in here? Why are there goosebumps covering my arms? My heart seems to be expanding in a rapidly shrinking vise. Claws dig into the sensitive organ and squeeze until I'm weeping blood.

"You don't have to worry, Bambi. No one will hurt you." Abel slings an arm over my shoulder, attempting a carefree, nonchalant persona, but only someone who knows him as well as I do can see the tightening of his eyes. The fear.

"I'm not worried," I insist immediately, knowing they need to hear that. "I trust you guys to take care of me." And I do. These men would move heaven and hell for me. I'm not dumb enough to believe that these men, these inmates, are the heroes in this story. If anything, they're the beasts, the monsters, the killers. But they're *my* beasts, monsters, and killers. They protect me with every ounce of darkness surging through their veins. They try to hide the truth from me, try to protect me, but I see them for what they really are.

And I love them for it.

"Why don't we watch a movie?" I suggest, pulling out of Kai's head and submerging myself once more into my customary darkness. Blindly, I reach out until I'm able to intertwine my hand with Abel's and then Cain's. Both twins grip me with a bruising intensity, as if they're afraid I'll disappear at the slightest gust of wind. "Will the others join us?"

"Damien, Rion, and Bron are...busy," Abel admits, choosing his words carefully. I don't even react to the ominous statement. Using Kai's eyes, I saw Bronson drag the man away, Rion and Damien following in their wake. I'm pretty sure they're not going to be painting each other's nails, if you know what I mean.

"That's okay." I throw them an easy smile, despite being unable to see them. "We'll hang out, just the four of us."

Their hesitation is evidence enough that they're still uneasy with what just transpired. I wish to soothe them, calm them, remind them that I'm still standing and will continue to stand. They can't get rid of me that easily. They may have claimed me, but I've claimed them as well. These men? They're mine. Soon, we'll be married and have...

I allow that thought to trail off. Damien has been working

tirelessly to find a cure for my predicament, but he admitted that it's hard to unwind a spell that he doesn't know the ingredients to.

Alyssa, my mother and torturer, placed a spell on me that prohibited me from giving birth until she was ready for me to. She may be dead, but the spell remains, a way for her spirit to haunt me beyond the grave.

Pain bombards me, as it always does, when I think about what I have to give up. Namely, a family. I know I have my men and I wouldn't trade them for anything or anyone, but I always expected to have tiny versions of me running around. Maybe it's the wistful fantasies of a child, but I want a kid. *Kids*. Desperately. And I want these men, my future husbands, to be the fathers.

Abel lightly raps his knuckles against my forehead. "Where did you go, Bambi?" he asks lightly as the twins drag me forward.

My tongue nervously snakes out to lick my upper lip. "Here and there," I answer evasively.

"We talked about this." He clicks his tongue in mock disapproval. "You can't keep thinking about my cock. You'll make the other guys jealous."

A snort of laughter escapes before I can wrangle it back in. Trust Abel to know how to dispel the tension currently permeating the room. Even Kai releases a bark of laughter, and I have no doubt Cain's lips are twisted into a wry grin.

"Trust me, brother. It's not your cock she's thinking about."

"Is too," Abel retorts immediately. "Isn't that right, Bambi?"

"Err…" Abruptly, my back hits a wall, and the hard planes of Abel's chest press against me.

"There's no 'er' about it." He leans forward to lick up my

neck, and goosebumps follow in his wake. "Tell them you love me best."

"Nope!" Cain grabs my hand suddenly and pulls me to the side and into his arms. "She loves me best."

"I believe it's me she loves the best," Kai adds with another snort. "But you two assholes can measure your cocks all you want."

"If we measure, I'll win." That's Abel of course. His voice is practically dripping with cockiness like venom drips from a snake.

"We have the same cock," Cain says with a scoff. "But mine is prettier."

I cover my mouth with my hand, but it's no use. Peals of laughter burst from my lips unbidden. The more I try to contain them, the louder they become, until I'm gripping my stomach with tears cascading down my cheeks.

"You guys are...ridiculous," I say around my laughter, a rather unladylike snort punctuating those words. That sends Abel over the edge, and his laughter joins mine, followed immediately by Cain and Kai. We probably look stupid—standing in the halls of the prison, dopey smiles on our faces and tears running down our cheeks. But we need this. Sometimes, we laugh because the only other option we have is to cry and fall apart, something I refuse to do.

WE WATCH *MARLEY AND ME*...AND I SORT OF BEGIN TO HATE Abel for suggesting this movie in the first place. I'm a sobbing mess as I wipe at the snot and tears intermingling on my face.

"I don't...want...the puppy...to die," I sob out as I cuddle into Kai's chest. In the distance, I hear the distinct sound of flesh hitting flesh—no doubt, Cain punching Abel for putting this movie on in the first place. Through Kai's eyes, I watch the ending credits appear on the screen, but my heart is broken, in shatters.

"Shit, I'm sorry, Nina," Abel says, and Kai swings his head to stare at the trickster demon. His face is pale, a red mark already forming on his cheek from where Cain slugged him. "I thought it was a cute kids' movie. I didn't realize… Well…I didn't know it would end like *that*."

"He's a fucking dumbass," Cain grumbles, rolling his eyes. He turns towards me, winces at whatever he sees in my expression, and shifts uncomfortably on the musty couch in Rion's prison cell. None of the guys like to see me in tears, Cain especially. "What if we buy you a puppy?"

"So you can kill it?" I whine, pressing my face against Kai's chest and inhaling his citrus scent.

I hear harsh whispering, random words floating to me, "You deal with this. It's your mess."

Finally, Abel crouches down in front of me and tenderly brushes his hand through my hair.

"I'm sorry, Bambi. Will you ever forgive me?"

"Maybe…" I sniff, pulling out Kai's head and sliding easily into Abel's so I can see through his eyes. His gaze is fixed firmly on me, still in my dragon's embrace. "For a kiss."

Kai snorts, face twisting with amusement before he plants a reverent kiss to my scalp and reluctantly releases me.

"Bambi…" Abel begins, tone accusatory. "I feel like you were playing me. Is this a ruse to get me naked and in bed with you, naughty girl?"

I watch my face distort until an evil grin materializes on my face. "Maybe."

Cain and Kai both break into raucous laughter as Abel shakes his head in amusement.

"You are in *so* much trouble." He begins to tickle up and

down my sides, and I shriek, attempting to escape his relentless attack.

"Stop!" I say as I fall backwards, and he lands on top of me. He holds himself on his elbows so as not to hurt me, his eyes roaming my face and setting my skin ablaze.

"You're so beautiful," he whispers as he grips my hips. He wrenches his gaze off of me for only a second, turning towards the door as Cain and Kai slip out of the cell, matching mischievous smiles on their faces.

"They're leaving us alone?" I question as Abel focuses once more on his hands gathering up my white dress.

"I can't punish you with an audience, now can I?" he asks teasingly, but his words only cause pleasure to flood my system. An audience? Why does that sound like the best idea in the world?

"What are you going to do to me?" I ask, attempting to be coy. My friends, Haley and Rebecca, have been teaching me how to be sexy, using winks, hair flips, and seductive phrases. I think...I think I've got the hang of it. "Are you going to penetrate me with your missile, shitface?" I continue, and he stills.

Before breaking into laughter.

"Did you just call me shitface?" he gasps out, and I watch my face turn crimson.

"I was trying to think of a romantic nickname, and I panicked," I defend, embarrassed. Immediately, his laughter dissipates, and he cups my cheeks tenderly.

"Hey, I'm not laughing at you. Okay...I was a little, but you're so fucking adorable and perfect that I can't help it. Do you have any idea how much I love you? Do you even comprehend the lengths I would go for you? I would die for you, Nina. I would *kill* for you. I'd lasso the moon if that was what you desired. Fuck, I love you." His eyes travel to the glistening ring on my finger, and I don't need eyes to know that he's smiling. "Soon, you're going to be mine in every single way."

"I love you too, Abel," I whisper, throat clogged with the enormity of my emotions for this man. "So, so much."

As if he can't help himself, he presses his lips to mine, caressing them. Each brush of his tongue against my own sends fireworks shooting down my spine. He tastes like heaven and as pure and crucial to life as sunlight.

"Say it again," he murmurs against my lips before devouring them once more with a vengeance.

"I," I breathe, and he kisses the corner of my lips. "Love." Panting, he begins to kiss down my throat, and I arch my neck to grant him better access. "You."

"You're going to be my wife soon," he whispers as his teeth graze the straps of my dress. "Mrs—"

"Doe," I cut in before he can finish. Since I first said yes to them, all six of my men have been trying to convince me to take their last names. I've been adamant that if anyone is going to change their last name, it's going to be them. To Doe. Abel Doe. It has a nice ring to it, wouldn't you say?

Instead of answering, Abel merely uses his teeth to pull my right strap down until it slides off. He then repeats that process with my left strap. My dress slides down until my breasts spring free. I skipped the bra this morning, not feeling the need when the only people I'm ever with are my men and best friends, and I'm so grateful for that now. My nipples are already hard and beaded, the pink color contrasting with my porcelain skin.

Abel groans low in his throat as he lowers his head to one nipple and sucks it into his mouth. It's oddly erotic to watch through his eyes as he plays with my breast, kissing my areola before claiming my nipple once more.

"Are you in my head right now?" Abel asks roughly as he peppers kisses across the valley of my breasts. At my nod, he leans back and surveys my bare upper body—my swollen lips and lust filled white eyes, my heaving chest, and my pink, pointed nipples. "I want you to see what you do to me."

Getting to his feet, he lowers his gaze to his pants, where I can clearly see the outline of his erect cock. I whimper, feeling wanton and needy, as he slowly unzips his pants and pushes down his boxers. His cock springs free, already dripping with pre-cum. It bobs against his stomach as he begins to touch himself. I nearly unravel at the erotic sight as his other hand cups his balls.

"This is what you do to me, Bambi. This is what you always do to me."

"Abel," I moan as he continues to stroke himself from base to tip. Since meeting my men, since becoming intimate with them, I've been nearly insatiable. I could die happily with their cocks between my legs or in my mouth.

"Take your dress off, Bambi. I want you to see yourself."

Trembling, I make quick work of pushing my dress the rest of the way down, then climb to my feet until I'm standing in front of him in only a pair of panties. I bite down on my lower lip, tasting blood, as I hook my thumbs into the waistband and push them down.

"Fuck," Abel mutters as he strokes himself faster and faster. "Do you see how beautiful you are? How perfect?" He drops to his knees before me and stares up at my glistening pussy, already wet and aching for him. Through his eyes, I see the pink lips and engorged clit. When his tongue meets my center, I nearly explode then and there. "Look at that perfect pussy. Do you see how pretty it is? How wet it is for me? Do you want my cock, Bambi? Do you want my big fat cock in your perfect pussy?" Normally, I'm not a fan of dirty words, having been on the receiving end of unwanted ones more times than I care to admit. But Abel's words make my legs shake and knees wobble.

"Yes," I beg, reaching for his shoulders. He pulls his head back to stare up at me, giving me an unrestricted view of my soaking pussy, large breasts, and flushed face. The entire sight has my eyes rolling into the back of my head.

Getting to his feet, and ignoring my cry of protest, Abel whips his shirt off and steps out of his pants and boxers. Both of us are naked now, and it occurs to me that anyone can walk down this hall at any time and see us through the bars of Rion's cell. It only amplifies the lust pulsing straight to my core.

"Come here," Abel says, grabbing my hand and pulling me after him. I must make a face, as he begins to chuckle darkly. "Trust me."

We stop only a second later as Abel steps up behind me, facing a mirror. In the reflection, I can see his glazed over eyes, flushed cheeks, and golden skin glistening with sweat.

"I want you to watch us together," he whispers in my ear, nipping down on my lobe. I squeak, jumping, and my boobs bounce as well, which only makes Abel groan.

"I want you so bad," I whimper as Abel lines up behind me, his cock rubbing against my juices. "Abel, please." I don't want teasing. Not anymore. I want him to enter me, consume me, until I can't tell where he ends and I begin. I want him to make me his in every sense of the word. "Make love to me."

He bites my shoulder before slowly pushing himself inside of me. He pauses halfway in before pulling out. "Fuck, baby, you're dripping for my cock."

"Abel…" Now my voice comes out more as warning than a plea, and Abel doesn't disappoint. He sheathes himself inside of me, allowing me only a second to adjust to his length. I lean forward and press my palms against the wall on either side of the mirror, waiting for him to move. He begins to rock slowly, almost as if he's afraid he's going to break me, but I can't have that. I *won't*. I'm not made of glass, despite what they believe. After what I survived both at the Compound and then after with Alyssa, I don't think anything could ever truly break me.

"Harder," I whisper, and I have the pleasure of seeing his eyes widen in surprise.

"Are you sure?" he questions as his pace increases, his hands gripping my hips.

In answer, I begin to press back against him until his balls touch my skin. That, more than anything else, seems to be his undoing. He fists my hair and drags me back until my body is flush against his. He pounds in and out of my pussy with reckless abandon, eyes open and meeting mine in the mirror before us. Each thrust of his hips sends me closer to careening over that steep edge, but I want to fall. I trust Abel to catch me at the bottom.

"Nina…" he groans. "Fuck!"

"Yes! Yes! Yes!" When his hand lowers down my stomach to pluck my clit, I detonate. Explode. My orgasm crashes through me with the strength of a tsunami. I see stars as my body shakes and shakes.

Abel continues to pound into me through my orgasm, my pussy clamping around his cock like a vise. With a curse, he roars his release, coating my pussy lips and thighs with his cum.

He doesn't immediately pull out of my channel when we crash down from our high. Instead, he plants soft, tantalizing kisses across my shoulder. I shudder, my body feeling leaden and weak, as I collapse against him. Very gently, he pulls himself out of me and grabs a towel from the corner. Placing it beneath the rusted sink, he wets it and returns to me, dropping to his knees.

I pull myself out of his head as he gently wipes at my thighs and lips.

"That was…amazing," I say, and I hear the smile in his voice when he speaks next.

"You're amazing. And perfect. And beautiful. And…now you can tell my brothers that I do, indeed, have the best cock. That they all have micropenises compared to mine."

I giggle, grabbing his hand and helping him to his feet. He wraps me in his arms immediately, and I rest my head against his sweaty chest.

"Okay. I'll make sure to tell Damien that you said that he has a tiny cock."

The gasp of fear and horror he makes? Priceless.

CHAPTER 4

DAMIEN

The man's a screamer.

You can tell a lot about a person from how they scream. From their final words when faced with impending, inevitable death. Do they beg for mercy? Remain firm and stoic? Sob for their mothers?

I've been tortured once before, many years ago. I didn't scream, and I didn't cry. The pain was unbearable, my veins imploding with pure agony. Yet, you wouldn't have been able to tell from the expression on my face. I retreated to a part of my mind I reserved for moments like that—a tiny recess where the dark and scary monsters hide until they're needed once more. They say that monsters hide underneath beds, but that's not true. No, there's a particular spot in hell reserved for men like me, men who feast on pain and blood like it's an oasis in a desert.

As this man thrashes, incoherent words falling from his lips, I feel...nothing. No sympathy, no guilt, not even anger. I know the latter emotion will consume me at a later time, when I unlock my beast from the relegated section of my mind where I house it.

This…this spineless creature tried to *kill* Nina. He tried to take away my very reason for breathing. That isn't just something I can forget, let alone forgive. He'll pay for what he intended to do to her, what he tried to do to her. His spilt blood will be the offering on a sacrificial altar and gifted to my goddess, my angel, my Nina.

I know that if she saw me now, she would be disgusted, maybe even afraid. She sure as fuck wouldn't smile at me as if I handcrafted the ring on her finger from sunlight. However, she needs my darkness, my demons, my beasts. She needs me to fight in the shadows so she can thrive in the light.

Keeping my face impassive, I plunge my fifth knife into the trembling, sniffling man's stomach, twisting as I watch blood pour from the open wound. Rion, behind me, begins to cackle. I don't have to look to know that the crazy psychopath is perched on the table in the corner of my chamber, his legs swinging back and forth as he hums beneath his breath.

This is the one room in the prison I'm allowed to embrace my inner desires, allowed to unleash the monster prowling just beneath the surface. It's located down one of the many twisting hallways of the prison, on the opposite side of the throne room, cells, and cafeteria. Less chance of someone stumbling upon it.

The walls are gray like the rest of the prison, constructed of roughly hewn stone, and a single chair rests in the center of the room. A table sits behind it, currently dripping with contraband. Knives, axes, daggers…anything sharp, you'll find it here. It's amazing what power and money can do for you, even twenty feet below ground and in a maximum security supernatural prison.

Of course, I can use my powers to torture as well, but where's the fun in that? I like to get my hands dirty, to watch the blood drip from my porcelain fingers like fresh paint. One would think that my skin would be rough and calloused, but it's smooth. Gentle to the touch. A pretty mask that hides the monster, the savage.

"You should let me take a round with him," Rion says, a malevolent excitement to his voice that makes the disgusting man cry harder. Snot drips down Ben's face, intermingling with the blood already present there. But it's not enough. It'll never be enough.

Instead of answering Rion, I merely grunt, turning back towards the table to grab a bear trap.

"We could play a game," he rambles. "Twister with his body parts. Okay, you ready for this? We each cut off a body part—say, a hand or a foot or even a finger—and then we draw shapes on the floor with his blood. Actually, let's draw the shapes first. We can easily cut a vein in his wrist to get the blood, or we can just use the blood already dripping from him. I'm cool with either. Anyway, we draw a row of triangles, a row of circles, a row of squares, and a row of hexagons. Now, since he pretty much has two or more of every important body part, such as hands and eyeballs and feet and lungs, we place one of each off to the side. And then we grab a body part at random, and the first one to grab the correlating body part from Ben's actual body has to put it on the designated blood shape. Sort of like, eyeball to hexagon. You get me?"

I have no idea what the fuck he just said.

"You see, Ben," I purr, stepping closer to the crying, naked man currently hanging from my ceiling. I sit on the plastic chair and cross my legs, steepling my hands together. "You better tell me what you know, or else I'm going to have to get Rion involved. And he's a little crazy."

"I take offence to that." Rion jumps to his feet and moves to stand beside me, peering up at Ben with narrowed, slitted eyes. "I'm a whole shitload of crazy. It's rude to assume otherwise. On a scale of one to one hundred, I'm a solid one thousand, and not just in the good looks department." He nudges me with his elbow, and I just barely resist the urge to stab him.

Abruptly, Rion leans forward until his face is level with Ben's, any and all mirth diminishing from his dark eyes. He looks positively savage, the embodiment of darkness and sin. Pure madness reflects on his face as he presses his thumb into a wound on the man's chest.

"You tried to kill my buttercup," he hisses, his voice nearly guttural. The man begins to scream as Rion plunges his finger deeper and deeper into the hole. "Tell me why, and I'll kill you semi-quickly. Of course, I'll still make you suffer, but I can promise you that I'll leave your penis alone. But if you don't…" He drops his gaze to the man's flaccid dick, his grin growing. "Have you ever seen a skinned penis before?"

"Fuck, I'll tell you. I'll tell you anything you want to know," he sobs out, snot dripping from his nose.

Rion straightens abruptly and turns towards me with his signature jovial smile.

"See? All you have to do is threaten a man's rocket launcher, and you'll get the goods. Wait. That sounds like I'm talking about getting a man's rocket launcher…but I don't want his dick. Unless it's served on a silver platter. Oh! Can we do that? Can we feast on his dick tonight? I haven't had a good dick in a while. I'll even let you have the balls."

Ignoring him, I face Ben expectantly.

"Well?" I cock one eyebrow as his body shakes.

"The dead pool," he whimpers. "The fucking dead pool."

"What the fuck are you talking about?" I ask curtly. If there's one thing I hate more than disgusting, pathetic men like him, it's being left in the dark.

"A couple days ago, we got word about a dead pool in the

prison." He begins to pant erratically, pure terror emanating from his sunken eyes.

"Like the movie with that sexy Ryan?" Rion waggles his eyebrows suggestively. "I might even allow Nina to ride his dick and let him live. Honestly, I wouldn't blame her. He's a sexy hunk of meat." His eyes turn ten shades darker. "Actually, I'd still gut him."

"It's a..." Ben swallows. "It's a list. With names of people to be killed and their price."

My body freezes as I exchange a terse look with Rion. What the fuck? Why haven't we heard about this? We know everything that goes on in this prison—or so we believe.

"And Nina's on the list," I surmise as that familiar tendril of rage slithers through me like a snake. I immediately try to suppress it. The last thing I need is my emotions getting the better of me. Until I get the answers I need, I can't afford to lose my head.

But the thought of how close this man came to snuffing out Nina's life...

Of never hearing her twinkling laugh...

Seeing her eyes sparkle...

Holding her in my arms...

My hand tightens around the bear trap as I set it by my feet. I'll play with that toy later.

"N-Nina's on the fucking top of the list," Ben stutters, releasing a humorless laugh. "There's over twenty million dollars tied to her death. Do you know what that money can do for my family? For me? I only have a few more years left in this prison."

"Let me see the list," I say darkly, and when Ben's eyes flicker towards his pants discarded in the corner of the room, I stride in that direction, removing a folded piece of paper from his pocket.

My eye begins to twitch as I scan the words typed out.

1. **Nina - 20 million**
2. **Blade - 1 million**
3. **Rion - 1 million**
4. **Damien - 700k**
5. **Cain - 500k**
6. **Abel - 500k**
7. **Bronson - 500k**
8. **Braelyn - 50k**

"That is awful," Rion breathes from over my shoulder. When I glance at him, he appears genuinely affronted. "I'm worth at least two million, give or take."

"Who the fuck made this?" I hiss, staring intently at the tattered paper. Nina's name glares back at me defiantly. Twenty million dollars. That's a lot of fucking money.

And there's a lot of sick, soulless fucks in this prison who won't hesitate to take her out in order to get said money.

"I don't know." Ben's voice is heavy with defeat. No doubt, he already knows that his story will end with death by my hand. He has no reason to fight anymore.

"Where did you get it?" I ask instead as I shove the paper into my jacket pocket. Ben bites down on his lower lip.

Immediately, I grab the bear trap in one hand and his cock in the other. Without preamble, I drop his cock into the metal jaws, relishing his scream of agony as they snap shut.

"Where did you get it?" I repeat darkly as blood pours down his thighs from his mangled cock.

"Joseph Turner," he cries out at last. "I swear, that's all I know. That's all. Please. Oh, please—"

Rolling my eyes at his dramatics, I remove my dagger from my jacket sleeve and slice it from one ear to the next.

"Awww. No fun. I wanted to torture him a little more." Rion, honest to god, begins to pout.

"We got what we needed," I murmur, straightening out

the few creases in my pristine black suit. "We need to talk to the others. Is Bronson still on patrol?" The shadow wolf left shortly after the torture session began to search our cells and the cafeteria for any other nasty surprises. I wouldn't want to be in his way at this moment. Bronson's on a fucking warpath.

"Yes, sir." Rion salutes me before turning to stare at Ben's now dead body distastefully. "But I have an idea that I think you might like."

"I'm listening," I say evasively.

"How about we make Benny Boo here a reminder of what happens when you fuck with our girl?" He smiles, showcasing abnormally sharp teeth. "Let's show the inmates what their punishment is for getting on our bad side?"

He's right.

I really, *really* like that idea.

CHAPTER 5

BRONSON

There's nothing more satisfying than sticking my fist into some motherfucker's face. Well, except for maybe sticking my cock inside Nina's pussy.

I stare at the pathetic excuse for a man as he trembles, no doubt sensing my raw, animalistic rage permeating the room.

Shortly after I arrived in the cafeteria, the rest of the inmates cleared out, recognizing me for what I am—a monster. A predator.

And them? They are my prey.

The man's name is Joseph Turner, though no one here calls him that. Instead, he goes by the dumbass nickname of One Shot. Rumor has it that before he was sent to Nightmare Penitentiary, he worked as an assassin in a guild that rivaled Damien's. If his name is any indication, he's able to take his targets out in one fatal shot.

Unfortunately, his background means he's also immune to most torture techniques. If we want to find out the truth about the dead pool, we're going to need him to talk.

My wolf prowls beneath the surface of my skin, making me feel more animal than human. In the reflection above

Joseph's shoulder, I see long fangs contorting my mouth and dark, pitch black fur on my arms. It's a stark contrast to my messy blond hair and golden skin.

Joseph releases a moan of pain, and satisfaction races through me.

This…this…this *monster* was directly responsible for what almost happened to Nina. I can't allow him to live.

"Are you going to talk, motherfucker?" I roar, slamming my fist once more into his stomach. He's currently tied to a chair in the center of the cafeteria, the rest of the tables moved away. When Damien told me the truth about Ben, about the dead pool, rage like no other slithered across my skin like a fucking viper. That rage…it needs an outlet. And Joseph's face is looking rather punchable.

I've been trying to be better for Nina. But I'm a protector first and foremost, and that job requires me to do what most would deem immoral. I'm sure I could get Damien and Rion to come interrogate this pathetic man, but where's the fun in that? Joseph Turner is *mine*.

"Fuck you," he hisses, blood coating his teeth. He turns his head to the side to spit it out, and I just barely contain my grimace as the dark red liquid lands centimeters from my boot. Motherfucking asshole.

Smirking like a savage, I land punch after punch into his face, my smile widening with every speck of blood. By the time I'm done with him, he'll be nearly unrecognizable.

"Tell me about the dead pool," I seethe, pulling my arm back in preparation to land another blow. "We know you gave it to Ben."

"Fuck you."

This time, teeth fly from his mouth with the force of my blow.

"Are those the only two words you know how to say?" I ask

darkly. Movement over his shoulder captures my attention, and I can't help but flash him a malevolent smile. His face instantly whitens, because let's be honest—any smile I direct at anyone other than Nina is most likely not a nice one. This one in particular promises bloodshed and pain. Lots and lots of pain.

"You don't have to talk." I shrug nonchalantly as Damien stalks forward, each step controlled and precise. He wears his customary black suit and pressed white shirt, the cuffs rolled up slightly. His dark hair is smoothed away from his face as he steps around me to stop in front of Joseph.

When a wet stain appears on Joseph's pants, I practically cackle with glee.

"You good?" I ask Damien, clapping a hand on his shoulder. The crazy mage doesn't even turn around as he procures a blade from the inside of his jacket sleeve.

"He'll talk," he vows in a deadly voice—a voice that's made of nightmares. Of monsters and beasts and spiders and creatures that go bump in the night.

With one more punch aimed at Joseph's head, I turn on my heel and leave the cafeteria. I have a mate to attend to.

My skin itches with the need to take her in my arms, hold her to me, protect her. I need to see with my own two eyes that that asshole hadn't hurt her. Hearing it and seeing it are two entirely separate things. I need her more than I need air to breathe and water to drink.

I move quickly down the cellblock until I reach the section we delegated for ourselves. No one is allowed in our sanctuary.

"Bronson!" a cheery voice says, and I feel my heartbeat increase as I turn in Nina's direction.

She's sitting on Abel's lap as she plays a game of chess against Cain. My eyes immediately travel over her heartbreakingly beautiful and perfect features, cataloguing any changes. Is she hurt? Did she get nicked with Ben's blade? If any of her blood left her body…

I take a deep breath to quell the rage percolating in my stomach, instead choosing to focus on her. Only her. Gradually, the rest of the world falls away.

Her dark hair hangs around her like molten obsidian stones. It frames her heart-shaped face and milky white eyes. Her lush lips are quirked into a mischievous smirk, one that I wish to kiss away. How did I get so lucky? How did I find someone as perfect and as beautiful as she is?

She must sense something hanging stagnant in the air around us, my need for her perhaps, because she stealthily jumps down from Abel's lap and runs towards me. I hold her in my arms, inhaling her sweet scent as she clings to me just as fiercely.

"Mine," I growl, sliding my arms beneath her ass to hold her steady. With a rumble, I turn on my heel and stalk towards my cell. I need to feel her in my arms, feel her heartbeat thumping beneath my hand.

"You can't just take her," Abel objects, annoyed. I whip my head around to level him with a piercing, glacial glare. If he even attempts to take Nina from me, I'll rip him apart. He must see that in my gaze, or maybe he just sees the pure insanity emanating from my eyes, since he holds up his hands placatingly. "You know what? Carry on."

"Fucking pussy," Cain murmurs to his brother, and Abel shoots him a dark look.

"I didn't see you fighting for our girl, brother."

I turn around just as Cain throws himself across the table, the chessboard clattering to the ground. Nina giggles at their antics, her thin arms tightening around me.

When I enter my cell, I drop her carefully onto my bed and hurry to cocoon her in my blankets. She needs to be safe and warm.

"Bron," she murmurs as I grab a second quilt and tuck it around her body. Soon, only her eyes, pert nose, and plush lips are visible. Not even her cascade of black hair can be seen. "Is this really necessary?"

"*Mate*," I rumble out as I move to sit behind her, pulling her against my chest. Her cushioned head rests just above my heart, and I stroke up and down her covered arm. "*Protect.*"

Fuck, I can't even talk like a damn human. The thought of how close she came to death, of how close she came to leaving me, makes me both terrified and furious. Terrified of living in a world without her in it, and furious at the fucker who dared attempt such a thing in the first place. A part of me wishes I had been there to see Ben die. Maybe then my beast would be pacified.

"You can't leave me," I growl out as I plant kisses across her cheek and then down to her lips. "You. Can't. Leave. Me."

"I'm not going anywhere," she whispers, her voice merely a breath of air. "You're stuck with me." She giggles self-consciously, almost as if she believes that's a bad thing, but I practically preen at those words.

She's wrong, though. It's not me who is stuck with her. It's her who is stuck with me. My brothers and I have claimed her as our own, as our woman. She came barreling into our life with doe-like eyes, innocent smiles, and a light so blinding that it chased away our darkness.

Now that we have her, now that we've gotten a taste of what life can be like with her, we'll never let her go.

CHAPTER 6

There are no new attacks in the weeks that follow, but all of my guys are still on guard. They barely even allow Braelyn to be alone with me for longer than a few minutes. It's cute...but annoying, a word I never would've associated with my men before. I love them all, but there's only so much I can take before I feel as if I'm going to explode.

Even now, sitting in the crowded cafeteria with my girl-friends, I can feel Damien's eyes on me like a physical caress. No, not just a caress—a brand. It sears into my flesh like molten lava, leaving behind a mark that is distinctly Damien.

"Stalker alert," Braelyn murmurs conspiratorially, nudging me with her elbow. I simply roll my eyes, not bothering to respond. I understand their paranoia, I honestly do, but I can't even pee without one of them hovering over me. Do you know how awkward that is?

Rebecca snorts. "Girl, what I wouldn't give to have a sexy hunk like that watching my every move."

I slide into Braelyn's eyes just as Haley gives Rebecca a fist bump. Rebecca is an older, robust woman with mousy brown hair, teal eyes, and a plump body. Her smile is conta-gious, nearly cleaving her face in two, and it reveals dimples on both of her cheeks. Haley, on the other hand, is slender, with golden hair that frames an angelic face.

"So you never answered us," Haley presses, placing her elbows on the table and leaning forward. "Which one of your husbands has the biggest dick?"

Rebecca breaks into laughter, and even Braelyn chuckles. Jenny, on the other side of the Braelyn, smiles softly, covering her mouth with her hand.

"Err...they're not... I mean, we're not married...and, um..." I pretend to glance down at my wrist. "Oh, would you look at that? It's time for me to leave."

"You don't even have a watch on," Haley snarks petulantly.

"And you're blind," adds Braelyn, a smirk evident in her voice. She leans against Jenny's side, and just before the two can exchange kisses, I slide out of her head, once more succumbing to darkness.

Shoving the remaining piece of toast in my mouth, I hurry in the direction I felt Damien's presence.

Then abruptly slam into a hard body.

"Ow," I lament, rubbing my bruised nose.

"Shit, I'm sorry," an unfamiliar voice exclaims, sounding terrified. "I didn't see you—"

"It's okay," I assure him immediately, just as an arm snags around my waist and pulls me against a chiseled body. I tense instinctively before relaxing as Damien's familiar arctic scent surrounds me. Smiling softly, I lay my head against his chest as silence ensues.

I slide into Damien's eyes just in time to see the second man lower his head subserviently, a tiny whimper emitting from his lips. He appears to be young, maybe my age, and abnormally thin and sinewy. I can see every bone protruding from beneath his shirt. His garnet red hair is messily pushed to the side, one lock hanging longer than the others and brushing against his cheek.

"I didn't see her," he says softly, refusing to lift his head. The terror radiating from his pores is almost palpable, and I can't help but sympathize with the poor man. There was a point in my life when I was just as scared. I would jump at my own shadow and pray for a death that never came for me. I can see all of those feelings and more in his azure gaze.

When a wet splotch appears on his pants, and the cafeteria roars with laughter, I turn in Damien's arms, wrenching myself out of his head once more.

"Dam, it's okay. It was my fault. I wasn't paying attention. It's okay," I assure him gently, stroking up and down his arms. He's trembling beneath my touch, muscles rippling. He's an untamed beast, savage and unpredictable, and the last thing I'll ever want to do is leash him. At the same time, I'm afraid that he'll snap and kill this inmate simply because he ran into me. I'm not oblivious to Damien's darkness. Sure, they try to hide it away from me, but I see him—the good and the bad. There's a light that sparks inside of him, a light I wish to feed until it becomes a brilliant, all-consuming flame, one I can get burned by.

"Damien," I press softly, cupping his cheeks and forcing his gaze to meet my blind one. "I'm okay. But I'm tired. Can you walk me back?"

Finally, my words seem to get through to him. His muscles gradually relax beneath my hands, almost incrementally, as he rests his forehead against my own. In a voice too low for anyone to hear, he whispers, "You're the only thing capable of pulling me back from the darkness."

My throat clogs with emotion, but instead of answering, I merely brush at his dark hair, soothing him through touch alone.

When he pulls away, I know I calmed the raging, prowling, feral beast. Maybe not completely—I doubt even *I'm* capable of that—but enough for us to leave this place without a trail of bodies in our wake.

"Apologize," Damien growls darkly at the young man. I can't tell what supernatural he is. A vampire, perhaps? No, that can't be it. I would've seen his fangs when he got scared. Maybe a shifter or even a demon.

"I-I'm…I'm sorry," he stutters out.

"It's okay. Accidents happen," I assure him. I hear his footsteps retreat as he scurries away before tugging on Damien's sleeve. "Come on."

Without a word, Damien intertwines his fingers with mine and leads me towards the cells. At one point, Damien's room was a guard's station at the very back of the hall, but now, that room belongs to me.

It's there he leads me, opening the door and guiding me inside with a hand on the small of my back. I pop into his head once more just to get my bearings.

A single bed rests against the wall, its sheets so white, they practically shine. Unlike the rest of the prison, which has variations of cement and stone for flooring, this room has rich brown carpeting. Two dressers flank either side of my bed, and Damien's acoustic guitar still rests against the far wall. This is the only room in the entire prison that has an en suite bathroom connected to it.

"Hey, are you okay?" I ask Damien tentatively as I move to sit on the edge of the bed. Instead of immediately answering, he lowers himself to his knees before me and wraps his arms around my stomach, nestling his head between the valley of my breasts. There's something almost empowering about a man as strong and as proud as Damien kneeling before me. At the same time, it's terrifying. He treats me as if I'm his queen and he's nothing more than a loyal servant, but

I don't want that. I want him to see himself the way I see him, the way I see all of them—as my kings.

"You were brilliant in there," Damien whispers, his breath feathering against my collarbone as he tilts his head up. I easily slide out of his mind, focusing instead on the way he feels. His addictive scent. The thundering of his heart.

"Brilliant? That's a pretty badass word," I tease, and I don't need vision to know that his lips curved upwards at my use of the word "badass." Abel's been trying to get me to swear more often, and so far, my favorite swear words are cum stain and cock bitch.

"You're so fucking cute sometimes," he murmurs as he twists his head to plant a kiss to my breast over my shirt.

I gasp, my hands clenching Damien's arms.

"You're their queen," he continues, sliding down my dress sleeves until my chest is bare to him. "You're my queen."

"I'm no one's queen…" I pant as he begins to plant kisses up the arch of my boob, never touching my aching nipple. "I'm just me."

"And that's what makes entire worlds bow down to you, Angel," he whispers fiercely. Finally, *finally*, he takes my aching nub in his mouth, grazing it with his teeth. I moan, gripping his head and shoving my entire breast into his wet mouth.

"Damien…" I swear, with every tug of his teeth, fire races through my veins, until I'm drowning in blistering flames.

He turns his attention to my neglected breast, giving it the same treatment as the first. He's not gentle. No, not this time. He's rough and primal, and every bite of his teeth feels as if he's marking me as his own. Maybe he is, in a way. Only certain supernatural species have fated mates, and mages aren't one of them. Still, I can't deny the burst of light that erupts inside of me at the thought of him marking me, claiming me as his own.

When he pulls away from my aching, needy breasts, it's only to kiss the ring adorning my finger.

"Soon, my love," I whisper, understanding his tender gesture. Soon, I'll be tied to him irreversibly. He'll never be able to change his mind.

"Soon, Angel," he responds, pulling me in for a desperate kiss. His hands knead my breasts as his tongue devours my own. I fall into him, losing myself in his embrace, in him. Though I can't see him, I can feel him everywhere, his touch a direct line to my pulsing center.

"Damien…" I plead as he pushes up my dress and slips my underwear to the side. One of his fingers rubs down my wet slit before teasing my clit. "Dam—"

Before I can finish my needy plea, the door to the room is thrown open. Immediately, Damien's presence leaves me, and I slip into his eyes to see him standing protectively in front of me, guarding me from the intruder's view. He doesn't need to worry, though, because Abel is standing in the entrance, eyes wide with panic.

The lust dissipates instantly at the emotions swirling in his gaze.

"Abe?" I question, jumping to my feet and slipping my straps back over my shoulders. He doesn't make a quip about the position he found me in. He doesn't even dip his gaze to my breasts.

"Nina, I need you," he says urgently, stalking around Damien to grab my arm.

"What's going on?" Damien demands, and through his vision, I watch as he slides a dagger out of his sleeve, holding it at the ready.

"It's Cain," Abel whispers. "He needs you."

CHAPTER 7

I hurry after Abel, the cloying darkness pressing in on me from all sides. My heart hammers in my chest as I remember his choked voice.

What's wrong with Cain?

Oh, God. What's wrong with him?

I quicken my pace as Abel leads me down the twisting hallways of the Labyrinth. I don't know where we are, but my heightened hearing is able to make out distressed, strangled gasps.

"Cain!" I breathe in horror, sliding into Abel's mind instantly. His eyes are latched on his twin brother, who is currently pressed against the far wall of the room, rocking back and forth. Tears brim in his eyes as he lifts his sightless gaze in my direction. I know a part of him can hear me, can recognize my presence, but he's too lost in his flashback to respond with anything more than a guttural cry. I notice that his zipper is undone, his shirt untucked. "What happened?"

It's only then that I see *her*. I've never seen her before in my life, but I have no doubt in my mind that this woman is behind Cain's breakdown. She's pretty enough, I suppose, though my anger momentarily clouds my judgement. Her black hair is cut just below her chin in a surprisingly stylish and modern cut, considering where we are. Tattoos line her arms and neck, and even from this distance, I can see that one of her tits is hanging out of her shirt.

"What happened?" I demand again, wrenching my hand free of Abel's and stumbling in Cain's direction. His arms are extended, reaching for me, and I easily slide into his warm embrace. He rests his cheek on the top of my head as he inhales my scent, his body still trembling. Being mindful of the state he's in, I gently zip his pants back up, ignoring his flinch and the sob that's wrenched from his throat as I do so.

Abel turns to stare at the unknown female, and I don't need to see his expression to know that pure and unencumbered rage will be emanating from his eyes.

"New inmate," he hisses, smoke wafting around him. "Since the others were busy, Cain offered to go meet her."

When inmates arrive in the Labyrinth, they're usually unconscious so they won't see the entrance and exit, though the constantly changing pathways make it virtually impossible to escape anyway. Usually, the inmates are confused and groggy when they first wake up. Oh, and terrified, especially the females. My guys make certain that no one is taken advantage of when they first arrive. But after that? All gloves are off.

"I misread the situation," the girl protests immediately.

The growl that leaves my throat is utterly inhuman and unlike any sound I've ever emitted before. Even Abel whips his head in my direction, and I know shock is splayed across his face.

This...this...

I try to think of an appropriate curse word but come up blank, too lost in my rage.

This *woman* hurt Cain. And though it was unintentional—

no doubt, she was merely trying to seduce him—I still see red. Surprisingly enough, there is no jealousy intermixed with my other emotions. I know that all of my guys are completely, one hundred percent faithful to me.

But my anger lives inside of me like a living, breathing entity.

Through Abel's eyes, I watch as my glassy white gaze turns a bleeding, crimson red. My face begins to change and contort as pure and unfiltered *power* rushes through me. All I can think about is hurting the woman the way that she hurt Cain. Making her pay—

I allow that thought to cut off abruptly.

What am I doing? This isn't me. I don't hurt people, even when they deserve it.

Cain continues to tremble in my arms, his breathing coming out in shallow gasps, and I rein in my turbulent emotions. Still, guilt swallows me whole, like the swooping, gigantic maws of a monster.

"Cain," I whisper, coming back to myself and allowing my rage to abate. I'm shaking almost as erratically as Cain is, but for an entirely different reason. But I can't focus on me right now, not when one of the loves of my life is falling apart in my arms. "Baby?" I say the endearment almost hesitantly as I brush through his unruly blond hair.

"N…in…Nina," he stutters out, gripping my arms like they're life vests and he's adrift at sea.

"Yes, my love." I slide out of Abel's head and focus instead on how soft Cain's hair feels underneath my fingers. How his heartbeat steadily recedes to a normal rhythm. How his breathing evens out as he relaxes in my embrace. I'm dimly aware of Abel instructing the girl, Natalia, to leave, but I'm not able to hear her response.

"Fuck, Nina!" Cain curses abruptly, and then his lips plunder mine. I can feel his tongue sweeping across my lips, but before I can open for him, he pulls away. "Fuck. Fuck. Fuck. She wouldn't stop touching me. I tried to get her to stop. I tried. She wouldn't stop. Fuck. Fuck. Fuck. Why didn't I fight harder? Why did I just collapse, crying? Fuck. Fuck. FUCK!"

"Cain…" I hesitantly place a hand on his shoulder, and his entire body stiffens.

Voice muffled, he confesses, "I didn't want you to see me like this."

Indignation fills me as I grab his cheeks, forcing his hands to drop to his sides. I can't see him, but I imagine his eyes are focusing anywhere but on me.

"You don't want me to see you like this?" My voice comes out harsher than I intend it to. "You don't want me to see you breaking apart, is that it? Cain, I love you. I love you so freaking much, it's surreal. I want to see all of you—the good and the bad. I want to be able to help you, the way you guys so often help me. Why won't you let me?" Throughout my entire speech, I stroke my thumbs up and down his cheeks. With each track I make, I catch a new teardrop.

"Because I'm supposed to protect *you*," he whispers, his forehead pressing against mine. "I hate that I do this. I hate that I fall the fuck apart all the damn time. What type of husband will I be to you if I'm such a goddamn mess?"

And *I* hate the way he speaks of himself—as if he's anything less than pure perfection. As if he thinks I'll ever judge him because of his past and the consequential flashbacks. Kai once explained what it was to me—PTSD. Apparently, it happens when someone experiences something traumatic.

The twins were apparently unwilling prostitutes in a club created by some sick man named Boris. They were often sold to both men and women for pleasure. I can't even imagine the type of pain they went through.

That type of trauma…it leaves a scar on you, one that isn't always visible. There isn't a simple bandage you can slap over the wound to call it healed. No number of stitches can staunch the steady flow of blood from the opened wound.

I hate that my men are hurting, and I hate even more that they feel they need to hide it from me.

If I could, I would take all of their bad memories and…

A lightbulb metaphorically turns on in my head.

Uneasiness skirts through me at the absurdity of my idea, followed immediately by overwhelming happiness. Because if this works…

For now, I continue to brush through Cain's tangled hair with my fingers, peppering kisses across his scalp and down his cheeks. He sighs in contentment, and I know the worst of his panic attack has subsided.

"Nina?" Cain's raspy voice circles around me, warming me from the inside out.

"Yeah?" I don't dare raise my voice above a whisper, almost as if anything else is capable of disrupting the tranquility we have found ourselves in.

"I love you," he whispers hoarsely.

"I love you too."

And I make a vow, right then and there, that I'll protect them from any monsters who dare try and harm them. Even the monsters raging a battle inside of their own heads.

Even myself.

ABEL IS *NOT* HAPPY WHEN I TELL HIM I NEED TO CONFRONT Natalia by myself.

And honestly? I'm not either, but she needs to understand that what she did was wrong. I have no doubt that if any of my other men had bared witness to Cain's breakdown, she would be six feet under by now, female or not. Metaphorically speaking, of course. According to Damien, there's no location here to bury bodies. Instead, you need to bring the bodies to a private shoot that sends them straight to an incinerator.

I use Abel's eyes for guidance until I spot Natalia in conversation with a stone-faced Braelyn and her girlfriend, Jenny, all three of them crowded around a table in the cafeteria. They turn in my direction when I enter, their conversation instantly abating with my presence. I notice that Braelyn's lips are curled into a prominent frown, wrinkles appearing around her eyes, and Jenny looks troubled. Natalia, on the other hand, does *not* look upset. Instead, she sits smugly at the table, resting her head on her arms.

I pull out of Abel's head as soon as I'm near enough and slam my hands down on the table.

Resisting the urge to snarl, I begin, "Look, I understand you're new here—"

"Is this about the fucker who freaked out?" Natalia asks with a scoff, and instantly, the sound grates on my nerves. The precarious control I have on my emotions, on my anger, is slipping through my fingers like butter. I take a deep, fortifying breath, attempting to get myself under control.

The last thing I need is angel-ing/demon-ing/human-ing out, as Rion calls it.

I don't *trust* myself. Not completely. There's so much about my lineage that I don't know, and I'll never put other people in danger because of it.

"His name is Cain," I manage to say, my hands gripping the table so harshly, I'm afraid my fingers are going to snap in two.

"Fuck off." She releases a disgruntled snort. "He was practically begging for it. If anyone should be under investigation, it's him. As soon as I arrived, the bastard was pawing at my tit and pinching my nipple. He was going to rape me!" Her voice raises to a deafening pitch, and behind me, I hear Abel hiss. I can tell his demon is near the surface, wanting to be set free and obliterate this horrible girl who dared to imply such a thing.

But he'll allow me to handle this, both as the Queen of the Labyrinth and his fiancée.

My voice is the equivalent to thunder rumbling over the ocean at night, where the only sound you hear is the whoosh of the waves and the growl of the sky. "I know what rape is, Natalia. Cain knows what rape is. And I'll always take an accusation seriously. But this? This is a blatant lie, and you know it. By lying, you're invalidating the feelings of thousands and thousands of other women, and men, who have actually faced sexual assault." I'm...shaking. My body trembles as if someone placed a live wire beneath my skin and it's currently jerking back and forth, leaving sparks in its wake.

"Oh, please. The bitch baby wanted it." Natalia releases a semi-desperate laugh, almost as if she's willing Braelyn and Jenny to join in. Both women remain silent. "He was practically sucking on my nipple. Maybe that's it, huh? Maybe you're just jealous that he wanted me. Though I don't understand why you would be. You already seem to be in a relationship with his brother. Unless...unless you're the prison whore? Hmmm. I can see that. The poor little blind girl passed around by the inmates. I can't say I wouldn't mind tasting your pussy, though. I imagine it's the same as sucking cock? I'm pretty good with my tongue...as your demon lover can attest to."

Rage steals the air from my lungs. I can barely think straight over the incessant pounding of my heart.

And for the first time in my life, I slap someone.

I remember from before that she's nearly a head taller than me, so I make sure to raise my hand. I hear the satisfying crack of flesh meeting flesh, and then silence descends in the cafeteria.

A woosh of air betrays Natalia's intent, but before her hand can connect, she releases a wail of agonizing pain.

I slide into Abel's head immediately, unsurprised to see him directly behind me. The hands touching my shoulder now have onyx-colored talons where his fingernails once were. No doubt, he's almost completely demon.

And in front of us, sobbing pathetically, is Natalia, holding her hand to her chest.

Holding her hand with a *knife* in it to her chest.

Damien stalks from the shadows resembling a gorgeous avenging angel. *My* avenging angel. With a nonchalance befitting his status, he stops when he's mere inches from a sniveling Natalia and rips the dagger straight from her flesh.

"*No one* hurts Nina," he hisses, his voice laden with menace and a pinch of his trademark darkness.

"That was so fucking hot, Bambi," Abel whispers in my ear. "Do you feel how hard I am?" He presses his boner against my back as flames enter my cheeks.

"I don't know what came over me," I confess. "I just *hated* the way she was talking about Cain. Hated it. I didn't mean to hurt her."

"The bitch deserved it." Abel's voice loses the playfulness from only seconds earlier. We both watch as Braelyn and Jenny drag a still crying Natalia out of the room. I have no doubt that they're going to kill her. It's a dog-eat-dog world in here, and my guys didn't become the kings by showing leniency.

Technically, in the hierarchy of the prison, I'm supposed to deal with the female inmates. Oftentimes, I allow Braelyn to enact vengeance, so she'll decide if Natalia is allowed to remain alive. Female rapists are just as bad as male rapists, despite societal belief, and I won't shed a single tear if Natalia is deemed guilty.

For a brief moment, pain eats away at me, consuming me. I've never been this callous before, this desensitized to death, and I'm not sure I like the new Nina I'm turning into.

But at the same time, I can't find it within me to feel even an ounce of guilt.

I have no doubt that if Natalia had the opportunity, she would've raped Cain. It's one of the most horrendous sins, in my mind. Murder has all sorts of possible justifications, but no one who is sane can come up with one for rape. Which is why Natalia needs to die.

Maybe my time here is truly making me a monster.

Or maybe I've just learned how far I'm willing to go to defend and protect the people I love.

CHAPTER 8

RION

There are only a few things I like in the world.

Nina, obviously.

Pissing off Bitch Mage and the rest of his merry gang.

Oh, and world domination.

You know, the usual.

I lower myself onto my belly on the rafters above the throne room where Kai currently resides, ruling over his minions with an iron fist. Damien stands against one wall, arms folded over his chest as he adopts a nonchalant, almost impassive expression. His icy glare travels across all of the men and women present before resting on Nina, as they always do.

Abel and Cain are standing side by side, the latter leaning on his brother for support. I heard about what happened earlier today, and anger pulsates through my body at the thought. Some people...

I swear, some people are the embodiment of evil. And that means a lot coming from me.

Bronson remains in his wolf form, curled up on the floor

beside Nina, who has one hand in his fur. But I'm not fooled by Bronson's relaxed posture. He's more than capable of ripping your head off and tossing it across the room.

Dammit. I get a little tingly in my lower regions at the thought of bloody heads.

I allow my gaze to travel back to the assembled crowd. I count only about a handful of females and close to twenty men. All people Kai believes he can trust in this vicious world.

Nina's friends—Rebecca, Haley, Braelyn, and Jenny—stand near the front of the room, while behind them, a group of battle-hardened men linger. I catalogue each of their faces, counting the number of times their eyes flicker to Nina's face and darken with lust.

One murder.

Two murders.

Three murders.

I begin to sing it to the tune of "One Bottle Pop" as I sway from side to side. After a moment, I get bored of hiding and flip gracefully over the edge, landing in a crouch in front of a shifter I recognize from my own gang. Pete or something.

"Petey, Pete, Pete," I singsong, patting first one cheek and then the next. I lean forward and plant a tender kiss on his nose before inhaling deeply, my smile widening. "You smell like a pickle."

When his eyes widen in horror, the color draining from his face, I shift into my cat form and meander over to where Nina is standing. Clawing at her legs with my best puppy dog eyes—fuck, cat eyes—I wait until she caves and picks me up, nuzzling her face against my head.

"Mr. Scruffles," she says with a giggle as I lick her cheek.

I swear Bronson rolls his eyes at me, but considering he's still in his wolf form, I can't be certain. But if he rolled his eyes at me, I'll bite his—

Oh! Shiny!

I begin to bat at Nina's necklace, a gift from Damien, with my tiny paws, meowing enthusiastically when it sways back and forth. Back and forth.

Wait…

What was I thinking about again?

Oh, that's right. Murdering someone.

Hmmm…

I wiggle in Nina's arms until she puts me down, eyes alight with amusement, and then I make my way through the legs of my brother husbands. Abel smirks at me with mirth, but Cain just glares. I hiss right back at him, the fur on my back bristling.

Now who the fuck was I thinking about murdering?

Honestly, at this point, I might just have to take a coin and flip it. Heads, I murder no one. Tails, I murder the next person who looks in Nina's direction.

I make my way over to where Kai stands in front of his throne, addressing the dead pool issue. I'm not too worried. I'd like to see someone come at me. I can cut them up with my little kitty claws and then piss on their rotting corpse. Have you ever smelled cat pee before? Shit's rancid.

Doesn't it just give you the warm and fuzzies to think about the many different ways you can murder someone?

Kai eyes me with annoyance, his right eye twitching, as I pantomime lifting my leg up and peeing on him as if I were actually a dog instead of a cat. Of course, I'm not actually going to pee—

Dammit. A little sprinkle comes out.

Just a tiny one.

When Kai's eyes narrow, looking seconds away from lunging at me and wringing my adorable, fluffy neck, I race across the throne room until I reach Damien. I throw myself into his arms, and he instinctively makes a move to catch me.

And then I shift back into a real boy.

Naked and all.

"Hey," I whisper as his eyes harden. "Are you going to have your way with me, big boy?"

He drops me so hard, I swear I see stars. I'm not going to take offense to it, though. The bastard probably just wanted to see my cock bounce.

Ohhh new idea. Me. Bitch Mage. Nina. One in each hole.

Daddy likey.

And…

I just referred to myself as Daddy. Gag. Never again. That's one kink we're not doing, though I wouldn't protest to a little school girl action.

I can totally pull off the skirt and socks.

The audience begins to retreat from the throne room as Kai ends his speech, and a few glances are thrown my way. I immediately cup my cock with a low, threatening growl.

I mean, *hellooo*. Just because I'm naked, doesn't give them the right to look. These man nipples are reserved for Nina and Nina alone. And my cock, of course, which is probably the best cock that the big guy upstairs ever created. That's Nina's too.

"Did you pay attention to anything I said?" Kai asks me, annoyance clear in his voice.

I pretend to ponder the question, but the answer is abso-fucking-lutely not. To be frank, if he wasn't one of Nina's mates, I would probably kill him. No reason. We just don't share as profound a bond as I do with Damien. That dude is my bro soulmate, if you know what I mean.

Hashtag Dion for life.

And yes, I have the T-shirts already made. I'm just waiting for them to be delivered to the prison.

"I'm not worried," I say, pulling myself to my feet and

ignoring the pair of pants Abel tosses my way. Pants are for wussies.

Instead, I walk to Nina and pull her flush against my front, grinding my cock against her ass.

"Rion..." Her voice is half pant and half moan, but all it serves to do is amp up my lust. From the glazed expressions darkening the other men's faces, they're on the same wavelength as me.

"How are you not worried?" Abel queries, but he sounds slightly breathless and his eyes are glued to where I'm slowly inching Nina's dress up her porcelain thighs.

"Because no one will be fucking dumb enough to go against us," I say determinedly. "It'll be suicide. They know that they're only signing their own death warrant, and if there's one thing I learned from my time here—besides the fact that if you want to be my lover, you got to get with my friends—it's that people want to stay alive. It's human nature. Well, a lot of things are human nature. Cannibalism, for one. Not that I'm saying we should be cannibals. That's the first thing they taught me in elementary school." I adopt a firm, slightly high-pitched voice. *"Eating other people is bad. Really bad. Don't eat people. Eat vaginas."* I pause, allowing my words of wisdom to seep in, as they did for me many years ago. "Mrs. Trembal taught me that. Though...now that I think about it, I'm pretty sure she got arrested by the supernatural police for eating her husband, Mr. Trembal. Though we called him Mr. Tremballsack, because his balls were fucking huge. Nina, don't listen to me talk about his balls. Fuck! Are you envisioning them? Don't envision his ballsack, dammit!"

Way to go, Rion. Force your mate to picture some other dude's wanker.

And now I'm saying "wanker" like I'm British or some shit. I'm not. Well, I can be, if the mood hits.

I push Nina's dress up even further until my hand is able to graze her panties, already damp from just my words.

Was it the talk of Mr. Trembal's ballsack?

I jam my cock against her ass once more, as if to say, *"Here's a nice pair of balls for you to play with! Please forget about my teacher's husband's."*

I swear, if there was such a thing as Yelp reviews for my balls, I'd be getting the highest fucking star rating known to man.

Two out of two.

Because what fucker has five balls?

Mr. Trembal, that's who.

I run the pad of my thumb over her slit, only the thin material of her panties separating me from her bare flesh.

With an animalistic growl, I rip her panties straight from her body and go to shove them into my pocket...before remembering I'm naked, and instead, watch as it flutters to the ground. Whoops. Maybe I should've shoved it up my ass crack as a sort of temporary pocket.

Bronson, the sly dog-wolf, immediately bends down and grips it between his teeth, slowly backing away.

Finally, I have access to my buttercup's sweet cunt, and I waste no time stabbing one finger inside of her tight channel. I use my other hand to push down her dress until her tits are bared to the other men in the room.

All five of them—even Bronson, who is now in human form, wearing a pair of low-slung sweats—eye Nina with barely contained lust and wanton need. They look as if they're seconds from leaping forward and devouring her.

I begin to pluck at her nipples as I add a second digit to her sweet, sweet pussy. She moans, throwing her head back until it's resting on my shoulder.

"Rion..." she pants, digging her fingernails into my arms.

"Yes, Buttercup?" I bite down on her neck, no doubt

leaving a mark, as I begin to circle her clit. Removing my mouth from her porcelain skin, I smirk at the others, "We were talking, yes, *mi amores?*"

"Why the fuck are you talking in a French accent?" Cain demands, but he sounds breathless. His hand is dipped beneath the waistband of his pants as he touches himself, and fuck, the sight is hot. There's just something about masturbation that makes a man horny.

Well, hornier. I'm pretty sure my cock is ripping a hole through Nina's dress with how hard it is. My perfect, beautiful, amazing mate.

Fucking hell.

How did I get so lucky?

I never believed I would fall in love. It was an elusive concept, a daydream that I knew would never be my reality. Who would ever love a shifter like me? Sure, I had my fair share of hookups over the years, both males and females, but all of them pale in comparison to Nina. Hell, they don't just pale. They turn to dust and blow away on an imaginary wind.

The first time I saw Nina in one of the various tunnels of the prison, I knew I was a goner. How could I not be? I don't believe in love at first sight and all that crap, but my soul called to hers as keenly as hers did mine. A distant part of me knew we were meant to be together. Just Nina and her pussy.

Wait...

I pinch down on Nina's clit, just as she trembles in my arms, coming with a scream. I swear the sound of my name leaving her perfect lips is enough to get me to come as well.

As she clutches my arms, I move one of my hands to my cock and jerk myself—

Once.

A one-pump chump, apparently, because I swear the second my hand touches my dick, I explode across her back.

We will never speak of this moment again.

"I'll be in your cell, Buttercup," I whisper in her ear as she falls down from her high, continuing to clutch at my arms and whisper praises.

"Rion!" Kai calls to me, his expression frazzled and eyes molten. Dragon boy is totes lusting over our mate right now. "We need to talk about this."

I give him a two-fingered salute.

"No, we don't," I protest, continuing to walk backwards, my cock bobbing in front of me. I wink in Nina's direction, though I know she can't see me. "No one will touch a hair on Nina's perfect head. I made that message clear."

I smile wickedly when I think about the way we displayed Benny Poo in the gym. Think 'X marks the spot,' with the spot being his penis and the X his arms and legs.

We nailed the fucker to the wall, so any time someone walks in, they'll be reminded of what happens when you fuck with us.

Come to think of it, we're gonna need to ban Nina from going to the gym for the next week or so. At least until we remove his dismembered body.

"Well, we have people looking into things," Damien says casually, pulling a blade from his suit jacket and sliding it through his fingers. I kinda want to lick his blade right about now, but I like my tongue connected to my mouth, thank you very much.

"Can we trust them all?" Abel asks nervously, exchanging a glance with his brother. It's times like this where I wish I had a twin. Mom said I had a twin, but I ate him in the womb. Or maybe he ate me. Honestly, I can't remember the logistics, but if I'm eaten, then this is a pretty damn good heaven.

"They already know about the dead pool," Cain points out. "We didn't tell them anything they didn't already know."

"All we did was offer them rewards for giving us information," Bronson adds. "They need to know that if they help us, we can make their lives pretty good here in prison. But if they fuck with us…" He trails off with a growl, and I fan at my cock. Hot damn. Can I get Nina to growl like that?

As the five of them continue to bicker, I hurry out of the room and towards our cellblock. Nina's room is at the very end of the hall, in the room that used to be Damien's. Well, before that, it belonged to a guard. But a little murder took care of that issue.

I don't know how long Nina will remain with the others, but I know that the second she arrives here, I'll be ready. Maybe I should put some wrapping paper around my cock—

I pull the door open, my eyes automatically landing on the makeshift bomb on her bed.

And then everything explodes around me.

CHAPTER 9

The warden scares the shit out of me.

Not that I'll ever admit that, of course, but there's something about the man that oozes raw power. His trench coat hangs loosely around him as he takes a long drag of his cigarette, allowing it to balance between two fingers as he surveys me.

I throw him a cocky smile.

"Got me all alone in here, didn't ya?" I wink conspiratorially as those obsidian eyes of his narrow. Fucking hell. Those eyes look as if they're capable of ripping apart my insides and rearranging all of my internal organs. If the rumors about this man are true...

Then my fear is very, very justified.

But if there's one thing my years on the street have taught me, it's that a little smile and a shit ton of charisma and confidence can go a long way. And it doesn't hurt that I'm sexy as fuck.

I'm not gonna deny that I'm every male and female's wet dream. If you want me to be the innocent little priest, then just hand me a clerical collar. And if you want me to be a rocker bad boy, then I'll be the first to admit that I look pretty damn great in a leather jacket.

My blond hair and elegant features give me an angelic look, but the tattoos on my arms and torso remind the world that I'm anything but.

Sex… It's a tool you can use, and one that I've assembled into a weapon of mass destruction. The game is simple—get someone to fall in love with you, and then use them to your heart's content.

Does it make me a monster?

Most definitely.

Does it look like I give two shits about it?

Nope.

"Maybe we can take these cuffs off and I can show you a good time…" I allow my words to trail off suggestively as I raise my wrists, both of which are restrained by magical dampening handcuffs. Sure, I like cuffs just as much as the next kinky fucker, but I hate not having access to my beast.

When the warden snorts derisively, turning away to stare down at his paperwork, I flicker my gaze to the other occupant in the room. Some lowlife guard with auburn hair and a scruffy beard. His hooded eyes travel over my body as I bite my lip seductively, purposely allowing my eyes to drop to his rapidly hardening cock.

Yeah, this dude totally wants me to fuck him. I'll be more than willing to stick my cock up his pasty ass if it means having a guard on my side.

"Before we finish your processing, you have a visitor," the warden says gruffly, drawing my attention back to him. He stands from his desk, his eyes briefly roaming over my face with heady distaste, before he nods for me to follow him.

As he stalks ahead of me, disappearing through the shelves of magical artifacts he's collected over time, I make a show of stumbling.

"Damn. It's harder to walk than I thought it would be with these things on," I gripe, fluttering my eyelashes like some pathetic sap at the guard. Heat enters his cheeks as I stagger to the side, allowing my hand to caress his own.

"Oh…um…" Sounding flustered, he procures a key from his uniform pocket and removes my cuffs. He grabs them before they can clatter to the floor and shoves them into his back pocket. "I'll put them back on when we reach the visitation room."

"Thanks, friend," I purr, easily picking up on his thoughts now that I have access to my powers.

Fuck, he's so sexy. That tight little ass…

My hand brushes his again as I implant a vision in his head, one so vivid that he actually gasps in shock, not that he knows it was me who put it there. No one knows about this power but me.

The guard bends forward, allowing me an unrestricted view of his ugly, hairy ass, as I reach around his body to cup his balls. They're damn near bursting with how turned on he is.

I spit on my hand before sticking a single finger into his puckered hole. He moans low in his throat, arching his ass further against my cock.

"Now, now, my pet," illusion me whispers as I nibble on his ear. Abruptly, I grab his shoulders and spin him around, just barely containing my grimace of distaste. Because older men with slightly protruding bellies and hair fucking everywhere are not my kink. Fortunately for me, this is only an illusion.

I lick first one of his taut nipples and the next before dropping to my knees and kissing his belly. I continue to lower my mouth until my tongue snakes across the slit on his cock, already dripping with pre-cum.

As I swallow him whole, my other hand tugging at his balls, I can't help but smirk, releasing him with a slurp.

"You're mine now, pet. And you'll do exactly as I say."

My eyelids flutter open to see the guard with his pants tented, eyes glazed over with need. I adopt an innocent expression, taking a step closer as if I'm genuinely concerned.

"Are you okay?" My thumb brushes against his hand once more, and he jerks as if I was sucking his cock.

He blinks rapidly, attempting to orient himself, before turning towards me with undisguised lust and want.

"Yes." His eyes drop to my own cock just as I throw another vision into his head.

My hand closes around both of our dicks, holding them together as I jerk us off. I kiss up his neck, to his jawline, and then back down as our cocks caress one another with every pump of my hand.

He inhales sharply, staring at me as if he wants to bend me over the table and fuck me senseless, and my grin broadens.

Yup. It comes in handy to have someone in your back pocket. There's nothing a little lust won't do.

Of course, I have no intentions of actually fucking the guy, but he doesn't need to know that. He can go around thinking that we're in some forbidden love story or some shit.

I don't love.

And I sure as hell don't fuck my targets.

"Inmate! Gus!" the warden bellows, pausing where he stands at the end of his office, his eyes narrowed suspiciously. I once more push out my lips, the epitome of innocence, as his eyes drop to my freed wrists. "And why the fuck are his cuffs missing?"

Gus quickly makes up excuses as he reapplies the magical cuffs, abruptly restraining my magic. But it's okay. I already did what I needed to, if his lust filled eyes are any indication.

And when his hand brushes my dick through the hideous orange jumpsuit I've been wearing since my transfer from the upper levels of the prison, I know for sure. Hook. Line. And fucking sinker.

"I'm sorry I got you in trouble, Gus," I say with a soft smile. Do these fuckers actually fall for this shit? Women and men alike flock to me like a moth to a flame. It's sickening and maddening. I sometimes want to shake them senseless and ask them why they're so fucking stupid.

"I'm sorry I had to put these back on," Gus says with a blush almost as red as his hair.

Once more, I rub my fingers against his wrist, smirking when goosebumps dance on his skin.

"It's okay," I assure him with another megawatt smile. "I'll always remember what you did for me."

Before he can respond, I meander towards where the warden is waiting, his lithe body shaking with irritation.

"Are you done now, Brookes?" he asks, ire lacing his tone.

I flash him a sugary sweet smile. "Never."

The warden is silent as he leads me down a long, twisting hallway, Gus at my back. When we reach a set of small, private rooms, the warden stops abruptly and spins towards me, leveling me with a look capable of curdling milk. The vitriol in his eyes is clear as day. This man really doesn't fucking like me, and no amount of seduction or persuasion will change that. No big deal. I don't need everyone in this prison to like me...just the ones who matter.

"This little bullshit, innocent routine you have going on?" the warden begins, his voice a low growl. "It's not going to save you where you're going. If I were you, I'd cut the crap and pull on a pair of big boy panties. You're not going to last longer than a week."

"That's where you're wrong." I take a step closer, still beaming, and his eyes harden.

"I guess we'll see who's wrong when we're collecting your

corpse from down below. That is…if there's anything left to collect."

With that cheery statement, he pushes open the door and gestures for me to enter.

I swagger forward with all the confidence in the world, as if I'm not in a maximum security supernatural prison. As if I'm not in handcuffs. As if my life hasn't been inevitably altered because of one fucking mistake.

I trusted the wrong person, and you know what they say about trust—it's fucking stupid.

The door snaps shut behind me, the automatic lock engaging, as I survey the scarcely decorated room with a single metal table, two chairs on either side, and plain gray walls. Haven't they heard that a little color can go a long way? If I was the one who decorated the prison, I would've painted the walls a cheery yellow. Maybe a light blue.

My eyes snag on the camera in one corner, facing the table. The little red light isn't on, indicating that it's only for show.

Good to know.

"Logan," a dry voice greets, and I drag my attention towards the tall man sitting in the seat opposite me. As always, his illusion is firmly in place, making it impossible for me to decipher his features. When I try to focus, try to stare directly at him, my surroundings blur as a splitting headache threatens to rip me in two. All I know for certain is that he's an immensely powerful mage or warlock…someone capable of wielding spells that have been deemed illegal by the Council.

Hell, he might not even be a man. His voice is distorted, as if heard through a never-ending wind tunnel, and always has a distinct, raspy cadence to it. I'm assuming it's a man based on their broad shoulders, but for all I know, that's an illusion as well.

Either way, this bastard is my ticket out of here.

"You're looking well," he continues, nodding towards the seat opposite him. I offer him my winning smile, sliding smoothly onto the cold metal seat. It immediately hurts my ass, and there's not a lot of things capable of hurting it. Trust me. That thing has been poked and prodded and fucked more times than I care to admit.

"Orange isn't really my color," I say with a sultry wink. I've never been able to use my powers on this fucker, which is another reason I wanted Gus to remove my cuffs. Every time I've come into contact with him—or her, again I'm not sexist—I've been in magical cuffs. It's a real fucking pain in my ass.

"This is the last time we'll be in contact for a little while," he continues, and a moment later, his blurry hand appears in front of me, dropping a photograph on the table. I can't even tell what color his skin is. White, black, fucking pink. It's almost as if he's moving faster than an average human, faster than any supernatural, and it's causing his body to vibrate erratically.

"Why, Smith!" I place a hand to my heart in mock horror. "It feels like you're using me."

Yeah, *Smith*. That's the name he gave me to work with.

"You do have skills that we need," he deadpans, and I just barely restrain my eye roll. I swear, this man has no sense of humor to speak of. Everything he says is in a monotone voice that grates on my nerves.

"I'll get it done," I promise Smith cockily, glancing down at the photograph. Like the last time I saw it, a few weeks earlier, my pulse thunders in my ears as I stare at the stunning girl with obsidian hair flowing to the middle of her back. Heart-shaped face. High cheekbones. And the strangest white eyes I've ever seen.

I drag the corner of the picture off the table until it's resting in my lap.

"And I'll get my freedom for this?" I whisper, glancing down once more before I fold up the photograph and place it in my pocket.

"We don't back out of our deals," Smith reminds me curtly. "Send us confirmation that the job is done, and we'll get you out of here."

The picture feels like a weight in my pocket, but I manage another one of my infuriatingly cocky smiles.

"Consider it done."

CHAPTER 10

NINA

I stay behind when the others leave, knowing that I need a moment alone with Kai. He's been unbearably stressed since Ben's attack, and through Abel's eyes, I can see the strain it's taken on my dragon mate. His skin is sunken and pale, eyes appearing impossibly wide in his haggard face, with dark circles beneath them both, and his shoulder-length hair is wildly mussed. There are lines around his eyes and between his brows that weren't there prior.

"Kai," I say gently when the last of my men leave, once more pulling me into my customary darkness. I reach blindly towards him, and it doesn't take him longer than a second to pull me into his arms. I feel so safe when I'm in his embrace, as if not even the fiercest of storms can take me away from him. Because I know, without an ounce of doubt, that I'm meant to be with this man.

There are only a few absolute things in this world.

The sun will rise every morning and then fall at night, blanketing the world in a silvery darkness.

The ocean waves will kiss the shoreline before retreating in a never-ending tango of push and pull.

And my love for these six men is infinite and unencumbered, defying the laws of time.

Kai buries his face in my hair as he inhales sharply.

"Rion's right, you know," I begin gently, running my hands up and down his back, tangling my fists in his gray shirt.

"Those are two words I never thought anyone would say," he jests half-heartedly, but I can tell his mind is still millions of miles away.

"You guys are the biggest badasses in this place," I continue, and I can practically feel his lips twitch against my scalp at the use of the word "badasses." Abel would be so proud of me.

"If anything were to happen to you—"

"It won't," I say, cutting him off, positioning my hands so they're able to slide up his chiseled chest and cup his cheeks. "Do you want to know why?"

"If you say it's because you know we'll protect you, then I'll have to spank you, baby girl. That's a lot of fucking pressure," he teases, but I can hear a sliver of truth in his words. I think that's what bothers my dragon the most—he's afraid that he won't be able to save me. That one of the monsters lurking under my bed will grab my ankle and pull me under before he can stop it.

His fears are valid, considering what happened a few months ago, but it's not only him anymore. I'm stronger than I've ever been, and I'm growing stronger every day. I still feel pain and hurt and worry. I'm still weighed down and destroyed by the scars of my past.

But I'm not broken.

I don't believe I've ever been.

Sure, my edges aren't as smooth as they could've been,

but that doesn't mean the pieces don't fit. Just because they're jagged doesn't make them any less perfect.

I truly believe that's why the universe paired me with these six men—because we're all mangled, chewed-up pieces of a distorted puzzle, and only when we're together is the picture complete.

"Actually," I push up onto my tiptoes to kiss the corner of his jaw, "I was going to say that I'm capable of protecting myself."

He murmurs something nonsensically, twisting his head to chase my lips, and I take his moment of distraction to thrust my leg out and wrench his arm over my shoulder. It's a move Damien taught me, designed specifically to work on men larger than me.

I hear Kai's startled yell and the audible *whack* as he hits the cement flooring. A giggle escapes unbidden as I move to stand over him.

"You've been practicing," he murmurs from where he's sprawled on the ground, and I move to straddle his waist, placing my hands on his chest.

"Just a little." I wink, wiggling ever so slightly as his cock hardens underneath me. He moans low in his throat, a pained and heady sound, as his hands come to my waist.

"Fuck, baby," he groans as I wiggle. He moves his hand from my waist to my breasts, once more pulling down my dress sleeves until I'm bared to him. The tips of his fingers graze my sensitive nubs as I throw my head back, feeling wanton and needy.

Ever since Rion fingered me in front of the others, I've been in a constant state of lust. It was almost to the point where I was tempted to take Rion up on his offer and go with him back to my room. Or at the very least stick a finger inside of myself and finish the job. But as Rion once articulately told me, "Why masturbate when you have six willing cocks to please your juicy sweetness?"

"What are you thinking about, my love?" Kai pants as I lean forward, pushing my breasts into his face so his tongue can lick a pathway from the underside of my boob to my nipple. He circles the nub before gently pulling it through his teeth, and I swear the sensation travels straight to my core. "Are you thinking about what happened earlier? When Rion fucked you with his fingers in front of all of your other mates? How good your pussy felt when he touched that pretty little clit of yours?"

I whimper at his dirty words, jerking my hips wantonly against his rapidly hardening cock.

But one thing about what he said sticks with me.

"They're not all my mates," I pant breathlessly, and his hand slaps down on my ass cheek. The move is so sudden, so out of character for him, that I pause, my mouth dropping open.

"Don't you ever let them hear you say that," he warns severely. "Some of them might not be able to have fated mates, but that doesn't change their feelings for you. The stars themselves put you on a pathway to find them. They're made for you, just as you were made for them. Don't go thinking anything else."

The urgency in his tone has me freezing, my hands lowering to clench his muscular shoulders. I swallow the ball of yarn stuck in my throat as I realize how my words could be construed.

I never want the others to think that they're somehow less than because we're not mates. From what I gathered, only animal shifters have fated mates, but that doesn't make my feelings for the twins and Damien any less than what I feel for Bronson, Rion, and Kai. I love them all just as

intensely, as if my heart has been cut into six equally proportionate slices.

They were meant to be mine, of that I have no doubt. I
was born for them, just as they were born for me. We don't
need animal sides to see that.

"I'm sorry," I whisper as he plants a gentle kiss to first one
breast and then the other.

"It would break their heart if they heard you say that," Kai
repeats.

"I love you all so, so much." I lean forward to plant a
tender, reverent kiss against his lips. His stubble grazes my
cheeks and chin, somehow increasing my desire. "I know it's
technically not possible for them to be my mates, but it
feels…"

"It feels as if they are," Kai finishes for me as he palms first
one tit and then the next before releasing them. Before I can
cry out at the loss of connection, I feel his hand move to his
zipper as he frees his cock. "We don't know a lot about what
you are, baby. I mean, for all we know, you're more than
capable of having fated mates yourself. Maybe that's why you
feel so comfortable with them—because they're your mates
just as surely as I am."

His cock slides back and forth across my slick folds as he
positions himself, hoisting me upwards before pulling me
back down until he's fully sheathed inside of me.

We both groan at the sensation as my pussy involuntarily
squeezes his girth.

"Fuck, baby, you're so tight," he praises as I begin to ride
him. I found early on that this is one of my most favorite
positions to take my men. It gives me a feeling of control, as
if I can choose to stop this at any time I desire. Not that I
ever would, but I like knowing I have the option.

I lean forward, his cock hitting a new angle, as he once
more grabs at my breasts.

"I love your fucking tits," Kai gasps as he plucks at my nipples. "They're so big and perfect."

"I love your…um…nipples too," I murmur between pants as I struggle to reciprocate his dirty talk. I have to give him some credit—he doesn't laugh at me, though I know my mate well enough to tell he's amused.

"What else do you like about me?" He begins to thrust his hips harder, and I throw my head back, my black hair brushing against his thighs where his jeans still sit. The mere fact that we still have our clothes halfway on only amps up my desire. It's dirty and raw and animalistic…and I freaking love it.

"Your cock." I lower my hands to his chest as he drops his own to my slick opening. He begins to circle my clit with the tip of his rough finger as my body convulses around him.

"What else?" he demands.

"Everything!" I finally reach that blessed cliff and careen headfirst over the edge. I come with a scream, my nails digging into Kai's pecs as he shifts us abruptly, repositioning me so I'm beneath him and he's rutting into me savagely.

My pussy squeezes his cock like a vise as he comes with a roar, one I'm positive can be heard all the way across the prison.

"Fucking hell, baby." Kai lowers his forehead to my own, and I desperately wish I could see the expression on his face. Would he be smiling? Stone-faced? Dopey? "You're so perfect. If anything happened to you—"

"We already went over this," I say tiredly as I stroke his tangled hair. "Nothing bad will happen to me. I prom—"

The door to the throne room slams open, and Kai immediately crouches above me with an enraged, guttural growl. I easily slide into his mind to see Bronson standing before us, distress evident in every line of his face.

"Bron?" I amble to my feet, not caring that my dress is still pushed down beneath my breasts and that Kai's and my combined juices drip down my thighs.

Bronson whines low in his throat, more wolf than man, before hurrying towards me and wrapping me in his muscular arms.

"Bron? What's going on?" I bite down anxiously on my lower lip, breaking skin.

When Bronson says one word—just one word—I know it will change everything completely.

Panic steals the breath from my lungs as my heart stutters to an abrupt stop.

"Rion," Bronson whispers, and I feel myself shudder in his arms, falling apart at the seams. "It's Rion."

CHAPTER 11

NINA

I'm running out the door before Kai can stop me. Using Bronson's eyes for guidance, I maneuver the twisting halls of the Labyrinth until I reach the cellblock my men claimed for themselves.

My heart races faster than a herd of wild horses as I pause in the doorway, my hands coming to my mouth in shock. Bile rushes up my throat as I begin to slide forward, only for Bronson's arms to wrap around my waist, holding me steady.

"Oh god."

The entire cellblock is nothing more than tiny shards of gray cement, debris, and residual ash. Even now, flames lick at the walls located near the very end of the hall, closest to where my room was. Damien stands with the twins near the doorway, all of their faces grave.

"Rion?" I whimper, and three heads snap in my direction. "Where...? How...?" Panic rises to the surface, and I feel adrift, as if I'm thousands and thousands of miles away from the shoreline and steadily sinking beneath the unrelenting ocean waves. I claw helplessly at my throat, as if that will somehow stop the onslaught of emotions from consuming me. Drowning me. Killing me.

Rion said he was going to be here. To wait for me.

Here.

Where debris and soot cover the crumbly walkway.

Here.

Where flames devour the walls and ceiling.

Here.

Where my bedroom is nothing but charred furniture and peeling, brown wallpaper.

"Nina, listen to me." Bronson twists me in his arms and cups my face with his rough hands. His thumbs stroke leisurely patterns onto my sensitive skin as he presses his forehead against my own.

I immediately pull out of his head, embracing the darkness, as he tries to soothe me, tries to talk me off the ledge.

"Feel in your heart, my beloved. You know that Rion is alive and well. You can feel it."

I sob uncontrollably, gripping his wrists as if I mean to pull him closer...or push him away.

"Rion..."

"He's alive," Damien speaks up from behind me. "But he was injured in the blast. Badly. Fortunately, we arrived quick enough to contact the guards and have him sent to the medical wing with Brina."

"He'll be fine, Bambi," Abel cajoles, his voice closer than it was before, as if he snuck up behind me while I broke down in Bronson's arm. "He's a tough motherfucker. He's probably already on his way back."

"Look in your soul," Bronson whispers. "Feel him, Goddess."

I do as he says, retreating to a part of myself where I'm able to reach my men. My body unclenches incrementally as

I force myself to relax, force myself to focus on anything other than Rion lying in a body bag.

I would quite literally go insane.

Just like when I was training, I travel to the brilliant, energetic ball of light that symbolizes Rion in my...soul? Heart? Essence?

The part of me that declared him as mine.

The connection is strained, frayed almost, like a wire that has been cut, but I'm soon able to slide inside of his head.

His eyes are open as he stares blankly at a stark white ceiling. Pain radiates throughout his body—throughout *my* body—but he doesn't utter a single word as a pretty woman with red hair and a wicked scar on her face hovers over him.

"You have some nasty burns, little kitty," she observes, her smile widening and distorting her face even further.

But Rion is already retreating inside of his head and focusing on other things. On me.

In his mind, I can see my face, wreathed in a cocoon of gold and silvery light as if I'm the embodiment of the sun and the moon combined. The rest of the world is shaded in black and gray, but not my face. It's the only bright spot, disrupting the monotony of darkness.

Is that...?

Is that really how he sees me?

My throat clogs with the enormity of my emotions for this man, and I reach a mental finger forward to caress him.

He stills, the image flickering, and then his voice reverberates through my head, bone-weary and tired.

Buttercup?

I practically sob as my legs threaten to give out on me.

It's me, my love. Are you okay? What happened?

This isn't the first time I've been on fire, Buttercup. Am I mistaken, or does he sound almost cocky? As if that's something worth bragging about?

Still, my knees are weak with relief, and I want nothing more than to hold him in my arms and kiss him senseless.

But you're okay?

I'm okay, he assures me, his mental voice almost jovial. *Maybe I'll get a lollipop for being a good patient. I once got a lollipop stuck in my hair, so then my momma took a chainsaw and—*

What happened? I interrupt his ramblings before he can finish his tirade. I know my mate. Once he starts talking, he'll never stop.

I swear I feel the temperature in his head drop one hundred degrees. I don't know how else to describe it. One second, his warmth caresses me like a spring breeze, and the next, it feels like I'm in a tundra. The coldness seeps through my very skin and embeds itself in my bones. I imagine that goosebumps will be pebbling on my body, causing every hair to stand on end.

Someone left you a present, he hisses, and in his mind, I can see the tiny bomb placed on my pillow. *If you'd been alone...*

So that means he or she was nearby, I muse.

What do you mean? His tone is quiet, but it could never be construed as soft. There's a darkness to it, a menace, that both terrifies and arouses me.

I suppose that's what I get for falling in love with the monsters I should've feared.

The bomb wasn't on a timer, because no one knew what time one of us would enter the room. My guess is that someone was nearby and waiting. Though if I was truly the person's target...

It's not like he or she could've waited for you to show up, Rion laments bitterly. *I saw the bomb. Besides, he or she still would've been able to claim a million dollars for killing me.*

I'll relay this to the others. Maybe there's a lingering scent, I tell Rion, my heart lodging in my throat. Because someone tried to *kill* Rion. If he would've been one step closer to the bomb,

I have no doubt we wouldn't be having this conversation. Maybe fate is on my side for once and chose to save one of the men I love. After all, haven't I been through enough crap? I deserve to have a happily ever after.

Silence descends, his mind for once peaceful and serene. *Rion?*

Yes, Buttercup?

I love you.

Warmth suffuses me as I hear a distinct purr-like rumble.

I'll be back before you know it. Don't miss me too hard.

The connection snaps, and I find myself in my body once more, still in Bronson's arms.

"Angel?" Damien asks worriedly, and for Damien to be worried, it means I was extremely out of it.

I place a hand to my forehead, feeling flushed and over-heated, as Bronson scoops me up bridal style.

"Are you okay, Goddess?" His voice teeters the precarious edge between a growl and a question, his wolf making an appearance.

"I'm fine," I assure him. "But, Bron?" I tap his shoulder gently, waiting until he stops. I slowly reach my hand up and trace the contours of his handsome face. "Do you think you could sense if anyone was in this hall besides one of us?"

"Why—"

"Because I don't believe the bomb was on a timer. It's too much of a coincidence. And through Rion's eyes, I didn't see any wires that led back to the bomb for it to be tripped when he entered the room."

"You're so fucking sexy when you talk about tripping wires and bombs," Abel purrs from somewhere behind me.

"You think someone went into our home?" Damien demands sharply, ignoring the trickster demon. I reach blindly in his direction, only feeling comfort when his fingers interlock with my own and squeeze softly. I feel the barest graze of his lips against my knuckles before he drops my hand.

"It makes sense," Kai murmurs tiredly, and I wonder when he arrived. Probably at the same time I did with Bronson, though my mind was too consumed with pain and panic to notice.

"Rest assured," Damien begins curtly, "I will find the intruder and interrogate them myself. Whoever dared to hurt my family will fucking pay."

CHAPTER 12

My wrists ache from the cuffs scratching against my sensitive skin, turning it red and raw.

Fortunately, the women who hired me for the next few hours are more interested in each other than me.

I lay on the bed forgotten as Daisy Livingston and Mollie Bara, both of whom have prominent political husbands, fondle each other's tits. Daisy plucks Mollie's nipples and lifts her fake breasts as Mollie trails kisses down the other woman's neck.

I don't know why they even bother with me when they seem content with each other. Maybe so they don't feel as guilty fucking women when they're both already married. Hell if I know.

As they continue to kiss, I allow my mind to drift. Away. Away. Away.

I think of my brother, locked in a cage away from the rest of the world, and my resolve to escape solidifies. I'm blessed that most of the clients of this sick club choose me over my brother. Why would they want a trickster demon when they can have one that embodies sex?

Almost absently, I send a wave of lust at the two women, and they both groan heartily.

One day, I'm going to escape this prison.

One day, I'm not just going to be a body for people to use and discard.

"Hey, pretty boy," one of the women, Mollie, purrs, drawing my attention back to her. She leans her head down and licks at her lover's nipple before capturing it in her mouth. Her other hand reaches for my flaccid dick.

I try my hardest not to grimace as she begins to stroke me.

Thank the fucking stars that Daisy chooses that moment to cup both of Mollie's breasts before rolling her over, lowering her mouth to her cunt.

As they go to town on each other, I think of sunshine. Of blue skies and fluffy white clouds. Of sand beneath my feet and waves crashing against the shoreline. Of bustling streets and secluded forests.

Freedom.

So close, I can practically taste it.

The women end their session without touching me again, and I practically sag in relief when they leave. Of course, they don't bother to fucking uncuff me, so I'll have to wait for an employee to come by.

I don't know how long I sit in the dark, my arms aching from where they're positioned uncomfortably over my head, when the door shoots open, careening off the far wall.

"Hello?" I try to keep the ire out of my voice as I twist my head towards the intruder.

Only for all of the color to drain from my face and horror to grip my heart in an iron claw.

"No," I breathe as Lionel Green steps in the room. He's already naked, his hairy belly and small cock on display.

"I asked them to keep you right here for me." Lionel licks his puffy lips. His grin is predatory, the thing of nightmares, as he strokes his micropenis.

I try to envision another world. A better one. Anywhere but this hell. "Spread your ass cheeks for me, boy. Daddy wants entry."

~

I WAKE WITH A START. A HEART POUNDING, STOMACH clenching, hands sweating type of start. I can barely see through the haze of water in my eyes. Blinking rapidly, hoping to dispel the liquid, I scrub a hand down my face before flopping over with a sigh.

Nina stirs beside me, her pink lips slightly parted, and I take a moment to survey her in the dim prison lighting.

She's so beautiful that my chest hurts. With her hair shining like a cauldron of spilt ink, she's a vision to behold. And she's mine.

Because somehow, someway, this perfect girl chose me as her life-long partner. She chose to love me, scars and all.

When she moves again, the blanket slides farther down, baring her breasts to my hungry eyes. I bring the tip of my finger to one of her rosy-pink nipples and gently flick the tip. She shifts again, face creasing, but doesn't wake up. Slowly, keeping my eyes trained on her, I begin to circle first one nub and then the next, watching the way her skin pebbles beneath my touch. Consumed by an unexplainable need, I lean down and kiss her nipple while my other hand squeezes her breast.

Still, Trouble doesn't wake.

On her other side, I spot Abel sleeping soundly, one arm sprawled over her stomach. After the night the three of us had…

It's no wonder she's dead tired.

A tiny smirk of satisfaction curls up my lips as I wrap a strand of her pitch-black hair around my finger.

I suppose Boris's sex club for the fucked and depraved

taught me one thing—how to please a lady. There's nothing greater than knowing *I'm* the one who put that dopey smile on Nina's face. That *I'm* the one who brought her to orgasm.

Surprisingly enough, my brother and I didn't share any females when we were held captive. Mainly because one of us cost an arm and a leg. And two of us cost a fucking continent.

Thank fuck for small miracles. I like having something that belongs to Nina and Nina alone. Sharing her with my brother? Both of us feasting on her tender flesh and bringing her to the peak of orgasm? I'm grateful that we were able to save that for her.

My cock stirs down below, ready for round—what is it? Five? Six? But I will it into submission. Only a year ago, the thought of touching someone other than my brother would have brought me to hysteria. I'm not entirely healed now, but thanks to Nina, I don't have to face my demons alone.

I stare at her sleeping face one more time, marveling at how serene and peaceful she appears, before sliding out from underneath my blankets and moving on silent feet towards my box of clothes. I slide on a pair of loose basketball shorts before padding out of the cell.

Since the explosion, Kai moved us to a collection of abandoned cells near the cafeteria. We haven't gone back and completely cleared out our old cells, so for now, our belongings rest in duffle bags and boxes.

I pass Bronson's cell, where the growly wolf shifter is sprawled unceremoniously on his stomach, head tilted to one side in sleep, and then Kai's empty one. Unsurprisingly, our leader is nowhere to be seen.

Standing sentry at the end of the cellblock is Damien himself, arms clasped behind his back and eyes fixed firmly ahead.

He doesn't even fucking blink when I move to stand in

front of him.

"Where's Nina?" he demands, tone glacial. I hold up my hands in a placating manner, my lips quirking in a smirk.

A part of me wants to tease him, but I know that will only lead to pain and death—*my* pain and death.

"Safe. With Abel." A genuine grin erupts on my face as I think about last night. My tongue on her pussy while she kissed Abel passionately. We didn't take it any further than that…yet. Just a bunch of orgasms from our tongues and fingers.

But you can bet your ass we're planning to. Or *her* ass, as the case may be.

"Can't sleep?" Damien arches one eyebrow in understanding. Out of all the men, sans my brother, Damien understands what I've been through the best. Rumor has it that he was molested when he was just a kid by the leader of the assassin guild he trained with.

And just like me, his tormentor still lives.

Hell, I'm pretty sure he still *talks* to the sick fuck.

I grunt a reply to Damien's query and then glance in the direction of the gym. Well, makeshift gym, since the Labyrinth doesn't actually fucking have one. Only a select few have access to it, and even then, it's barely ever in use.

"Kai down there?" I ask, knowing there's nowhere else he'll be at this time of night.

Damien nods curtly, already dismissing me and staring at the wall with stoic indifference. That man…

I swear he could kill me with a flick of his wrist and not feel an ounce of remorse if I meant to harm Nina, even though we've been "friends" for many, many years.

Though, I can't say I wouldn't do the same. If it was their lives or hers, I'd choose hers. Every. Damn. Time.

Before I can take a step in the direction of the gym, Damien places his hand down on my shoulder, halting me. I turn towards him in surprise, but his lips are straightened into a thin line.

"Find a way to fight your demons, brother," he warns, "before they consume you completely."

With that ominous statement, he releases my shoulder and casually slides a blade out from his jacket sleeve. Probably imagining…I dunno…stabbing someone.

Whatever psychopaths do.

It occurs to me that I'm only wearing a pair of loose shorts and no shirt as I maneuver the twisting halls. If there's one thing I hate just as much as physical touch, it's being objectified. It's having eyes on you when you're least expecting it and feeling like your skin is crawling.

I don't run into anyone as I make my way to the dusty room we delegated as the gym—if you can call the room with a single punching bag, broken treadmill, and stationary bike missing a pedal a gym.

Kai is already there, shirtless and sweating as he levels punch after punch at the bag. I know he can sense my presence, but he doesn't turn around as he beats the bag to within an inch of its pathetic life.

"You know," I drawl lazily when it becomes apparent he's not going to acknowledge me, "if you want someone to kick your ass, I'm available."

Finally, he stops his brutal assault and steadies the bag before turning around. "You mean a chance to kick *your* ass," he corrects with a wry smirk, moving towards a broken stool we all use as a table. He takes a swig from his plastic water bottle before using a towel to wipe the sweat off his face. "I thought you were with Nina."

"Can't sleep." I shrug nonchalantly, even as an uncomfortable itch radiates across my skin. I want nothing more than to crawl back into bed with my lover, but I'm too *damaged.* Too broken for that.

No, what I need is to kick the crap out of someone.

"Nightmares?" Kai arches an eyebrow, and I rein in my urge to growl like a feral animal. How come everyone fucking knows everything about me all the damn time?

"Less talking, more ass kicking," I grunt out, already taping up my hands.

Honestly, with both of us shirtless and dripping with sweat, we're probably the stars of some porno out there. But there's nothing even remotely sexual about what we're doing.

Every punch, every kick, every tackle…

It allows some of the rage to deplete from my body. Some of the tension to drain away.

After an hour of fighting, we're both covered in a myriad of bruises, none of them visible in normal clothes, and a fine layer of sweat.

I drag myself to the stool and sip from Kai's water bottle, ignoring the disapproving look he gives me.

"You as stressed as I am about this damn dead pool?" I ask, wiping the water off my mouth with the back of my hand.

"It's more like a fucking hit list," Kai grumbles. "Usually, dead pools involve predicting the time of death. I've never heard of it actually involving murder."

"So you think there's a reason it's named that?" I query, my heart sounding like thunder in my chest. "Maybe a homage to Ryan Reynolds?" My joke falls flat as panic tightens my rib cage.

"Or maybe there are more than two lists," Kai surmises, "and over time, the names got confused."

"So a hit list…"

"And one that guesses when each hit will take place." His face turns contemplative, but somehow, that's even scarier than if he were angry. He may adopt a cool, calm front, but I know him to be a terrifying killer. He won't hesitate to slice your neck and then bathe in your blood if the need arose.

"But we don't know any of it for sure," I point out. "It's all theory at this point. All we know is that there's a hit list… dead pool…whatever, with Nina's name at the very top."

The thought of anything happening to her…

"We need to know why," Kai growls out, his thoughtful façade dropping as if it was never there to begin with. "Does it have anything to do with her bitch bio mom, Alyssa?"

"The Compound?" I add, remembering the horrific place she and Kai grew up in, where she was tortured and experimented on, turning her into a mutant tribrid.

Kai's eyes turn glacial, and I suddenly remember that he was there with her, at least at first. No doubt, he experienced similar horrors while trapped at this mysterious Compound.

"No," he grits out, hands balling into fists. "They would want her alive."

The implications of that send a cold chill coursing through me.

"They're not getting their hands on her, Kai," I say, using his real name instead of the one people in the prison refer to him as. His eyes snap to my face in surprise, but whatever he sees there has him relaxing incrementally.

"No one is fucking touching her," he agrees. "But we need to be careful. What happened with Rion…it can't happen again."

We both fall silent as we finally leave the gym, beginning the walk back to our new cellblock. This early, there aren't that many people walking about, but we still run into a few shifters who glare at us, eyes spewing murder. Kai simply glares back, his eyes resembling those of reptiles, before the cowards scurry away, their metaphorical—and in some cases, literal—tails hanging between their legs.

"You know," I begin softly, "this isn't a place for Nina to

live in. To start a family. And I'm not just saying that because of the fucking list floating around…"

Kai pauses, eyes staring blankly ahead as his hands twitch by his sides.

For a moment, I think he isn't going to answer, but when he finally does, his voice is a hushed murmur. "You're right." He releases a bark of dry laughter. "Hell, I always knew it, but you're right—our girl deserves better than this fucking dump."

But there's nothing we can do, no way we can get Nina acquitted for her crimes. She murdered a councilwoman, for fuck's sake. Her own mother.

She's stuck in here, just like the rest of us. Forgotten by society as a whole.

Kai's eyes glimmer with something I can't name as we finally step into the cellblock, and I can't help but wonder what he's thinking about.

If it's the same thing I'm thinking about…

No! I shake my head vehemently. I know, more than most, that escape from this hell is impossible.

Still…

Foolish dreams of escape and babies and houses on the ocean flicker through my head before I can contain them. And when I finally reenter my cell, unsurprised to see Nina and Abel still asleep and tangled around each other, a genuine smile crooks up my lips.

A future out of this hellhole…

Sometimes, it's nice to dream, even knowing it'll never become reality. Then again, there is no freedom without Nina. I'd rather be trapped in a cage with her, than free alone.

CHAPTER 13

The next few days are relatively uneventful. No more attacks. No strange bombs. No one even *talks* about the list circulating the underground prison.

Yes, we call it *the list* now. Not the dead pool. Not the hit list. Just…the list. It somehow demotes it from bone-chillingly terrifying to only slightly nauseating.

To be completely honest, it makes me queasy to think that there might be two lists, one predicting our deaths and the other offering money for it. Why us? Why me? Logically, I understand why people might want to take action against my guys, but I don't understand why I'm at the very top. I'm practically useless, with very little control of my powers. Besides, it's not like anyone *knows* the truth about what I am. Only my men and Braelyn do.

So *why?* Kai seems to believe that the Compound isn't involved. After all, they would want their investment alive and unharmed.

Maybe it's someone against the Compound?

Or heck, maybe we're looking too far into this and it truly is just a fellow prison mate who's rich and hoping to eliminate the guys once and for all. And if they take me down, that's a surefire way to do it.

I shift on the steel bench as the raucous shouts and jeers ring out around me. There's the distinct sound of flesh hitting flesh, but I don't bother to slide into anyone's mind. I know what I'll see.

Every grievance between inmates takes place in the fight ring. If you're issued a challenge, you're forced to fight for your life…or you're hunted down.

I was in that ring once when Tessa, a girl who I thought was my friend, became jealous over my relationship with Rion. I chose not to kill her, but my men still deemed that she was too dangerous to have around.

Rion…

The thought of my shifter lover still in the medical wing of the prison tightens my stomach into dozens of knots. The last time I talked to him, he promised he would be released today. I'm practically holding my breath in eager anticipation.

Braelyn places a reassuring hand on my shoulder and gives it a squeeze.

"You doing okay, Nina?" she asks softly as one of the fighters begins to moan and another one roars in victory. The crowd goes positively wild, and a few steps behind me, I hear Kai's slow clapping as he watches the exchange. I don't need eyes to know that he's standing beside Bronson and Damien, both of whom are watching me more than the fight itself. I can feel their eyes on my flesh like a physical caress.

But of course, the crowd of bloodthirsty prisoners don't know what this fight is truly for—a distraction.

While men and women beat the shit out of each other in the ring, Abel and Cain are traveling from cell to cell, searching for any leads. I think the silence and tranquility of the prison is worrying them almost as much as it is me.

Besides the arrival of a new prisoner, nothing overly exciting has occurred, and I don't know if I should be glad or wary.

Or both. Definitely both.

"Just thinking," I respond, shivering as I huddle into Damien's suit coat, pulling it close. The air is uncharacteristically frigid today, almost as if a vent has been left open. Since my wardrobe consists of nothing but dresses, Damien gave me his jacket as soon as we arrived, with the promise to procure me warmer clothes.

"A penny for your thoughts?" She nudges her shoulder against my own as I fiddle with one of the buttons lining the open flap.

I laugh lightly, remembering the first time she asked me that and I didn't understand the saying. I simply held out my hand and waited for her to give me a penny, thinking if she wanted to pay me for my thoughts, that was her choice.

She still teases me about it to this day.

"It's just...everything." I shrug helplessly. "The list. Rion. My powers." Almost absently, I push up one of the long black sleeves and scratch at the skin of my wrist.

"Damien still working with you?" Braelyn queries, and I nod once, nibbling on my lower lip anxiously.

While it's true he's been helping me harness my powers, that's not the only thing we've been working on. My mage fiancé is still working tirelessly to lift the spell my mother put on me that prohibits me from having kids. He describes it as a thorny vine squeezing my uterus. Slowly but surely, he's removing the weeds and demolishing them in a ball of flames.

But we still don't know what effects Alyssa's magic will have on me. Will I ever be able to have kids? Do I even want to, especially while I'm trapped here? It sure as heck isn't an environment I want to bring babies into.

"Well..." Braelyn trails off for a moment, her arm

brushing my side. "If you ever need a break from all of the dick energy, let me know. Jenny and I would love to have you."

My lips can't help but twitch into the beginnings of a smile. She talks as if we're neighbors visiting each other's houses and making dinner, not inmates in a maximum security prison.

"What's this?" Braelyn questions suddenly, and before I can comment, she reaches into my jacket—Damien's jacket—pocket.

"You shouldn't be doing that," I hiss, cheeks flaming. "This isn't mine. It's Damien's."

Braelyn is silent for a moment, so silent, I almost think she left when she breathes out, "It's a love note."

"A...love note?" I parrot dumbly as something uncomfortable settles in the pit of my stomach. Why would Damien be carrying around a love note in his pocket?

Panic threatens to consume me, already beginning to cut off my air supply, but the knowledge that none of my guys will ever hurt me keeps it adequately subdued. Still, that doesn't stop the lingering jealousy that persists like an annoying mosquito buzzing around my head.

Why would he have a love note? Did someone slip it into his pocket when he wasn't paying attention? Or did he keep it purposely? Why—

"It's not for Damien," Braelyn continues, voice nearly inaudible. "It's...it's for you."

"For me?" My eyes widen in disbelief. "Damien wrote me a love note?"

"I don't think he's the one who wrote it," Braelyn states cryptically, and this time, my curiosity takes over and I slip easily into her head.

Fortunately, she's still staring down at the crisp sheet of paper, so I'm able to see the words written in blood-red ink.

My precious, white-eyed darling,
You're mine. My sun. My moon. My world.
I will find a way to get to you.
Love,
Me.

"What the heck?" I gasp as I reread the words. The ink still appears to be wet, almost as if someone just wrote it. "Who put this in my pocket?"

"I have no idea," Braelyn confesses, but her attention is no longer on me. She glances in both directions warily, as if preparing for an attack.

In the ring, a shifter and a vampire partake in a bloody fight, one that involves claws and fangs, but Braelyn's gaze sweeps over them without stopping. Finally, she focuses on my three men still standing slightly behind me, whispering amongst themselves.

"Come on," Brae says, gripping my upper arm and hoisting me to my feet. Our sudden movement garners the attention of all three of them, and they turn to stare at me with varying degrees of confusion. Well, except for Damien. His face is as blank as always, his ice-cold eyes traveling over my body and assessing me for injuries...as if I could've possibly gotten hurt in the hour since we've been here.

Braelyn doesn't speak as she thrusts the note into Kai's hand.

"What is this?" He doesn't immediately open it. Instead, he keeps his dark gaze on me.

"A love note," Braelyn responds curtly. "I found it in Damien's jacket pocket."

At that, I see the first hint of emotion cross Damien's face. Shock and anger color his cheeks crimson as he grabs the note from Kai's hand and unfolds it.

"I don't know why anyone would send me a fucking love

note," he seethes, staring directly at me. "Would you like me to kill her?"

"Calm down, psychopath," Brae placates lightly. "It's not for you."

"It's not for...?" His brows furrow as he finally reads the note, and then a chilling coldness overtakes the previous shock and disbelief. His eyes harden until they're chips of ice in his arresting face, and his lips flatten. "I see."

Without a word, he hands the note to Kai and tugs me forward, wrapping his arms around my waist. I pull out of Braelyn's head and simply *exist*. His scent surrounds me, coddling me, and his arms make me feel secure, loved, and protected.

"Thank you for bringing this to my attention, Braelyn," Kai says, and his words are accompanied by an enraged growl. No doubt, he handed the note to Bronson to read.

"A threat?" my shadow wolf rasps out, more animal than man.

"I don't think so," Kai replies, and though his tone is casual, almost nonchalant, it does little to belie the barely veiled violence lingering just beneath the surface. "I think it's just some sap taking a romantic interest in our girl, nothing more."

"Not a surprise," Braelyn mumbles. "Half the guys here are in love with her, and the other half want to fuck her." Her matter-of-fact tone causes both Bronson and Kai to hiss sharply, and I can imagine my friend shooting them a "what can you do about it?" look.

"But it is concerning how they got it in my coat pocket," Damien muses in a cold, detached voice. His hands tighten almost imperceptibly around my waist. "They would've had no way of knowing I'd give Nina my jacket, and we had our eyes on her the entire time we've been at the ring. So how did they slip it in?"

"Magic?" Kai guesses, sounding supremely pissed off, as Abel would say.

"It takes powerful magic to make an object materialize in a new location," Damien agrees.

"Fuck, I need to fight," Bronson snaps, and I hear the heavy thud of his footsteps as he stomps away, no doubt to find an opponent willing to fight him—there usually aren't many. He returns only a moment later and rips me away from Damien. He nuzzles his face into my hair, inhaling my scent, before whispering, "I don't like the thought of having competition, Goddess."

I giggle into his chest—because heaven knows I'm not tall enough to reach his neck—and say, "There's no competition. You're my mate, Bron, for now and ever."

This time, the noise he makes is all male satisfaction. "Damn right I am."

Kai's strident bellow interrupts our conversation.

"Next up in the ring, we have my chief enforcer, Bronson, versus Piggy!"

The audience immediately breaks into roaring cheers, and I can't help but crinkle my nose.

"Piggy?" I ask in disbelief. "What type of name is that?"

"The name of someone who's going to have his ass beat in the next five seconds," Braelyn mutters from behind me.

I just know that Bron is smirking smugly, agreeing with her assessment.

"What will you give me if I win, Goddess?" He once more rubs his nose up and down my neck, ignoring the chants from the crowd. He seems content to make them wait as long as he likes.

Bron-son. Bron-son. Bron-son.

"What do you want, my love?" I reach my hands up to cup both of his cheeks, loving the way his whiskered face feels against my soft palms. He's in desperate need of a shave, but honestly? I love the rugged look on him.

And that gives me an idea…

Remembering my last talk with my girlfriends, when they were discussing their favorite sex moves, I say, "If you win, I'll give you a blow job."

His breath hitches, and I'm suddenly acutely aware of his hard cock pressing against my stomach. Behind me, I hear someone—Kai more than likely—choke on air.

"Motherfucker," Bronson grits out.

"And if you lose," I lick my dry lips, trying to remember the correct terminology, "you'll have to watch while Kai reams my ass and I swallow Damien whole. Or Kai can pound my pussy. I'm not picky."

Totally nailed it.

Bronson doesn't speak. Heck, he doesn't even move. Even Kai and Damien have become unnaturally quiet behind me, almost as if they're holding their breaths.

All at once, Kai releases a ragged gasp and whispers, "Fucking hell, baby."

Damien adds, "You're going to lose, Bron, or I'll cut off your dick and feed it to Piggy."

"Not a chance in hell, assholes," Bronson retorts, claiming my lips in a bruising, possessive kiss. He captures my wrist and brings my hand down to his fully erect cock. I instinctively palm it. I've given my guys blow jobs before, but this feels different somehow. I don't know how to even explain it.

Maybe it's because I initiated the playtime? I'm usually so timid and unsure when it comes to pleasuring my guys. But throughout the year, my confidence has increased and I've learned to embrace my sexuality.

"Tonight, this big fat cock is going to be sliding between your perfect lips, goddess," Bronson murmurs, releasing a low moan as I squeeze down hard, just the way he likes it.

"Then win." I shrug as I release him, and he lets out a low, almost threatening growl. It's a noise a predator would make the second it locks eyes on its prey. And I can't say I'll mind being hunted and devoured by the likes of Bronson.

"Have fun fighting with a boner!" Braelyn calls as Bronson stomps towards the ring. She giggles wickedly before once more jabbing me with her elbow. "I taught you well. 'Reams my ass'? Classic!"

"You taught her that?" Kai demands in disbelief.

"Well…porn did, technically."

Damien makes a weird noise in the back of his throat, and Kai growls sharply. But Braelyn? She just laughs her ass off as she retreats, no doubt to sit back down beside Jenny.

I soon find myself alone with two very horny and very pissed off monsters.

"What's this about porn, Angel?" Damien asks darkly, running his finger down my neck and then back up. "Are we not pleasing you enough?"

I blush. "She's joking… I don't… I mean…I wouldn't…"

I mean, I know what porn is. Sort of. Maybe? But I don't…

I haven't…

"We know that, baby." Kai's voice is dark as sin. "And fortunately for us all, we can have a lot of fun tonight." He leans forward to lick the shell of my ear. "Because Bronson's going to lose."

Bronson? Losing? That's laughable. He's one of the best fighters in the prison.

"How is he—"

My question is answered when Bronson releases a hiss of pain. I slide into Damien's eyes immediately to see his gaze fixed firmly on Bronson, my wolf shifter held immobile by his magic. His eyes are a glowing yellow as his opponent, Piggy, lands another punch to his midsection.

"Motherfucker! Damien, you're a dead man!" Bronson snaps.

Instead of answering, Damien moves behind me and wraps his arms around my waist. He places his lips directly to my ear and whispers, "All's fair in love and war. And sex. Definitely sex."

CHAPTER 14

ABEL

Prisoners are very, very good about covering their tracks.

If they don't want you to know something, there's no chance in hell you'll discover it.

Unless you're me or my brother. We can be very sneaky when we need to.

I do a somersault, jump gracefully to my feet, and then put my back flush against the wall, holding my finger gun at the ready.

"What the fuck are you doing, dumbass?" Cain demands, his eye twitching.

I shush him, and I swear he looks ten times more murderous. "I'm being a secret agent," I stage-whisper, kicking out my leg like some sort of ninja.

"You're gonna hurt yourself," he deadpans, folding his arms over his chest.

"I'm not going to hurt myself." To prove my point, I kick my leg up even higher, like some sort of Dutch dancer, and then… "Holy shit! I broke my nards, man. I broke them." I cup my junk, because fate somehow hates me. I'm going to be so fucking pissed if I broke my penis, dammit, now that I actually have a reason to use it.

Cain actually cracks a smile, and his eyes, the same grassy green color as mine, twinkle.

"You're a dumbass."

"A dumbass with broken nuts," I groan, leaning forward. "Send Nina! I need kisses to make 'em better."

Because, yeah, I'm just enough of a masochist that I would break my elephant trunk in order to have Nina's lips wrapped around it. Wait, no. Retract that statement. My junk is definitely not comparable to an elephant trunk. Those are gray and wrinkly, while my manhood is golden and thick and perfect and long and—

Cain places a hand on my chest, stopping me in mid-step, and puts a single finger to his lips. At first, I think he's messing with me for shushing him earlier, but then I hear the distinct sound of sheets rustling.

What the hell? Is someone down here? Everyone is supposed to be in the arena during the fights.

Fucking? Cain mouths, and I waggle my eyebrows suggestively. It wouldn't be the first time two people snuck away to do the dirty.

But who the hell would be stupid enough to fuck in our old cellblock?

I exchange another glance with my brother, and any previous humor dissipates. We were sent down here for one reason and one reason alone—find out which prisoners wish to see us dead. Discovering who created the list is important, yes, but right now, we need to face the immediate threat.

And to know that someone is in an area that only a few days prior had been ravaged by a bomb…

It's suspicious as fuck.

As one, we move through the halls until we reach the old cellblock. My eyes briefly assess the charred cement and debris littering the floor, before another sound reaches my ears. Closer this time.

Cain stealthily moves forward, not making a single sound, as I follow behind. When we reach Bronson's old cell, where an unfamiliar figure is bent over the bed, applying sheets to the mattress, I move to one side of the open archway and Cain moves to the other. He holds up three fingers and begins to count down.

Three.

Two.

On one, we both move forward, Cain pushing the man against the wall with me at his side.

"What the fuck are you doing?" Cain growls out as the man's eyes widen.

I'm almost positive I've never seen him before in my life. He's a handsome man, I'll give him that, with white-blond hair cut short and an innocent face. But that innocence is contradicted by the tattoos visible on his arms and neck.

Those baby-blues harden briefly before they're replaced by a cocky, almost sultry look.

"What's the matter, handsome?" this new man purrs, tilting his head to encompass me as well. I feel something probing the edges of my mind, but I swat it away. Power? It feels like power, but there aren't a lot of creatures that are capable of entering someone's mind, Nina excluded. I must've been imagining it.

Cain tightens his arm around the intruder's throat, and the cocky swagger dissipates as confusion swims in the asshole's eyes. That confusion is replaced by something infinitely colder and more dangerous.

"What are you doing here?" Cain demands.

"Don't be like that," the man tries again, his voice soft. He even fucking bats his eyelashes.

Is he...?

Is he seriously trying to flirt with my brother?

Even if Cain wasn't head over heels obsessed and in love with Nina, he's still as straight as an arrow. I literally have to cover my mouth to hide my laugh.

"Sorry, dude," I say with a chuckle. "We don't like dick."

Once more, that hard expression distorts the man's angelic face as he glares at Cain.

"I don't either," he confesses. "Now get the fuck off of me."

"Not until you tell us why you're here." Cain pushes down even further, no doubt cutting off the man's air supply, to emphasize his point. Only when the man's face turns a bright red does Cain release him, taking a step back and crossing his arms over his chest. "Talk."

"Fuck, man." He begins to cough, hurling daggers with his eyes at first my brother and then me. "I was just looking for a cell. It's not safe to be without a cell at night, you know?"

I eye the man suspiciously as he glowers.

"Look," Cain begins, taking a step forward, "you can't be—"

Before he can finish speaking, the man has Cain flipped over his shoulder and a knife to my brother's throat. Terror briefly immobilizes me before I spring into action, lunging at the attacker. Just as I'm about to make contact, he waves a hand, and I'm flung across the room, my head careening against the cell wall.

"I can kill you at any second," the man says almost lazily. He digs the blade at Cain's neck in deeper, drawing blood, but my twin doesn't wince. He just continues to glare up at the fucker defiantly. "But fortunately for you," he pats Cain's cheek condescendingly and then jumps to his feet, "I don't feel the need."

Rivulets of lava begin to form on Cain's skin, almost like it's cracking, and dark horns push through his blond hair.

His fingers elongate into keen claws as he takes a threatening step closer.

"I'm not an enemy of yours," the man says in a low voice. "I actually have information for you…for all of you." He turns to stare at me as well, his face grave. But just as quickly, that expression is replaced by a jovial smile. "So why don't you guys take me to your leader, okay?"

"This isn't some fucking alien ship," Cain growls out, still half demon. The stench of sulfur permeates the room.

The man simply rolls his eyes, leaning casually against the wall with his arms crossed over his chest. His angelic face belies something dark and wicked. Something dangerous.

"Nope," he pops the P with a sly grin. "It's just prison, and trust me, you're gonna want to hear what I have to say."

I exchange a glance with Cain, and he nods his head subtly. Because why the fuck not? The worst that can happen is this guy is full of shit and we'll have to kill him. And the best? Well, when it comes to Nina's safety, snitches don't get stitches. They get fucking gold and pearls and the favor of every last monster in this hellhole.

The fight must've already ended, because the halls are crowded as we march towards the throne room. Everyone purposely looks away when we pass. They know a dangerous fucker when they see one.

When we reach the throne room doors, I pause, glancing over my shoulder at the grinning asshole.

"As soon as you enter, bow. Don't fucking hesitate. Don't make any wiseass jokes. Don't fucking attack. We'll hear what you have to say."

"Yeah. Yeah. Yeah." He waves his hand in the air dismissively. "This isn't my first time dealing with an evil dictator."

For some reason, his words make me bristle, mainly because I didn't even realize that that was how the other inmates perceived us. Dictators. Huh. Dictator Abel.

Has a nice fucking ring to it.

I don't bother knocking as I push the door open and stalk inside, Cain and the asshole at my heel. And then I pause, my eyes widening to the size of saucers as I take in the sight before me.

A naked Nina is on her hands and knees, her gorgeous tits swaying and her pretty pink nipples on display. Kai is fucking her from behind while Damien—still in his suit—has his cock in her mouth, his fingers in her gorgeous black hair and his eyes closed in pleasure. Bronson is glaring at all three of them where he sits on the edge of the raised dais, a scowl on his face but lust emanating from his gaze.

Oh shit.

All three of them turn towards us in surprise, though that expression quickly turns to murderous rage when they stare at the intruder at my side.

The man's mouth is slightly agape, but there's no mistaking the lust oozing from his pores. His eyes are latched on Nina's breasts before moving to the curve of her ass. I don't need to be a lust demon to know that he has a boner the size of fucking Texas.

I think…

I think I just may have inadvertently gotten a man killed.

And honestly? I don't feel a fucking ounce of shame. He put a knife to my brother's throat, is a fucking cocky ass bastard, and is now staring at Nina with something akin to reverence.

This fucker's going down.

CHAPTER 15

NINA

Kai's kissing me before I even enter the throne room. Behind him, Bronson releases a growl of irritation, but he doesn't protest as I'm led through the doors and onto the rough stone floor. There's a bed in a tiny room located behind Kai's makeshift throne, but we're too eager to explore each other's bodies to use it. No, this is going to be raw and dirty.

"You lost, wolf." Damien's voice is almost taunting as he strolls up behind me and pushes my dress down. His hands immediately move to my breasts, kneading the heavy flesh and plucking my nipples.

"Because you cheated," Bron snarls, though the noise sounds more lust filled than anything. "Oh…fuck."

I don't bother submerging myself in any of their minds. I want to focus on the sensations their touches evoke, their unique scents, their hushed praises and whispered reverence.

I feel Kai move to his knees to kiss my stomach as he lowers my dress down farther. His tongue enters my belly button before he licks a path down to the waistband of my panties and then to my core. Embers of need burn hotly inside of me as he kisses my mound through the lacy material.

I whimper, arching my back, as Kai continues his ruthless assault. Damien's lips move to my neck, and I feel over- whelmed. By sensations. By the feelings they bring out of me. By love.

Kai pushes my panties to the side, and his tongue spears my pussy lips, running up and down the length of me. I moan, throwing my head back against Damien's chest as my silent assassin continues his assault on my aching breasts. I can hear rather than see Bronson pacing, his footsteps brisk as he releases low growl after low growl. The sound is rough and primal, shooting liquid heat straight to my center.

My orgasm comes hard and fast, but it doesn't take me by surprise. I was balancing on that precipice for quite some time, and Bronson's lust filled snarl only forced me over the edge, tumbling head over feet until I crashed at the rocky, beautiful bottom.

But my guys aren't done. Not even close.

I'm dimly aware of being pushed onto my hands and knees, my position changing so that I'm now facing Damien. I blindly place my hands on his thighs, loving the way his muscles clench beneath my touch, before fumbling for his zipper. His cock hits my face, and it takes considerable effort to feed it into my mouth. I run my tongue over his slit, moaning at the taste of his salty pre-cum, as his hands tangle in my thick black hair.

I can feel Kai line up at my entrance, his cock prodding my already soaked pussy, and he doesn't waste any time thrusting into me. The force pushes my mouth farther down Damien's cock, and I remember to hollow my cheeks like they taught me. He's so deep inside of me that I want to gag, but I resist the urge and take him even *deeper*.

I fist Damien's pants as Kai makes love to me from

behind. Damien's cock slides in and out of my mouth, and I feel a trail of saliva dripping down my chin from the force of his brutal thrusts.

"Fuck. Fuck. Fuck. Fuck," Bronson murmurs, and I half wonder if he's fisting himself. If his eyes are trained on the way Kai destroys my pussy and Damien claims my mouth like it's his and his alone. Or maybe he's staring at my tits swaying with every forward thrust of Kai's hips.

Kai's hand lowers to my clit, even as his punishing pace increases.

I'm so close…

The door to the throne room is pushed open, and all three of us freeze.

Before I can even catch my bearings, I'm on my feet and pushed behind two strong bodies. Another large figure comes up beside me and places a hand on my waist, holding me still. Bronson, if his pine tree scent is any indication.

I slide easily into Kai's head to face the intruders, my smile growing when I spot the twins. But that smile fades when I notice the man standing between them, his mouth agape and his eyes swimming with deep and undiluted lust. He quickly tries to clear his expression, adopting a nonchalant frown, but that doesn't stop the threatening growls pouring from my men. Even Abel and Cain, the two who brought him into our throne room, appear pissed as all can be, their eyes brimming red as their demons make appearances.

The first thing I notice is that the man is beautiful. That might be a strange thing to say about a guy, especially one in prison, but there's no denying that he has the face of an angel. His blond hair, so light it's almost white, frames a decidedly cherubic, innocent face—high cheekbones, thick lips, golden skin, long, sooty lashes. I spot tattoos on his arms and chest that give him a rough vibe, directly at odds with his angelic appearance.

There's something in his eyes that gives me a pause, something hard and cold and not entirely unlike Damien's.

"Kill him," Kai says instantly, taking a threatening step closer, and the man's face pales significantly, though he continues to offer us that bored, almost lazy expression.

"He says he has information," Cain sneers as he pushes the man a few steps forward, towards the group of monsters just waiting to unleash all of their pent-up anger onto their prey. A sliver of fear snakes down my spine as I stare at the man. It's not the fear one would expect. I don't believe he's going to hurt me. No, if anything, I'm afraid he's going to hurt one of my men.

Or one of my men is going to hurt him.

I feel something touch my head, but I don't protest as Bronson dresses me in a baggy shirt, the smell revealing it to be Kai's. It reaches my knees, the fabric swishing around me when I move. Through Kai's eyes, I watch as Damien calmly walks forward, shoving his dick back into his pants in an almost lackadaisical way, as if it's an inconvenience for him to *not* be flashing the world.

"What is your name, runt?" A knife appears in Damien's hand as he tilts his head curiously to the side. His gaze is cold. Icy. Emotionless.

And I know that I'm not looking at Damien the lover, but Damien the killer.

"Logan," the man replies without preamble, flashing my assassin a charming smile, one that makes two dimples pop out.

I swear if it was even possible, Damien looks *more* murderous, his icy blue eyes flashing. Logan's smile wavers slightly, even as confusion creases his features. He glances from Damien to the twins before finally settling his attention on me over Kai's shoulder. That confusion is replaced by curiosity and lingering lust. I want to tell him to look away, that he'll only make things worse, but Logan is either an idiot or he has a death wish.

"Don't look at her," Bronson growls out, moving to stand in front of me. When Kai turns away from Logan and focuses on me once more, I pull out of his head and into Bron's. Of course, my broody, overprotective shifter is glaring at the new prisoner as if he's mentally planning to rip his head off his body.

I stumble forward until my cheek is against Bron's back and then wrap both of my arms around his waist. I physically feel the tension drain from his rigid body at my touch, and his gaze lowers to where my hands touch his abs. He's too large for me to connect them, but he doesn't seem to mind when he places his large paws over mine.

"You okay, Goddess?" he whispers, too low for anyone but me to hear.

"Of course."

I know what he's asking and *why* he's asking. There's no doubt that this Logan person saw me in a compromising position with two of my men. But instead of the self-consciousness I thought I would feel, I am…

Calm? Is that the right word?

Maybe I don't know how I feel necessarily, but it's not anger or hurt.

"What did you have to tell us?" My soft voice has everyone turning to face me, but I focus my white gaze in the general direction Bronson was looking earlier. At Logan.

"Maybe if the information is good enough, we'll let you live," Kai snarls, and I just barely contain my eye roll. I love all of my guys, but sometimes they can be a teeny tiny bit… psychotic? Murderous? Overprotective?

"It's about the list." Logan doesn't beat around the bush,

and Bronson reluctantly turns away from me to face the blond-haired man once more. "The hit list. And the dead pool."

Logan is across the room in a span of seconds, his back against the wall and Damien's knife at the hollow of his throat. I take an automatic step forward, but both Kai and Bronson reach out to stop me.

"How do you know this?" Damien presses the knife in just enough to draw blood, and I watch as it travels down Logan's creamy skin, marring the colorful tattoos already present there. Logan doesn't even flinch, which is more than I can say for most men who face Damien's wrath.

"Because," Logan lifts his head to meet Damien's ice-blue gaze defiantly, "I was sent to kill her."

CHAPTER 16

LOGAN

I am so dead.

It's actually not even funny how dead I am. On a scale of one to ten, with one being alive and ten being twenty feet underground with maggots crawling out of your eye sockets and dirt on your decaying bones, then I would be a fifty. As in, I'm pretty sure I won't even have bones left for the maggots to feed on.

In my head, I picture sad music playing as a tiny little violin floats around my head, its soulful tune permeating my very soul.

At least if I die, I can stare at something nice.

Unbidden, my eyes drift to the girl's face once more. Nina. Nina Doe. My file told me a lot about her, but she's even more beautiful in person. It's an effortless type of beauty, something unnatural and ethereal. I imagine she climbs out of bed appearing like every man's wet dream… and then some. Heaven only knows how many spank banks her mere presence has filled.

My cock instantly begins to harden as I picture the dragon shifter pounding into her pretty pussy. Those soulful, plump lips of hers locked around the mage's cock. Her perfect tits bouncing, with those pretty pink nipples just begging to be sucked.

Down, you fucking hussy, I mentally chastise my cock when it feels as if it's going to cut a hole through my pants. I'm pretty sure that if I'm not already dead, then I will be soon if the guys catch wind of my boner—

Oh, hell. The demon is looking, his eyes narrowed.

Which one is he again?

The sex demon. He's the only one able to sense the lust wafting off of me in tangible waves.

Think gross thoughts, Logan. Grandma's saggy tits. Lionel's peachy ass. A naked mole rat-looking cock.

My boner gradually turns limp, and I give myself a mental pat on the back.

Oh, wait. The scary mage with the scary knife and the scary blue eyes is staring at me in a—you guessed it—scary way. Dammit. Apparently, I couldn't get rid of my boner fast enough for his scary liking.

"What do you mean you were sent to kill her?" he demands, his ebony hair sweeping across the pale skin of his forehead. He really is a beautiful man, and for a brief moment, I wonder if it's possible for me to seduce him with my gifts. But as quickly as the thought occurs to me, I dismiss it.

My powers don't seem to be working on the people associated with Miss Nina Doe. It's almost as if she's blocking my powers, which is impossible. Or maybe…

Or maybe they're all her fated mates.

The thought has me tilting my head to the side to study her in abject curiosity—well, as far to the side as I can while being pinned to the wall with a knife at my throat. If they're her mates, it would make sense why my magic doesn't work on them.

Though the thought of this beautiful girl, with the white eyes and the delectable, sexy body, being unattainable sends a surge of jealousy through my system. It's completely unexplainable and quite frankly, ridiculous. But dammit, I've never met a pretty face I couldn't seduce. And Nina? I have a feeling she would be one hell of a catch. I would fuck her and leave her, just as I do with all of my conquests, but I would cherish the memories of our time together forever.

What a shame.

I suppose I'll have to find someone else in the prison to fuck in the meantime. It shouldn't be too hard, considering what I am.

Someone with long, black hair…

Milky white eyes…

"Answer him, you piece of shit," the volatile dragon demands, stalking forward until he's shoulder to shoulder with the mage. Blade, I believe his name is. Or Malakai, though don't call him that if you want to live. Only Nina and the men from his inner circle are allowed to call him Kai in this prison.

"It's exactly as I said." I adopt a cocky, take no shit smile, one that will most certainly drive them both crazy. What can I say? If I'm going to die, I want to at least annoy the shit out of everyone before I go. "I was placed in this prison with one purpose and one purpose alone—killing Nina."

There's a sharp intake of breath, and I don't need to look to know that Nina is staring at me with those damn white eyes of hers. I want to look towards her, want to gauge her reaction to my words, but I don't pull my attention away from Asshole One and Asshole Two. At this point, I don't even know which asshole is which, and honestly, I don't give a damn. They both take up residence in the asshole compartment of my heart.

The knife at my throat digs in even deeper, and a trickle

of blood slides down to my shirt collar. Fuck. This is the only shirt I have in this godforsaken place, and it took me hours to find a man in my size to steal it from. I guess this means I'll have to go shirtless for the time being. What. A. Shame.

"Give me one good reason why I shouldn't kill you right now," the mage, Damien I believe, snarls, and I can practically taste his power on my tongue. It sort of reminds me of eating a spicy pepper that causes your entire mouth to inflame and then turn numb. So much power…

"Because I'm telling you what I know," I drawl lazily, my eyes once more slipping to Nina. For some reason, I can't seem to look away. It's not just because of her beauty, though that definitely plays a part. It's…everything. She enchants me, as cliché as that sounds. And that mere fact annoys the shit out of me. Maybe I should spank myself to rid the crazy from my system.

"And what exactly do you know?" Blade demands, but instead of addressing him, I flick my attention back to the glowering mage.

"I'll tell you once Tall, Dark, and Sexy here backs up a few steps. I mean, seriously, man, have you ever heard of personal space?" And just because I'm an asshole, I thrust my hips against him so he can feel my raging hard-on, which reappeared the second Nina made eye contact with me. He doesn't need to know that the boner isn't for him, though I'm not sure announcing it's for his mate would do me any favors. "Unless you want to excite me…"

He backs away from me with a scowl, his eyes darkening with disgust. To Blade, he says, "Can I kill him?"

"No!" Nina exclaims, at the same time Blade deadpans, "Not if I do it first."

Awww. Couple murders. How cute.

"Look," I begin, once Damien's knife is no longer at my throat. I hesitantly put my fingers against the skin there, unsurprised when they come away red. The copper stench of my blood fills the air. "I'll tell you what I know if you promise not to kill me."

"Deal," Nina interjects immediately, stepping around the large shadow wolf. He immediately places his hands on her thin hips, pulling her against his front.

"Yes." Blade flashes me a smile that would make babies cry. Or grown men. "Deal."

Yeah, we have no fucking deal. He's going to slit my throat the second Nina's away and then say I ran away to join the circus or some shit.

"So here's what I know, *mi amigos*." I place one foot up against the wall, as if we were having a casual conversation instead of…well…a death threat one.

"I would recommend cutting the bullcrap." The trickster demon makes a face at me. "They get a little stabby when you try to have fun."

"A little stabby?" His twin raises a blond eyebrow.

"A lot stabby," the trickster demon amends.

I lick my dry lips as I focus on each of them. Nina's mates. The most fearsome men in this entire prison. Wasn't there a sixth one? A shifter?

"Basically, the council is pissy that little Ms. Doe over there murdered first Raphael Turner and then Alyssa," I begin, nodding my chin at the girl in question. Doe really does fit her. With those wide eyes, she resembles a cartoon deer.

"So they sent the hit after her," Blade concludes, his expression turning dark and even more stabby than before. This does not bode well for me.

"They created the hit list, yes," I confirm. "But they also created the dead pool. They, and some of the other high society members, bet on when they believe you guys will die." I shrug my shoulders as if I don't give a shit either way.

"Both lists are completely different, but the one floating around this prison is the actual hit list. The council is willing to spend a lot of money to see you guys dead."

"And they hired you…?" The shadow wolf trails off, a question lingering in his voice. I smirk.

"Because I'm an assassin. One of the best assassins, actually." I face the stabby mage, my grin broadening. "You remember Narian, don't you?"

I watch his lips pull away from his teeth in a snarl. Oh, yes. Damien most definitely remembers Narian.

I always heard that Damien was the old man's favorite… and that's not a good position to hold. And trust me. I would know.

When Damien left, Narian set his sights on little ole me…

I shove those memories in a steel box. And then, for added effect, wrap said box in barbed wire and a sickly poison, one that will kill me if I even stare at it. It's safer that way. For everyone.

"Narian." Damien spits on the ground, as if even saying that name causes his mouth to fill with bile. "He's involved with this?" His ice-blue eyes flash dangerously, and he begins to twirl that damn blade around his fingers. Though the blade gets precariously close to his skin, it doesn't cut it. Not once. He's too well-trained for that.

"*Every* assassin guild is involved," I reply with an eye roll. "That kind of money? It's an assassin's wet dream." I snort, because while it might be their wet dream, it's not mine. Mine has luscious curves, pitch-black hair, smoky white eyes…

Shaking my head against the thoughts clogging it like a wad of toilet paper stuck in a pipe, I continue, "And rumor has it, the bounty on each of you guys will increase over time. Some people are even lying in wait, hoping that the inflated price will make it worth their efforts."

"And how do we know that's not what you're doing?" Damien demands, still looking seconds away from wrapping his bare hands around my throat and squeezing until my face is as blue as his eyes. I always heard that knives were his preferred choice of weapon, but apparently when it comes to Nina, Damien won't hesitate to use any methods at his disposal. Kinky. I like it.

"What do you mean?" I blink my eyes at him innocently, pushing a tiny bit of my power at him. Of course, it doesn't fucking work—it's like trying to penetrate a steel fortress—but I can't help but try. Survival of the fittest, and all that.

"How do we know that you're not just waiting until the price of our deaths increases?" the wolf shifter finishes, suspicion lacing his tone. His voice is guttural with his growl. Oh. I love it when they're feisty.

"Why would I tell you the truth if I had something nefarious planned?" I demand with another exasperated eye roll. "I would just stay silent, wait until the price increases, and then kill you all." I swear, these men have a healthy amount of trust issues. They should really consider seeing a therapist.

"Why are you telling us?" a quiet voice queries, and we all pause as Nina takes another timid step forward.

I turn to face her completely and, ignoring Blade's threatening growl, stare at her. I mean, *really* stare at her. Study her face like a painter would his muse. There are tiny, silver freckles dotting her pert nose. I wonder what they would feel like beneath my lips? Her own are thick and bright red, still slightly swollen from being wrapped around the mage's cock. Her hair is still tousled too, from her recent fucking. Silky black strands are matted to her skin with sweat.

I've never seen anyone more beautiful.

And that's coming from a man who has seen and fucked a lot of men and women. Models. Actors. Actresses. Musicians.

Philosophers. Hell, even a few married couples from time to time.

But none of them excite me like staring into Nina's gossamer white eyes do.

"I'm an assassin, Miss Nina Doe," I begin, choosing my words carefully. My heart pounds a daunting rhythm beneath my rib cage. I can hear each consecutive heartbeat as if there's an entire marching band playing beside my ear. Drums. Symbols. Annoying as fuck trumpets. "I choose the side that I think will win. Always. And you, my dear girl..." I give her another cursory once-over, trying to ignore the way my heart plays leapfrog in my chest. The way it quite literally jumps from its confinement and crashes at her feet like a fucking offering. "I see something in you. Something that reminds me of myself. Maybe I'll come to regret my decision, but until then, I know which horse I'm backing."

Even if that horse kicks me in the head and kills me.

Even if that fucking horse kills us all.

CHAPTER 17

"What do you think?" I ask Damien a short while later. We sit opposite each other in the throne room on soft, fluffy pillows while he walks me through meditation techniques. Because apparently, I need to better understand my powers. And what better way to understand them than reaching my center or whatever? Honestly, I think he's pulling my leg, but since most of these sessions lead to sexy times, I can't complain too much. So for now, I'll sit across from him, close my eyes—even though I already can't see—and focus on my inner self.

"You're not focusing," he reprimands in a soft voice, a voice that slides through my system like tepid, melted ice.

"I am!" I protest immediately, fidgeting on the pillow. My legs are beginning to ache from sitting cross-legged for so long. "I mean, I'm trying…"

Damien releases a heavy sigh, and a moment later, I feel his slender fingers beneath my chin as he tilts my head up.

"What's on your mind, Angel?"

At his nickname for me, my heart flutters and begins to soar like the organ actually possess fluffy white wings.

"Nina," Damien prods, continuing to grip my chin between his fingers.

"Logan," I blurt, twisting my head to the side to kiss the inside of his wrist. His pulse skitters beneath my lips, and I can't help but smile. How did I get so damn lucky with him? With all of them?

"What about him?" Damien's voice has taken on a dark undercurrent, and I know he's not pleased with the direction of my thoughts. My guys don't like it when I talk to other men. Heck, they don't even like it when I think about them. Their possessiveness is both sexy and annoying, because *hello*? I can't really get through life avoiding any and all men, no matter how much my guys would like me to.

"What do you think of...everything he said? Like, do you believe him?" After the "meeting," Kai led Logan in one direction, while Damien took me in the other. Abel assured me that they didn't plan to kill or even hurt Logan—they just wanted to talk to him. I don't know if I believe that, and I made it very clear that if they kill him, I'll never forgive them. We don't just kill people because of something they might do in the future. What type of people would we be then? No better than Alyssa and the other men and women at the Compound who tortured me relentlessly.

I can hear the wheels in Damien's head grinding as he thinks of his answer. "I think," he begins carefully, "that there's still a lot we don't know. I do believe that he's telling the truth about the origins of the list. That's exactly what I would expect from the Council and..." His breathing hitches. The sound is barely noticeable, and if it were anyone else with him, anyone besides me, they wouldn't have heard it. "And Narian."

"Narian..." I gently wrap my hands around his wrists and pull them away. Only then do I climb into his lap, curling myself against his lithe, muscular body, my head under his chin. "I still hate him." Tears burn my eyes as loathing sears my flesh, branding itself in my very soul. "For what he did to you."

"Don't hate on my behalf, Angel," Damien pleads, peppering kisses along my hairline. "Don't turn bitter and cold. Not for me."

Indignation rears its head. "How can I not, Damien? This man hurt you." I twist to kiss his chest, directly over his rapidly beating heart. "He hurt the man I love." His entire body freezes under me, before he exhales noisily.

"Fuck, I'll never get tired of hearing you say that."

"What?" I blindly reach for his fingers and begin to fiddle with them. I play with the band of his silver ring, our engagement ring, before dropping his hand back into his lap.

"That you love me," Damien murmurs in wonderment. He sounds almost…shocked, as if the mere possibility that I could be in love with him is as surreal as snow falling in the tropics. Of a unicorn prancing through the prison right here and now and spearing everyone with its magical rainbow horn. I tell him every day, but he still sounds stunned. Awed.

"Of course I do." I plant a single kiss to the underside of his jaw. "How could I not?"

He snorts bitterly. "There are probably a billion reasons why you shouldn't, but I'm happy you're too damn stubborn to listen to any of them."

His lips claim mine, and for a brief moment, we exchange the softest, sweetest kisses imaginable. All too soon, he pulls away, leaving me feeling oddly bereft, like my soul isn't complete without his lips on mine.

"I'm sorry you were hurt." I drag my hand down his face, reveling in the way his silky skin feels beneath my palm. "That's actually something I wanted to talk to you about."

He pulls away slightly, still keeping his arms locked around me, and I drop my hand back to my lap.

"About me being hurt?"

"No." I shake my head, struggling to articulate the idea I came up with a few days earlier. "I can go inside your mind, right? Hear your thoughts. See what you see. Hear what you hear. And we've been practicing seeing memories…"

His arms have tensed around me, every muscle in his body coiled and ready to flee.

All I can do is pray that it's not me he wants to flee from.

"Nina, where are you going with this?"

Nina. Not Angel.

Pain slashes at my heart, sharper than any whip they used at the Compound, but I force myself to continue.

"What if there's a way for me to remove bad memories?" I rush to get out. "For you and Cain and Abel and Kai… What if there's a way for me to rip the bad memories from your head? Or heck, maybe I could leave the memories but get rid of all the hurt and pain associated with them. Is that possible? I mean, I don't know if it's even possible. It's just a random idea…"

I trail off when I realize that Damien has become very, very still. I'm not even sure he's breathing. His body seems to be hewn from ice.

"That's…" He seems to be struggling to formulate his own thoughts. "That's what you want to do with your power? Remove our bad memories?" He sounds stunned, almost breathless, and I can tell that I took him by surprise.

"Well, yeah." I shrug sheepishly, suddenly feeling shy and naïve and stupid. "I love you guys. I can't stand all of the pain you had to endure before I found you." I place a closed fist over my own chest, directly above my pounding heart. I understand pain just as much as anyone. I've endured it for years. I can handle my own pain, my own past torment, but what I can't handle is the pain of my mates. My loves. I wish I could scrub the hurt away like a marker on a whiteboard, but I know it's not that easy. Pain never is.

Suddenly, Damien's kissing me again, his teeth nipping at my bottom lip as he tugs on it. He releases me just as quickly and pulls me tight against his chest, resting his cheek on my hair.

"Fuck, Nina. Fuck."

I tense instinctively. "Did I do something wrong?"

"No, Angel. Not at all. You're just… You're just so damn perfect, you know that? Fuck, I love you so damn much. I'd kill the world for you, Nina. You know that, right?"

Heat inflames my cheeks at his dogmatic statement. At the sheer intensity radiating from him in palpable, stomach-churning waves.

"I just want to help," I confess breathily. "That's all I ever wanted."

"I know, Angel. I know." He kisses my forehead, then my cheek, and then my lips. All the while, his arms continue to constrict around me, his grip both loving and punishing. "But my pain…it made me the man you see today. The man who loves you with every ounce of darkness in his entire being. What I endured…it didn't break me. I could never truly be broken, even though I thought I was. You healed me. You took all of my shattered pieces and reconnected them with gold and glitter and everything beautiful in the world. So I thank you for offering to remove my bad memories. And fuck, I love you even more for thinking of it. But I don't want to take away the pain. I don't want to forget. I'll let my pain, hatred, and anger fuel me in the war to come. I'll let it fuel my love for you and desire to protect you. And when Narian comes again—and mark my words, he will—I'll be ready." His arms tighten around me almost imperceptibly as a surge of love flows through my body like the currents of a grand river, constantly swirling and frothing and battering the rocky shore. "I can't speak for the others, but I suspect Cain and Abel feel the same way. You can always ask them, though, but I'm going to have to refuse your offer."

"Dam, are you sure?" I ask gently, my voice choked with barely suppressed emotion.

"I'm only more sure about one other thing," Damien responds. "That I love you."

I sniffle, attempting to smother the noise by pressing my face into his chest once more. Desperate to say something, I try for a teasing tone. "See? You can totally be romantic. You're actually a big softie, aren't you?"

He grunts before reluctantly releasing me. "Don't get used to it. Now, come. If you refuse to focus and practice your powers, then I want to work on unraveling the spell Alyssa put on you."

The spell...

The one that prohibits me from having kids.

And just like that, the elation I was feeling from Damien's confession turns dark and gloomy, like a sun being speckled with black and brown dots, before the darkness consumes the light entirely.

Alyssa and Raphael once tried to destroy me, and they very nearly succeeded. I refuse to allow them to take this away from me. The possibility of having kids. Of having a family with the men I love.

To Damien, I whisper, "Let's do it."

There has to be a way to break the spell.

There has to.

CHAPTER 18

RION

"I'm back, bitches!" I spread my arms wide on either side of me as I wake from the sedation the guards put me under. I expect streamers and balloons and a "We're Glad You're Still Alive" banner to be hanging from the ceiling. Instead, I wake in an empty tunnel of the Labyrinth. Alone. And in an uncomfortable, paper hospital gown.

Well, suck my cock and call it a candy cane. Where's the red carpet? The party? My sexy as fuck mate in a sexy as fuck nurse's costume, prepared to kiss my boo-boos better? I explicitly told Damien that I wanted him to purchase a sexy nurse's outfit for Nina. The bastard didn't answer, obviously, because we're not telepathically linked despite how loudly I mentally scream. Either way, I thought as bros, he would know to do it for me automatically, especially since he'd benefit from it as well. And I've been injured, so that deserves some benefits. Nina in a short white skirt?

Oh, fuck.

The thought of my precious mate in an itty-bitty, teeny tiny, little nurse's outfit, one that shows the bottom of her ass cheeks and her perfect cleavage, makes me hard as a rock.

On a scale of one to ten, would it be horribly weird if I stroked one out in the middle of the tunnel? Just a quickie.

I fucking need that relief after the day—week?—I had.

Being treated by Brina, the sadistic fae doctor of the prison, is not my idea of fun. The bitch relished in every scream of pain I made as she applied skin grafts to the burns on my body. It wasn't too long before my natural healing capabilities kicked in, but that didn't stop the psychopath from stabbing me with her rusty needle and smirking like the devil she is.

I swear my dick has never been more limp in my life. Even memories of Nina weren't enough to penetrate the consistent haze of pain I found myself in.

Nina…

I miss my buttercup with an intensity that leaves me breathless. Or that could maybe be because of my depleted oxygen from smoke inhalation.

Just keeping it real.

I yearn to set eyes upon her beautiful, heart-shaped face. Those porcelain cheeks that always seem to flame when she's embarrassed or turned on, both emotions I love to see on her and evoke from her. That silky black hair that looks fucking great around my fist.

Before I realize what I'm doing, my gown is pulled up and my hand fists my erect cock. I start at the tip, collecting the pre-cum, and use the liquid as lube, stroking myself from base to tip. My other hand reaches down to fondle my balls, and I push down on them, balancing that precarious and blurred line between pleasure and pain.

Instead of my hand around my dick, my imagination changes it to Nina's luscious mouth, her eyes hooded as they stare up at me, half-mast.

Fuck. Fuck. Fuck.

Squirts of cum erupt from the head of my cock as I come,

covering my hand and my stomach. I continue to stroke myself through my orgasm, until it no longer feels as if I might physically die of cock-icitis. That's a real thing. Look it up. Seriously, type in Google, "death by cock." You'll thank me later.

Humming beneath my breath, I push my hospital gown back down, not bothering to clean myself up first, and awkwardly wipe my hand on the scratchy fabric. As soon as I get back to my prison cell, I'm going to enjoy a nice warm shower. Preferably with Nina.

Naked.

Oh, yes.

Don't be getting another boner yet, Rion, I tell myself sternly. And then, to my dick, I add, *You behave yourself, mister, or no orgasms for you.*

I swear my cock depletes like a puppy being kicked, when its tail lowers itself between the dog's legs.

Now, where the fuck am I?

I survey the graffiti-stained walls of the unfamiliar tunnel the guards have dropped me in. If my calculations are correct…the sun sets in two point five hours, and the moon is at a horizontal seventy-degree angle, and I'm approximately twenty-two point seven feet below ground, which means that the large hand on the clock is nearing a three while the short one is at five…

Which means I've been unconscious in the tunnel for about two hours.

And no, I'm not full of shit.

Shut up.

The guards always drug us prisoners when they bring us into and out of this level of the prison. We're not supposed to know how to maneuver the ever-changing pathways of the Labyrinth. Of course, it'd be impossible to do that in the first place. The halls of the Labyrinth are constantly twisting and changing, almost as if they have a mind of their own. As if they're a sentient being that breathes and bleeds. And even when you think you have a handle on the pathways, you have to account for the traps—everything from walls of nails to poisonous halls to crumbling floors.

Only the section that houses the cafeteria and cells remains still, though that has been reported to change at random as well.

Okay, so where the fuck am I?

I try to search for any location that seems familiar, but there's nothing but gray walls, busted, rusted pipes, and clay floors covered in dried blood and dirt. It's not the usual bloodstains from Damien's torture sessions...because trust me, I can tell the difference between normal blood and the blood from Damien's enemies. That blood almost seems... darker, if that's even possible.

Which it is, because I say it is.

As I walk through the winding hall, I can feel an open breeze on my bare ass. Yes, my hospital gown is only secured by a single tie at the back of my neck. My back and butt are on display.

Which makes me even more excited to see Nina. The things we can do...

I suddenly have a vivid image of dirty nurse and sick patient foreplay.

"Nurse, I need your help."

"What's the matter, sexiest shifter in the world?"

"There appears to be something wrong with my cock. Can you have a look?"

"Of course. But I'll need to get up close and personal. Would you be okay if I use my mouth? I can get a more accurate reading that way."

I laugh giddily as I squeeze my eyelids shut, focusing on the bond I share with Nina. I would almost describe it as a silver cord laced with glittering gold stars. It seems to connect my heart to hers, my soul to hers. Obviously, the cord doesn't actually exist, but it sure as fuck feels real when I caress it like one would a pet and get an answering tug in return.

I'm coming for you, Buttercup, I think with another gleeful laugh. I'm pretty sure that if anyone were to see me, they would think I was insane. Which is just plain rude, if you ask me. What societal definition decides who is insane and who is sane? Maybe what they actually mean is that sane is in. So, if you're considered insane, you're actually on the in of sane. Obviously.

It's not rocket science.

As I continue walking, following the direction of the silver cord, I suddenly become aware of something in the distance. It almost appears to be a...a door. There are multiple padlocks prohibiting anyone from entering the room. Or maybe keeping whatever is inside the room from escaping.

You know that curiosity killed the kitty cat, Rion. Don't be an asshole, I think to myself, even as my stupid feet glide me towards the locked door. What can I say? I have a fetish for death.

This close, I can see that there's nothing overly significant about the door. It's simply...a door. Made of wood. And a knob.

So a door.

But there are numerous chains crisscrossed over the surface, with more padlocks than I care to count. What is the prison protecting? Or maybe they're hiding something?

Or maybe it's another way out of here.

My curiosity is instantly piqued as I stick my ear against the door, listening intently.

I know that guards come and go when they need to

collect inmates for one reason or another. And I also know that my shifters scouted the usual entrance and never saw them arrive or exit. We always suspected that they had more than one way in and out of the Labyrinth, but since the maze is always shifting, always changing and distorting, we could never be certain.

Is this another exit?

Is this potentially a way out of this hellish prison?

The thought makes my heart beat erratically.

And with my connection to Nina…

Is it possible for us to explore more of the Labyrinth? With the mate bond, we'll always find our way back to her, which means we can never get lost. At least not truly. Not if we have her as our guiding compass, leading us back to safety like a lighthouse adjacent to a roiling ocean, helping wayward sailors return home.

Curiosity my guiding force, I get on my belly and attempt to peer underneath the door. While the door appears to be made of wood, I detect powerful magic vibrating around it, almost as if a mage or warlock placed a spell on it. But if there's anyone who can defeat a spell like this, it's my very own bro ho, Bitch Mage.

"Hello? Is anyone in there?" I ask in a singsong voice. I don't expect anyone to answer, I honestly don't.

But a guttural growl reverberates through the still air, and the entire door begins to shake. And shake. And shake. I can hear the sound of claws running down the door, accompanied by louder growls, which are immediately followed by distorted screams. Screams of agony and pain and anger.

I jump to my feet so quickly that I get whiplash, my head spinning faster than the cars on a rollercoaster as fear crashes into me. Like, I totally want to find a litter box and take a scared shit into it right about now. Maybe I'll call it a *shitter* box.

What the hell is that thing?

I begin to back away as the door continues to shake and shake and shake, almost as if the creature on the other side is trying to get out. Trying to escape. Trying to stick its claws in my skin and turn me into human confetti. And I rather like being whole and in one piece, thank you very much. This sexy ass body would not look good as confetti.

But why would the prison have a monster guarding the door?

Unless…

Unless it truly is a way to escape.

Before the thought can solidify, before I can act on one of the thousands of thoughts running rampant through my head, the Labyrinth releases a creaky groan. Suddenly, the world begins to spin, and I stick my hand against the stone wall, struggling to remain on two feet. The pathways around me begin to change with the magic of the prison, and I watch in horror as the mysterious doorway fizzles out of existence, replaced by an empty hallway interspersed with flickering torches. Now, instead of my connection with Nina leading me to the right, it directs me to the left.

As my feet begin to move in that direction, I can't help but think about the mysterious doorway and the monster on the other side.

What, exactly, is the prison hiding from us?

NINA

"Trouble!" Cain's breathy voice sounds in my ear, and I jump, spinning around with my heart beating a mile a minute.

"You scared the daylights out of me," I scold, attempting to calm my wayward organ before it sends me into cardiac arrest. I sit on the uncomfortable cot in the cell we have taken to using. Bronson was in the cell beside mine before he explained he had to check on Logan, who they are still keeping prisoner, and told me someone would be here shortly to look after me. I wanted to be offended that the guys thought I needed a babysitter twenty-four-seven, but I know they're doing it out of a place of love. As Bronson eloquently told me when I confronted him, I'm "precious cargo" and they would all be "lost" without me.

My heart turns to goo whenever I think about his words. Love for him, for all of my men, floods my system like fire. I always heard that fire, at some point or another, hisses and sizzles, before petering out, while other fires continue raging, growing and growing until the flames consume entire towns and forests. My love for them falls firmly in the latter category. Nothing can douse my love for them and theirs for me.

I don't need sight to know that Cain is giving me an impish smirk, one more suited for his brother than my normally surly demon.

"Maybe you should work on your reaction time," Cain comments, only half teasing. "If I were a murderer..."

"But you're not," I defend immediately, and silence stretches between us, pulled taut like a rubber band seconds from snapping and pelting one of us in the face. I bite down on my lip when I realize how my words could be construed. Because, truth be told, Cain *is* a murderer. His past is full of dark shadows and secrets and horrors that I hate that he had to face. I don't blame him for the people he killed to save himself and his brother. How can I, when I would've done the exact same thing to save any of the men I love? Plus, I have killed before—Alyssa.

My birth mother.

And the woman who enslaved me for years, experimented on me, and then attempted to breed me like a broodmare.

A pulse of lightning skitters down my spine as I shove those memories away in a tidal wave of anger. Now isn't the time to focus on me, not when I can so keenly sense how much Cain is hurting.

But then that anger shifts from what happened with Alyssa, to what Cain endured at Boris's club, where he was paraded around as a sex toy and not a human being. Where he was raped by men and women alike, his body used for their sick, sadistic pleasure.

"Nina..." Cain's voice is as grave as it was when we first met, so long ago. The change in his tone from gentle and calming to cautious has me slipping into his head automatically, seeing through his eyes.

My entire body freezes as if electrical currents are sparking through my veins.

Dark horns, similar to the ones I know belong to demons, sprout from my silky black hair, the tips curling like the horns of a ram. My eyes look almost crimson in the flickering bulb of the prison, the pupils rimmed in coal. And from my back, two majestic wings spread on either side of me, the color as white as snow and sparkling with a pearly luminescence. I've only looked like this once before—seconds before I killed Alyssa.

"Trouble," Cain begins slowly, and instead of backing away from me as I thought he was going to do, he takes a step closer. "Trouble, I need you to calm down. Tell me where your mind went."

I struggle to find the words that are rooted at the very tip of my tongue, tasting sour and moldy like some type of acid. My thoughts are swirling faster than a tornado coming full force down a street, catching asphalt in its windy grasp.

"It seems…" I bite my lip as I pull out of Cain's head once more, embracing my darkness. "It seems as if all of the people I love have pasts that I can't protect them from. That I can't save them from. It *hurts* me, and then I feel selfish for being hurt, because I'm not the one who endured it. Does that make any sense?"

Cain's silent for a moment before he closes the distance between us and grasps my hand in his, pulling me forward. I stumble slightly, my hands coming up to fist the collar of his shirt, but he doesn't let me fall. He'll never let me fall.

"Come on." Without waiting for me to respond—heck, without even waiting for me to gather my wits—he begins to drag me down the hall. With every step we take, my power fades until I begin to feel like myself once more.

"Where are we going?" I ask, loving the way his hand feels in mine. I swear my stomach gets all fluttery, as if thousands and thousands of bees have been set free, buzzing around and stinging me intermittently.

"On a date," Cain replies simply, and that buzzing from before? It drowns out all other sounds, until I can barely think straight. Barely breathe. Barely function.

We continue to move through the twisting hallways of the Labyrinth as Cain guides us to an unspecified location.

Meanwhile, my mind is spinning, twirling, doing somersaults as a giddy elation fills me like helium in a balloon. I only went on one date before with Bronson, and that led to…

My cheeks flame when I think about Bronson using his hand to bring me to the peak of pleasure. His growly voice whispering, "Goddess," with all the reverence he's capable of possessing. He always treats me like a queen, *his* queen, and I love the way he makes me feel. Sometimes, you want those dark men with tainted pasts, but other times…

Other times, you need men like Bronson. Men who make you feel treasured and adored, like a precious gemstone you find beneath layers and layers of muck and grime.

I hear the telltale sound of a heavy door being pushed open, and I know immediately we're entering the throne room. The last time I was here, my men were carting Logan off to press him for more information. For some reason, that bothers me. A lot. Maybe it's because I know what it's like to be a prisoner, what it's like to be a captive in a war you don't even understand. I know Logan claimed he was going to kill me, but he also told us the truth. About the lists. About the Council. About all of it. Surely he's not a bad guy if he was willing to do all of that.

I shake my head, pushing all thoughts of Logan to the deepest recesses of my mind. Today, I'm going to focus on Cain, my darkness twin. The demon who was the slowest to open up to me, the slowest to love me. Sometimes, it feels as if I'm walking on broken glass around him and one wrong move can pierce both of my sensitive soles, causing me to bleed out. And other times, there are nothing but fluffy, wispy white clouds. I feel bereft and free, as if no one can harm me so high up in the sky. Cain is so mercurial, but that doesn't make me love him less. I always knew about the duality of his nature—the lightness that seems to emit from his very soul and the darkness that shrouds him like a second skin. They're just two facets of the man I love with my entire being.

"Are you in my head, Trouble?" Cain asks, pulling me from my thoughts. I turn in the direction of his voice and give his hand a soft squeeze.

"No. Do you want me to be?"

"Get your fine ass in here, baby," he teases, and I comply immediately, sinking into his mind like a swimmer diving into the ocean.

The throne room, as always, is furnished with a single high-backed chair on a raised dais, but besides that, the room is empty. Well, almost empty.

Directly at the front of the room, sitting at the end of the red carpeting that creates an aperture towards the throne, is what looks like...white things. Their shapes are odd, almost curvy, with larger bottoms that shift inwards. Red stripes adorn each of them, but that doesn't help me understand what I'm seeing. Near them are two round balls with three tiny holes in the center.

"Is this...some sort of sex thing?" My voice comes out as a conspiratorial whisper as I try to think of what the toys could be used for.

Cain releases a bark of surprised laughter, his breath ruffling my hair.

"No! Why would you think...?" He trails off at whatever answer he comes to. "Of course. I'm such a fucking idiot. You've never been bowling before, have you?"

"Bowling?" I believe I've heard of it before, but my mind can't quite correlate the word with what I'm seeing.

"It's a game, Trouble," Cain explains patiently, not at all upset with or annoyed by my limited knowledge. I've been doing much better due to the movies the guys sneak into the prison, but there are still certain things I'm not overly familiar with. Like, just a few weeks ago, I learned that bondage could be used for torture...but also for pleasure. You can imagine my guys' surprise when I threatened a jerk in the cafeteria with bondage and spankings. Suffice to say, they were *not* happy with my threat.

"A game," I repeat, eyeing the white things with newfound appreciation. "What's the purpose?"

"You have to knock those pins down," Cain explains. A wide grin spreads across my face, and before Cain can stop me, I run forward and aim a kick at the pin at the very front and center. All ten of them topple with loud clunks.

"Did I just win?" I ask, spinning around to face him. Through his eyes, I can see that my face is alight with excitement and there's the slightest red tint to my cheeks. I don't know what expression Cain is wearing, but it takes him a long moment to answer. When he finally speaks, he has to clear his throat multiple times, but his voice still comes out slightly raspy and choked.

"You need to use one of these balls, Trouble," he manages to say, and I can't quite tell the emotion lacing his tone. It almost sounds like...awe, maybe. Love?

"One of your balls?" I lower my gaze in the direction I know his crotch to be, and this time, his gaze lowers to his rapidly hardening cock. To my immense pleasure, he sticks his hand into the waistband to adjust himself.

"Just get your cute ass over here, and I'll explain the rules," he instructs, though he doesn't immediately take his hand off of his cock.

I do as he says, stopping when I'm directly in front of him. My hands automatically lower to his thighs, being very careful not to startle him, before I cup his dick through the material of his pants. His breath hitches as I continue to palm his rapidly hardening cock.

"Trouble," he hisses out.

"You said I need to play with balls," I singsong, and he releases a snort before he can stop himself.

"You're sounding way too much like Rion and Abel these days," he admits with a shake of his head. With a groan of great reluctance, he steps away from me.

Through his eyes, I watch as my bottom lip protrudes in a pout, but he simply chuckles and taps a finger beneath my chin.

"Enough of that, Trouble. We're on a date, and we're going to have fun, dammit. But after..." His voice turns seductive, husky, and I just know his eyes are hooded with desire. "After, we can have fun."

My core tingles at the promise and threat in his words, and I nod my head excitedly.

"What are the rules?" I ask, rocking back on my heels. Cain moves to grab one of the two balls I noticed earlier and hands me the smallest, a pretty pink one. "And where did you even get this stuff?"

"Damien," Cain answers, as if that one word is self-explanatory. Which, in a way, it sort of is. Damien can quite literally get almost anything he desires sent to this level of the prison. I don't know if he uses his connection as an assassin or a mage, but he's powerful enough to have stuff delivered to him. "And about how you play..."

For the next few minutes, Cain walks me through the rules of the game. Stand at the end of the red carpeting and throw the ball down. However many pins you knock down is how many points you get. You're allowed two turns each time, unless you get all ten pins down on the very first try. That's called a strike. And if you get all ten pins down by your second time, that's a spare. And…it does something to your points, but I don't pay too much attention to that. Cain said he'll keep score for us.

The ball is surprisingly heavy, even though Cain assures me that the pink ball is the lightest you can have. Even still, my fingers ache as I stick them into the holes the way he directed.

And then I think about sticking my fingers into *other* holes while he watches…

"You do realize I have the muscle mass of a ten-year-old, right?" I ask Cain with a smile as I line up at the end of the rug. Years of captivity have made me weak and frail, and though my body is steadily getting stronger, it's still nowhere near where it should be, much to my men's displeasure.

"Suck it up, Buttercup," he quips immediately, and I smirk when I hear Rion's nickname for me leave his lips. If Rion were here, he'd be furious.

Pain clamors for my attention at the thought of my shifter mate, but I refuse to wallow. Not when this moment is about Cain and my relationship with him.

I try to pull my arm back the way Cain instructed, but the ball is too heavy and my arm is too weak. Instead, I use both hands, crouch down, and push with all of my might. I watch through Cain's eyes as it slowly rolls down the rug, curving sharply to the right, and missing all of the pins.

"Does that mean I get extra points?" I ask excitedly as Cain rushes forward to return the ball to me. "It takes talent to not get any pins, wouldn't you say?"

I can hear the smile in Cain's voice when he speaks next. "Sorry, Trouble. That's a big fat zero." He very purposely grabs a red marker and draws a zero in the first box.

"That's not nice," I say teasingly as I crouch back down,

prepared to throw the ball a second time. "You're my fiancé. Shouldn't you want to cheat for me?"

"Hmmm…let me think about it. Have my girl win…or kick my girl's ass?" He pretends to contemplate, his finger tapping against his chin. "I think I'm going to go with choice number two. Sorry, love. You're going down."

"We'll see about that," I huff, filled to the brim with newfound determination. I stare at the pins through Cain's eyes, aiming for the one directly in the middle. If I can hit that one, the momentum should push the others over as well. And then… And then I'll get a sparey. Or whatever Cain called it.

I line up, take a deep, calming breath, and then push the ball forward. I watch as it rolls slowly down the rug, directly towards that elusive center pin…

My heart thrashes in my rib cage, and my arms begin to lift in a celebratory cheer—

—when the ball veers to the right and knocks over the pin at the far edge.

"Oh my gosh!" I squeal like a banshee, jumping up and down and clapping my hands. "Did you see that, Cain? Did you? Look! I got a pin!" I run towards him and wrap both of my arms around his neck, my feet dangling off the ground. "In. Your. Face!" I release him to continue my little dance as his body shakes with laughter.

"Fucking hell, Trouble! If I would've known that bowling would get you so damn excited, we would've played months ago." His body shakes with amusement as he once more pulls me towards him, holding my body flush against his. "Fuck, I love you so damn much."

"Are you still going to love me as much when I kick your demon butt?" I tease, stepping onto my tiptoes to kiss the corner of his mouth. My lips linger there, tasting him, before I force myself to pull away, ignoring his low, heated moan.

"Want to make this more interesting?" Cain asks deviously, and my curiosity is instantly piqued.

"Depends," I answer, curious.

"How about a bet?" His voice is smug, taunting, and it instantly has my toes curling in the slippers Damien purchased for me.

"A bet," I repeat, my grin widening. I always love bets with my men, especially when the reward for winning *and* losing brings me immense pleasure.

"If I win, I'll let you ride me." He begins to kiss up the hollow of my throat, and I swear my soul leaves my body and orbits around the galaxy, before becoming nothing more than molten lava in the blistering rays of the sun. "And if you win…"

"If I win…" I parrot breathlessly, arching my neck to grant him better access.

"And if you win, I'll eat you out. I'll put my tongue between those sweet little pussy lips of yours and bite down on your clit. I'll make you thrash, mindless with pleasure, and scream my name. And when you come, I'll jam my cock so far into your heat, you see fucking stars."

My body trembles at his dirty words, my mind vividly picturing the fantasy he so crassly detailed.

"Do we have a deal?" he continues in a low, seductive voice.

"Deal. After all, I am the bowling pro," I tease, my voice still breathless from the lust coursing through me, burning white-hot.

Cain wins. By a lot. I think the final score was two hundred to twenty.

And when I ride him in the middle of the throne room, his hands kneading my breasts as I bounce on his huge shaft, I can't help but think…

I'm the true winner here.

CHAPTER 20

NINA

"Buttercup, did you miss me?"

The familiar, sultry voice causes goosebumps to race up and down my arms faster than an Amtrak train. Immediately, I spin to face him, my heart jumping up my throat and becoming lodged there.

"Rion," I breathe, half wondering if his presence is an illusion and at any second, he's going to dematerialize like an oasis in a desert, returning to dry sand once more.

"The one and only. Well, that's not technically true. Mama Rion told me that I had a twin that I ate in my womb. So I suppose the correct terminology is 'two and only.' But don't quote me on that."

As he continues his diatribe, I sprint in his direction, leaving Abel behind in our cell. My sunshine twin gives a halfhearted protest, reminding me that I promised him sexy times after I arrived smelling like Cain with sweat soaking my skin, but he doesn't stop me as I blindly reach for my shifter mate.

I tangle my hands in his obsidian hair, tugging gently, and he growls in satisfaction. The primal sound travels straight to my clit, and I have the irresistible urge to bring my thighs together and rub them.

"You're okay." Through touch alone, I familiarize myself with his striking features. With the lip ring that feels amazing against my mouth...and against other areas. With the second bulb in his eyebrow. With his broad, muscular shoulders that lead down to a tapered waist. With the smooth contours of his stomach and every dip and cranny of his six-pack. The fabric beneath my hands isn't the familiar cotton shirt Rion prefers to wear. It's scratchy, almost papery, in texture.

I didn't even realize how worried I was about him until now, when he's standing in front of me, safe and unharmed. My heart thrashes once before singing a jovial song complete with confetti cannons and handfuls of glitter.

My mate.

My love.

He's okay.

"You're not wearing your uniform." Rion sounds almost petulant, like a child who wasn't allowed a cookie after dinner. "Didn't Damien give you the sexy nurse costume I requested?"

"Sexy...nurse?" I cock my head to the side curiously as his hands land on my hips, pulling me flush against his already erect cock. Even though I've just made love to Cain less than an hour ago, my pussy is slick with moisture, ready for more. Ready for him. Ready for everything he can ever give me and then some.

But then I think about where he was, in the medical wing of the prison, and a sliver of self-consciousness and irrational jealousy slams into me like a thousand-ton wrecking ball.

Does he want me to wear a sexy nurse costume...because

he spent the jarring two weeks apart with a bunch of sexy nurses?

"What's with the frown, Buttercup?" Rion demands abruptly. I feel two of his fingers push against the outer edges of my lips, attempting to maneuver them upwards. "Who do I need to murder? Or maim? Or mutilate? I call them the three M's of torture. It's actually a song my mother taught me. *Maim, then mutilate, mutilate then murder. Murder. Maim. Muti-late—*" I place a hand over his mouth mid-verse, and behind me, Abel releases a bark of sharp laughter.

"It's just..." I struggle to articulate my thoughts, not wanting to come across as naïve or petty or jealous. Even though I am naïve and petty and jealous.

"It's just?" He waits for me to continue, and I don't need vision to know his striking eyes are fixed firmly on my face. Watching. Waiting. I once found it unnerving to be the sole focus of all of these alpha men, but I don't know if I feel that way any longer. I love the way their eyes caress me, even when I'm not speaking. The way that I can sense them across the room, like their very souls cry for my own.

Instead of answering Rion's innocent inquiry, I duck my head, suddenly embarrassed.

A slender finger rests under my chin, attempting to tilt my face up, but I stubbornly swat his hand away.

"Someone's feisty today," Rion muses, sounding pleased as can be by the fact.

"Someone's jealous," Abel singsongs, and I whip my head up from its subservient position and level a penetrating glare on the traitorous demon. I have no idea if he's affected by my ire, but I can definitely hear the telltale sign of his amusement when he speaks next. "Nina thinks that you've been fantasizing about nurses while you were in the medical wing."

Rion's silent for exactly ten seconds before he demands, "Is that true?"

"It's just—"

Abel interrupts me. "I think you better introduce our girl here to the world of porn and kink."

"I know about kink," I interject with a scowl. "Didn't you guys just get into an argument with me a few weeks ago about bondage and spankings?"

I can practically feel the temperature in the room drop a couple degrees as their moods sour.

"You can't tell any guy other than the six of us that you want to tie him up and spank him," Abel states gravely. The distinct smell of sulfur permeates the air as his demon makes an appearance. I know that when he gets like this, his spindly, bat-like wings protrude from his back and dark horns erupt from his blond hair. Usually, his eyes turn crimson and rivulets of lava crack open his skin like an egg that has been dropped one too many times.

Like with Rion's growl, the possessiveness in Abel's voice sends heat shooting through my bloodstream like fallen stars. I want nothing more than to have him pin me to the dirty stone floor and use his claws to rid me of my simple white dress. And then, I want his cock to slide into my wet folds while Rion twists my head to the side so I can suck and lick his long, thick girth.

"Do you really think that I would ever in a million years fantasize about a girl who isn't you?" Rion asks me at last, directing my attention to the conversation at hand. Is my face on fire? It definitely feels like it is. He sounds genuinely hurt.

Shoot. *Think of something to say, Nina.* Maybe I should call him Daddy and see if he reacts the way Abel did when I said it to him. Think of something sexy. Something…scandalous.

"I'm not wearing any underwear," I blurt, and flames

immediately enter both of my cheeks at my impromptu confession. I feel like a freaking idiot—even more so when silence descends. Desperate to rectify the situation, I add, "I mean, I had some on in the morning. I don't just walk around with my cooch out on display. Did you know that cooch is another word for vagina? I didn't. Not until I heard Rebecca talking about fanning her cooch. I asked her what she needed to fan, and she said her plantation. I was confused. Aren't plantations immense buildings in the South? But then Braelyn told me that she meant her...err... vagina. Well, her vagina region. Anyway, I had underwear on. Until Cain took it off and kept it."

Oh. My. God.

Did I just turn into Rion?

Did my crazy mate's crazy ramblings finally rub off on crazy me?

"Did she just...?" comes Abel's voice. Breathless. Husky. Laced with unrestrained desire.

"She just fucking rambled," Rion says on a sigh, sounding like a proud dad. "Like me."

"Oh my fuck. Are there two of you?" Abel's voice hitches with his terror.

Before I can respond, Rion grabs my hand and begins to drag me away, my short strides barely able to keep pace with his long ones. "We are definitely going to go back to my cell and have a long conversation about porn and acting out some of the popular kinks. Then, we're going to fuck on my bed. Or on the ground. Or against the wall. Or on the moon. Well, once I get you the moon, I mean. Do you want it? I'm pretty sure I can ask Damien to steal it for you. He's my precious mage bitch, after all. Ohhhh. That's sparkly!" Before I can enter his mind to see what has enraptured his attention, he continues, "Just kidding. It's dried blood. And I also wanted to ask you...why the fuck did Cain allow you to walk around without any underwear on? Actually, don't answer that. I don't think I'll ever want you to wear underwear. Unless you're with other guys. Or girls. Or anyone who isn't me."

We reach his cell in record time, but before I can make myself aware of his surroundings, he pushes me back onto the bed. I place my palms on either side of myself as he hovers over me, his breath warm against my face.

"Do you remember the first thing I said we're going to talk about?"

"Um…sex?" Please say yes. Please say yes. Please say yes. I'm pretty sure my pussy might die if she doesn't have a cock in it soon. At least his cock. I missed him fiercely while he was away, and being with him once more, feeling his arms around me… It's like my soul is complete. Like it's been lying in fractures and is only now in one piece. Whole. He makes me feel whole.

"Nope." He pops the P as he continues to tower over me, his strong arms emitting an almost palpable heat. Licks of flame dance on my sensitive skin, and my lips part instinctively. He brings his hand to my throat and slowly trails his fingers down to the strap of my white dress, fingering it as if it's fine silk he yearns to purchase. "Porn and kink, remember?"

"Porn and kink," I repeat, though my voice isn't as strong as his. It's breathy and subdued. I'm barely able to think past the lust percolating in my stomach, twisting tighter and tighter with each passing second. I'm nearly mindless by it.

"Porn and kink." His body releases a low, animalistic purr as he runs his nose down my neck, sliding it across my shoulder, and then repeating the pattern. Up and down. Down and up. Up and down… "Slide into my head, Buttercup. We're going to watch a little video."

I do as he says, my nipples pebbling beneath the thin

dress, and see that Rion has moved the ancient television closer to the bed. He sifts through the DVDs before pulling out one that says *Naughty Nurse* on the front.

"Now, I haven't watched this since I met you," Rion begins as he slides the DVD into the player. "So it doesn't even compare to my fantasy."

His fantasy?

My mind swarms with confusion as, on the screen, a striking man with sandy-blond hair perches himself on a cot. I recognize the room as one that would belong in a hospital.

"Are we watching a movie?" I wish we had popcorn. Abel got me addicted to that snack, and I haven't been the same since.

"Shhh." Rion's eyes can't help but flicker in my direction, his gaze lingering on my chest a beat before traveling to my lips. With a muffled curse, as if remembering he's supposed to be my eyes for the movie, he turns away again, focusing on the screen once more.

A busty bombshell of a nurse enters the room and closes a curtain behind her. She has the largest breasts I've ever seen, and her tiny nurse's outfit only enhances that.

"I heard that you've been injured," the nurse says in a low, sultry voice.

She's a horrible actress. You would think that a movie would hire someone who actually had a lick of skill, but what do I know?

"What's the plot of this movie?" I whisper to Rion, and his eyes leave the screen once more to focus on me.

"There is no plot, Buttercup. Well...maybe you can consider it a deep and meaningful masterpiece about people in power taking advantage of people beneath them. Very, very deep. It probably deserves a thousand Oscars."

"Oh. Interesting!" I nod my head in understanding, but when he doesn't immediately turn back to the movie, where the breathy nurse is asking the patient to undress—even though his injury is on his leg. Why would he have to completely undress? Couldn't he simply pull up his pants leg? —I grab his chin and force it in the direction of the screen. Rion's hand immediately clamps down on my thigh.

On the screen, the male is now completely naked. My eyes travel across the broad planes of his chest, to the splatter of hair traveling down his chest, and then to his large, erect cock with the mushroom tip. I can't help but think that my guys are better looking. Sexier. And their cocks are way bigger.

"Maybe we shouldn't have fucking watched this," Rion growls, his hand tightening on my thigh possessively. I shush him.

"Shhh. I want to know what happens. Does the patient live?"

"Does the patient...?" Rion trails off, and his vision distorts as he shakes his head slowly from side to side.

The sexy nurse lowers herself to her knees and begins to palm the man's dick.

"Let me take care of you," she coos before her tongue snakes out to lick the tip of his cock. The man squeezes his eyelids shut, falling back onto the cot with a breathy, pained moan.

"Is that what happens in hospitals?" I ask, aghast. Did some sexy nurse lick Rion's cock during his treatment? The thought poisons my stomach and makes me sick. Physically ill, as if any second, I'll expel the contents of my stomach.

"No!" Rion rushes to reassure me. "It's fiction. It's a... Fuck, Buttercup! This is a porno."

"You said that before," I point out. The patient grabs the nurse's upper arms and yanks her to her feet, kissing her swollen lips intensely. In a decidedly caveman move, he rips open the front of the nurse's dress, buttons flying through the air, and bares her heavy breasts to the camera. She really does have a good…rack? Rake? What's the word?

She has good boobs.

Easily a handful each, with pink nipples that the patient doesn't hesitate to suck in his mouth. I watch as he slurps on each of her nipples like a man starved…

Then Rion turns his attention away from the television and focuses back on me.

"Rion! I was watching that," I protest. For some reason, the sight of the two of them together has made me…hot. Did someone turn up the temperature in the prison? My breasts are unbearably heavy, my nipples sharp, and my pussy is already wet.

"And I didn't realize how jealous I would be knowing you're staring at another man's dick," he growls.

"Actually, I was staring at her boobs," I say without preamble. Out of the peripheral of Rion's vision, I can see that the nurse is now on the cot with the man between her thighs, his long tongue stroking the inner walls of her pussy lips. She squeezes both of her large breasts together before plucking her nipples.

"Fucking hell, Buttercup," Rion curses. "You can't say shit like that to me."

"Why not?" I tilt my head to the side curiously. Rion shifts on the bed slightly, so he's not able to see the movie at all. Which means I'm not able to see the movie at all. Through his eyes, I watch as he slides the straps of my dress down the rest of the way, freeing my breasts. Instinctively, I bring my hands up and begin to rub my fingers around my nipples, causing the buds to become even sharper.

"Fuck. Fuck. Fuck," Rion curses.

And then…I get it.

What he meant when he was talking about kink and porn and his dirty fantasy. I know he's still wearing that hideous hospital gown, which means all he needs is a naughty nurse…

I've never…err…acted before, so I have no idea what I'm doing. But if it makes Rion happy, I'm willing to do just about anything.

"I heard you've been injured," I begin softly, attempting to replicate the sultry tones of the woman in the movie. I can hear her breathy pants and the guy's harsh moans. Are they fighting? No, they definitely didn't look like they were about to be fighting. Which means that they're…having sex. On television.

The thought makes me impossibly wetter, especially when the woman cries out in bliss.

"Huh?" Rion, for once, sounds speechless.

"Injured," I repeat, standing gracefully from the bed and placing my hand on his shoulder. "Lie down. Let me get a good look at you."

He does as I say, his pulse skittering beneath my palm, and from his new angle, my breasts dangle enticingly over his face.

"What hurts?" I question, trailing my hands down his delectable, tattooed body. I wish with a fierce intensity that I could see every inch of him, but I have to settle for this. Seeing through his eyes. Experiencing what he feels.

I sink a little deeper into his mind, allowing his thoughts to sweep over me like a heavy gust of wind. It's much easier to sense his than it was the first time I attempted it. Rion's essence—the sheer brilliance of his soul—intertwines with mine like slithering snakes. His thoughts pinball around in my head.

Are we actually doing this? Are we actually playing dirty nurse? Fuck, what do I do? I didn't think she would actually do it! I've never roleplayed before. Think, Rion, think. Say something charming. Or witty. Or amazing. You're a bad bitch shifter. You personify sex.

What Rion says is… "I have a booboo on my cockadoodledoo."

Fucking dammit, Ri. What is wrong with you? Well, besides the fact that you've been dropped on your head twenty-seven times from the age of zero to two. They called it 'Crack the Egg,' but instead of using real eggs, they used babies' heads and—

Holy, fuck.

Rion's thoughts taper off when I pull up his hospital gown and wrap my lips around his length. I know I'm supposed to be in character or whatever, but all I want is to pleasure my mate. To watch him fall apart beneath me and lose himself to the sensations I evoke. I want him to see stars as his eyes roll into the back of his head.

I wrap my hand around the base of his cock and lick the tip, loving the taste of his pre-cum. Working my mouth and hand in tandem, I take him as deep as I can, making sure to hollow my cheeks, and bob my head up and down his shaft. When I pull away, it's only to lick his cock like a lollipop, paying particular attention to a vein that runs down the side.

"Fuck. Fuck. Fuck. Fuck."

There's something immensely erotic about seeing the scene through Rion's eyes. Seeing his cock in my grasp as I lean over him, my bare chest brushing against the tops of his thighs.

Before Rion can come, I gently slide off of him, pull my dress the rest of the way off, and then move to straddle his toned waist. He grips his cock and rubs it through my juices, lubricating himself even further, before he grabs my hips and pulls me down onto him.

Both of us groan at the connection. I feel too full, almost to the point of bursting, as his cock caresses my inner walls, the piercing at the very tip of his dick rubbing against me in a way that has me seeing stars.

I place my hands on his chest, only then realizing that he still has the hideous hospital gown on, and begin to bounce on top of him.

"Yes, Buttercup. Use me. Take me. I'm yours." Rion's hands travel from my waist to my stomach, before cupping both of my breasts. His fingers twist my nipples in unison as I continue to ride his dick desperately, throwing my head back so my black hair doesn't obstruct his vision. *My* vision.

"I want to try something," I murmur desperately, and when his vision dips with his nod, I don't hesitate to climb off of his cock. I don't feel embarrassed as I twist my body so my face is near his cock and his own is level with my pussy. From his eyes, I can see that my pink lips are glistening, desperate for his tongue.

"Fucking hell." Rion runs his pierced tongue up my slit as one of his fingers probes my tight entrance. "Buttercup...are you in my head right now?" He sounds so turned on by the prospect, so aroused, that more liquid seeps from my pussy.

"Yes," I moan as my searching fingers wrap around Rion's cock and I guide him towards my mouth. "I want you to eat my pussy, Rion. Please. I need you."

My pleading words, combined with the knowledge that I'm staring at my own dripping cunt right now, is enough to have Rion's dick twitching in my hands. He begins to feast on me like a man possessed, his fingers sliding in and out of my pussy as his lips latch on to my clit.

I move my own mouth over his hard length, fondling his balls the way I know he likes. With a wicked smirk around his cock, I trail my finger down his thigh and then to his back hole, sliding one of my lubed up fingers through it.

Rion jumps in surprise as my finger begins to move in

and out of his ass while my mouth swallows his cock, but he doesn't relent his ruthless pursuit on my clit.

His cock jumps in my mouth, and he releases a curse, the noise muffled from where his head is between my thighs. "I'm gonna—"

"Come for me," I murmur around his dick. I don't know if he can even hear my words or just feel the vibrations, but either way, his cock twitches once, twice, three times, before he shoots ropes of salty cum down my mouth. I try to swallow all that I can, but the weird position I'm in, combined with the pleasure of Rion's mouth and fingers, has more than a few swallows dripping down my cheeks.

Rion bites down on my clit, and I swear my soul leaves my body. Sparks of light fly across my vision as my entire body shakes and shakes and shakes. A scream escapes my lips before I can contain it, and I bite down on Rion's sweaty thigh to muffle the sound.

I collapse on top of him, sweat and cum sticking us together, but I'm too weak to even care, content to remain like this for the rest of my life, with my head on Rion's thigh and his dick inches from my face.

"Come here, Buttercup," Rion instructs, his voice just as breathless as I feel.

I slip out of his head and blindly twist towards him, crawling up his muscular body until my head is snuggled beneath his chin. He must've turned the movie off. I no longer hear the contented grunts and moans of the actor and actress.

"Are you tired?" He rubs a hand down my sweat-soaked spine.

I nuzzle against his chest as my eyelids flutter. "Yeah," I confess. My body feels as if it weighs a million pounds. I don't know if I'm even capable of lifting my head.

"All right." He kisses my temple. "Sleep, my love."

As darkness encroaches on the edges of my vision, I can't help but whisper, "And Rion?"

"Yes, Buttercup?"

"I really want to see how the movie ends."

I don't get to hear his reply before sleep claims me.

NINA

I snuggle against Rion's chest, the epitome of contentment and calm. I imagine I would feel this way about any of my mates, any of the men I love. A giddy, half asleep part of me wishes I could stare intently at the engagement ring on my finger like they do in the movies. Revel in the knowledge that soon, I'll be a Mrs. Soon, I'll be married.

Instead of doing that, I simply trail my finger over the edge of the ring, tracing the design. Kai gave it to me from his personal vault—the place where his dragon likes to hoard all of the gold and jewels he's capable of acquiring.

I love it.

I love it so freaking much, my heart feels seconds from bursting, splattering the walls of the cell in vibrant red blood.

Lazily, I draw pictures into Rion's chest as he continues to sleep, but after only a few minutes, my bladder begins to protest. Being extra mindful not to wake up my serene, sleeping lover—and he needs all of the sleep he can get, especially since he's still healing—I stumble towards where I took off my dress. It takes me a few tries, but I'm able to slip it on in some semblance of modesty.

Before I leave this section of the small cell, I plant a chaste kiss on Rion's forehead, and I swear I hear him murmur my name in his sleep. The thought makes me smile. It's *me* he's dreaming about. Me. I bite my lip as I brush my fingers through his thick hair...before my hand catches on something.

My smile dissipates when I realize that the object in question is sharp to the touch. No, not sharp, necessarily, but thorny.

A stem.

I run the pad of my fingers over the thorny stem and then feel the edges of the flower. I'm not positive, but I would guess based on the shape that it's a rose, maybe a tulip.

Did Rion get this for me?

Love for him consumes me, bursting like water in a kettle, and I bring the satiny petal up to my cheek. One smell confirms that it's definitely a rose. Fresh, too. When did Rion have time to grab this for me? We fell asleep immediately after sex, and I would've known if he left for even a second.

Maybe it was there before...? And I didn't notice...?

Choosing not to focus on this, I place the flower gently on the edge of the bed and then wander towards where I know the toilet is. It's slightly embarrassing to have to pee in front of your sleeping lover, so I pray that he doesn't wake up.

I quickly take care of business and then wash my hands in the metal sink beside the toilet. It makes a weird, deafening, creaking sound as I turn the knobs to adjust the temperature. I wince, half expecting Rion to jump out of bed, instantly alert, but my shifter remains asleep, his soft snores filling the air.

I wonder what he looks like right now. Would his arms be stretched behind his head? Is he still wearing that paper hospital gown? Would he look younger in sleep? Gentler? That's one word I never thought I would use to describe any of my mates. They're a lot of things, but gentle isn't one of them. Except with me.

I suppose I'm the exception to a lot of things.

A tiny smile begins to play on my lips as I face the direction of Rion's breathing. My handsome, perfect, eccentric shifter. Mr. Scruffles.

Biting my lower lip, I debate the merits of waking him up with my lips wrapped around his cock. My pussy throbs when I think about the night before, when our bodies were twisted together on the small, twin-sized bed. All I would need to do to ensure a repeat episode would be to climb on the bed, grab Rion's cock, and—

Music drifts to my ears, the noise hushed and distorted, as if I'm hearing it down the end of a long tunnel. My entire body goes rigid as the blissful, enchanting noise pounds against my eardrums. I can feel my heart race in my chest, and I'm suddenly consumed with the need to move. To walk. To leave this cell, leave Rion.

What...?

Before I realize what I'm doing, my feet are propelling me out of the cell. I stumble slightly, my face hitting the edge of one of the silver bars, but even my shout of pain doesn't stop me from moving. It's almost as if I don't have any control of my body, as if I'm being controlled by a puppeteer and I'm nothing but the poor, dusty marionette he decided to use for the day.

No!

I try to open my mouth, try to scream, but the lilting voice continues to corral me forward.

Everything will be okay.

Everything is fine.

You're fine.

It feels as if someone is speaking those words directly into my brain, despite the fact that the only noise in the hall is the soulful singing. I don't recognize the song or the language, but the words blend together. Beautiful. So beautiful.

Abruptly, my feet stop moving, though I don't know where I am. The music cuts off as quickly as it began, causing an emptiness to blow through my body. I suddenly can't breathe. Can't think.

What...?

Where...?

How...?

I know I should be alarmed, but there seems to be a perpetual cloud of confusion hovering over my consciousness. I bring both of my hands up to my head instinctively, a low groan leaving my throat.

Rion...?

Where is...?

I struggle to articulate his name, though my mind conjures up images of my handsome shifter mate. But it isn't long before those too are lost in a sea of confusion.

"Nina Doe," a soft, masculine voice whispers. A moment later, I can feel a single finger trail up my cheek and then back down. It touches the very edge of my lips before dropping from my face. "The Queen of the Labyrinth. The mate of the kings."

His voice is musical...magical. My entire body sways towards his like a flower in a grassy field, desperate to capture every ray of sunlight. I wilt. Burn.

For him.

For this stranger.

For his voice.

"You don't know who I am," he continues, and I can hear his footsteps as he walks around me, stopping when he's at my back. Still, I'm unable to move. Unable to turn towards him. Talk to him. Acknowledge him.

All I can do is sit in my customary darkness, his voice slithering through my body like dozens of insidious snakes.

"But I know who you are." His hands move to my breasts and give them a quick squeeze. I want to scream at the violation, but my lips remain stubbornly pressed together. All that manages to escape is a single tear that cascades down my cheek, leaving behind a blotchy red smear. His fingers tweak my nipples through the fabric of my dress, but instead of the love and lust I felt when Rion did that last night, all I can muster up now is disgust and horror. Pain.

But even those emotions are soon swept away, replaced by an icy numbness that shrivels up my lungs and freezes my heart. Am I even pumping blood anymore? I'm not sure.

"You must be wondering why you're trapped. Why you're captivated by my voice, even when your head tells you that you hate me." He leans forward to nip at my earlobe, and I shudder. "I'm a siren," he continues at last, and the species sparks a tiny bit of recognition, though it's hard for me to focus through the mind-numbing haze. "But I'm also a greedy man, Nina. A very greedy man. And when someone offers me a lot of money to kill your pretty cunt..." He lowers his hand to touch me under my dress, and I want to sob. But my stupid, traitorous body is incapable of doing anything besides standing there like prey.

I hate it.

I hate him.

The intensity of my emotions almost takes me by surprise. I've hated a lot of people in my life—Alyssa, Raphael, Lionel, Narian, and all of those men and women who hurt my twins—but I can't remember a time when my hatred was so sudden and pronounced. There's no buildup.

One second, this man's a stranger, and the next, he's my enemy.

And I hate him. I hate him for making me lose control of a body I just became proud of. I hate him for taking advantage of me when I'm incapable of fighting back, just like a coward would do.

And I hate him even more for trying to take me from my mates.

I have no doubt in my mind that he's here to kill me. Obviously, he wishes to collect on the money from the hit list. A demented part of me can't even blame him. Not really. Even the sanest of people can be corrupted by greed and money. By power and influence.

"I wanted to take my time with you," the siren continues, his husky voice reverberating through me. Calming me. He removes his hand from my body, and I hear rather than see him step away. "But I don't think I'll have enough time. So instead, I want you to kill yourself."

His silky words…

I'm helpless to resist them. They compel me to do the unthinkable, but I'm unable to swim against the currents. They continually pull and tug at me until I'm drowning, my head sinking beneath the turbulent ocean waves.

My mates…

Immense sadness fills me as my feet move me forward, my body desperate to adhere to the siren's command, even as my mind screams at me to stop.

I place both of my hands on what I assume is the wall of the tunnel…

And then I slam my head against the hard cement.

Once. Twice. Three times. Four times.

Pain explodes behind my forehead, shooting through my bloodstream like thousands of colorful, explosive fireworks. Blood trickles from the wound on my head and into my eyes.

I can feel it touch my lips, but even the salty taste isn't enough to stop me.

Madness.

This is madness.

You don't want to kill yourself, Nina.

You don't want to die.

Fight this!

But even as I think this, I continue to bang my head against the cement. Again. And again. And again.

The Labyrinth shakes, almost as if the building itself is furious at me for hurting myself, for daring to leave it, but no one intervenes. Darkness closes in on me from all sides, the monotony of blackness interspersed with shooting white lights.

Am I dying?

What's happening to me?

More blood cascades down my cheeks, following the path that my tears took earlier, but I can't stop. My body refuses to let me, forcing me to obey the twisted, sadistic desires of the siren.

"What the...?! Hey!"

I don't immediately recognize the new voice, but the next thing I know, the haziness is ripped from my mind like a string being cut. I'm suddenly keenly aware of the blistering pain in my head and the heaviness of my heart. I hear what sounds like a neck being snapped, and then a gentle hand touches my hair.

"Nina, stay with me. I got you."

That voice...

Logan.

But before I can focus on that, before I can focus on anything, my body sways precariously to the side and I fall unconscious.

CHAPTER 22

BRONSON

othing can prepare me for the horror I feel when Logan, our recently released prisoner, rushes into the throne room, a bleeding Nina in his arms.

"She needs a doctor!" he screams as I spring into action. The rest of the guys are in the fighting ring, supervising a match between a jaded vampire and his incubus lover. Rion should've been with Nina in his old cell.

"What the fuck happened?" My heart jumps up my throat as Logan gently places her on the red rug. I feel lightheaded and dizzy, my stomach a tumultuous mixture of distress and anxiety.

My love is so pale, so ashen. She looks frail beneath the hanging bulb, her black hair an obsidian waterfall around her shoulders. And her face…

Her face is a mottled canvas of already blue and black bruises. Blood flows from a wound on her head, and her nose is at a crooked, unnatural angle. Horror fills me, inflates me, until I feel as if I might burst from it. I can feel tears stinging the back of my eyes as I try to tamp down the rapidly rising panic. No. No. No. No.

Darkness blankets my vision as I stare at my mate, my entire fucking world.

And then...

The anger sets in, eroding away the initial panic like an odorless acid.

"What. Did. You. Do?" I demand, though my words are barely intelligible around the canines in my mouth. I want to tear this pathetic excuse of a man limb from men. How fucking dare he? How dare he hurt a female? How dare he put his hands on the woman I love?

Just as quickly as the anger consumes me, it drains away, leaving me bereft and empty. One glance at Nina's sunken face, at the blood pooling down her cheeks and the hideous bruises, at her lashes fluttering against her cheekbone as she embraces unconsciousness, has panic taking its place.

No. No. No. No.

"What happened?" I'm not sure he understands my words around my growl, but he can guess the gist.

Logan releases a heavy sigh, almost as if the weight of the universe is settling on his shoulders, pushing him thousands of feet below ground. "A siren," he explains, and my hands curl into fists. Fucking sirens. They have the capability of stopping you with a single word, their magical voices making it so you want to please them. Making it so you want to do whatever they say. If one of them used his or her powers on Nina...

I gently grab her tiny hand, being extra mindful not to accidentally skewer her with my claw, and rest my forehead on her bloody chest. She's in desperate need of a shower and medical care, but I don't know if I'm capable of moving. I feel numb. My mate...

She got hurt.

Again.

And I wasn't there to protect her.

Immense self-loathing threatens to swallow me whole, and for a brief moment, I allow it to consume me completely. It festers in my lungs, making breathing difficult, before unfurling like a tulip in spring in my chest.

My head is knocked to the side with the force of the punch, and instantly, my wolf comes out to play. Coarse, dark fur sprouts on my arms and face, and it takes considerable effort not to turn into an animal right here and now and maul Logan into shreds.

The blond-haired man glares down at me, body radiating an almost elemental fury, something deserving of its own place on the periodic table. His lips curl into a scowl so cruel, you'd think someone cut it into his face with a blade.

"Get your head out of your ass, man, and help your fucking mate!" Logan bellows, his chest heaving. "Don't just wallow like a punk ass bitch."

A part of me still wants to punch him, maim him, kill him, but a larger part is too relieved that he forced me out of my self-pity to do any of that. Right now, my mate needs me. She needs me to take care of her and nurse her back to health.

My goddess needs to be worshipped.

With a nod more to myself than him, I set to work cataloguing each and every one of her injuries. It looks as if—I swallow heavily, bile rushing up my throat—she hit her head repeatedly against a hard surface. The wall, perhaps? There's too much blood on her pretty face for me to see the full extent of her injuries.

"Grab me something to wipe this blood off of her," I direct Logan gruffly, grateful when my voice doesn't come out as a guttural growl. Before Logan can walk away, I snap my arm out and capture his bicep, ignoring the blood of my beloved that stains my fingers. "And don't even think about running away." I know my eyes flash with the darkness of my wolf. "You claim that you didn't do this, but until we know for sure…"

I have to give him credit—he doesn't look away and he doesn't cower. Instead, he lifts his chin ever so slightly before nodding once.

"Understood." His eyes flicker to Nina's broken, bruised form, and his features soften considerably. One glance at me has them hardening once more. Brick by brick, he rebuilds his apathetic front. "And the siren? The asshole who did this to her?" He waits until I give him my full attention before continuing. "His body is in pieces down the hall."

With that, he turns on his heel and stomps away, hopefully to find me what I need.

My hand shakes as I bring it to Nina's hair, wiping away some of the blood-soaked strands. I'm extra mindful of her injuries. Fuck, so many injuries…

When Logan returns, he has a medical kit and a washcloth in his hands. I have no idea where the fuck he got them from, and at the moment, I don't care enough to ask. What I care about is the woman lying on the ground, her face distorted with hideous bruises and gaping wounds.

Blood.

So much blood.

But if there's one thing my sister's death has taught me, it's that I'm capable of compartmentalizing my pain for the time being. For now, I'll focus on Nina and only Nina. Later, when her other mates are around, I'll allow myself one second to fall apart. Just one.

I almost wish Logan hadn't killed the siren who did this to her, if only so I can kill the man myself. I hope it was painful. I hope he screamed in agony and pain as Logan ripped him limb from limb.

As I begin cleaning Nina's injuries, my mind begins to wander.

How many assassins are lurking in the prison right at this fucking moment, waiting for a chance to kill the woman I love?

How many prisoners will be willing to sell their soul for the money the fucking Council is providing?

And which council member is spearheading this…this witch hunt? Make no mistake, that's what this is. If they truly got the chance to know Nina, they'd realize she's the sweetest, strongest person that ever existed.

I work mechanically, cleaning her wounds and washing blood from her face, neck, and arms. My work in the pack back home has made me skilled in healing, though I wouldn't have been able to help Nina if her injuries had been any more severe. Fuck, just thinking about her with even worse injuries…

Bile rushes up my throat, but a lifetime of steel-enforced will keeps it adequately subdued.

"I can't…" I barely even realize I'm speaking until the words leave my mouth. "I can't lose her, man."

"I know." Logan's voice is soft from where he stands just off to the side, eyeing Nina curiously. "You really love her, don't you?"

"She's my entire world," I answer without preamble. And she is. The moment she arrived at the prison and my wolf declared her as my mate, no one else has mattered. Everything that I am, everything that I will be, centers around her. Just this tiny slip of a girl with raven-black hair, smoky white eyes, and a heart that is capable of loving even the most damaged of souls. "I didn't know I was capable of feeling like this, you know? It's like…" I struggle to explain the thoughts in my head. "It's like I've been living in a black and white movie, and suddenly, she's brought color to the world, disrupting the monotony I've grown accustomed to."

It seems silly to be spilling my soul to a man I don't like, let alone trust, but I can't stop the words from leaving. The pain, the panic... They both pile on top of me like dirt burying a coffin. Only in this case, the body inside is still alive, still breathing, still fighting tooth and nail to escape.

"And the others...?" Logan queries. There's no judgement in his voice, just curiosity. He stares at Nina as if he's never seen a female before. So many questions linger in his bright baby-blue eyes, but I don't know if even *I* have the answers to them.

"The others..." Guilt fills me instantly as I drop the rag I've been using to clean Nina's forehead. I swallow heavily. "The others are going to freak the fuck out and then murder me for not getting them sooner."

Fuck. I was so focused on Nina that I've forgotten about my brothers.

I scrub a hand down my face, not even caring when Nina's blood smears across my forehead and cheeks.

"She's going to be okay, man," Logan says softly, his eyes fixed on my girl. Normally, that would bother me immensely, but I'm too wound up to care. I swear my stomach is in more knots than a dozen jump ropes being found in a dusty attic would be.

"She's strong." I brush the back of my fingers across her cheek. She stirs slightly in her sleep, her face twisting into a pained grimace, but she doesn't wake up. My throat clogs, and I can feel tears burn my eyes. "She's resilient. She's been through so much already. I know she'll survive this."

And when she wakes up, I'll worship her. Not just her body—though I'll definitely worship that too—but *her*. I'd spend my life on my knees if that's what would make her smile. You can tell you love someone when suddenly your own happiness is secondary to theirs.

"You should..." I swallow heavily, the enormity of my emotions for this woman nearly overwhelming me. "You should grab the others. Um…” I hesitate, peeking a glance at him over my shoulder. “No guarantee that they won't kill you when you deliver the news.”

They deserve to know, but there's no way in hell I'm leaving Nina's side. Not again.

Every damn time I leave her, she gets injured.

“I'm sorry, Goddess,” I whisper softly, bending down to kiss her clammy forehead. The ground is beginning to become uncomfortable beneath my ass. I know I have to move her, have to bring her to a bed, but my body is numb. Just…numb. I don't know if I'm even capable of lifting an arm at this moment.

Why didn't Rion protect her? He was supposed to be with her. Where is the shifter fucker?

Dark thoughts continue to surround me, until in the landscape of my mind, all I'm aware of is darkness. Pitch-black, absolute darkness. So many monsters are capable of hiding in this shadowy wonderland. So many beasts.

My wolf gives a mournful howl, and I give in to the need to shift. Pain explodes in my nerve endings, but it only lasts a second before my wolf takes over. I place my furry head in Nina's lap, distantly aware of the pounding footsteps as Nina's other lovers enter the throne room. But I don't focus on them. I can't.

Nothing matters at this moment except my broken and bruised fiancée. My mate.

The woman I failed to protect.

CHAPTER 23

NINA

Darkness. Cloying, intense, absolute darkness.

It's the type that makes the hairs on the back of your neck stand on end and your hands tremble. It's the type that sends insidious fear slithering down your spine like a snake, though you don't know why.

I'm used to darkness, having lived my entire life embracing it.

But this…this is different.

Mainly because I know I'm not alone.

I can sense the eyes on me, the softest of caresses, and goosebumps ripple up my arms. Every hair on my body stands on end, saluting the world, as I attempt to orient myself to the stomach-churning darkness on every side of me.

"Hello?" My voice wavers ever so slightly, fear clogging my airways. Where am I? The last thing I remember is… falling asleep with Rion, his arms constricting tighter around my waist than a python. And then, nothing. Is this a dream? It has to be, though my dreams are usually vibrant with color and light. Dreams are a place for me to escape, after all, and why would I ask for more of the darkness?

Heart hammering, I take another step forward in the pitch-black abyss. Anything could be lurking, waiting, lying in wait. A monster. A killer.

Anything.

Or anyone.

"Hello?" I feel stupid, like one of those girls in the horror movies Abel makes me watch. One of those heroines who knows all of her friends have been murdered, but still goes into the creepy, abandoned house and screams, "Hello," as if the murderer is going to pop up around the corner and reply.

That's me.

I'm the stupid girl.

But I can't seem to stop myself.

"Nina..." The voice floats all around me, the noise seeming to echo. Instantly, I freeze, my hands trembling by my sides.

"W-Who are you?"

Silence reigns as I spin in a wide, desperate circle. Those invisible eyes, those penetrating eyes, seem to be burning a hole through my skin in order to peek at my very soul. The sensation is unnerving and sends nausea swirling in my stomach.

"Nina." This time, the voice comes from directly beside me, only a hair's breadth away, and I yelp, jumping backwards a few feet. "You are here."

"Who are you? And where is here?" My head scrambles to put together everything I know, but try as I might, the memories evade my grasp, shattering on the floor in thousands of irreparable pieces.

"You may call me...Nick." He stumbles over the word, almost as if that isn't his real name and he made it up on the spot. My hackles raise as I continue backing away from the masculine voice.

"Nick," I repeat. Can he hear the way my heart is racing? The way it threatens to grow limbs, rip apart my rib cage, and then crawl its way out? It suddenly feels too heavy for my body. I wouldn't be surprised if I found it on the ground, beside the broken shards of my memory. "Nick, where am I?"

"You are in my home." Once more, his voice sounds from directly beside me. He says each word slowly, carefully, as if he isn't used to speaking. I can dimly make out a posh accent, though I can't decipher the origins. "You have been injured," he continues, and I feel the slightest pressure of fingertips against my cheek. There and gone in a breath.

"Injured?"

Once more, I focus on my splintered memories, struggling to recall what happened. I was with Rion in bed…

And then…

And then the voice! The song! The lilting music that was impossible for me to resist.

I cling desperately to those memories, my metaphorical knuckles turning white and the veins popping, as the rest of the scene replays in a loop.

The hands on my body. The voice instructing me to bang my head against the wall. The pain.

And then…

And then Logan arrived and snapped the siren's neck. Kai told me once that they were some of the only paranormal creatures capable of luring people to their deaths with just their voices. Once you were under their thrall, it was impossible to resist.

"Nick, where am I?" I repeat. My heart races, and sweat beads on my forehead.

"You are with me," he states simply, his soft, melodic voice washing over me the same way the siren's did. Only, unlike the siren's, I don't sense any malice from this man. Just curiosity. Confusion. Warmth.

"Your home?" I try to feel my surroundings, try to gauge how far away I am from my men, but my searching hands feel nothing but air. Now that I'm thinking about it...

It almost feels like I'm floating. There's nothing tangible or solid beneath my bare feet.

Just wispy air.

Panic settles in, a heavy pressure on my chest, but I'm able to breathe around it as I turn in the general direction I heard Nick's voice.

"Where is your home?" I begin carefully, regarding him like a fuse that can explode at any moment. I need to tread carefully.

"Everywhere." His voice resonates from every direction. "And nowhere."

"That doesn't make any sense." My brows furrow together as another feather-light finger brushes down my cheek and pauses on my pulse.

"Did you like the gifts I have bestowed upon you?" he asks suddenly, before I can probe him further for information.

Bestowed upon?

"Gifts?" I choose to ask instead, ignoring his weird, formal language.

"The note," he explains, and I can hear the smile in his voice. "And the rose."

"Those were from you?" I distantly remember the creepy, borderline possessive note someone slipped into Damien's jacket pocket. And then the rose on my pillow after my night with Rion...the rose I thought came from him.

I try to ignore the unease that crawls up my spine like millions of fire ants. First, he left a note in my pocket that conjures images of serial killers and stalkers and crazy murderers—I may have been watching too many horror movies—and then, he went to Rion's cell while we were both sleeping and naked and left a rose.

Who does that?

"You are upset." Nick sounds baffled, if not a little bit hurt.

There are a thousand things I want to ask, but I settle on, "Why did you do it? What do you want? Tell me the truth."

Why go through all of this trouble for me? I'm not oblivious. I know that a lot of the guys in the prison find me attractive, mainly because of my status as the unofficial Queen of the Labyrinth and because of my overprotective mates. People want what they can't have.

But no one has ever taken it to the extreme "Nick" has. Maybe because most people know they'll be ripped to shreds if they lay a finger on me. That's enough of a deterrent as anything.

"Soon, little one," Nick says softly. There's a lapse in conversation, and for a moment, I think he's left. But then his voice reaches me from all directions, making it impossible for me to pinpoint an exact location. "I will try to protect you, but my power is limited. It has only recently become active again."

"I don't understand what you mean—"

"You need to wake up now, little one." His hands touch my shoulders, and for a horrible, nauseating second, I think he's going to kiss me. Instead, he shoves me.

I spin wildly around, tumbling through wave after wave of air, before darkness mercifully claims me one final time.

I WHEEZE, MY LUNGS CONSTRICTING WITH PANIC AND MY PULSE thundering in my ears.

The first thing I'm aware of is pain. My head is throbbing as if...

As if I hit it repeatedly against a cave wall.

"Careful," a growly voice reprimands, and I feel a hand touch my chest, guiding me onto my back.

"Bron?" I reach with shaky hands for my lover, and he nuzzles my palms, a low whine leaving his throat. "Where am I? Where is everyone?"

"We're here," Abel says softly, his voice sounding from the other side of me. I can't help but notice how subdued he sounds. He's normally so upbeat, full of life and energy, that this drastic change leaves me reeling. I must've been in pretty bad shape for him to sound like that.

"Everyone?" I reach with my free hand, and someone—my guess is Abel—immediately takes it.

"Damien and Blade are with Logan, helping to dispose of the...err..." Cain trails off as Abel gives my hand a reassuring squeeze.

"The body," I finish for him, once more attempting to sit up. Wincing, I bring a hand to my forehead, unsurprised to feel a fresh bandage over the wound.

"And Rion is..." Cain's voice tapers off again, and he swallows audibly.

"Where is he? Is he hurt? Is he okay?" I rapidly fire off question after question as my mind imagines the worst possible scenarios. Did the siren hurt him? Did I hurt him while I was under the siren's thrall? Is he alive?

I search for the big ball of energy inside of me that I've come to associate with Rion and find him alive and well, just a few feet away. It doesn't seem as if he's in the room with me, though. Why would he be sitting just outside of it?

My confusion must've been plain to see on my face, because Cain rushes to explain, "He feels a lot of guilt over what happened." Darkness coats his words when he speaks next. "As he should."

"Don't." I remove my hands from Abel and Bronson, ignoring the latter's growl, to whack Cain gently. "Don't blame him for what happened. It wasn't his fault."

"He was supposed to be watching you, Goddess," Bronson says in a calm voice. Too calm. I know my wolf shifter well enough to hear the fury lacing his words.

"It was my fault," I defend immediately, hating that they're putting the blame onto Rion. And worst…that he's accepting it. "I got out of bed to go to the bathroom. Rion didn't even know I was up. And besides, if the siren's song made me… um…" I allow my words to fizzle out when Bronson begins to growl and the smell of sulfur permeates the air. Taking a deep breath for courage, I add, "What I'm trying to say is, if Rion was under the siren's spell, he wouldn't have been able to resist. It could've happened to any of you, so please don't blame him for something he had no control over."

I need to go to him, to check on him. He's hurting. I can sense that as sharply as I can feel my own pain.

"Easy there, Bambi." Abel wraps an arm around my shoulders. "I can see the wheels in your mind turning."

"But you're still injured," Cain adds, his voice rough with emotion. "So you need to be resting."

"Do you remember what happened?" Abel takes over one more.

"I remember…"

Cuddling with Rion.

The siren.

His horrible, unwelcome, nauseating touch. One that even now sends bile racing up my throat.

Pain.

And then…

Darkness.

But I feel as if there's something I have to remember, a tiny piece of the puzzle I need in order to understand everything bombarding us. Try as I might, I can't hold on to it longer than a second.

"The siren..." I bring my thumb to my lower lip and pull on it gently. "You said he's dead?"

"Logan took care of him," Cain answers in a dark tone. And then, almost under his breath, he adds, "Though I wish he left the fucker alive. I would've liked to get my hands on him."

"Same, brother," Abel murmurs.

I nod once, hating the immense wave of relief I feel at knowing the siren is dead and can't hurt me ever again. It's a strange thing, to be targeted by a man you don't even know. I'm almost positive I never talked to this person before, someone so blinded by greed that he would be willing to kill an innocent female.

Is it wrong that I'm glad he's dead?

Does that make me a horrible person?

Why is it so hard to differentiate right from wrong? When did that line become blurred?

"What was his...?" I swallow, trying again. "What was his name?"

"Brett," Bronson growls out, and I automatically bring my hand up to his hair, trailing my fingers through the short blond strands. He whines low in his throat and leans against me. "He's been in this prison for almost five years now. We thought he was a good man."

"Though how good can anyone be if they're down here?" Abel laments with a harsh sounding chuckle.

"We found the hit list in his room," Cain tells me, putting a hand on my foot and rubbing gently at the sole.

"It's scary," I begin, trying to wrangle the moan that wants to escape as Cain continues to massage my foot, "the power money has over people. And it's even scarier what my life is worth."

Cain freezes, his hands closing around my ankle, and Bronson emits a fierce growl.

"No one is going to get to you, Trouble. You know that, right?" Something dark and broken, something made up of shadows and nightmares, fills Cain's voice. "Not again. We let it happen one too many times."

"Things have to change," declares Abel resolutely. "We can't stay here any longer. Not with the list against you."

Before I can ask him to elaborate on what he means, I hear the sound of a door opening and closing and nearly inaudible footsteps stopping just at the edge of my bed. Only one man moves that silently.

"Angel," Damien says gently, and a second later, I feel his fingers on my calves. "How are you feeling?"

"I hurt," I confess, "but it's not horrible."

"Good. That means your natural healing is kicking in. You should be back to normal soon," Damien explains in his soft, melodic voice. "Would you mind if I used my magic to check the progress of your healing?"

I can't help but note that I'm the only one Damien will ever ask permission from. Usually, he takes what he wants without remorse, without thought to the people he might hurt. But not with me. Everything is my choice with him. It's been like that from the very beginning, when I sauntered up to the blue-eyed man and fed him.

"Of course." As he leans over me, I bring my hand up to cup his cheek. He pauses, twisting his head to kiss my palm, before placing his own hands on both of my shoulders. I can't see his face, but silence descends as he does whatever magic he needs to do. I can feel heat emitting from where his hands touch my skin, but besides that, I feel nothing.

One minute turns into two. And two turns into ten.

I don't think I'm the only one becoming concerned when Abel asks, "Damien, man. Are you broken? Do we need to reset you? Did someone unplug you?"

Damien pulls away from me with a gasp—a gasp that is completely unlike my stone-cold assassin. It's broken and raspy.

"That's impossible," he breathes, horror lacing his tone.

"What's impossible?" I fidget on the uncomfortable bed I'm sitting on. I haven't gone into anyone's head, so I'm not sure where I am, but my guess is the small bedroom located in the back of the throne room.

"I need to... I need to talk to Kai."

Before any of us can comment on Damien's abrasive, uncharacteristic behavior, the door slams shut, signaling he already left.

"What was that all about?" I ask, anxiously chewing on my lower lip.

"I don't know." Bronson touches my cheek. "But I don't like it."

I agree. Anything that ruffles my apathetic assassin...

It can't bode well for me.

CHAPTER 24

NINA

I don't see Damien and Rion the rest of the day. Or the following day.

Though I suppose "see" is the wrong word to use in this context.

I do, however, spend my days being coddled by Bronson, the twins, and Kai. I swear that almost every second, at least two of them are touching me in some way, shape, or form. I want to feel suffocated, annoyed, but all of those negative emotions are overshadowed by the overwhelming love I feel for them.

My injuries have already healed themselves, though I still feel phantom pain from where my head banged against the wall repeatedly.

I don't dare tell my guys exactly what happened—how the siren touched me, violated me. That's a secret I'll take to my grave. Besides, what could they do about it? The siren is already dead. They'll simply blame themselves even more, wallowing in misplaced guilt.

My worry for Damien and Rion grows each hour I don't see them. Why did Damien run out the way he did? Even though he claimed he was going to talk to Kai, my dragon shifter remains just as in the dark as I am. And Rion…

Does he really blame himself for what happened to me? He was asleep. There's no way he could've known. I don't doubt that the siren placed some sort of spell on him as well, something that put him into a blissful, serene slumber. He has absolutely nothing to feel guilty for, though trying to tell him that is like talking to a brick wall. A brick wall who is never in a room with me for more than a second.

He always finds a convenient excuse to leave whenever I enter. Go to eat in the cafeteria? Rion suddenly remembers he has to train in the makeshift gym. Go to the throne room? Rion declares he has somewhere he has to be…and then proceeds to hide in the rafters, watching me. I know, because I can see through his eyes.

Something he seems to forget.

I want to confront him—confront *both* of them—but I'm forced to play by their rules…even if their rules are extremely stupid and maddening. I'm sorely tempted to dive inside of their heads and read their thoughts, but I'll never disrespect their privacy like that…even if it is killing me every day.

"Goddess," Bron places a gentle hand on my shoulder, pulling me out of my thoughts, "are you ready?"

When Bronson asked me on a date the second I started feeling better, I was overjoyed. I missed my shadow wolf shifter with a fierceness that took my breath away. I feel this way about all of my guys, all of my mates I haven't been able to see and talk to in a while.

Braelyn and Jenny helped me dress in a white gown Damien somehow procured. It hugs both of my biceps, stopping at my elbows, and conforms to my breasts before cinching at the waist. The skirt cascades outwards with a delicate lace frill, ending just above my knees. Through Braelyn's eyes, I watched as she brushed my silky black hair until the color almost seemed to glow. Even now, envisioning myself in my mind, I feel an odd thrill.

I don't look anything like myself.

For a brief moment, I imagine what life would've been like if I was never a prisoner in the Compound. If I never lost my eyesight. If I never went to prison for a crime I initially didn't commit.

But then I think about the guys, my loves and mates, and I sweep those thoughts away in a tidal wave of annoyance. My past may be horrible, it may be filled with dark shadows and monsters that hide under the bed, but as Damien said, it made me who I am today. I wouldn't be where I am without every horrible thing I endured. Going to prison was the best day of my life, mainly because it brought me to the men who own me—heart, body, and soul. Everything I am belongs to them, and I can't help but think that fate gave me to them for a reason.

It takes a special kind of woman to love every inch of their tattered, beautiful souls. I'll cherish and love them until the day I die, whether that be minutes from now or centuries.

"You look beautiful," Bronson whispers, his lips tracing the shell of my ear. Goosebumps immediately erupt on my skin at his close proximity. I love the way his slightly whiskered face feels against my skin.

I slide into his head, using his eyes, as he gently places my hand on the crook of his elbow. From this angle, I can vaguely see that he's wearing a black shirt, though the rest of his outfit is just out of view.

We move from the cell, down the hall, and to the cafeteria that is empty at this time of day. At first, I think he's going to treat me to another fancy dinner, but instead, he moves past the tables and to a kitchen carved into the wall. The room consists of nothing but a stainless steel table, an oven, a microwave, and a fridge covered in spots of reddish rust.

Though most of the food arrives by magic, there is an area that the inmates transformed into a kitchen. Somehow, Damien was able to barter for most of the items in the kitchen, though I have no idea what he gave up.

Bronson leads me to the center island, where there's an assortment of mixing bowls and bags.

"What is all this?" I ask, running my hand over the smooth surface. It's cold beneath my fingers, though the room itself is tepid, turning hotter by the second due to the oven currently pre-heating.

"I thought..." Bronson forks his fingers through his hair, and I imagine he's aiming a sheepish smile my way. "Now that you're feeling better," he swallows heavily, "I thought you might want to bake with me."

"Bake?" I quirk an eyebrow

He almost sounds embarrassed when he speaks next. "Yeah. Bake. My mom...she used to teach me and my sisters. She worked at the local bakery for our pack and made everything from pies to cakes to cream puffs." His tone turns wistful, and I can tell almost immediately that he holds the woman in high regards. A pang of sadness infiltrates my system. I'll never be able to meet his family. Not while I'm stuck here, hundreds of feet underground with my life locked away.

"I never baked anything before," I confess, though I know there's no reason for me to feel upset by that. Is that what I'm feeling? Upset? Guilty? Angry? So much of my life has been spent in a tiny six-by-six cage with only just enough room for me to stand and lay down. And when I wasn't in my cell, I was on a cold slab of cement, prepared to be tortured and experimented on.

"I'll teach you." He gently wraps an arm around me and

pulls me against his chest, resting his chin on my head. We sway rhythmically from side to side, and I allow the sense of security, comfort, and love to seep through my skin, warming me from the outside in.

When Bronson moves away, I reach for the edge of the steel counter and grip it until my knuckles turn white. Through Bronson's eyes, I watch as he moves throughout the kitchen with an ease that suggests he spends a lot of his time here. At least, more than I would've expected. He grabs ingredients from a cupboard, a few more mixing bowls, and a glass pan. But at the very corner of the pan…

"Is that blood?" I ask, unsure if I should be horrified or amused.

"Maybe I'll use a different pan…" Bronson trails off.

After a moment, the ingredients are laid out in front of us and Bronson is pushing a carton of eggs in my direction.

"Have you ever cracked an egg before?"

Surprisingly enough, I don't do that badly cracking the first egg. I only get a few eggshells in—which Bronson diligently picks out—so I call that a win. But the second egg…

I release a startled yelp as the yolky egg slips from my fingers, tiny white shell pieces scattering throughout the mixture of flour and sugar.

"Oh crap."

"Here." Bronson gently steps up behind me, his arms curving around my small body, and begins to grab the egg shell pieces. I bite my lip at the heat his body emits and instinctively shove my butt backwards, against his rapidly hardening cock. He releases a breath of air, his muscles going rigid, before he forces them to relax. "Careful, Goddess," he murmurs.

"Careful?" I feign innocence, but I know Bronson can see right through me when he chuckles, the sound low, dark, and more delicious than the chocolate chips we're planning on putting in our brownie batter.

"Behave," he growls with a playful smack to my butt. I yelp but can't contain the ridiculous smile that erupts on my face.

We work in comfortable silence for a few minutes before I dare to ask the question nagging at me.

"What do you think is going on with Damien?" I question, attempting to sound nonchalant. I can't help but think about Damien the last time I saw him, through Kai's eyes. His striking features haggard, the waves of his pitch-black hair falling riotously around his face, almost as if the most meticulous man in the prison hadn't bothered to brush it. And then the glint dancing in his blue eyes, the unfathomable depths capable of rivaling the ocean they stole their color from.

His rejection and avoidance of me is beginning to hurt. A lot. More than I'll ever admit.

But Bronson has always been able to see me too clearly. My hurt and pain…it's all laid bare before him.

"I don't know," he growls out, his tone sharper than it was mere seconds before, reminding me of a frosted over sword. Apparently, just discussing someone hurting me is enough to send his wolf closer to the surface. "But I swear to you I'll find out."

"No," I respond automatically, heaving out a sigh. I begin to stir the mixture once more as Bronson adds a cup of cocoa powder. I tried a spoonful earlier, believing it would taste like normal chocolate, which Abel got me addicted to, but it was disgusting! Bronson simply laughed at me, explaining that this is cocoa without any sugar. Why would anyone eat this stuff? "No, Damien will tell me when he's ready," I continue.

But the question is…

When will that time be?

And what does it have to do with me?

"You know," I continue as Bronson grabs a clean baking pan, "there's still so much I don't know about who I am."

"What do you mean?" Bronson grabs the bowl from me and flips it over so the batter falls into the blood-free baking pan, using a spoon to capture every last drop of chocolatey goodness. He smooths it evenly over the bottom of the pan.

"I mean, what I am." I tap my fingers against the counter as I watch him work. Well, watching through his eyes as he works. "We know that I'm part angel and human, but the Compound placed demon DNA inside of me," I continue. "But from what we gathered, none of those species are capable of having fated mates. So why am I different? Why do I have mates? Is it mainly because of you guys? I mean, is the bond one-sided? Am I not technically mates with the twins and Damien?" My heart thumps loudly in my chest at the thought. As if somehow, my claim on them isn't as valid as my claim on the others. As if any second, they could leave me and not think anything of it. I think a part of me would die if that ever came to pass.

"Does any of that matter?" Bronson asks, and there's nothing malicious in his voice. Just curiosity and worry. Probably for my mental stability. "You're Nina Doe. *What* you are doesn't negate *who* you are. And who you are is the sweetest, strongest woman I've ever met." He pauses. "Don't tell my mom that."

"I want to meet her," I say wistfully. "And your sisters."

"They'll love you," Bronson assures me, a smile in his voice. "Maybe I can schedule a visitation. Would you like that? Would you like to meet them?"

"Could I?" I spin to face him fully, hope and anxiety warring within me. On one hand, I would love nothing more than to meet the family Bronson speaks so fondly about. And on the other...

What if they hate me? What if they don't want their son sharing his mate with other men? What if I'm too weird or naïve or—

"Hey." Bronson places his large hands on my shoulders and gives them a quick squeeze. "Quit overthinking everything, my goddess. I can promise you already that they'll love you. And when have I ever lied to you?"

My lips part on a breathy exhale as I tilt my face to his. All I want is for his lips to meet mine...

Bronson goes rigid, his muscles turning taut, and throws me to the side, forcing me to instinctively leave his head. Agony reverberates up my side, though that does nothing to dampen the confusion and horror I feel. Why did Bronson just push me like a sack of discarded meat?

A deafening growl echoes in the kitchen, followed immediately by a gun being fired. The growl turns into a whine of pain, and I know in my heart who that whine belongs to.

Bronson.

CHAPTER 25

KAI

We gather in a small room that once served as the guards' break room. The sparse area is lightly furnished with a single table that can fit up to twelve and a collection of mismatched chairs—plastic, a few wooden ones, and even an armchair covered in a variety of holes, the fabric weathered away by age.

I sit directly at the head of the table with the twins to my right and Damien to my left. Next to the mage sits Rion, his gaze downcast as he stares intently at the table. Bronson has decided to take Nina on a date...though that's more so she won't bear witness to these proceedings if things take a bloody turn.

Across from both of us rests Logan, a decidedly nonchalant expression on his pretty boy face. His arms are crossed over his chest as he reclines back in his seat, his legs kicked out. Normally, I would've cut him a new one for showing me such disrespect, but that's not the point of this meeting. For today only, we're on the same team. How could we not be when he saved Nina's life?

"You wanted to see me, my lord and grace?" Logan quirks

a light blond eyebrow, his lips twitching with a smile. I try to remind myself to remain calm, to not attack, but it's so fucking hard when he's sitting across from me, looking for all intents and purposes like an angelic sculpture warped into a sadistic demon. Asshole.

"As you know, we were able to hear from Nina herself what transpired a few days prior," I begin formally, and I can't help but note that Rion goes rigid on the other side of Damien. His hands curl into fists where they rest on the table.

I haven't talked to Rion since the incident, and not for lack of trying. He's been avoiding everyone, including his second-in-command, Braelyn. A part of me wants to blame him for allowing Nina to be injured, but the more logical part of me understands that it wasn't his fault. He was nothing more than a pawn in the siren's malicious game. There would've been no way he could've resisted the siren's song, even if he had been conscious. I may be a lover and a mate, but I'm also a leader. And a leader knows when the blame has been misplaced.

"So does this mean I'm free to go?" Logan maintains that cocky smirk as he holds up both of his hands, which have been tied together with barbed wire in place of handcuffs. Damien glares at the other man silently, tilting his head to the side so a lock of black hair falls into his eyes. Why does he look so…disheveled? He's another member of my inner circle I need to speak to. Soon. What secret is that analytical mind of his hiding?

"It depends." Damien slides a dagger out from his jacket's sleeve and rests it calmly on the table in front of him. The damn thing is already coated in a fine layer of blood, the blade glinting menacingly in the hanging bulb of the room. Fucking psychopath. I have no doubt that before Damien entered this room for the meeting, he stabbed some poor soul just to get his blade wet. He sort of treats it like a cock in that respect—it must be dipped into a wet hole every few days in order to keep him sated.

"Depends on what?" Logan tries for another broad grin, but it wavers as his blue eyes lower to the bloody dagger. He gulps before quickly smoothing over his expression.

"Depends on what you are."

Silence descends as all five of us stare at Logan with varying expressions of distrust and suspicion. Abel seems more curious than anything, an easygoing grin plastered on his face. Cain appears murderous, though that could be his standard expression. Some people have resting bitch face, while others, like Cain, have resting "I want to murder you in your sleep" faces. Rion is still staring at his hands on the table, his face shadowed, while Damien regards Logan with cool indifference. That's a lie, though. I know my assassin well enough to detect the barely veiled chaos lurking just beneath the surface, waiting for a chance to be set free.

"What am I?" Logan tilts his head to the side, though his apathetic front does very little to hide his growing panic. "I'm just a man. A man without a plan. A man who wishes to stand—"

"Is this a joke to you?" Cain cuts in, his tone dangerous. Tiny fissures of lava erupt on his skin as his demon comes out to play. Only Abel's hand on his shoulder prohibits him from launching across the table and wrapping his hands around Logan's throat.

Logan's tongue darts out to wet his lips. His discomfort shouldn't amuse me as much as it does, but I can't deny that I receive immense pleasure from watching him squirm. I half wonder if I should just kill him now and rid us of his presence once and for all. But alas, I have a woman to think about now, and she doesn't take very fondly to murder, especially the premediated kind. Shame.

I sigh heavily as my eyes lower to the ring on my finger. I can feel my lips begin to quirk into the beginnings of a smile, though I quickly blank my face.

Soon, my beloved. Soon, you'll be my wife.

The thought makes me fucking giddy, like cannons of confetti and glitter are being detonated in my stomach. It's sickening and horrifying, and I fucking love it.

Logan seems to be hesitating, his eyes flickering from face to face, before Abel says, "You know we'll be able to tell if you're lying." He leans across the table to boop the other man's nose. "We're very, very good at what we do." And then, just because he's an asshole, he gives Logan's nose a sharp twist, and the other man releases a pained hiss. "Whoops." Abel reclines back in his chair, still maintaining that bright smile. "My hand slipped."

"Didn't you say that last night when you fingered Nina?" Cain whispers, too low for our unwanted prisoner to hear.

"It was an accident," Abel counters, aghast. He places a hand to his chest in mock horror. "One second, we're in bed. And the next, my fingers are beneath her panties. It could've happened to any of us."

Great.

Now I'm interrogating the prisoner with a boner. He's going to think I'm like Damien, who gets off on pain and torture.

"I'm a..." Logan trails off, forcing me to tune the twins out.

"Yes?"

Logan seems to decide something, and I watch all of the tension drain from his shoulders. He reclines even farther back in his seat, uncrossing his arms so they're draped lazily over the armrests. "I'm a cupid."

We all blink at him, at a loss for words.

"You're a what now? You're stupid?" Abel squints at him.

"Impossible," Damien says with a huff. "Cupids are extinct."

"Actually, they're not." Logan gestures vaguely down his body with a salacious eye waggle. "And I'm proof of that, big boy."

Damien's eye twitches. "I will stab you and eat your innards for breakfast," he deadpans.

Logan shrugs casually. "Figured my mojo wouldn't work on you. It never does." The last statement is said almost bitterly, and instantly, my curiosity is piqued.

"You tried to use your powers on us?" I demand…though I still have no idea what powers he even has. Hell, I don't even know what a cupid *is*. All I can think about are babies in diapers with bows and heart-shaped arrows.

"It didn't work," Logan murmurs, not at all affected by my ire. "The mate bond is too strong between you guys and Nina."

Is that…?

Is that jealousy I detect in his voice?

"Mate bond?" Cain's voice has turned quiet, almost somber, but his eyes are glimmering with something akin to hope. "Wh-What do you mean?"

Logan rolls his eyes, seemingly more comfortable now that we haven't made a move to kill him. "That's part of my cupid power. I can sense mate bonds between species. And the bond between all six of you and Nina? It's stronger than I've ever seen before."

Cain and Abel have gone rigid, their eyes wide and their mouths agape. Damien is also deadly still, only his eyes moving to pierce Logan with an unreadable look.

So it's true, then—Nina is able to have mates of her own. Which means that Cain, Abel, and Damien are also her mates, along with Bronson, Rion, and me. I try to bite down on the smile that wants to escape, but fuck, I'm happy for them. I honestly didn't think I would be, mainly because the thought of sharing Nina made me want to vomit at first, but there's a lightness in my chest that wasn't there prior. They needed to hear this, needed to know that they're just as loved and important to her as we are.

Cain reaches for his brother's hand and clasps it tightly, both of their eyes sparkling with endless emotion.

"So what else can you do?" I ask, clearing my throat to redirect Logan's attention to me. He'd been staring at the twins with an almost curious expression, his head canted to the side to display the tattoos on his neck.

"Well," Logan smirks once more, "I'm also capable of traveling inside of people's heads. Creating illusions. Reading their desires. It's not that different from what your girl can do."

"And why is that?" Damien finally seems to have pulled his head out of wherever it was. Probably up his ass, alongside the twins'.

Logan shrugs with a wry twist to his lips. "Probably because a cupid is a nearly extinct branch of angels, but our powers are considered more demonic in nature. And at the same time, we spend the majority of our lives in the human realm."

His words make sense, but…

Icy fear skates down my spine. "How do you know the truth about Nina?" I demand. All eyes turn to stare at me.

"What?" Logan's brows furrow.

"I hear what you're implying. Don't try to deny it, runt." I sneer at him, my anger rippling across my body. "How do you know the truth about Nina's lineage?"

"Oh, that she's part demon, angel, and human?" Logan questions casually…not at all like he just dropped a bomb the size of Kansas in our laps. We've been so diligent in keeping the truth about Nina a secret. How did he discover it? How the fuck did he— "Calm down, dragon breath." He rolls his blue eyes and straightens in his seat. "I can sense the power in her. It's another gift us cupids have—being able to tell what species a person is. I mean, *hello*. We're the ideal match-maker. Our entire job depends on creating couples that can procreate. We usually need the couple to be the same species for that, but not always."

Once more, Damien has turned rigid, even more rigid than when he discovered the truth about his mate status with Nina. "Procreate? What do you mean?"

"It means that my magic encourages little babies to be born," Logan replies dryly. "Among other things."

"Among other things," Abel mutters with a grunt.

Logan gives him a narrowed-eye look.

"My powers are similar to Nina's," he reiterates, "and as such, I'd be willing to train her myself. For a price, of course."

"What makes you think we'll ever work with you?" I growl out, though I can't deny that the idea holds merit. I want nothing more than for Nina to be able to understand and control her powers. To protect herself. And though Damien is a patient teacher, he doesn't understand every-thing Nina can do. Fuck, none of us do. But if Logan can teach her...

"Because you want the best for your mate," he retorts immediately. "And all I want is protection."

"Protection," Cain repeats, shoving a hand through his blond waves. "In exchange for helping Nina with her powers?"

"Correcto!" Logan throws his hands up into the air like his favorite team just scored a touchdown. "Score one for the sexy demon."

Cain scowls. "Fuck you."

"Ohh. You offering?"

"If we agree to do this," I interrupt, knowing a fight will

break out at any moment, "then you'll be under our protec-tion. The prison will know that any harm that comes to you will be retaliated tenfold. But that also means if you betray us—"

"Then death, pain, and an eternity of torture will befall upon me, blah bah blah." He waves a hand in the air dismissively, but I'm not done. I'm determined to drill this point home so he knows the consequences of his actions.

"And if you hurt Nina—"

"I won't." Some of the carelessness dissipates from his eyes as he levels me with a dark glare. "I'll train her to the best of my ability and protect her, just like I did when the siren attacked. You have my word." The sincerity in his voice is impossible to deny, though another sliver of unease skitters down my spine. I can't quite put my finger on why. "Besides," Logan reclines once more, "I can guarantee you that I'll never actually be alone with the queen. One of you assholes will always be around to supervise."

"Damn right." Abel lifts a hand for a high-five from Cain, but the sex demon simply rolls his eyes. Instead of being discouraged, Abel places his palm against Cain's forehead and whacks him.

"Fucking hell, Abel," Cain gripes, rubbing his head and glaring daggers with his eyes at his twin.

"My hand slipped," Abel replies unrepentantly.

"Your hand can slip with me anytime," Logan responds coyly, and all five of us glare at him.

"And that's another thing." I make a face. "Stop with the fucking flirting, man."

"Can't really help it." Logan shrugs. "I'm a cupid. Flirting and love are all I'm good for. But rest assured," he swivels to meet each of our eyes, "I'm not into any of you."

His tone implies that there *is* someone he's into, and I have a horrible feeling that I know who she is.

Fuck.

I'm gonna have to keep a close eye on the bastard.

"Okay." I squeeze my eyelids shut and take a deep breath. "That's all I wanted to discuss today. You guys can go—" Rion is off his chair and out the door before I can even finish. "—but Logan?" I turn towards the cupid, allowing him to see my distrust. "You're on thin fucking ice. If I catch even a whiff of deceit—"

"You'll tie me up like a bad boy," Logan finishes, winking. "I get it. But trust me, the last thing I'll ever want is to hurt Nina. She's the only one here who has been remotely kind to me." His expression turns wistful, almost dreamy, and I stalk forward before I can stop myself.

"And that's another thing." I lower my voice to a hushed murmur. "She's not yours. She'll never be yours. Get that out of your head, runt."

The dopey expression vanishes as quickly as it appears, replaced by something cold and cruel.

"Trust me." His eyes narrow into unforgiving slits. "I hear the message loud and clear."

Without another word, he turns on his heel and storms out of the room, leaving me alone with the twins and Damien. Before the latter can leave, I lift a hand in the air.

"Damien? A second?"

The twins exchange a loaded glance but hurry out of the room. Damien, with heavy reluctance, stalks forward, his expression drier than the desert. He begins to flip his blade between his fingers as his icy blue eyes fix on me.

"Yes?"

"You've been acting weird." There's no point beating around the fucking bush. "I noticed it. The others noticed it. Nina sure as fuck noticed it." He blanches, a reaction that would've been imperceptible if I didn't know the sadistic fucker as well as I do.

"I'm handling it," he responds curtly, turning to walk away. My words stop him cold.

"If you're having second thoughts about her—"

My back is against the wall with a blade at my throat before I can catch my breath. For the first time in forever, Damien's gaze isn't hewn from ice. It's pure fire, sparking with all of the madness he contains inside of himself.

"Never say that again," he says in a low, deadly voice. "Never question my love for my mate."

"Dam," I growl sharply, reminding him that I'm the alpha of this pack. I'm the leader.

Though if there's anyone who wouldn't give a damn, it would be Damien.

"I told you," Damien continues, "I'm handling it." He shoves me away from him, his breathing erratic and his shoulders heaving. "Now get the fuck out of my sight before I gut you."

I bare my teeth at the challenge in his voice, my dragon demanding that I put him in his place. But I know that fighting Damien is the last thing any of us need. He's not naturally disrespectful to my authority. Whatever is weighing on him must be beginning to take its toll. For now, I need to give him space, allow him to gather his own thoughts.

And then I'll kick his ass.

I watch the mage storm out of the room, his power crackling around him, and wonder once more what could've happened to have brought this meticulous, apathetic man to ruin.

CHAPTER 26

NINA

Red engulfs my normally pitch-black vision, the color so deep and vibrant, I'm barely aware of anything else.

All I can hear is Bronson's pained whimper, followed by the roar of our unknown assailant.

No. Not Bron. Not him. Please, not him. I can't live without him.

That thought plays on repeat in my head as I stagger to my feet, my stomach roiling and my hands shaking slightly as a heady combination of fear and white-hot, toe-curling anger rumbles through me.

"Bronson?" My voice is a breathy whisper, but when I receive no response, not even a rumbly growl from my over-protective wolf shifter, I...explode. There's no other word I can think of to use for it. Tendrils of darkness creep at the edges of my vision, coiling around the garnet color like slithering snakes, hissing and biting. I can feel something happening to me, but I don't stop the change. I physically *can't.*

All I know for certain is that Bronson is injured and that someone is trying to kill him.

And that makes my inner beast *furious.*

Murderous.

Deadly.

I slip easily into the intruder's head to see that he's staring down at Bronson. And my poor, sweet, protective wolf shifter…

There's a gaping wound in his chest where the bullet hit him. His blond, tousled hair is matted with sweat, and his gorgeous eyes are currently closed, his lashes like shadows against his cheeks. The only relief I feel is the knowledge that he's still alive, that his chest continues to rise and fall steadily, even though blood pours from his wound at a rapid pace.

And then the assailant's eyes flicker to me, and he actually staggers back a step.

Dark horns poke through my mane of obsidian-colored hair, curling at the ends like a ram. My eyes are red. And not a pinkish-red either, but the color of blood. Something cold and deadly and macabre. Luminescent white wings erupt from my back, fluttering in a breeze I don't feel. Each feather seems to shine with its own inner light, appearing almost pinkish and pearlescent in the sparse lighting.

For the first time ever, I give in to my wrath. My anger. My pain.

No one hurts my men.

No one.

The assassin—I have no idea if it's a man or a woman—takes another step backwards as I descend on them like an avenging angel. No, maybe angel is the wrong word, despite the nickname Damien gave me. There's nothing angelic about the scowl on my face and the fire burning hotly in my eyes. I'm death and vengeance, all wrapped up into one. But no amount of pretty packaging and immaculately placed bows can hide the truth from both of us—I'm dangerous. And maybe, just maybe, I'm evil too.

I don't allow myself to fixate too long on that epiphany as I continue to stalk forward, my wings rising behind me until it blocks out all light.

"Please," the voice—masculine—begs, his vision distorting with his full-body shakes. I want to laugh haughtily, though a distant part of me recognizes that it's not truly me who wants to do that. It's my power, exacerbated by my rage and incandescent fury. By my need for vengeance against this man who hurt someone I love.

"There will be no mercy." I don't recognize my voice. Surely I don't sound like that. Right? Goosebumps ripple even across *my* skin.

But I don't give myself a second to ponder that as my arm shoots out, capturing the man by the throat. My face fills his entire vision, and I can't help but note, with a mixture of both morbid fascination and growing horror, that cracks of lava have opened up on my skin, leading to my hand still wrapped around his throat. It's what happens to the twins when they "demon-out," as Abel likes to joke.

It has never happened to me before.

"You will pay!" I scream in his face, the red of my eyes devouring the irises and pupils completely before expanding outwards. I want to be scared of myself, horrified even, but a dark, sadistic smirk tilts up my lips instead. It's weird on my face. Unnatural, as if that smile belongs to someone else entirely.

As he begins to sob, I shove my fist through his chest, just as I did with Alyssa, and grab his heart in my hand, relishing the amount of power I hold. One squeeze...

That's all it would take.

One. Squeeze.

"You shouldn't have touched my mate," I whisper, and then I pull his heart from his chest cavity and crush it in my hand.

~

I MUST'VE PASSED OUT.

I don't remember it happening, but when consciousness returns to me, I know innately that I'm being watched. Again. The darkness is not the one I have grown accustomed to.

This one hides beasts and monsters, shadows and silhouettes.

"Nick?" I spin slowly, attempting to orient myself to my new surroundings as my mind struggles to remember what just occurred. I was with Bronson in the kitchen, baking. And then...

And then the assassin.

What did I do?

I place a hand to my forehead as my brain screams at me, taunts me. I know in the deepest recesses of my soul that something horrible happened. I *did* something horrible, something that even now, with no memory of it, turns my stomach.

Is Bronson hurt?

Oh, God. Please no.

Why can't I remember?

Panic thrums through me, electrifying my already frayed nerves, and the pounding in my head intensifies.

"Nick!" This time, my voice is more of a scream than a plea. I will quite literally kill him if he had a hand in what happened.

The morbid direction of my thoughts momentarily startles me, but not enough for me to regret them.

I will do anything to keep my mates safe, even if that means killing other people.

When did my life come to this?

Nick's honeyed voice answers me immediately, "You are safe."

"Where am I? What happened?" I fire off the questions in rapid succession, turning in the general direction I thought I heard his voice. It's so hard to know for sure—it seems to bounce off of every wall. Off the floor I don't feel under my feet. Off the ceiling I can't see or touch.

Everywhere.

And…

Nowhere.

"You are safe," Nick repeats, and I feel something touch my cheek, soft and warm. When I spin towards him, my heart in my throat, the pressure disappears as quickly as it arrived, leaving me feeling oddly bereft. "You used your powers. You are strong, little one. Stronger than I initially suspected." His voice turns contemplative, and I imagine he's eyeing me like I'm some sort of exotic specimen beneath a magnifying glass. Something for him to watch and observe. Study. Poke and prod at.

When I take a step away, he releases a heavy sigh. "I am not going to hurt you."

"Am I in your…home?" I question, testing the word out softly. *Home.* Where is his home again?

Everywhere and nowhere.

That doesn't make any sense, but then again, none of this does. I half wonder if this is nothing more than a demented dream that I'm having, a way to compartmentalize everything I've been through. Maybe I hit my head? Again?

Why do I remember every interaction perfectly when I'm asleep but never when I wake up? What does he do to me?

"You are in my home," he confesses, and then his voice turns despondent. "But I have a feeling you will not be for long."

"What does that mean?" I ask, agitated and confused. "How do I keep…coming here? *Why* do I keep coming here?"

And why am I struggling to articulate the questions I so desperately need to ask?

"I bring you here," he admits from directly behind me. Hot breath ruffles the hairs around my ear, and I shiver involuntarily, trying to squash my immediate and instinctive reaction. "You have always been here. Sometimes, I get… lonely. But then I hear you and see you, and I am no longer alone. When you arrived, I sensed you immediately, and you woke me from my slumber. I have been too weak to visit you until recently. I am sorry I have not been able to protect you the way I should have."

"That doesn't make any sense." I can feel my nose begin to scrunch together. It sounds as if…as if Nick's been watching me for a long time. As if he's been waiting for an opportunity to meet me himself. But who is he? Have I seen him before? I nearly snort at my unintentional pun, but it's the truth. I feel like I would've noticed a stalker. Or at the very least, my men would've. And what does he mean about waking up when I arrived? Does he mean when I arrived in the prison?

Thousands of questions settle uncomfortably on my tongue, tasting of poison, but I can't figure out how to ask any of them. I need to tell Kai about this encounter. That is, if I remember it when I wake up.

"Everything will make sense in time," Nick cajoles, answering the question I forgot I asked. Another sigh escapes him, this one heavy with emotions I can't even begin to untangle. "But for now, you need to wake up, little one. Your other mate is worried."

"Wake up."

"Wake up."

"WAKE UP!"

CHAPTER 27

RION

If anyone were to see me now, they would think I was *sulking*. But Rion No Middle Name Doe—I'm already prepared for our wedding—doesn't *sulk*. He just broods in relative peace and contemplates stabbing anyone who stares at him for longer than a second. And Rion has a lot of sharp, pointy, orgasmic knives. He cuddles with them at night and asks them to run away with him.

And…

And apparently, he also talks in third person. Dammit. I mean, I talk in third person. At least it's better than if I chose to talk in second person. Can you imagine how annoying that would be?

You step through the halls. You stab a ho. You smile manically. Surprise…you're a deranged serial killer.

But back to the matter at hand.

I. Don't. Brood.

But fuck, all I can see when I close my eyes is Nina's pasty face mottled with hideous bruises and thick, never-ending blood. I still get sick to my fucking stomach at the thought. And then I murder any poor sap who gives me a funny face. What constitutes as a funny face? Any face that isn't Nina's.

Or Bitch Mage's.

Because we have a bond.

It's inseparable.

Dion for the win.

My good mood instantly evaporates as my thoughts drift back to Nina, as they always do. I know I'm being cold and aloof towards her, but I can't help it. What good am I to my mate if I can't protect her? Fuck, she was my responsibility that night, and I slept through an attack that could've taken her life. If Logan hadn't gotten there when he did…

Self-loathing percolates in my gut, rushing up my throat and tasting vaguely of acid, but I try not to drown in that emotion. I don't deserve to.

What I deserve is Nina to slap me in the face and tell me that I'm not man enough to be her mate. That I don't deserve her. Then, I'll turn into a cute little kitty and lick my paws while Celine Dion's "My Heart Will Go On" blares in the background. Of course, I won't leave Nina—it's literally impossible and the mere thought makes me ill. But I won't bother her. I'll remain in the shadows, always stalking, always aware, always protecting. What happened before will never happen again. I'll make damn sure of it, even if it costs me my life.

But alas, I'm weak, and I can't go another minute without seeing with my own two eyes that Nina's alive and well. It's like an itch that I know I shouldn't scratch but I can't seem to stop myself. I still having fucking nightmares of that night, and I wouldn't blame Nina if she never forgives me for letting her down when she needed me.

Hell, I don't think I'll ever forgive myself.

The meeting with Logan has left me shaken in more ways than one. I don't know if I want to kill the smug fucker or get down on my knees and kiss his shoes. He saved Nina, my mate, when I couldn't, and that's a metaphorical kick to my dick.

I know Nina is in the kitchen with Bronson on a date, so it's there I head, skirting past a group of inmates heading in the opposite direction. I give them a narrowed-eyed, frosty glare, one Damien would be proud of.

Are they giving me funny looks? Do I need to kill them? Nah. I'm pretty sure that fucker is just constipated. Or he just had some serious anal, because his butt looks mighty tense.

Humming beneath my breath—a sad, despondent song because I'm still depressed as fuck—I head past the row of tables in the cafeteria and towards the little nook in the wall that serves as our kitchen. At least when the magic of the Labyrinth doesn't automatically replenish our food supply.

I expect to hear Nina's sweet giggles or Bronson's grumbly voice, but only silence greets me.

Instantly, I'm on alert, my spine prickling with unease.

Did they leave?

I wouldn't be surprised if Bronson took Nina back to his cell for a little…one on one time. You know, the apple dumpling surprise. The sausage highway. The puffin in the muffin. The polka-dot daydream.

You know—S. E. X.

As I hone in my senses, I become aware of two heartbeats. Soft. Subdued.

The shift takes over me before I can stop it, and where once a man stood now stands a beast. My tiger shakes out his furry head before stalking forward on silent paws, his mouth opened and his teeth bared.

Shit. I'm doing it again. Talking in third person.

Because fuck everyone. I *am* the tiger.

I prowl forward, using my head to open up the swinging door, and then I freeze, my fur bristling.

Directly in front of me is a runt of a man, his eyes wide and vacant and a bloody heart resting haphazardly on his chest. Not just any bloody heart. *His* bloody heart. In his hand is a gun—a gun that I recognize as belonging to a guard. How the fuck did he smuggle that in here? No doubt, he paid good money for it. I'll have to find the guard involved and kill him. Painfully.

I twist my large head to see my beautiful, perfect mate resting unconscious a few feet away, the pool of blood around the guy having not quite reached her yet.

Panic thrums through me, just as prevalent as it was when she was attacked by the fucking siren, and I shift back to my real boy form, dropping to my knees at her side. I brush a shaky hand over her face, capturing a strand of her obsidian hair before resting my fingers on her pulse. Steady. She's alive.

My eyes flicker from her serene face to the man missing a heart, and diminutive pieces begin to click together. I have no doubt that Nina raged out and killed him—something that will destroy her when she awakes. And I also know that she overworked herself and her powers. Using your powers is like using your muscles. You need to train them and build up an endurance.

"You'll be fine, Buttercup," I assure her sleepy form, planting my lips against her clammy forehead. She stirs in her sleep, almost as if she's subconsciously reaching for me, but doesn't wake. But that's okay. She doesn't need to wake up yet. I'll watch over her until she does.

Though…

Though what caused her to rage out the way she did?

She didn't do it when the siren attacked her, though I have no doubt she's strong enough to have resisted his allure and killed him.

She only embraces her inner darkness, her beast, when one of us is in trouble.

My head snaps to the side, just as a pained groan echoes through the air. Bronson lies slightly behind one of the tall, metal tables, blood sticking his shirt to his chest.

Fuck!

I scramble towards him, ignoring the way my dick accidentally touches his hand—I totally shredded my clothes when I shifted the first time—and hover over the poor fucker.

"You better not die, Wolfie," I say as I begin to fondle his bullet wound like some sort of sick pervert. I need to get the bullet out if he's going to be able to heal himself. "I'm too fucking lazy to dig you a grave. Though…I don't really know where we would put a grave for you. There's not really a lot of dirt in the prison. Oh! Maybe I'll shove you in a plant and staple flowers to your decaying corpse so you can be a pretty tree. Would you like that, Wolfie? Would you like to be a pretty tree?" As I talk, my searching fingers finally clasp the bullet. Bronson releases another anguished whine, but I don't hesitate pulling it out and tossing it to the side.

There.

Hopefully, his wolf healing will kick in and close the damn wound.

Or else he's a goddamn human tree. I refuse to take no for an answer.

Not that he could say no. He'd be fucking dead.

"Is he going to be okay?" a soft, breathy voice inquires from behind me. I turn to see Nina sitting up, her white eyes wide in her unnaturally pale face. She's always been ashen—a product of years with little to no sunlight—but I've never seen her like this before. She looks…sickly. My girl doesn't have enough meat on her bones.

"He'll be fine." I try to make my voice cheery and lighthearted, but it probably comes across like I'm taking a major shit and then quickly spraying Febreze so no one will smell it.

Not that that has happened to me before.

"Rion." Her lower lip trembles as she turns her blind gaze in the general direction of the dead body. "I killed that man, didn't I?"

Anger momentarily darkens my vision. I may be a dumb man, but I'm not a *dumb* man. I'm able to understand exactly what happened. This fucker, whoever he was, tried to kill Nina and Bronson. Bronson, of course, put himself in front of Nina and caught a bullet to his chest for the action. Nina freaked and attacked the fucker, ripping out his heart.

I'm so fucking proud of my girl, I could kiss her.

"You did what you had to do," I state firmly, hoping that she hears the sincerity in my voice. I don't ever want her to apologize for taking care of herself and our family. Ever. It's a dog-eat-dog world out there, and my lover will be on the fucking top of the food chain if I have my say in things. If it's between her life and anyone else's, she should always choose hers.

Always.

"I thought you were mad at me," she finally chokes out, and the sheer emotion in her voice makes me feel like a piece of shit. Broken. It makes me feel fucking broken, like she stuck her hand in my own chest and pulled out my heart, instead of the heart of the assassin. "And then this assassin attacked me and Bron. And Bron got hurt. And I used my powers. And then I had a strange dream, and I think this one guy—"

"Hey." I crawl towards her on my hands and knees until I'm able to pull her in my lap. I try to ignore the way her ass feels against my cock, because now is not the fucking time to get a boner. "I was never, *ever* mad at you, Buttercup. Don't even think that."

"Then why have you been ignoring me?" She twists until her face is pressed against my neck, her tears burning my skin. I think the events of the last few days have finally begun to catch up with her. First, her attack. Then, my own shitty behavior. And finally, Bronson getting shot. I can feel how badly she's itching to crawl towards him, but I refuse to let her go. Not yet. Not until she understands.

"I've been feeling…guilty," I confess at last, swallowing heavily. I rub my hand up and down her back, attempting to soothe her. "Because of what happened. I felt…" I struggle to articulate my thoughts, but fuck. For the first time ever, I'm at a loss for words. "I felt as if I didn't deserve to be your mate."

She reels away from me as if I struck her. Confusion splays across her pretty, angelic face as her white eyes widen.

"W-what? W-why?" She sniffles. "Did I make you feel that way?"

"No!" I rush to assure her, bundling her in my arms once more and holding her against my chest. She's still tense, her muscles taut, but she finally rests her head back on my shoulder. "It was my own fucking fault. I'm not used to feeling so many feelings, and you, my dear buttercup, make me feel them all. I was scared that I almost lost you. Angry that I didn't protect you. And honestly? I was jealous that Logan was there to save you when I wasn't. I'm so sorry—"

"Don't apologize." Her voice is harsher than I ever remember hearing it. Certainly harsher than she's ever talked to me before. I freeze automatically, and I'm pretty sure I gape at her like a fish out of water, flopping uselessly on land. "You have nothing to apologize for. Do you hear me, Rion? Nothing. At all. What happened was in no way your fault. I love you, you stupid…you stupid butthole!" She jabs a finger in my chest, and I don't bother to contain my smile at her insult. Fuck, I love her. Especially when she's feisty.

She crawls out of my lap, and for a heart-stopping moment, I think she's leaving me. I quite literally panic and make a pathetic, desperate mewling noise that totally ruins all of the street cred I've managed to gain.

But she only crawls over to Bronson, as if it pains her to be apart from her injured mate for too long, and checks his pulse. The tension physically leaves her shoulders when she confirms that he's alive and well, before she positions him so his head is in her lap and she's stroking his blond hair.

Fucking hell. I almost want to get shot just to have her do that to me.

Is that fucked up?

Don't answer that. Unless you're going to say, "No, that's not fucked up. That's completely normal. Go shoot yourself in the chest, Rion, and ride that pony."

I crawl towards both Nina and Bronson and claim her hand that isn't stroking Bronson's hair.

"Don't shut me out," Nina says softly, tiredly, her eyes looking as if they've aged fifty years in a span of minutes. I hate that I caused that reaction. Fucking loathe it. "I love you. I can't bear to think…" She trails off with a choked sob, and I press a tender kiss to her shoulder, where her strap has slid down.

"Never again."

If my buttercup wants me by her side, then I'll get super-glue myself.

Nothing and no one will tear us apart.

CHAPTER 28

NICK

I wait with bated breath for her to sleep.

Watching. Always watching.

Protecting.

Loving.

And when she finally gives into unconsciousness, when her face turns serene and peaceful in slumber, I push my will into her mind as I have done countless times before. If I had a tangible body, I imagine my heart would be beating erratically, owned by this girl who has yet to see me in the flesh.

But alas, I have a heart constructed of nothing but shadows and memories, and though it beats in this strange darkness I have found myself in, it is not real.

Though it certainly feels real when I am around Nina.

Like before, I move forward through the darkness as her soft voice reaches my ears. At first, I cannot understand the words she is saying, but as I get closer, my name leaves her lips on a breathless exhale.

Nick.

That is not actually my name, though I suppose that does not matter. Nick is who I am now.

"Nina," I whisper as I approach her. I cannot see her in this inky, cloying darkness, but I can sense her as keenly as if she were an extension of my body.

Some might see the darkness as an absence of light, an absence of everything good and pure in the world, but I see it as *everything*. After all, before the world was made, the universe was shrouded in nothing but darkness. How can it *not* be everything? It is the one place suspended between life and death, the one place where time stops. It is where light cannot penetrate, but when has light been the deciding factor on the validity of something?

The darkness is not nothing.

It is the footsteps rapidly approaching you, the warm embrace from a lover and friend, the tears stuck on your eyelashes but refusing to fall.

It is not nothing.

My heart races even faster when I move to Nina, envisioning the way she looked the last time I saw her—sleeping between Rion and Bronson. Her long, silky hair cascading across her pillow and somehow making her features look even more stunning and softer. Those long, ebony lashes fluttering against her cheekbones. The delicate swoop of her neck as she twisted into her shifter lover's embrace, pressing a kiss to the shell of his ear, before turning towards the shadow wolf and falling back to sleep.

"Nick," she repeats, and I imagine her cute little nose is scrunched adorably. "What am I doing here?"

"I wanted to see you," I confess, resisting the urge to brush my fingers across her cheek. Only here, can I touch her. Only here, can I be with her.

For now.

I will spend the rest of my life finding a way to get to her.

But if she discovers what you are...

I allow that thought to trail off as I focus once more on

the stunning female. And she is not just stunning because of her physical appearance, though there is no denying she is the most beautiful woman I have ever set eyes upon in all of my years of existence. It is because of her soul. Her pure and gentle soul that laps at my rough edges like the calming, gentle waves of the ocean. Someone as pure as her...

She should not exist.

"You wanted to see me," she parrots, confusion lacing her tone. "Why?"

"Because you are everything," I state plainly. There are no other words capable of encapsulating my thoughts. I am nothing, but with her, I am someone. She freed me, and I doubt she is even aware she has done so.

"You don't know me," she protests immediately.

I bite down on my lip to stop myself from saying everything I want to. I imagine she would not take kindly to the truth—that I have been watching her long before I made her aware of my existence.

But that is all there is to do in my world. Watch. Listen. Wait.

And I *do* wait. I wait every single day until I can finally gain enough power to reveal myself to her. For now, I have to find solace in these few stolen moments.

If she would like me to get to know her the traditional way, then I will do so.

"What is your favorite sound?" I ask abruptly, cocking my head to the side, though I know she cannot see me.

She releases a strangled noise in the back of her throat. "What?"

"Favorite sound," I repeat. "What is it?"

"I-I..." She pauses, and I hear her suck in a breath. "I guess I never really thought about it before. No one has ever asked me that." She sounds far away and distant, an unfamiliar lilt to her voice as if she is holding back tears. The thought makes me want to tear this world apart, but I settle on distracting her instead.

"There is a pipe in the Labyrinth that has broken apart," I begin, keeping my voice soft and soothing as to not scare her away. "It is deep inside the tunnels, almost a mile or so away from here." I scratch absently at my chin as she takes a step closer. I cannot see her, but I can sense the heat her body emits as if it is palpable. "A tiny trickle of water always cascades from the broken pipe and rushes against some of the rocks there. The noise..." I pause again, thinking through my words. "I imagine it is how a waterfall would sound."

"You've never seen a waterfall?" Nina asks.

"No," I confess, swallowing roughly. "I have never. But I have heard others talk of them before. Have you seen one?"

"No." She takes another step closer, and something explodes across my flesh. I am unused to such a sensation, and I cannot help but stare at my arms in wonder. Are those goosebumps, perhaps? I have never experienced them myself before, though I know others have. "So you *are* an inmate of the prison!" It is not a question, though I choose to take it as one.

An inmate...

Maybe.

A prisoner?

Most definitely.

"I will answer you if you answer me," I say at last. I want her to know everything there is to know about me. I want to bare my soul to her, all of the black and twisted edges of it, and know that she will accept and love me unconditionally, as I will her. Is it too much for me to hope for?

"Answer you...?" she begins in confusion before she seems to remember what I had asked of her. "I suppose my favorite sound is—" Cutting herself off abruptly, she steps away from me, mumbling something under her breath too low for me to hear.

"What was that?" I cock my head to the side curiously as she continues to back farther and farther away.

"My favorite sound… It isn't appropriate." The last word is spoken as a whisper, and I feel my smile broaden. Is she embarrassed? Flustered? I try to think through all of the adjectives that could describe her suddenly chagrin attitude.

Anxious? Distressed? Upset?

"Are you…embarrassed?" I decide to ask her.

"No!" she protests automatically, though her panicky voice is a direct contrast to her dogmatic statement.

"No?"

"No," she repeats more firmly. "It's just…"

"What is just?"

"Next question!" she blurts out.

"But you have not answered this one."

"Oh my god, Nick!" Her voice is muffled, as if she is covering her face with her hands. "Fine. My favorite sound is mygushorgnaize."

"My gush organized?" I have never heard of that sound before. How peculiar. Perhaps I will need to find away to—

"Myguysorgasming," she repeats, her words jumbled together.

My brows knit. "Huh?"

"My guys coming!" she practically shouts. "Okay? That's my favorite sound."

I pause as I consider her words, my heart pounding unevenly before returning to a steady rhythm.

Her words…

They make no sense to me.

"Your guys coming?" I repeat, and she releases an agonized moan. "Where are they coming from?"

"What?" Her voice is no longer muffled, almost as if she snapped her head up to drill a glare in my general direction.

I try to keep my tone patient. It is apparent she does not understand my question, so I will have to explain myself to her carefully. "They have to come from somewhere, little one. So where do they come from? And where do they go?" They are simple questions, so I do not understand why she sounds like a dying fish.

"That's not what I meant..." She trails off once more, and I make a mental note to discover what other synonyms there are for the word "coming." Nina groans before whispering, "Why am I even telling you all of this?"

"Maybe because a part of you knows that I would never do anything to harm you. That I will never use your words against you." Unable to stop myself, I place my palm on her cheek, relishing the smoothness of her skin, and she lets me. "Maybe a part of you recognizes that your soul belongs to me, just as mine belongs to you."

"But—"

I cut off her mounting protest. "But just because it belongs to me does not mean it cannot belong to others as well." The last thing I want is for her to think I am trying to steal her from her other men. They need her just as much as I do, if not more so.

I become distantly aware of her shifter mate, Rion, peppering kisses along her neck, hoping to wake her up and apologize to her with his body once more. I sigh heavily, knowing that my time with her is coming to an end. The knowledge makes me feel oddly bereft and empty, as if I had something in my hands and then lost it.

"Nick..." She says on a breath, oblivious to the world outside of this bubble. This perfect, diminutive bubble I constructed for her and her alone. A place where the darkness is everything and she does not have to hide.

"Wake up, little one." I press my lips to her forehead, the gesture too chaste and fleeting to be considered a kiss. I can feel my fake heart racing in my chest, and I know that any second now, it will gain arms and legs and crawl out from beneath my rib cage, burrowing itself inside of Nina Doe. "Wake. I will see you soon."

Sooner than you think.

CHAPTER 29

DAMIEN

How is this possible?

How the ever-loving fuck is this possible?

Those thoughts play on repeat in my head as the guard once more checks the magic-dampening handcuffs securing me to the table. Pathetic. As if something as insignificant as metal cuffs could restrain me if I really wanted to escape.

I don't. At least, not without my angel by my side.

But how the fuck could this happen?

I have no doubt that new fuck, Logan, is somehow involved. I'd gut him if I wasn't…

If I wasn't over the moon with fucking happiness. The feeling is foreign to me, invasive almost, and I have the irresistible urge to scratch at my skin where an itch has taken up residence. Of course I fucking can't, considering the fact I'm chained like a common prisoner, but the need is there. Driving me. Pushing me.

Just like the need I have to claim Angel.

My mate.

Just the thought of her conjures up a memory from a few weeks earlier, before the dead pool and hit list. Before I discovered the truth about her.

She's sitting in the porcelain tub in the bathroom, her perky breasts on display, even with the water rippling around her. I used almost every favor I'm owed to procure this bathtub for Nina, and even then, I had to carry the water from the shower to the bath by hand, unbeknownst to my beloved.

Still, it's worth it to see that smile on her face, the one capable of making angels weep and demons renounce hell.

The water sloshes over the basin of the tub as she turns her blind gaze to me. My breath catches at her expression, a heady combination of lust and wanton need. Love. Affection. All of the things she shouldn't be feeling for a man as sick and depraved as me.

"Don't look at me like that, Angel," I say huskily, my eyes scouring every bare inch of her perfect body. When she shifts in the tub, the peaked points of her nipples brush the rim, and I have the irresistible urge to take one after the other in my mouth and suck on them until she screams for me. There's no sound more beautiful than my name leaving her plush lips.

"And why can't I look at you, my beloved?" she asks with a breathless giggle, her cheeks taking on a rosy quality. I'm not sure if it's from the heat of the water or her own arousal. If I touch her right now, would her pussy be slick with need? Would her nipples pebble beneath my hands as she gasps out my name? "You're my fiancé, are you not?" She still says that word with a giddy sort of wonderment, as if she can't truly believe that she's engaged to all of us. Honestly, I can't believe it either.

The knowledge that fate put this tiny slip of a girl in my path to love and cherish me...

To be my wife...

It's almost too much.

"Because..." For a brief, brief moment, I allow all of the self-

loathing I feel to enter my voice, making my words nearly unintelligible with bitterness. "You trust and love me, but I'm the true monster of this prison, Angel. That'll never change."

And someone like me will only tarnish someone as pure and as innocent as you. As perfect as you.

That thought plagues me constantly, along with the feeling that I'll never be good enough. That I'll never deserve her. That I'll break her, just as I break everything I ever touch. It's quite unnerving, having gone from never experiencing any emotion to feeling that strong one daily.

"Tell me this..." She moves closer to me until she's practically leaning over the edge of the tub. Her black hair hangs in wet, enticing streaks down her porcelain skin, obscuring her rosy nipples from view. Her next words stop me short, pulling my gaze away from where I've been ogling her breasts. "Would you hurt me?" I blink at her wordlessly, but she continues. "Would you ever hurt me, Dam?"

I know my eyes flare with a fierce, possessive fire as I shake my head vehemently. "Never." And again, louder, hoping to drill this point home, "Never, Angel. You're the one person in this entire godforsaken world that I'll never hurt."

But I'm breaking that promise to her. Every damn day I keep my secret, every fucking day I keep *her* secret, I'm hurting her. She may not realize it yet, but she will the second I tell her the truth.

Fuck, I'm going to have to tell her and the others, and soon, before they bite my fucking head off. Before I lose the precarious trust she placed in me forever.

But for now, I'll do what I always do—protect my family from anyone who seeks to do them harm. Just thinking about the attack on Nina and Bronson a few days earlier causes my heart to palpitate, and I know I need to dig out and destroy the root of the problem first and foremost.

As if my thoughts summoned him, the door to the visitation room opens, and Narian himself strolls in, cocky as can be. He's gotten older since I've been locked up, though he's always been up there in years. His hair is thinner, a few strands just barely covering the bald spot on the top of his head, and his face is lined with wrinkles. Still, he's as toned as I remember him being, all muscle and bulk, and his eyes glimmer with malicious mirth.

"Damien, my boy! I was surprised to get your call." He speaks jovially, spreading his arms out on either side of him as if he wishes to hug me. As if we're best friends instead of cold-blooded assassins. As if he hadn't destroyed my childhood for his own sick pleasures and depravities.

I don't answer, simply watching him with narrowed eyes.

Unperturbed, he moves to sit in the chair across from me and folds his arms over his chest. Unlike when I was younger, his eyes don't roam over my body as if he's mentally undressing me. I no longer fit his tastes.

Sick, disgusting, perverted asshole.

"I heard that another one of my children have joined you," he continues on, merriment evident in his sparkling eyes. "Logan. How is he?" For the first time, I detect a hint of lust in his gaze, and his tongue snakes out to lick his upper lip. I don't even like the cupid, but I feel livid on his behalf.

If I love Nina with every ounce of darkness within me, I hate Narian just as much.

"And I heard that you're still seeing that one girl..." He trails off, tilting his head to the side curiously. Reading me. Gauging my reaction. And fuck, if there's one thing he could possibly do to get a rise out of me, it's mentioning Nina's name. I don't want her anywhere near this sick fuck, even if it's just her name leaving his mouth.

But I've been trained by the best, by the asshole himself, so I simply give him an indolent look, like he's not even worth my fucking time.

My nonchalance works. If there's one thing Narian hates most in the world, it's not getting the reaction he so desperately desires. He wants me to beg him, plead with him, get on my fucking knees if I were able.

"How's the little bitch doing?" Narian's lips twist cruelly. "Is her pussy still keeping you occupied? Rumor has it that it's made from solid gold. Is that true?"

Again, I give him no response. Not even a fucking eye twitch.

I'm that good…especially considering the fact I want to break free of these magic-dampening cuffs and rip him apart, piece by piece. Maybe I'll skin him first, just to hear his screams. Maybe I'll bathe in his blood like the sadistic fuck he molded me into.

Either way, this man is going to die by my hand.

"I hope you don't mind if I test out her pussy," Narian continues, flashing me a dark smile. It doesn't quite reach his eyes. He's still too pissed at me for not reacting the way he wanted me to. "Push her down on a bed. Spread those creamy thighs… Yum. I'm getting hard just thinking about it. Is it weird staring into her eyes when you fuck her? I mean, those are pretty fucking ugly eyes. I probably wouldn't want to look at them."

I turn towards the camera in the far corner of the room, where I'm sure some sweaty pig is watching this entire interaction, utterly unaware that he has two of the most deranged killers in one room, and lift a hand, signaling I'm ready to leave.

And Narian fucking snaps.

"It'll be a good thing when that girl is dead," he bites out, his body trembling with rage. "She's making you soft, my son. Weak. She's a disgrace. You should've just killed her yourself and got it over with. Fuck," he laughs harshly, the noise instantly grating on my nerves, "maybe that's your plan. Maybe you wish to collect the money from Lionel, is that it? Are you using the dumb, blind bitch for the money?"

I keep my face impassive, blank, but my mind is spinning.

Lionel.

The fucking dickhead Lionel Green was the one who put out the hit on Nina.

Fuck!

He can claim all he wants that it's because she was behind the deaths of two of his fellow councilmembers—though technically, Nina only killed Alyssa—but I know the truth.

Lionel is practically obsessed with the twins. He'll kill for them. Hell, he'll even *kill* them if he can't have them. I know from my sources that he was one of the patrons who purchased them the most when they were prisoners of Boris at the depraved sex club.

And now, he's going after our girl.

My girl.

And our—

That train of thought shuts down fast.

I can't wait to stick my hand in Lionel's chest, pull out his heart, and then use his internal organs as a noose. It's completely possible. I've done it before, and I'll do it again for my angel. Maybe I'll blood eagle this disgusting fucker. The possibilities are limitless when you have an imagination like mine. An imagination that's full of blood and guts, shadows and monsters, knives and guns.

Or maybe…

Maybe I'll ask the twins what they want to do with their tormentor.

One thing is certain.

Lionel fucking Green is going to die soon.

But not before Narian does.

Now that I have the information I need, I finally turn to

face Narian completely, the man still ranting and raving away without a care in the world. A slow, malevolent smile curls up my lips, and his words falter for just a moment. He knows that smile—it's the one I always wear when I'm playing death.

That hesitation is all I need. Before he can scream, before he can even get off of his chair, I spit at him.

And the poisonous dart I've tucked under my tongue hits him square in the neck.

I have the pleasure of watching his eyes widen in horror as his gaze flickers from me to the dart sticking out of his skin and then back to me. The fucker doesn't even have enough strength to rip the damn thing out.

His entire body convulses as the poison works its magic, and he falls off the chair, his head careening against the side of the table and leaving behind a bloody imprint. White foam erupts from his mouth as he shakes and shakes and shakes, his skin turning an ashen color and his eyes and ears leaking blood.

I watch it all with the same detachment I do everything. It doesn't matter to me that this is the guy who, for lack of better term, raised me. Taught me everything I know. He's nothing but my enemy, using his assassins to go after me and my loved ones.

No more.

The guards run inside, and I feel a jolt of electricity course through my body as I'm tasered. But fuck, a little dose of electricity is worth it to see the life finally bleed out of Narian's eyes. I don't know how many times I imagined this exact moment. A hundred? A thousand? A million? An odd thrill shoots up my spine as a slow, languid grin curls up my lips.

As more and more guards crowd the room, screaming

and yelling into their walkie talkies, I hang on to a sliver of consciousness, refusing to let the darkness claim me.

I'm tased again by one of those asshole guards. And again. And again.

My last coherent thought is, *I need to tell Nina the truth,* before shadows consume my vision.

CHAPTER 30

NINA

Two days.

It's been two days since Damien went to go see his mysterious visitor and returned to the Labyrinth covered in bruises. When he awoke a day earlier, he took one look at me and instantly retreated into himself. Mentally, of course. Physically, he remained as vigilant as ever, watching me with an unnerving intensity that made goosebumps ripple up my arms and down my spine.

I can feel his eyes caressing my skin, the heat his gaze emits almost palpable, as I sit in the cafeteria with my girl-friends. And then when I'm in the throne room, listening to the newest grievances, his gaze doesn't stray from me. Whenever I enter his head, the only thing I can see through his vision is myself. Always myself.

A part of me wants to prod further, hear his thoughts and deepest desires, but I would never betray his trust like that, even if the need to know his secrets is riding me.

Instead, I ignore my aloof fiancé the way he's ignoring me, even though it's killing something inside of me, crushing it in a meaty fist until the pieces are almost unrecognizable.

At least Bronson woke up, though my growly wolf shifter is upset and frustrated that someone got the drop on us. He doesn't even care that I killed someone with my bare hands. If anything, Bronson appears relieved that we'll have one less threat to deal with. Apparently, the attempted killer wasn't even an assassin, but some weaselly man looking for extra money. I discover that he's the sniveling, fearful man that I accidentally ran into in the cafeteria, the one Damien threatened bodily harm to.

And now he's a dead man.

Because of me.

Because I can't seem to stop hurting people.

On the third day, Kai gently wakes me where we lie in bed together, my head resting on his muscular bicep as he strokes a hand down my back.

"We need to train today," he whispers in my ear, his lips creating a pathway from my lobe to my neck and then back up. I shudder delicately, overcome by the sensations he evokes within me, before turning in his embrace and twining my arms around his neck.

"Do we have to?" I wrinkle my nose. "Can't we just sleep for eternity? I'm comfy." I wiggle my hips against his rapidly hardening cock to emphasize my point.

Kai groans low in his throat, his nose lightly touching my cheek before traveling to my jawline. "You're a fucking temptress, baby."

I release an evil laugh, one that Abel would be most proud of, and kiss the hollow of his throat. "Then I'm being trained well, young grasshopper."

There's a moment of shocked silence, before Kai's body shakes with his laughter. "Did you just call me a young grasshopper?"

"It's from the karate movie I watched with Abel and Cain!" I protest, feeling slightly indignant. When Kai continues to laugh, I can't help but giggle as well. Lowering my voice to mimic the actor's, I say, *"Patience, young grasshopper. Maybe the force be with you."*

Kai begins to laugh harder, and I can feel the vibrations rippling through my own body. "Fuck, I love you. Even if you are horrible at quoting movies."

"Hey!" I use his chest to sit up slightly, my curtain of black hair falling around us. "I'll have you know that I'm making up for a lot of lost time. Years in a tiny cage will do that to you."

I know the second the teasing mood dissipates.

Kai goes rigid underneath me, his muscles bulging beneath my hands, and I know his mind has traveled back to when we were both prisoners in the Compound and best friends. Before he unwillingly left me and was thrown into prison, simply for being my mate.

A part of him blames himself for not being there to protect me, but I never held that against him. Not even for a second. The time we had together was precious, and it's something I'll cherish forever, but I'm grateful he wasn't with me the entire time I was a prisoner in that hell. The things they did to me…

I still have nightmares. I still wake up in a cold-sweat, my heart pounding rapidly as terror blinds me and steals what little warmth remains from my body. When I close my eyes, I can feel their hands on me, their sharp tools digging into my skin, the ropes around my wrists and ankles…

"If I could, I would bear the pain so you wouldn't have to," Kai whispers as he cups my cheek, his thumb tenderly rubbing against my lips.

"And if I could, I would take away all of this misplaced guilt you feel," I counter immediately.

He groans, mumbling something inarticulate under his breath, before he reluctantly sits up, taking me with him.

"You should change, baby girl," he murmurs, squeezing my butt. "You're not going to have your usual teacher today."

Damien's not teaching me? The thought sends a pang through me, a surge of potent longing, followed by a trickle of unease.

"If he's not my teacher, then who is?"

THROUGH KAI'S EYES, I WATCH LOGAN STRETCH IN THE center of the throne room. He bends himself at his waist until his hands touch his toes, his silky blond hair falling forward. For a moment—for a brief, guilty moment—I admire the lithe, muscular build of his body. Once I realize what I'm doing, I shake my head rapidly, schooling my features the way Damien always does.

What the heck is wrong with me?

I don't ogle men who aren't my mates, even ones as attractive as Logan.

His head snaps up when he hears us enter, his eyes landing first on Kai before trailing to me. His baby blues dance beneath his gorgeous blond hair, and a fine layer of sweat covers his muscular build. This close, I can see the tattoos peeking out of his tank top, though the details are impossible for me to decipher.

"Do you know why you're here today, Nina Doe?" Logan asks as he moves to perch on Kai's throne. Immediately, my dragon releases a low, threatening growl, and Logan casts him a frosty look before lowering himself to sit on the raised stone platform instead.

"Because you're training me?" I can feel my brows furrowing in confusion. Why is Logan training me? What *is* he? I suspect my mates know the truth, but I haven't bothered to ask. It's not my place to know, especially when most of the prison is still oblivious to my own powers and lineage.

"I'm a cupid," Logan begins without preamble, clasping his hands together on his lap. He leans forward until his elbows rest on his knees.

"A cupid?" I repeat, sifting through my limited knowledge of supernatural species.

Logan releases a breath of air. Somehow, he's able to make that barely inaudible noise sound irritated.

"You didn't explain anything?" He directs the question at Kai, who I can practically feel bristle.

"I figured you would handle that," he retorts.

Logan twists his head to face me once more, and his entire face seems to soften, warmth appearing in his bright blue gaze. "A cupid is a subspecies of angels. We can sense romantic love and pairings. Sometimes, we're able to see mate bonds." Which is how my guys learned that they're my true mates. I wondered where they came to that conclusion, but I was too ecstatic with the knowledge to prod. "Other times, we can pick up a person's innermost fantasy. Warp it. Twist it. Project images and videos into a person's mind." He begins to pick at one of his nails, feigning a nonchalance I can tell he doesn't truly feel. His shoulders are too tense, nearly brushing his ears, and his eyes spark dangerously. "It's why we were killed off, hunted for sport. Even angels consider our traits to be too...demonic for their liking." He finally stands, towering over me with his full, impressive height, and stalks forward. "It's why I've been tasked with training you, Nina Doe. I'm an angelic creature with demonic traits that lives in the human realm. And you're a mixture of all three."

"How did you...?" I trail off breathlessly. As far as I'm aware, the truth of my heritage is a closely guarded secret. Not even Braelyn knows the truth.

But when Kai doesn't immediately attack Logan, I allow myself to relax.

"And you're going to teach me?" I inquire, lifting an eyebrow in disbelief. Internally, hope blossoms like an errant firework, shooting sparks in every direction until my entire bloodstream is alive with it.

Logan's smile is sharp and predatory, a shark circling blood in the water. "Of course, Nina Doe." I make a face at his usage of my full name yet again, but he continues on, unperturbed. "I'm going to teach you how to control your boyfriend here."

"What?" I gasp, staggering back a step. Only the sudden appearance of Kai's hands on my shoulders stops me from fleeing.

"It's quite easy," Logan continues, either oblivious to my sudden unease or choosing to ignore it. My guess is on the latter. "As a cupid, I can help steer people in the right direction when it comes to love matches by pushing my will into their bodies. I imagine that you can do the same."

"Make people fall in love?" I ask in disbelief, and his grin widens, revealing pearly-white teeth.

"Are you in Blade's head right now?" Logan inquires, and when I nod, still hesitant, he smiles eagerly. "Perfect. I want you to focus on all of his senses, just as you've been trained to do. What he tastes. What he smells. What he sees. What he hears. What he feels. Are you doing it?" He pauses, and I bob my head again. "Perfect. Now, I want you to slide into his thoughts, the way Damien taught you. I know you can do it, Nina Doe."

I do as he says, losing myself in the sensation that is Malakai, my childhood best friend turned lover and savior. His warm essence washes over me, only comparable to the heat and fire of a dragon. It smells vaguely of smoke and ash.

Logan's voice comes to me as if in a distant dream.

"I don't want you to merely sense Kai. I want you to *be* him."

Be Kai?

I want to scoff.

Kai is more than just one thing. He's…everything. He's joy and hope. Strength and security. The innate sense of protection. The calm before the storm. He's the one constant in my life, the anchor keeping me at bay when the currents try to pull me away.

I know immediately that something is different.

Because when I open my eyes, my lashes fluttering against my skin, I'm able to *see.*

Shock ripples through me as I blink, staring at my hands in wonderment. But they're not my hands. No, they're way too big and are covered in pale scars.

Kai's hands.

"What the heck?" The voice that erupts isn't my voice either. It's deep and masculine, sending a fine, delicate tremor through my body.

Kai's voice.

Kai's body.

Holy crap.

I whip my head in Logan's direction, who's currently grinning at me like the cat who ate the canary. He rubs his hands together eagerly as he takes in my wide, probably fearful, expression.

"Nina Doe?" he questions, quirking an eyebrow. When I nod, a wide, brilliant smile appears on his face and he releases a loud whoop. "It actually worked."

"Where's Kai? What's going on?" I fire off, spinning once more. Directly to my right is…me. My face is slack, white eyes wide, lower lip pushed out slightly in a pout. The only indication I'm breathing is the steady rise and fall of my chest. Otherwise, I'm as still as a statue.

I can feel my precarious control slipping the longer I stare at my motionless body, panic setting in.

"Wait! You need to maintain—"

Before Logan can finish his instructions, I feel a metaphysical snap as my powers propel me out of Kai's body and back into my own like a taut rubber band being broken. Darkness engulfs my vision, and I stagger back a few steps, holding my hand to my cheek and sighing as my familiar soft palm touches my skin.

"What the fuck?" Kai murmurs, sounding disgruntled and dazed.

"Kai!" I turn in his general direction, throwing myself into his arms with the knowledge that he'll catch me. His arms immediately band around me, holding me steady as he breathes in my scent, his body shaking.

"What happened?" he questions softly. Abruptly, he releases me, and I slide into his head just as he whirls on Logan. Whatever expression is on his face has the cupid taking a step back, his hands raising in a placating manner. "What did you do to me?"

"I did nothing," Logan insists, that smirk still firmly in place, despite the impending danger. "But your girl? She did it." He sounds so freaking proud of me that my heart stutters once before returning to its normal rhythm. I want to blush and duck my head, but I don't know if I'm horrified or ecstatic with what just occurred.

I controlled Kai's *mind*.

But at the same time...

"You don't remember what happened?" I ask softly, resisting the urge to chew on my nail. Kai turns to face me, and my face fills his vision.

"I remember we were talking about..." He trails off as realization dawns on him. "You controlled me, didn't you?" I can't quite read his tone of voice.

"I'm sorry. I'm so, so sorry. I was just doing as Logan instructed, and then the next thing I knew, I was using your body, and—" My ramblings are cut off by Kai's sudden, and very insistent, kiss. His tongue enters my mouth, tangling with my own, as his hands move down to my butt once more, squeezing and kneading. When he pulls away to rest his forehead against my own, we're both breathing heavy.

"I'm not mad, baby. Why would I ever be mad with a new skill you learned that can protect you? I'm so fucking happy." He kisses me again, this time sweeter, before he reluctantly pulls away and turns towards Logan. "I suppose I'll have to thank you."

Logan clears his throat, his cheeks bright red, even as he tries to smother his reaction to our heated kiss. I can feel my own face burn hotly with embarrassment, but Kai simply holds me tighter, radiating male smugness. "No thanks necessary. I'm just doing what we agreed upon."

"Either way, I'm thankful." Kai sounds as if he's in physical pain, and I giggle into my palm. Men and their egos. "Are there any other—"

Whatever Kai is about to say is interrupted by the door to the throne room being thrown open and Damien stalking inside. I can only tell it's him by the way Logan freezes, his face draining of all color.

Only one person in this entire prison is capable of evoking such fear in the inmates.

My heartbeat turns from a mere gallop to a trot as Damien moves to stand directly in front of me. Through Kai's eyes, I take in every detail of my meticulously-groomed mate. From the black hair, to the cold, icy eyes, to the suit that looks as if it was physically made for him. I haven't even realized how much I missed him until now, when he stares down at me like I'm the only thing in the entire world. The only thing in *his* world.

"Nina," his voice catches on my name, the only indication that something else is going on, "we need to talk."

DAMIEN INTERTWINES HIS FINGERS WITH MINE AS HE LEADS ME out of the throne room and down to the old cellblock that was destroyed in the explosion.

"What are we doing?" I ask, allowing him to lead me along and trusting him implicitly.

He doesn't immediately answer, pushing aside a precariously hanging rafter so we can enter what was once his bedroom. The last time I was here…

Rion had nearly been killed. Because of me. Because of the bomb that was meant for *me*.

Guilt engulfs me instantly, but I stomp it down, knowing that the only people to blame are the ones attacking my family.

The flooring and walls of Damien's old bedroom are still charred, but the pungent smell of smoke no longer permeates the air. All of the furniture Damien acquired over the years has been destroyed except for a lone chair, leaving behind nothing but residual ash that has yet to be swept up and black remains.

"Damien." I tug on his arm insistently until he stops, turning to face me. At the same time, I slip out of his head and once more embrace my customary darkness. "Why did you bring me here?"

"My guitar still remains," Damien says evasively, and the abrupt change in topic gives me whiplash. He guides me to the chair that has somehow survived the blast, at least well enough for me to perch on it, and then moves silently away. My tall, dark, graceful shadow. "I placed a spell on it," he continues, and after a moment of silence, I can hear the melodic notes of his guitar as he plucks the strings. Goose-bumps erupt on my skin instinctively, and I don't even bother to hide my reaction.

"Damien…" I lick my suddenly dry lips as he continues to strum an unfamiliar tune. "What's going on?"

He releases a bark of laughter, the noise a direct contrast to the soulful music he's playing. "What isn't going on, Angel?" He asks the rhetorical question with a derisive snort, the noise so unlike my normally stoic mage that I blink at him. "Everything is changing, and it's my job to protect you. But I can't protect you in here. I can't. I just fucking can't."

Gracefully, I rise from the chair and step towards him. He immediately stops playing his guitar and reaches out to tug me into his arms, as I knew he would.

"Tell me what's going on," I plead, smoothing my hands over his wrinkle-free suit. He trembles beneath my touch, his breath fanning across my face, but he doesn't immediately respond. "Damien, please. Let me help."

"I don't know how it happened." His words rush together. For once, he's not the impassive, icy man with a heart enclosed in solid steel. He's flesh and blood, weeping red and utterly vulnerable. I wonder if he ever allowed himself to be like this with anyone else. If he ever allowed the walls he constructed around himself to shatter in a plume of dust. A small part of me hopes that he hasn't, that I'm the only one who's ever seen the man beneath the killer. The gorgeous, beautiful, gentle man who believes the blood staining his hands defines him.

"Damien," I prod gently, and his grip on my arms tightens. Not to the point of pain, but enough for me to go quiet and tilt my face up in his general direction.

"I don't know how it happened," he repeats. "I believe it's a product of a lot of things. The spells I've been performing on you. Your age—maybe Alyssa planted a failsafe in case anything happened to her. Maybe once you reached a certain age, the spell wore off. Fuck, I even think Logan's arrival played a huge part. You know what he is, don't you? His species was created purposely to encourage matches capable of maximum reproductive capacity."

"Maximum reproductive capacity?" My lips curl slightly at the scientific term. "Damien, what the heck are you talking about?"

He takes a deep breath, the gesture unable to dissipate the tension I can feel lining his body, before he whispers, "The spell Alyssa placed around your uterus is gone."

Everything freezes. The world, Damien, me... I'm not even sure I'm breathing. The darkness has never felt more suffocating, more pronounced, closing in on me from all sides until I'm practically drowning in it.

Gasping.

I'm gasping for air, but current after current continues to pull me under, until I'm bobbing through the ocean with no chance of survival.

"What?" I manage to gasp out, my voice shaking ever so slightly.

"The magical ropes I noticed around your uterus? The ones that prohibit you from having kids? They're gone. Completely. I don't even detect a trace of the magic."

His words feel like a metaphorical freight train barreling towards me at one hundred miles per hour. It runs me over, but instead of dying instantly, I topple head over heels while my entire life rotates on its axis. What was up is now down. What is down is now up. What is left is right.

And what is right...

Well, I don't have the answer to that question anymore.

There are numerous facets of human nature, and the black and white colors I've grown so accustomed to have merged together, painting the world in a murky, stomach-churning shade of gray.

"And there's something else." Damien's voice lowers to a whisper so soft, I can barely hear him.

I can barely think, barely breathe, only aware of the pounding reverberating through my head. Pound. Pound. Pound. It's symbols and gunshots and explosive bombs and fireworks... They all merge together in a cacophony of sound.

"Yes?"

Somehow, I know what he's going to say. Even before he says it, I know the next words that will leave his lips.

And everything changes.

"You're pregnant."

CHAPTER 31

NINA

His words are a verbal freight train, plowing me over and then continuing on to demolish everything in its path. My heart feels like a rocket ship in my chest, vibrating erratically before taking flight and barreling up my throat. I can barely breathe through the pounding in my ears, so deafening that stars replace the darkness of my vision.

Without immediately responding to Damien's proclamation, I take a moment to analyze my own feelings. My own emotions. They're a tumultuous mixture, all of them threaded together, making them impossible for me to unravel. The second I grab one and begin to pull, the ball of yarn gets tighter and even more tangled.

Deep breaths, Nina. Deep breaths.

There's panic, obviously. So potent that I'm practically drowning in it, the taste of decay filling my mouth. And intermixed with the panic is fear. Even a little anger at Damien for keeping this a secret.

But then there are the bright ones, shining like beacons and infusing me with warmth.

Joy.

Excitement.

Hope.

The toxic cocktail of emotions leaves me breathless and panting. I'm dimly aware of Damien placing a hand on my elbow, guiding me back to the chair I abandoned. When my body tilts precariously to the side, he automatically catches me, and I can tell how rigid he is through touch alone. Every plane of his chest is held tautly, as if he's seconds from snapping entirely.

And I don't know what I'd do with a snapped Damien.

His voice, however, is gentle when he speaks next, as he kneels in front of me and places his hands on my knees. "Talk to me, Angel."

"I don't know how I feel," I confess in a breathy whisper, still attempting to unravel the emotions squeezing my heart in an iron vise. So. Many. Emotions. They bombard me from every direction as if I'm standing in an open field during a hailstorm. "I'm...I'm excited. And terrified. And confused. And horrified. And..." I place a hand over my mouth as Damien's grip tightens almost imperceptibly on my thighs. "Oh God. Damien, I don't want to deliver a baby here."

Not in this place that breeds monsters.

Not in prison.

I can't think of a worse fate.

But I also know that a piece of my soul will shrivel up and die if I'm forced to give the baby up. *My* baby up.

"You could tell the warden." Damien's voice is nearly inaudible, merely air that blows across my face. It's colder than icebergs, the frigid nature of it in direct contrast to the tender way he touches my legs. "If you tell the warden, he'll send you to a safer part of the prison until you give birth. And once you give birth—"

"No," I say, cutting him off vehemently and shaking my

head from side to side. "I'm not leaving you guys. Besides, is anywhere really safe with the hit still out on me?" I instinctively bring my hands to my stomach, where there's apparently *life* forming inside of me. A product of the love I feel for my men. I want to ask Damien more questions—if he knows who the father is, if he can tell the species of the baby or even the gender—but I don't. None of that matters at the moment.

"I'll protect you and our child with every power I possess," Damien vows, placing his hand over mine. His breath hitches. "I don't give a damn if that baby isn't biologically mine. I'll protect and love you both."

My heart fills with love for this man.

Removing my hand from my stomach, I cup his smooth-shaven cheek.

His lips meet mine in a tender kiss as my other hand travels up his arm to cup the side of his face, bringing him even closer to me. His own arms band around my waist, practically lifting me off the chair.

We're still kissing as he leads me to the ground, shifting our positions so I'm on the charred floor and he's hovering over me.

When Damien pulls his lips away, I cry out automatically, needing my mage with an intensity that leaves me breathless. I hear him moving around, and a moment later, his bundled up jacket is underneath my head, serving as a makeshift pillow, and his lean, naked body is hovering over mine.

"Damien," I pant as he pulls down the straps of my dress and takes one of my nipples into his mouth. His tongue swirls around the pointed peak as his other hand crawls underneath my dress, pushing away my underwear to spear me with his finger.

I gasp, my back arching instinctively, as he continues to shove his digit in and out of my pussy.

"This pussy is mine," Damien growls out, the possessiveness in his voice nearly taking me off guard. It's a reaction I would've expected from Bronson or Kai, not my normally stoic and apathetic mage.

He adds another finger to my tight channel as he moves his lips to my neglected breast, pulling my nipple through his teeth.

"These breasts are mine." His hand grabs my tit and begins to knead the flesh as I writhe, almost mindless with pleasure. When I don't answer, struggling to even get enough air in my lungs, he removes his fingers and stops playing with my aching breasts. "Answer me, Angel."

"Yes," I manage to rasp out. "They're yours. I'm yours."

"Damn right you are." He pulls his lips back to mine and kisses me with a bruising intensity, one I feel in my very soul, incinerating any doubt or fear I might've had and replacing it with an all-encompassing and consuming love. "You and our baby…" I can practically sense the darkness permeating from him in tangible waves. But instead of scaring me, as it no doubt would a sane person, I cry out in pleasure. *"Mine."*

"Yours," I agree, desperate to touch all of him. I run my hands down his bare shoulder blades, and surprisingly, he lets me. Damien is always very cautious about touch. He doesn't let anyone besides me touch him, and even then, he still gets twitchy and anxious. Not in the same way Cain does, but more so in the sense that he isn't used to it. That he doesn't always associate touch with pleasure instead of pain.

His back muscles dip low, and I allow my hands to fondle his chiseled, rock-hard butt. I want to reach between us and grab his cock that I can feel pressing against my stomach, leaving behind a wet streak, but I can't grab it in this position.

"Damien." It's a plea. I'm begging for him, needing him with every fiber of my being. He's as essential to me as breathing. I need to breathe him in and devour him like oxygen.

"Angel." His fingers begin to scissor inside of me, and I can feel myself on the verge—

But before I can topple over the edge, Damien removes his fingers from my channel. A second later, his hot cock slides against my sensitive folds as he slowly pushes himself inside of me, inch by inch. I gasp when he reaches the hilt, loving the way he fills me so completely, and buck my hips so he's forced to move.

He doesn't. At least not right away.

Instead, he stills over me, his arms braced on either side of my head and his lips a hair's breadth away from my own.

"I never thought I would have this," he whispers, and the sheer vulnerability lacing his tone has my heart pounding, hands shaking, lungs shriveling.

"A girl underneath you?" I tease, but I know that's not what he meant.

"Someone to love. Someone who loves me. A family." He clears his throat seconds before planting a tentative kiss to my lips. It's a slow, almost careful kiss, and I can feel how tense he is above me. I want to remind him that I'm not made of glass, that I'm not going to break the second he applies too much pressure, but there's something so alluring about the tender pecks he plants to every inch of my lips. I deepen it further, my fingers threading through his hair as he lets out a low, pained sound in the back of his throat. I shiver, my toes curling as he moves away from my mouth and back to my sensitive, aching breasts, sucking on my nipple.

"Damien…" I pull his face back to mine and part my lips automatically, searching for his tongue, and sigh in pleasure when it tangles with my own.

"I'll never let you go." Something malevolent enters his

tone, evoking images of bloody knives and dark streets. "I'll kill anyone who tries to take you away from me."

Without giving me a chance to respond, he begins to move, his hips thrusting against my pelvis as his cock slides in and out of me. It starts off slow, almost as if the news of my pregnancy makes him think I'm breakable, but those notions quickly dissipate as he becomes consumed by a fervent hunger.

His hands fondle my breasts as he pounds into me, leaning forward to capture my lips in another one of his bruising kisses. I love the way his lips move against my own. As if he's claiming me. Owning me. Loving me in a way only a monster like him can. I'm not oblivious to the darkness that resides inside of Damien's soul, but it also doesn't scare me. I know he'll use every ounce of his darkness to love and protect me and our unborn baby. There's not a doubt in my mind.

He doesn't love often, but when he does, it's fiercely and unconditionally.

I know he'll move heaven and hell to see me safe and happy.

My pussy squeezes his cock as his lips travel to my throat, marking me with his teeth. I scream out my release as his hips judder, seconds before he spills his seed inside of me. His lips clasp down on my sensitive neck, hard enough to bruise, but the sensation only makes me explode again, milking him for all he's worth.

Damien releases a heavy breath, nuzzling his face against my neck, before moving so he's on his back and I'm lying half on his chest and half on the ground, his cock still inside of me, rapidly hardening.

Silence descends as he strokes my bare back, his fingers as soft as moth's wing against my overheated skin.

"We need to tell the others," I whisper, planting a kiss to his chest.

I wish desperately I could see his face when he sighs once more.

"We need to get out of this fucking prison," he murmurs curtly, and I find myself nodding before I remember where I am.

There's no escape. Not for me and not for the men I love.

We're defined by our pasts, trapped in this prison by both metaphorical and physical chains.

Until death claims us, I have no doubt that this is where we'll remain.

Sadness fills me as I think about the unborn child growing inside of me. Of the life she or he will never have.

I'm sorry, my sweet baby.

I'm so, so sorry.

CHAPTER 32

KAI

"I told you, I'm fine," Bronson growls out, directing a narrowed-eyed stare at Rion, who holds his hands up innocently.

"Dude, I just don't want you to fall over and become a werewolf pancake. I don't think Nina would be too happy. Actually…" The crazy shifter puts a finger to his chin in contemplation. "If she gets to eat you, she might be happy. I, on the other hand, am *not* gonna eat you. Unless you're into that sort of stuff." He waits, raising a pierced brow as Bronson glares at him, moving stiffly until he's finally sitting on a chair in the throne room. "No? Fine. Spoilsport."

"You should take it easy," I tell my chief enforcer, watching the relief splay itself across his face when he's finally able to sit after being on his feet all day.

"I'm fine," Bronson retorts immediately. The same damn thing he's been saying every time one of us asks him. I know his natural healing has begun kicking in, but he was shot, for fuck's sake. That's not something that will heal overnight, even for an immensely powerful shadow wolf. "Now what did Nina want to talk to us about?"

"Dunno." That's from Abel, who tosses another grape in the air. Of course, the asshole misses it when he tries to catch the fruit in his mouth, and we both watch as it rolls towards his brother. Cain gives Abel an annoyed look. "Nina just told me to gather everyone in the throne room."

"And are you sure that meant him?" Cain asks with a venomous look in Logan's direction. To be quite honest, I've almost forgotten the cupid was in the room with us, which isn't a good thing. I don't trust him. At all.

And the last thing I need is for him to stab me in the back while I'm distracted.

Abel shrugs again in answer to Cain's question. "Again, dunno. He was just sitting there looking lost and shit, so I took pity on him and invited him to join the popular table."

Logan glares at the trickster demon, eyes hurling daggers. "I wasn't looking 'lost and shit,'" he argues. "And I don't want to join your table of psychopaths."

Abel places a hand to his chest in mock pain. "Psychopaths. I'm hurt, Logan. I prefer the term 'sexy and deranged lover.'"

Logan's pretty boy face twists, but he wisely doesn't comment.

A moment later, Logan has completely left my mind when the door to the throne room opens and Damien and Nina step inside. My love looks…pale. Her onyx hair appears even darker around her washed-out face. Even her pure white eyes seem brighter in comparison, those glorious depths glimmering with unshed tears.

"What the fuck happened?" Bronson jumps up from the chair, wobbles when he's greeted with the fresh pain from his wound, and then grits his teeth together as he steps in front of Nina. "Who do I have to kill, Goddess?" He eyes Damien warily, as if he's half expecting Nina to name the mage. I have no doubt Bronson will try to kill Damien if Nina wished it.

I wonder who would win that fight.

"Nina," I growl, my dragon unfurling inside of me and demanding to be let out. Demanding to claim his mate and protect her from whatever put that haunted, doe-eyed look on her face. "What happened?"

"I'm..." She swallows heavily, and my eyes drop to the swan-like arch of her throat.

"You're desperate to ride my cock, Bambi?" Abel asks with a forced laugh. His joke manages to garner a tentative smile from Nina, one that she quickly squashes. She fiddles with the hem of her white dress, tension bleeding from every pore of her body. Damien stands directly beside her, one hand on the small of her back while he gifts us all with an impassive look. It's obvious he knows what's troubling her, but you'll never get him to admit it. There's only one person he ever drops his mask with, and she's the one currently shaking like a leaf in the wind.

"Trouble." Cain's voice is practically a bark as he stalks forward, stopping only inches in front of her. Damien's eyes narrow at his tone of voice, but he doesn't comment when Cain places his hands on her shoulders. "What the fuck is going on? You know I hate when you do this shit."

"What shit are you referring to?" Rion pipes in. "The sexy kind? I didn't know you liked that kink, my naughty demon friend." Despite his words being addressed at a glowering Cain, Rion doesn't peel his eyes away from Nina. His face is grim, even as his tongue plays with his lip ring.

And then Nina says it. In the throne room. Miles underground. In prison.

The words that barrel me over with the force of a wrecking ball. The words that cause every organ in my body to freeze. The words that make my hands shake erratically as blinding terror courses through me.

"I'm pregnant."

No. No. No.

No!

I drop to my knees, my legs unable to hold my body up, as I stare at my beloved. Simply stare. I'm dimly aware of Bronson howling, the noise low and tormented, of the twins gripping one another tightly, of Rion dropping his face into his hands. Only Damien's expression remains blank, hewn from stone and utterly unreadable.

"You can't be," Bronson finally manages to say, his voice sounding distant to my ears. "The spell—"

"Is no longer there," Damien cuts in, a frown curling his lips down. "It hasn't been there for a while."

"How the fuck didn't you notice something like that?" Rion snaps, and for once, I don't see the crazy, eccentric shifter. I see the rival gang leader. The fierce and terrifying tiger.

"You're not…" Nina's voice trembles slightly, and she wraps both of her arms around her midsection. "You guys aren't happy we're going to have a child?"

Her wobbly voice…

It fucking breaks me.

All of our heads snap up at once, and I can see my own horror reflected on each of their faces.

"That's not it at all, baby," I murmur, finding my voice when all I want to do is wage a war against this goddamn world. Tears prick my eyes, and I don't even try to hide them. "We're going to be dads." I take another breath, searching for the right words. Because overshadowing the joy and wonderment of this discovery—*we're going to be a fucking family*—is godawful terror.

My kid is going to be born in the Labyrinth.

"We need to leave," Bronson interjects, his words a guttural growl. I wonder how close he is to losing his shit and shifting. I know that the second the throne room is empty, my dragon will explode out of me.

"You're talking about escaping prison." Abel turns towards Bronson, mouth agape. "Fuck, Bron."

"Do you have a better idea?" Bronson snaps, running a shaky hand through his tousled blond hair. "My child—*our* child—is not fucking growing up here. I can't..." His voice hitches slightly. Wolves in general place a huge emphasis on family and kin.

The knowledge that his own kid will be stuck inside of this fucked-up place, or removed from our care as soon as she or he is born, is a literal knife to the gut.

"The door..." Rion whispers softly, his long lashes fluttering. And then, with more animation, he repeats, "The door."

Yes, this mysterious doorway Rion believes will take us out of the Labyrinth. It sounds like a dream. A good dream, but a dream all the same.

"The halls are always changing. There's no way we'll be able to find it again," Cain says, his voice tired and unsure. His eyes are locked on Nina as if she's the only thing he sees. The only thing in his entire universe.

I understand completely, because God knows that she's mine.

Bronson turns towards me, his eyes beseeching my own. There's a sharpness to his face that wasn't there prior, almost as if his wolf is lurking just beneath his skin, waiting for a chance to be set free.

"We need to leave, Blade. We can't stay here. Not with the hit list against us. Not with..." He gestures wildly towards Nina.

"He's right," Rion adds gravely. He forks his fingers through his dark hair. "Fuck, he's right—we can't stay here. Not now."

Nina is silent as her blind gaze volleys between all of us. I know she's dying to ask Rion about this door he found, but she remains silent, allowing us to gather our thoughts.

Though all I want to do is grab her, kiss her senseless, and then lock her in my treasure vault so no harm can come to her and our...

My eyes lower to her stomach. Obviously, I don't see any visible signs of her pregnancy, but I know it's only a matter of time until her belly rounds enticingly. My cock hardens at the thought, but I shove those lustful thoughts aside.

"Okay." My voice is soft, but as I expect, it silences everyone instantly. Cain and Abel both stare at me in disbelief, but Bronson sags in physical relief. Rion and Damien, though, are impossible to read. "Okay. We'll leave."

"Take me with you."

We all jump at the unexpected voice. All of us, surprisingly, except for Nina, who simply turns her head in Logan's general direction. Even Damien seems shocked, his mouth parting slightly before he hardens his features and glares at the other man.

Logan holds our gazes stubbornly, his teasing smile nowhere in sight.

"I can help," Logan continues, a hint of desperation in his voice. "I can continue to train Nina. I mean, who knows how long we're going to be down there, searching for an exit? And I can fight if it comes to that. I'm also capable of sensing minds, as you guys are well aware. Romantic thoughts, lust, any sort of attraction, past or present... It'll give us an advantage if a guard is approaching."

His words hold merit, but at the same time...

I don't fucking trust him.

But it's Nina who speaks, her windchime voice causing all of us to wilt in her direction like flowers seeking sunlight. I would feel fucking pathetic, if I gave a shit about anything or anyone other than the woman before me. "Logan," she begins, moving away from Damien until she's able to stand by me. She places her hand in the crook of my elbow, her eyes remaining fixed on the cupid. The cupid who's currently staring at her with love-struck eyes. "What did you do to land yourself here?" She pauses. "And don't lie to me."

"Enter my head. Hear the sincerity in my thoughts," Logan all but pleads, continuing to give Nina these obnoxious puppy dog eyes that make me want to stab him.

"Me thinks he has a little crush on our fiancée," Rion murmurs to Bronson.

"I stole," Logan confesses at last, his gaze lowering to the ground. Nina's eyes have glazed over, the only indication she's entered his mind and is now listening intently to his thoughts. "From Councilman Lionel Green. I was living on the streets after an incident with Narian..." Horror etches itself across his face at whatever memory he's remembering. Nina sucks in a sharp gasp but doesn't interrupt. I place a hand on the small of her back and begin to rub soothing circles as Logan collects himself. "I heard that Lionel had recently acquired a priceless artifact—a feather from a cockatrice." He blows out a breath. "I tried to steal it, and I was caught."

I exchange a look with first Damien and then Bronson. We all know what the twins went through at that monster's hand. And to discover from Damien that he's behind the hit list?

Anger burns white-hot inside of me, but I attempt to snuff out the flame before it can blaze into an inferno.

Nina tilts her head to the side, weighing his words, before she finally nods.

"He's telling the truth, and I think...I think he should come with us." The skin between her brows creases as she struggles to articulate whatever is running through that beautiful mind of hers. "I don't know why, but I have a feeling that we need him." She turns her gaze towards mine, her white eyes pleading. "I don't know how to explain it, Kai. I know you don't trust him—"

"But I trust you," I interrupt forcefully. She blinks at me in surprise, and I kiss the tip of her nose to soften my harsh tone. "And even though it kills me, if you think we should bring the cupid with us, then we will."

"What about my friends?" She places her hands on my arms, her fingernails digging into my skin. "Braelyn and Jenny and—"

"There's a reason they're in prison, Buttercup," Rion says softly. "I know you don't want to hear that answer and I know that you care about them, but I don't think it's a good idea to bring them. Besides, the less people who know about this plan, the better."

Nina's face falls, but I agree with Rion wholeheartedly. Nina's friends...they adore her. I trust my girl with them, no questions asked, but they're a danger to society.

Braelyn herself went on a murdering spree, killing approximately fifteen people before she was caught and sent here. The only reason she ended up in the Labyrinth is because one of the people she killed was the son of a councilwoman.

Not that we're any better. It's completely hypocritical, I know that, but I also know that my men won't kill anyone now unless it's needed to protect our family. To protect Nina and our child.

But Braelyn and the others?

They're wild cards, and for a mission like this, we can't afford to have any.

"Nina, I'm sor—"

"Don't, Kai." A frown tugs at her lips, and I desperately

wish I could kiss it away. "I understand. I don't like it, but I understand."

I kiss her forehead, reveling in the heat that seems to radiate off of her, before placing a hand on her flat stomach.

By this time next year, my child will be born.

And hopefully, we'll be out of this godforsaken prison.

CHAPTER 33

"Come with me."

Damien's curt words have me glancing in the assassin's direction, but he's already stalking away, his muscles rigid beneath his black suit.

I exchange a wary glance with Cain, but he shrugs and follows.

It's been two days since we discovered the truth about Nina. Two days since we've made the decision to escape the prison. Two days since we've spent every waking moment planning and planning and...guess what? More planning.

"If you're taking us somewhere dark and spooky to murder us and hide our bodies, I'll have you know that I'm a screamer," I tell Damien with forced cheer. It's become natural for me to hide my anxiousness with quips and barbs. No one can know that, internally, I'm freaking the fuck out.

I'm about to be a father.

Me.

A father.

It's a word I never thought would be associated with me.

When I was a prisoner at the sex club, Cain and I both

had spells placed on us, similar to the one Alyssa placed on Nina, that would prohibit us from fathering children. Fortunately, the spell had an expiration date, but that didn't change the fact we were meticulous about using condoms. Neither of us wanted to be fathers, wanted the responsibility of loving someone that way.

But to know that Nina is pregnant…

I feel nothing but joy. It inflates me like helium in a balloon, making me feel weightless and buoyant. Fuck, I'm gonna be a father.

It's a gift I didn't even know I wanted, and impossibly, I fall even more in love with Nina fucking Doe. My Bambi. My world.

"I think you'll do more than scream if I decide to murder you," Damien says, his voice almost casual. Fuck, is this his way of making conversation? Of being friendly? We're gonna need to have a long talk about what's appropriate conversation starters. Talking about screaming and murdering? That's on the no-no list. As in, fuck to the holy no. "You'll probably piss yourself," Damien continues in his cold, detached voice. "And sob hysterically. But that will only be the beginning. As tears stream down your face, I'll stick my knife in your abdomen, cutting a straight line to your cock. I won't cut it off…at least not right away. Instead, I'll put tiny cuts all down the length. Cocks bleed, you know. And if it has enough cuts, you might pass out from the pain. Only then will I take your balls and rip it from your body, then shove them down your throat. Before you die, I'll allow you to see your cock in my hand as I take my razor blade and slice off tiny pieces."

Holyyy fuck.

Cain's face has turned green beside me, his hands moving to cover his manhood, as I stare at Damien with growing terror. We're buddies, right? He wouldn't truly chop up my dingle dwarf?

And then he fucking smiles. The sadistic, serial killer, psychopath honest to fuck smiles and throws his head back in laughter, patting me on the shoulder.

"You should've seen your face," he says between bouts of laughter.

Do I awkwardly laugh? Cry for my dead mommy? Hide behind Cain and offer him as a sacrifice? Where's Nina when I need her to rein in Damien's crazy?

I settle for laughing through my tears like a true champ.

I think being Damien's friend is even more terrifying than being his enemy.

"You look as if you're going to shit yourself," Cain whispers in my ear when Damien's expression turns aloof once more and he turns to walk in front of us.

"You're one to talk," I reply, jabbing his stomach with my elbow. "You're green as shit."

"Let's just make a pact right here and now to never, and I mean *ever*, get on Damien's bad side," Cain says as we resume walking. He holds out his pinkie with a wry grin playing on his lips. "Pinkie promise."

I practically squeal like a teenage girl attending a One Direction reunion concert. "You want to do a pinkie promise with me? I knew you loved me, brother."

Cain's eyes roll so far, I can see the whites of them.

"Honestly, I think the only way we'll ever piss Damien off enough to murder us is if we hurt Nina. And I for one have no intention of ever hurting that perfect human or our child. Do you?" Cain gives me a glance out of the side of his eye as I shake my head vehemently.

"Fuck no." The mere thought of hurting her makes me sick to my stomach.

"Then I don't think we need to worry about Damien stabbing us in our sleep." He pauses, his head tilting to the side.

Damien simply caresses the tip of the curved blade against his cheek. "You can't frame someone who's already guilty," he whispers. "You should've done a better job at hiding the girl's body."

It suddenly makes sense, in a sort of vague, distant, dizzying way.

Lionel murdered a girl and thought he hid the body. But Damien knows everything and everyone, and somehow, the body was found and her death led back to Lionel fucking Green. With nothing else to do, the supernatural police arrested Lionel and sent him to the Labyrinth...where Damien was happily waiting to surprise us with our "gift."

I think I have a little bit of a man crush on the crazy fucker. Sorry, Nina. She'll have to share my attention with my new bae.

"Tell us about the list," Damien repeats, ignoring Lionel's blubbering cries.

"Please don't hurt me. Please. I'll tell you everything you want to know."

Weak.

So fucking weak.

Lionel takes a deep, shuddering breath when Damien walks away, but screams in terror when the psycho returns with a pair of scissors. Humming beneath his breath, Damien cuts away Lionel's shirt, pants, and boxers, until the man is completely naked. The sight of his disgusting micropenis brings back horrible memories, memories I will to stay buried, but I don't allow myself to fall down that rabbit hole. I reach blindly for my brother, only breathing easier when his fingers interlock with mine.

Damien slides on a pair of gloves before kneeling in front of Lionel and grabbing his cock. His other hand still holds the curved blade.

"Tell me everything," he says, his ice-blue eyes swirling with darkness.

"I did it," Lionel tearfully admits. "I made the hit list. I just wanted that little bitch dead for stealing my boys from me." He turns towards us with pleading eyes. "I did it because I love you—"

Damien lowers the knife with a single swoop of his arm, and the crown of Lionel's cock falls to the ground.

His screams of agony are music to my fucking ears.

"Don't get off track, Lionel." Damien's reaches up to pet the man's head like one would a disobedient dog. "Tell us what we want to know."

"The councilmembers thought it was hilarious," Lionel gasps out, his body shaking. "They created the dead pool where we bet on how long it would take you guys to be killed. Please don't kill me. Please. I'll do anything."

"If that's all you know…" Damien raises his curved blade once more, and Lionel begins to sob harder.

"I gave the list to someone I knew in the Labyrinth. She was supposed to pass it on."

She?

That pronoun penetrates the rage thumping through me, but I can't focus on that. Not yet. Not until this disgusting piece of meat is destroyed.

Damien considers the squirmy, crying councilman with cold eyes before he finally stands and sets the blade back on the table.

Lionel practically collapses with relief.

"Boys," Damien turns towards us and gestures towards the table, "the floor is yours."

Is he suggesting…?

One look into his cold eyes confirm that I'm not misreading the situation.

He wants us to torture Lionel, the same way Lionel tortured us for years.

Cain's hand is bruising and tight around my own, nearly cutting off my circulation, but when I glance in his direction, his eyes are forged from solid steel. Tiny horns erupt from his blond hair as he stalks forward like vengeance personified.

"You're going to pay for what you did to me and my brother," Cain hisses, his voice nearly unrecognizable with the appearance of his demon. He grabs a blade at random from the table and tosses it to me. I catch it with a gleeful smile.

"No, please—"

"Your death is ours," I agree with another look at my brother. And then we begin to cut.

...

Blood drips from our skin and hair, painting the ground we walk on.

People give us a wide berth as we move towards the cell we left Nina in with Bronson.

When we arrive, she's fussing over him, completely oblivious to our presence.

But Bronson isn't. He takes one look at us, at the wings sprouting from our back and the pitch-black horns and the blood coating every available inch of skin, and excuses himself with only a small growl in our direction. He knows we'll never hurt Nina, our mate.

Our life.

"What—"

Her words are cut off by the force of my kiss, and I push her until she's flush against Cain's chest. His bloody arms band around her waist as I kiss her senseless, my tongue eagerly seeking out hers. I know she can taste the blood on me, the blood of our enemy, but she doesn't comment. Pleased gasps escape her mouth as I reach behind her to cup her ass.

"Abel. Cain," she pants, and our names leaving her lips sends a surge of primal satisfaction through me. A surge of possessiveness.

With a growl more like Bronson than me, I shred the front of her dress with my claws, making sure not to accidentally prick her skin. Only when they retreat back into my fingers do I touch her, running my bloody hands all across her supple belly and breasts. The red stains her skin as I flick her nipples, but she doesn't seem to mind, moaning wantonly and tossing her head back.

I fumble with the waistband of my pants, shoving them off and stroking my already erect cock. I might be crazier than Damien, but I legit got hard carving my name into Lionel's skin. And then I imagined fucking Nina over his bloody corpse, and I nearly came in my pants.

Behind Nina, Cain removes his own pants and shrugs out of his shirt. She doesn't hesitate to turn in his arms, running her hands all over his bloody skin. I push her hair to the side to plant kisses across her neck and then down her smooth skin. When I reach her pert ass, she gasps, clinging to Cain's shoulders, but I simply smirk devilishly and stab my tongue into her tight little hole. Using two hands, I hold her cheeks apart so I can tongue-fuck her properly, my tongue traveling from her pussy to her asshole and then back again.

"Abel," she gasps into Cain's mouth as he kisses her senseless, no doubt leaving bloody handprints all over her body. The thought only makes me harder, a feat I didn't think was anatomically possible.

"We want you, Nina," Cain murmurs against her lips. "At the same time."

She knows exactly what we mean, and I grin at the low moan that escapes her.

"Yes. God, yes." Like a good girl, she arches her ass in my face, and I lightly spank her cheek, watching it jiggle.

Satisfied that her ass has been properly lubed with my saliva, I move to my feet and wait until she's firmly placed on Cain's cock, his hands tweaking her beaded nipples, before I spit on my hand and rub it up and down my cock. That, combined with the juices from Nina's slick pussy, provides enough lubrication for me to slowly breach her tight ring of muscles. I work myself in slowly, desperate not to hurt her. Once I'm halfway, I pull out and drive back in, each thrust filling her ass until, on my third try, I'm all the way in.

We both groan at the contact, her back arching beautifully. Cain repeatedly peppers kisses across her face as she adjusts to our lengths inside of her.

"Is this okay, Trouble? Are you okay?"

"M-Move," she stammers. "I need you to move."

We fuck her with the reckless, primitive energy we felt in Damien's torture chamber, when we cut off Lionel's cock and tore him into pieces. When we spat on his dead body and laughed maniacally as his blood stained our skin.

But even his death pales in comparison the feeling of Nina wrapped around me.

I reach around us to cup her breasts, pinching her nipples, and she throws her head back with a cry of pleasure. The smell of vanilla invades my nostrils, and I breathe it in eagerly, allowing it to diminish the scent of copper permeating the air.

"Fuck, Trouble. Fuck," Cain groans out as he pounds into her. We find a rhythm that works for us—when he leaves her tight channel, I push in, my hands squeezing her breasts painfully. If it hurts her, she doesn't let it show, screaming our names with breathless wonderment and lust.

We work together to keep her constantly on edge, loving the way she cries out our names, demanding release.

My sweet, naughty little Bambi.

Cain lowers his hand to her clit while I tweak her nipples painfully, pulling them away from her bloody breasts and then releasing them.

"Oh my god!" she screams as she detonates around us. Cain grunts, his hips losing their rhythm as he explodes inside of her. My balls tighten, the feeling almost painful as I come as well, my cum dripping down her ass and legs.

And then we collapse on top of each other, a sweaty, bloody pile of limbs.

She doesn't ask us what occurred, but somehow, she seems to know. She always seems to know.

And somehow, someway, she was able to tame our inner demons until we slowly came back to ourselves, the darkness receding.

She accepts us—every bloody, dark, and dangerous facet.

Hell itself would have to come and claim me before I let anyone or anything hurt her or our unborn child.

Until death do us part, Nina.

Until death do us part.

CHAPTER 34

NINA

I wake sweaty and sated, comfortably nestled between my two twins. Sticky blood still coats my body from our lovemaking, but it doesn't negate what we did the night before. It was...perfect. From the rough way they grabbed me to the gentle kisses they showered me with afterwards.

For a brief moment, the two facets of my twins existed in harmony—the broken, rough edges combined with the smooth, gentle curves. Dark and light. Night and day.

I saw a side to my twins that I've never truly experienced before. Sure, Cain has always been curt and to the point, but I've never seen him completely unravel before. And Abel has always been my sunshine twin, emanating nothing but joy and positivity.

I'm grateful that they feel safe with me. That they're able to shed their skins and embrace their inner darkness.

My body is deliciously sore as I scramble out from between their bodies and fumble towards the sink. Fortunately, I'm familiar enough with the cell and don't need to rely on my powers to get there.

After using a washcloth to clean the dried, flaky blood from my body, I turn a blind gaze towards my sleepy twins. I can picture them with a startling clarity, despite my vision still being shrouded in darkness.

Their tousled, disheveled blond hair framing angelic faces. Their naked chest streaked with blood from my hands. Their mouths slightly open as they breathe deeply and evenly. The wanton part of me wants to wake them and demand a round two, but I know they need their sleep.

Instead, I reach blindly for my discarded dress, ignoring the copper blood I can smell on the fabric, and pull it on. It rubs deliciously against my sensitive breasts, and I rein in the urge to flick my nipples.

These men…

They're turning me into a sex-crazed fiend, and surprisingly enough, I don't care.

"Nina," a voice whispers, and I turn my head in Kai's direction automatically, a wide smile cracking my face in two.

"Hey, stranger," I reply back, keeping my voice low so as to not wake the twins. I stretch forward like a sunflower desperately seeking light, and not a second later, Kai's large hands are on my waist and his lips are traveling across mine. When I run my own hands from his shoulders down his chest, I realize that he's shirtless. I envision his impressive abs, covered in a myriad of colorful tattoos and scars, as my fingers dip into every nook and cranny. He shudders beneath my exploration but doesn't stop me until the tips of my fingers fiddle with the waistband of his sweatpants.

"Not here," he says simply, placing a finger to my lips. Before I can protest, he flips me over his shoulder, his hand smoothing over my butt, before moving to the bottom of my dress. His fingers slowly inch inside, touching my pussy lips—

"Baby." He freezes abruptly, his fingers in my swollen channel. "Are you not wearing underwear?"

"No," I respond innocently. "Is that a problem?"

He curses viciously, putting me back on my feet and straightening out my dress so I don't flash the entire prison. My silly, overprotective, possessive dragon.

"Fuck that," he snaps, grabbing my hand and dragging me behind him. I giggle at his tone, hurrying to keep pace with his long strides.

"You don't like the thought of the other inmates seeing my butt and pussy?" I tease, and suddenly, I'm pressed against the wall, his chest rubbing against my pebbled nipples deliciously as he leans in to nip my ear.

"That ass? That pussy? These perfect breasts…" His hands travel upwards to cup them, squeezing to the point of pain, before he releases them. "They're mine. Ours. Mine and your other mates. No one else can see them. You understand that? I'll kill anyone who looks. And that's not even an exaggeration, baby. I'll bury that fucker six feet underground if I have to."

I must truly be broken, for instead of instilling cold fear inside of me, his words make me unbelievably hotter. I attempt to rub my thighs together to alleviate the sudden ache there.

"You'll burn the bodies," I correct, panting, "not bury them."

He chuckles darkly before leaning down and kissing my nose.

"I'll do whatever the fuck I need to for you and our baby," he vows before pushing himself away from me, grabbing my hand, and then striding back down the hall once more. "Do you understand that, Nina? I don't care who I have to hurt. As long as you and the baby are okay, I'll do anything."

For some undefinable reason, a shiver works its way up

my spine. His words almost feel like a premonition, which is ridiculous.

I want to tell him that he can't sacrifice himself or the others for me, that a future isn't worth living if they aren't in it, but I keep my lips closed. Because for the first time in my life, I'm not just surviving for me and them. I have a new life I need to think about, one that is growing inside of me.

Instinctively, I drop my hands to my flat stomach, wishing desperately I could feel some sign that the baby is in there. A kick, perhaps. Or maybe even a fluttering heartbeat.

"We need to begin packing for the..." Kai doesn't voice the ending of that sentence, but we both know what he means. We need to finish packing for our escape.

It's decided that all of us—even me—will carry a bag with supplies. My men will have two each, while I'll only carry one. Even then, I have a feeling that within a few minutes of the journey, one of them will take the bag from me.

There's a lot of reasons for the multiple bags. For one, we don't know how long we'll be down there, so we don't know what we need to bring in order to survive. For two, if for some horrible reason we get separated, we'll always have our own supply of food and water to rely on. And finally, my men seem to believe that we'll need all the medical supplies we can find.

They attempted to travel through the Labyrinth when they were searching for me, and I saw through their eyes how dangerous and daunting it was.

The Labyrinth doesn't want us to leave.

Goosebumps erupt on my skin at the thought of what we have planned, and the cold wash of fear crashes through me like a tidal wave. The original anxiety squeezing my chest feels like a gentle hug in comparison to the sudden tightness now. My stomach roils dangerously, and my lips turn numb.

However, I push away the crippling fear and school my features before Kai can notice.

When we stop, I slip into his head to see we're in the kitchen—the same kitchen Bronson was shot in only a few days earlier and where I killed a man.

I swallow down the rising emotions, grateful when Kai's gaze doesn't flicker to the floor. I can still see the scene through Rion's eyes—the hole in the man's chest as blood pooled around him, his eyes glazed and unseeing, and then Bronson, his face ashen and sickly as he struggled to hold on to life.

Kai gives my hand a gentle squeeze, easily able to sense my distress, but thankfully, he doesn't comment. He doesn't poke and prod and demand that I give him more answers than I'm capable of.

Instead, he travels to one of the cupboards and pulls it open, grabbing cans at random.

"I have Rion grabbing medical supplies and Damien collecting weapons," Kai says, and I'm grateful that he's filling the silence with his voice. "You know what's funny?" He laughs, and there's a slightly hysterical edge to it that has me instantly on alert. "This Labyrinth has been operational for hundreds of years, and not once has someone attempted to escape. Most people know that it's foolish and suicidal." His hand trembles as he grabs another can. "But what can we do when the only other option is to die? To watch the woman you love die? To watch your unborn child die?"

"Kai..." I begin gently, but he continues on as if he didn't hear me. For all I know, he truly didn't.

"I don't know what I'd do if something happened to you. But at the same time, escaping isn't much better. There's a reason this is the most secure prison on the planet. There's no escape. It's foolish to even believe—"

"Kai." I move to stand in front of him, my face consuming his vision.

With a desperation I've never seen from him before, he places his forehead against mine, his breathing shallow and erratic.

"I'm so fucking scared," he confesses, trembling in my arms. "So fucking scared, Nina. I could lose everything in a span of seconds. My brothers. You. Our baby." His voice cracks, and I imagine that I'm the only one in the world he'll display such emotion to. He once told me that opening yourself up to someone requires a level of trust that is almost impossible to achieve. I'd scoffed at him, telling him he was too jaded and hard, but I know in my heart he was being sincere.

I'm probably the only person he'll allow himself to be vulnerable with, and he's terrified that he's going to lose me. I don't think he's ever experienced such gripping, stomach-churning fear before.

"I'm not going anywhere, Kai," I soothe, running my fingers through his shaggy hair. "I'm right here. I have you to protect me."

"But what if—"

"Nothing's going to happen to me." I plant a soft kiss to his cheek. "I have you to watch over me. Damien. Rion. Bronson. Abel. Cain. Heck, we even have Logan." I run my hands from his shoulders to his wrists and then back up again, repeating the circuit twice before I continue. "We're a team. All of us. You'll never let me down."

"But I did, baby," he says brokenly, his breath fanning against my lips with each exhale. I wish desperately I could see his eyes, those brown orbs that are so dark, they almost appear black in the right lighting. "In the Compound, I left you. I made you experience all of that shit by yourself."

"Hey!" I respond forcefully, removing my hands from his

shoulders to grip his cheeks. "Don't even talk like that. What happened was in no way your fault. You did everything you could to protect me in there. And it's *because* you protected me so well that Alyssa and Raphael decided to get rid of you." My voice wobbles as the enormity of my emotions for this man consumes me, eats me alive. "You were my best friend, Kai. I'm not sure if I truly knew what love was back in the Compound, but you were the one person I knew I could always rely on. You're like a beacon of light, disrupting the endless darkness I've grown accustomed to. I love you with every inch of my soul, Malakai. Forever and always."

"Fuck, I love you too." He claims my lips in a possessive kiss, one that speaks a thousand words he doesn't dare say out loud. I can sense his love and devotion for me and our baby, his fear that something will take me from him, his hope for a better future, and his guilt whenever he thinks about our turbulent pasts. "I thought about you every day while I was away," he confesses. "I never even looked at another girl because I knew I would somehow, someway find a way back to you. Of course, I wish the situations were different. I wish we weren't in this fucking prison and that we—"

I place a finger to his lips, cutting him off mid rant. "I wouldn't wish for anything else." Tears fill my eyes, but I don't bother to brush them away, wanting him to see my sincerity. "I found you again. I found the twins and Bronson. Damien and Rion. I found my family, Kai, and it's a beautiful thing. *We're* a beautiful thing. All of us." I feel my spine straighten as resolve settles in my gut, replacing the fear. "We're going to get out of this prison, Kai, and then we're going to start a family. All of us. I just wish... I just wish Jenny and Braelyn could come with us."

Kai smooths away my hair with hands so tender, no one would know they belong to a killer. But maybe it's because Kai's sins don't define him any more than mine do. To me, he'll always be that sweet, gentle man who loved me when I thought I was unlovable. Who saw the broken shards of me as something beautiful instead of things that needed to be thrown away.

"After our conversation the other day, Rion talked to them," Kai confesses. "We could see how unhappy you were, and we agreed that they should come with us. They're family." By the tenseness of his body, I can tell I'm not going to like the ending of this story. I wait with bated breath for him to gather his thoughts. "Nina, they chose to stay. I'm sure they'll talk to you about it at some point, but this Labyrinth is the only life they've ever known. They're happy here, and once we're gone, Braelyn will be ecstatic to be the queen." He chuckles darkly, and I can't stop my own grin from erupting on my face.

I can just picture my best friend cackling gleefully as she sits on Kai's throne, Jenny standing beside her. I don't know if Braelyn ever wanted a position of power, but I know she'll excel at it.

And Rion was right before.

She's one of my closest friends, all of the girls are, but I don't think any of them can survive outside of these walls. They're too bitter, too driven by bloodlust and hate, to be able to function in normal society.

That's not to say my guys are any different, because they're not, but I also know that they'll aim that bloodlust in the direction of my enemies, not random strangers.

That doesn't take away the sting I feel at leaving my friends behind. The guilt.

"There's something else I wanted to bring up to you while we're alone," I confess, chewing on my lower lip. Kai's eyes fixate on that before he forces himself to meet my gaze.

"What is it?"

"There's been someone...in my dreams." And then, I tell

him about Nick. About every interaction and the cloying darkness and the eyes I can constantly feel on me. I tell him about the note in Damien's jacket pocket and then the rose in bed with me, just before the siren attacked.

Kai goes rigid, his muscles like granite beneath my palms, but he doesn't interrupt until I finish speaking, my breath leaving me in a swooping exhale. It feels as if a heavy weight has been lifted from my chest, freeing me. I hadn't even realized how guilty I felt for keeping this a secret until now.

"Kai?" I ask worriedly when he doesn't immediately answer. Kai's silence is sometimes worse than his immediate and volatile anger.

"There's no one named Nick in the Labyrinth," Kai finally grits out, his voice like ice and chilling me to my very core. "He gave you a fake name." His hands grip my shoulders with an urgency I'm not familiar with, at least not coming from him. "And you're positive he didn't give you any more information? You never saw a face in your dreams?"

"No." My brows scrunch together as I think. "The only thing he said…" I lick my numb upper lip as anxiety floods me. "He claimed he was everywhere and nowhere. What does that mean, Kai? Who is he? Why is he entering my dreams? *How* is he even doing it?" Question after question bombards me as Kai's grip on my shoulder turns punishingly tight, the stress he feels over this situation bleeding through.

"I don't know, baby, but I promise you, I won't allow this *Nick* to hurt you." His voice shakes slightly with an almost incandescent rage. Warmth migrates through my body from where his hands press down on my shoulders. "No one will ever hurt you for as long as I live."

CHAPTER 35

NICK

I watch her with the dragon, her head resting on his chest as he wraps his arms around her thin waist. Her black hair falls around her, creating soft shadows on her high, chiseled cheekbones. The contrast of those onyx locks against her pale face only serves to make her more alluring, more haunting. When she turns, her eyes remind me of streaks of bright, white sunlight, warming my frigid bones.

Mine.

She is a thing of beauty, something so ethereal that I find myself unable to peel my gaze away. As dark as she is light, she is the perfect dichotomy.

The shadows have been my home for as long as I can remember, for as long as I have *existed*.

But the moment my gaze landed on Nina Doe, I knew I would do something I never thought myself capable of—leave the darkness and embrace the light.

For her, I will climb out of the abyss. For her, I will no longer merely stalk the shadows, but the light as well.

Everything is for her. Always.

But for now, I watch. Observe. Listen.

The time will come when I will claim my sweet girl, but until then, I will remain in the dark.

CHAPTER 36

LOGAN

I don't have a lot of belongings.

Actually, I have nothing but the clothes on my back, and even they don't belong to me.

Once a thief, always a thief.

Nobody notices me as I stand near the back of the throne room, counting the number of cans we decided to bring with us on our trip.

Inventory. That's all I'm good for, apparently. But I find that I don't give a damn if I'm the group's whipping boy, their little bitch. As long as it gets me out of this prison once and for all.

As long as I can stay with *her*.

Nothing matters anymore except that. Not what I was supposed to do when I was sent to this prison. Not what I *should* do. Only her. If I were a religious man, I would think she was sent here by God himself to free me from my past, from the chains that bind me.

But I'm not. And if a higher power does exist, he surely doesn't give a fuck about me.

My feelings for her...

They're unnatural.

One second, we were strangers, and the next, I wanted to worship at her feet, a humbled man bowing to his queen.

It's almost as if she's my fated mate, which is completely ridiculous. Laughable even.

A girl like her? The universe would never choose a man as fucked up as me to be her mate. And despite the tugging in my chest drawing me to her, I don't dare look and see if the sensation I feel is a mate bond.

Because if it isn't, if I discover she truly isn't meant to be mine, then I would give up. What's the fucking point when the one thing I want can never belong to me? Despite my wistful fantasies, I know in the darkest recesses of my heart that she can never be mine.

But maybe…

Maybe I can be hers.

I will my eyes not to flicker towards her face, though it's damn hard. It takes every ounce of self-control I possess to keep my gaze on the worn backpacks, even though I can sense her presence. It's…like sunlight. No, maybe sunlight is the wrong descriptor for Nina Doe. It's moonlight, pure and simple. The type of moonlight that bathes a starless night with rays of silvery white, disrupting the darkness we've grown accustomed to. Maybe living in the shadows isn't the worst fate a person can have, if it means having someone like Nina.

Bitterness engulfs me when I remember that I *don't* have her. She doesn't even know I exist. But why would she, when she has six doting mates following her around like besotted puppies? And what good am I to her anyway?

I'm just a pretty face whose entire life is made up of secrets and lies. A wet dream on the outside, a monster on the inside.

Once a liar, always a liar.

"We only get one chance to do this," I hear Bronson say from behind me, his gruff voice more wolf than man. I pause in my counting to listen intently to their conversation. "If we attempt this and fail, the entire Labyrinth will know. It'll be nearly impossible for us to regain our power, even with Braelyn backing us. And if the warden or the guards discover the truth…"

"We'll make it," Kai snaps, though when I twist my head slightly to peer at his face, I see the skin under his eyes lined violet with exhaustion. "You wanted us to leave, Bron. Don't you forget that."

"And I do," Bronson insists. "You know that. But I just…" He releases a heavy sigh, and I imagine he's running a hand through his blond hair. It's something he always seems to do when he's stressed or anxious.

There are benefits to being a social pariah, virtually ignored unless they're in need of you. You notice things and behaviors. Develop the ability to read people.

"We'll protect Nina and our baby," Kai assures his friend softly, their voices moving across the throne room as they prepare for the journey.

Baby.

My heart skips a beat at the thought of Nina with child. I don't know why—she's not my…anything, and I'll have no spot in that child's life. I'll be lucky if the guys don't sacrifice me to ensure Nina's survival.

Though maybe I wouldn't mind being a delicious, bite-sized human sacrifice. Not if it meant keeping Nina and that kid safe.

A surge of protectiveness and *possessiveness* rushes through me, my veins alight with white-hot fire. I quickly tamp down those ridiculous emotions before I turn into a Gollum version of Bronson, hiding Nina in the corner of the room and baring my teeth while murmuring, *"My precious."*

"Hey," a gentle voice says from over my shoulder, and my damn, traitorous heart flatlines before picking up speed with a ruthless vengeance. I don't want to look at her, I truly, honest to God don't, but I find myself turning anyway, my pulse skittering pathetically, too enamored with having her near.

Nina smiles at me, all smooth curves and gentle edges compared to my straight lines and brutal cuts.

Maybe that's why I'm so attracted to her—because she's so inherently *good*. I never detect any malice in her voice or any ulterior motives in her actions. There's no deceit in what she says, and that's rare in most people. As a cupid, I'm capable of sensing bonds of love and lust between individuals, but I've never seen a love as pure as Nina's. I suppose on a color scale, you could think of the bonds to be some combination of black and white. The love that is tainted by abuse or scandal or cheating is as dark as pitch, thrumming erratically and violently like a live wire that's been cut and is now whipping around and sparking at everyone who comes too close. This dark bond makes people jaded to love.

And then there's Nina's love. So pure. So brilliant. So... clean. There's no bitterness or jealousy or fear. She trusts her men implicitly to protect and love her until the day she dies, and their responding feelings are the same.

I'm man enough to admit that I'm jealous. I want that with someone, a love so strong and fierce that it's unlike anything the world has ever seen before. Correction—I want that with *her*. But I can't, not with the secrets burying me beneath layers of concrete and sand.

The muscles in my shoulders are so tense, they physically spasm, and I distractedly scratch the nape of my neck, avoiding eye contact once more. Not that it makes a fucking difference, considering she's blind. Though if she decided to travel into my head, I'll be damned if she notices how intently I watch her.

"You know that we're grateful you decided to come with us," Nina begins in that sweet, soft voice that never fails to make my dick hard.

Would it be horribly inappropriate if I began to talk to it, warning it to calm the fuck down? My cock, I mean.

I huff out a dry, humorless laugh. "It's not like I have much of a choice, princess," I say, the endearment slipping from my tongue before I can stop it. Fuck. There's a reason I've been calling her Nina Doe, and it isn't because I particularly enjoy her made up last name. No, I need to start distancing myself from her. Reminding myself that these feelings…they're one-sided. The sooner I can vanquish them, the happier we both will be.

And maybe feeling indifference towards her will assuage the guilt that rises within me.

Unable to look too closely at the plethora of emotions churning in my stomach, I turn away from her and give her my back.

But she's not one to be deterred.

When her hand rests on my arm, I jump, trying to ignore the heat that migrates from her palm across my bare skin. I try for a smile she can't see, but my skin is tingling in the worst way, like electricity is trapped in my veins and I'm being burned alive. How can a simple touch do that to me? Unravel me so effortlessly? "Seriously, Logan. Thank you. I know that it isn't safe—"

"I want to get out of this prison just as much as you do." My tone is acerbic, almost bitter, but I don't pull my eyes away from the cans to see if it hurts her. "Leaving has nothing to do with you."

It has everything to do with you.

Her hand slides from my arm, and I immediately want to take the words back, want to shove them back into my throat and swallow them whole. But I don't. I can't. Not after—

Not after what I did. What I plan to do.

When Nina releases a heavy sigh and begins to walk away, I feel a piece of my heart shatter and crumble into dust. I know that I'll never get that tiny piece back, and a part of me doesn't want to. I deserve to bleed, to make peace with the darkness.

"Braelyn!" Nina exclaims abruptly, and I turn away from the cans just in time to see her embrace a short girl with light brown hair. A second girl stands beside the first, her shy eyes flickering from face to face without sticking on one person in particular. Braelyn and Jenny. I've seen them around the prison before, and of course I know who they are, but I haven't been formally introduced.

I mean, why would anyone introduce the stupid cupid? I'm nothing to these people. Just a means to an end.

But if their end correlates with my own...

"I'm so sorry," Nina chokes out as she tightens her grip on her friend. Braelyn shushes her and begins to stroke her hair like a mother would a child. "You've been such a good friend—"

"None of that," Braelyn reprimands, finally pulling away enough to stare Nina down. "You're not leaving us behind, Nina. We're *choosing* to stay." Braelyn releases Nina to grasp Jenny's hand, squeezing in a show of solidarity. Her eyes are sad, though, when she faces Nina once more. "The Labyrinth is the only home we've ever known. I don't think I could survive out there in the real world. I'm too...hard. I rely on bloodshed. I *like* it here, Nina. We like it here." Braelyn turns her soft glance onto Jenny, gently smoothing away a wayward strand of hair. Jenny offers her a smile of her own, and I can see the bright bond between them. Their pure love for one another.

"But—" Nina begins, and Braelyn cuts her off.

"They asked us if we wanted to go with them," she admits, turning towards first Kai and then Rion. The latter stands with the twins, his features uncharacteristically grave as he stares at his second-in-command and friend. "But we both agreed it's not worth it. I don't want to risk our lives on a 'maybe,' Nina." She smiles to take the sting out of her words. "But if anyone is capable of doing the impossible, it's you, my dear friend. You've managed to unite the gangs in prison. You became the fucking queen. So I'm asking you to leave me, to not feel any guilt, and find a life for yourself and your men. If anyone in this godforsaken place deserves it, it's you."

Tears stream down Nina's face as she grips Braelyn's hands. "You've been such a good friend, Braelyn. I'm going to miss you."

"I'm going to miss you too." Braelyn sniffles and scowls, as if she's holding back tears and is pissed because of that. "But don't worry about me and Jenny. Hell, don't worry about Rebecca or Haley either. You know we'll protect them."

At that, Kai's face distorts into a scowl, though he clears it before anyone can notice.

What the fuck was that about?

"I know you will." Nina gives Braelyn another squeeze, just as Kai slips out the side door. I watch him go with furrowed brows before I focus on Nina once more. "I love you, Braelyn. Forever and always."

"Forever and always." Braelyn steps away and begins to wipe desperately at her eyes, just as Nina embraces Jenny as well, whispering something in her ear too low for me to hear.

I'm struck again by this woman's kindness. By her ability to see past a person's sins to the soul underneath.

Feelings like I've never felt before burst to life inside of me, feeling unbelievably warm and toasty.

But these feelings? They can't exist. I can't allow them to.

Cupids are meant to sense love, not be *in* love.

The sooner I get out of here, the sooner I can forget about Nina Doe once and for all.

CHAPTER 37

KAI

I find Rebecca in her usual cell, one that she shares with Haley.

She sits on her cot, a blanket on her lap as she flips through the pages of a book. Despite her hands moving, her eyes don't appear to be reading the words, a forlorn expression in her teal gaze. The robust woman barely glances up when I enter, though I can tell she senses my presence when her hands freeze.

"You know." It's not a question or even an accusation. Instead, it's a tired statement that leaves her lips on a heavy sigh.

"I didn't. At least, not for sure." I fold my arms against my chest and lean against the opened bars of her cell. At one point, the guards closed them every night to lock us monsters away. But when we overran the prison and kicked them out, all of the cells remained open. It's both a blessing and a threat. You can never close your eyes in this prison when there's no place for you to hide and escape. It's why gangs formed and alliances began. People are desperate to protect themselves against the killers who stalk in the shadows.

Like me.

Like Rebecca.

"I know you used to work for Lionel," I continue, watching her reaction carefully. There's not a flicker of surprise as she finally drops her book and folds her hands together in her lap. They're shaking, tiny trembles that reverberate through her entire body, but I can't find it within me to care.

"I was his secretary," Rebecca admits without preamble, though I already knew that. I knew that years ago, when the older woman was first brought into the prison, sniveling and sobbing. I had Tessa take her under her wing and show her the ropes. Despite her previous relationship with Lionel, I never questioned her alliance to me and my people. Not until now.

"And you were his lover." I have the immense satisfaction of seeing surprise in her gaze before she smooths her expression out. Now, this...this I didn't learn years ago. I only put the pieces together recently when Damien told me what Lionel confessed to, how it was a woman inside of the prison whom he contacted.

There are thirty-three women in prison, but only one of them ever had contact with the disgusting, vile man. I placed a call to a released inmate in the outside world and confirmed that Rebecca had in fact been in a relationship with Lionel Green...until she went crazy and murdered everyone on his staff. She claimed that she did it because she was tired of his brutal nature, that she hated the man with a searing passion.

Passion was involved, but I don't think it was hate she felt when she killed those people.

"I didn't even put it together until recently," I continue,

watching as her face pales beneath her dark red hair. I shouldn't enjoy the fear I evoke in her as much as I do, but I never claimed not to be a twisted, demented monster. But I'm Nina's monster, which is why this conversation has to be made before we can leave. "You killed those people—Lionel's staff—with a bomb, didn't you?"

Her hands shake as she smooths them down her dark, faded skirt. There are numerous holes adorning the fabric, because unlike Nina, she doesn't have anyone to gift her new clothes. If she would've asked, we would've happily given her some, just because she was Nina's friend. Perhaps she was trying to avoid being on our radar. Perhaps she felt guilt. I suppose I'll never know for sure.

"I discovered Lionel was fucking his intern," she confesses in a breathy whisper. "But I swear to you, I didn't know he was fucking the twins as well. I didn't know about the sick sex club. Not until I arrived here. And I wasn't lying about hating the man. I *do* hate him." Tear tracks mar her pudgy cheeks as she wipes them away with the back of her hand.

"Then why did you do it?" I demand when she finally turns to stare at me. I'm not gonna lie—the guilt and regret in her gaze give me a pause, but I force my features to harden before she can see me crack. Nina has made me soft, but she hasn't made me weak. I'll do what I always do to protect my family, even if it means killing one of Nina's only friends.

"Lionel reached out to me a few months earlier." Rebecca's hands twitch in her lap as she holds my gaze. "He had the hit list, and he wanted me to pass it around the Labyrinth. He offered me—" She hiccups, squeezing her eyes shut as more tears cascade down her face. "He offered me money. A *lot* of money. Just to give the list to some of the men inside of here. I have children, Kai. You know this."

"Blade," I interrupt forcefully, and she winces at my acerbic tone. "You will call me Blade."

"Blade," she corrects automatically, her voice frail and tiny. "I have children, Blade, and this money would help put them through college."

I throw my head back in dry, humorless laughter. "But that wasn't enough for you, was it? Not only did you try to kill us all by handing out the hit list, but you also attempted to kill Nina with that bomb."

Rebecca's shaking her head vehemently before I even finish talking. "I *never* planned to hurt that sweet girl. That bomb was meant for Damien." She cants her head down to stare at her interlocked fingers, still resting on her lap. "He's a serial killer, an assassin, a monster. I thought I would be doing the world a favor if he was dead. And you can't judge me for that."

"And the reward money was just a happy bonus, wasn't it?" I scoff at her ridiculous mentality. If she truly thinks killing someone for money makes her a better person, then she's more delusional than I thought. We're all monsters here, and no sweet words or false promises will change that.

"If it makes any difference, I'm grateful no one was seriously hurt," Rebecca offers, her voice subdued. Defeated. She knows she's fucked up, and now she's paying the price. There's a reason I'm the king of this prison, why my nickname is Blade. Justice is always served in a quick, timely manner, usually by my hand. "I never wanted..." She takes a shuddering breath, her shoulders seeming to reach her ears before lowering. "I never wanted people to die. I did what I had to do to survive. You understand that, don't you? I did it for family."

And maybe...

And maybe I do understand that, in a twisted, demented way. I know I would do anything for the people I love. Sacrifice anything. Maybe we're not that different after all. Just two monsters struggling in a world full of shadows and malevolent silhouettes and moonless skies.

"Are you going to kill me?" Rebecca spears me in place with her teal gaze, her eyes glimmering with tears. It makes her look younger. Not months or even years, but centuries. In her gaze, I see the woman who befriended Nina, who loves her children fiercely, even from within the confines of prison.

"No." That one word shocks both of us. I can see confusion and hope splay themselves across her face, dashing away instantly with my next words. "But your fate will be left entirely in Braelyn's hands. I won't kill you because I know that would hurt Nina, but I can't promise you anything beyond that. If you die, it won't be at my hands."

Rebecca's lower lip trembles, because she knows as well as I do that Braelyn has never been lenient when it comes to her punishments. Maybe, just maybe, Braelyn will offer Rebecca a second chance, but we both know that chance is slim.

I watch a myriad of emotions cross her face, before it finally settles on grim resolve. She has accepted her fate, though I can tell it's taking everything within her not to argue. Not to fight tooth and nail.

After all, we only become predators because we want to survive.

"I agree to those terms," Rebecca whispers at last, lowering her gaze back to her hands. Hands that created a weapon that sent Rion to the infirmary. That could've killed Nina. They don't look like a murderer's hands, but then again…are they supposed to? Does a killer have a black stain somewhere that the entire world can see? And I'm not talking about the stain on a killer's soul.

My own hands are colored red with blood. Does that make me any better than Rebecca? Do I even want to be?

The inmates of Nightmare Penitentiary have simply accepted the shadows. Me? I command them.

As I leave her cell, my whole body sluggish and heavy, as if the entire force of Earth's gravity is pushing down on me, I notice Haley standing against the wall, her mouth agape and tears in her eyes. It's apparent she heard everything Rebecca confessed to, that she knows the truth about her best friend.

As her gaze hardens, I realize that death might be the best option for Rebecca. It might be her *only* option. Without us at her back, without Haley and Braelyn and Jenny…

She's alone.

And lone wolves never survive for long.

CHAPTER 38

NINA

It's funny how you can talk for hours about something you plan to do, but the second that moment actually arrives, you freeze. Insidious terror unfurls in your stomach like a wilted flower, its petals an inky black that droop in death and decay. Your heart stutters and gets caught in your throat, the feeling reminiscent of a garrote cutting into your neck.

And suddenly, you think of everything that can go wrong. Of all the people you're leaving behind. Of the pain you'll potentially endure. And you wonder…is it worth it?

Is escaping worth the risks?

I shuffle from foot to foot as I stand between the twins, using Cain's eyes for guidance.

The Labyrinth stands before us, numerous passageways leading in every direction. Some will lead us to salvation, others to death.

Kai stands near the front of the group, a large backpack slung over his shoulders as he stares into the endless abyss. He holds a flashlight in one hand and a knife in the other.

Finally, he turns around, focusing on each of us before his

gaze rests on me. Resolve settles across his face as he turns towards Rion and Damien, standing directly behind him and in front of me and the twins.

Logan and Bronson are watching our rear.

"Let's go."

Two words. That's it. But with those two words, my entire life changes irrevocably. Either we'll escape this prison and the horrors inside of it…or we'll die trying.

According to my men, the farther away we get from the main portion of the Labyrinth, the one that houses the cells and the cafeteria, the more traps we'll run into. The more the sentient maze will shift and contort in an attempt to disorient us, until we're trapped in its thrall forever.

I tentatively begin to follow the group forward, my heart racing and my blood spiked with fear.

"Hey." Abel places a hand on my bare upper arm as we walk, directing both my and Cain's attention towards him. His green-gold eyes remind me of spring with little bits of fall flecked through. I only recently learned about the seasons. When you're a prisoner for years, there are certain things that just aren't clear, like there are names for when the leaves fall from the trees and a blanket of snow canvases the landscape. It was only when I made a comment to Cain about the snowy months that he asked, "Do you mean winter?"

The memory makes me smile before fear twists my mouth into something between a frown and a grimace.

I can feel panic clawing at me, keener than the blades in my men's hands.

"Hey," Abel stresses again, pausing to grip my face between both of his hands. "Everything is going to be fine, you hear me? Nothing is going to happen to you or the baby."

My hands drop to my belly instinctively, as they always

do when anyone mentions the little ball of life growing inside of me.

"It's not us that I'm worried about," I whisper sincerely, distantly aware that my other men have stopped too. We've only made it one freaking step into the Labyrinth, and I'm already second-guessing everything, wondering if we made the right decision.

"Nina." Through Cain's eyes, I watch Abel's pink lips curve into a wicked smile. "Let's play a game." He releases my face to take my hand, and we begin to walk once more. Cain's eyes drift from my face, towards the walls on either side of us. This particular hallway is constructed from dark brick, the ground littered with loose rocks and disgusting puddles of sludgy-brown water. Even more water drips from rusted metal pipes running across the ceiling, though my guys told me we wouldn't be able to follow them to an exit. Apparently, there are hundreds and hundreds of them, and all of them stop in random places throughout the Labyrinth. It'd be impossible to find which one actually leads out of this place.

Just another tool designed to disorient and confuse us.

"A game?" I parrot robotically, pulling Cain's attention back to me. In front of us, Kai, after consulting quietly with Rion and Damien, veers to the right, under a large archway that's graffitied in what looks like dark, red paint.

Or dried blood.

"Would you rather...cut off your pinkie or lose all of your nails?" Abel questions cheerfully.

"Abel!" Cain snaps, but Abel simply throws his head back in laughter.

"It's an honest question!" he defends around his chuckles, giving my hand a reassuring squeeze. To me, he asks, "Well?"

"What type of game is this?" I mutter, wincing at phantom pain, but he simply laughs harder. "Um..." I tap a finger to my chin in contemplation. "Well, I had my fingernails ripped off before at the Compound. That hurt. A lot. So I guess I'll say goodbye to my pinkie."

Too late, I realize that every man present has heard my words. The mood around us darkens considerably, curling around me like smoke.

Abel frowns, his face so pinched, you'd think he just swallowed a lemon.

"Sorry." I blanch as Cain leads me around a particularly deep puddle, the liquid appearing thick and sappy like black tar. "Probably shouldn't bring up stuff like that."

"No, Bambi," Abel says sadly. "You should bring that shit up. You should be able to talk to us about what you went through. It's just—"

"Hard for us to hear," Cain cuts in. He gently runs his hand through my black hair, the color appearing almost purple from the dim light emitting from the walls, and I smile, feeling his warmth blaze through me. "Now," he continues, changing the subject, "would you rather eat candy for every meal for the rest of your life or never eat candy again?"

"Candy every meal for the rest of my life, man!" Abel rubs his hands together gleefully. "Maybe then my cum will taste like chocolate."

"There's medication for that!" Rion calls cheerfully from in front of us. "It's called Chocolate A La Dick."

"I want a chocolate dick," I exclaim automatically, and I swear every man groans.

"No more dicks for you!" Kai cuts in vehemently. "You have e-fucking-nough."

"But Rion said—"

"A big, yummy chocolate dick?" Abel interrupts, and I can hear the amusement lacing his voice. Though Cain isn't looking at his twin, I imagine Abel's eyes are sparkling with humor. "Do you think you can swallow an entire chocolate dick, Bambi?"

"Probably." I shrug my shoulders as we turn down yet another hall. I have no idea how Kai is choosing where to go —maybe just blind luck? Hope? Faith? "I think I could easily swallow a chocolate dick."

Bronson growls from behind me, the low, primitive noise heating my core, as Abel chuckles.

"You know that any cocks added to this arrangement has to be agreed upon by us first, right?" Cain snaps, sounding irrationally jealous. What the heck?

"Wait!" I remove my hand from Abel's and hold both of them in the air. "We're talking about a type of candy, right?"

"I once tried to eat my own dick," Rion chimes in conversationally. "I'd been working on my gymnastics skills, okay, and I grabbed a bottle of chocolate syrup. Keep in mind, I was extremely flexible at the time—"

"Everybody stop!" Kai's shout is so sudden that I nearly stumble over my own two feet at the force of it. Fortunately, Cain and Abel both grab one of my arms, pulling me even tighter between them.

"What?" Bronson snaps, but it's not Kai who answers.

Damien's ice-blue eyes snap to my face before he slowly lowers his gaze to the ground. Cain does as well, and a tiny gasp leaves my lips when I see what holds my men's attention.

Though the ground appears to be made from cement, it's...cracking. Cracking like it's actually a thin layer of ice. Like it's a pond that has frozen over and oblivious kids decided to traipse across its length.

The jagged lines start directly beneath Kai's feet and expand outwards, almost like the gossamer strings of a spiderweb. As we stand, breaths bated, more and more cracks begin to form on the gray floor below us.

My pulse races, the sloshing of blood in my head so loud and so deafening that I barely hear Kai when he bellows, "Run!"

Cain and Abel tighten their grip on my upper arms as they run as fast as they can towards a section of the flooring that is a darker gray than the rest—the only part that isn't mottled and distorted with cracks.

And then...

The floor crumbles beneath our feet, caving in on itself, just as we reach the dark gray cement.

"Bronson!" I scream as I watch my shadow wolf's arms pinwheel as he attempts to find solid ground. Diminutive shards of stone crumble beneath his feet, and then he's falling, falling, falling—

It's that type of moment when time stops. I'm actually sure it ceases to exist, suspended between now and the uncertain and precarious future, like a snapshot you're unable to look away from. Wild, primal fear takes over me, a tiny voice screaming in my head but the words are incoherent. Desperation streaks through me like lightning.

No. No. No no no no. Nononono.

Logan materializes in my vision, his lithe body leaning over the edge, and grips Bronson's arm, just as the final section of floor falls away, leaving nothing but a gaping pit behind. Before even a second can tick by, the rest of my men are at the ledge as well, pulling Bronson onto solid ground.

Where there was once solid flooring is now nothing but a dark, endless abyss. It seems to go on for miles and miles and miles. Honestly, I wonder if it ever ends, if you'll fall and fall and fall until your heart eventually gives out.

That could've been Bronson.

I don't even realize I'm crying until my burly wolf shifter crawls towards me. I throw myself into his arms without preamble, squeezing him like the fate of the universe depends on it.

And since he just so happens to be the center of mine at that moment, I guess it really does.

"Are you okay?" I ask desperately, pulling myself away long enough to run the pads of my fingers across his face, down his smooth-shaven cheekbones, through his shaggy blond hair, much longer than it was when I first met him.

"I'm okay," he assures me, but all I can think of is, *what if?*

What if Logan hadn't been with us, hadn't grabbed Bronson's arms before he could fall with the rest of the floor?

What if I lost Bronson?

Oh God.

I curl my arms around Bronson's neck and brush my lips against his, the simple touch igniting my desperation and need. My fingers dig into his blond hair, and I know that I could fall forever into him and he'll never let me hit the ground.

"I was so worried," I whisper when we finally part, his forehead resting against my own.

It only lasted a few seconds, but I swear my soul was wrenched from my body. I imagine it would've followed Bronson into that abyss without a second thought. Because without him, without all of them, I'm not sure I'm capable of being whole.

I truly believe that our jagged edges fit together perfectly, making it so we no longer feel as broken.

I twist my head to face where I know Logan to be standing, allowing my sincerity to bleed through my voice. "Thank you," I whisper. "Thank you for saving him."

And then I turn back to Bronson and kiss him like the entire world will stop spinning if I don't.

CHAPTER 39

BRONSON

I thought myself to be desensitized to death. That's not to say that I'm completely clueless to the Grim Reaper lurking in the shadows, holding a shining scythe and dressed in a dark robe, but I've seen too much of it to really give it a second thought.

But that feeling of falling, the weightlessness…

It's a harsh reminder that death waits around every corner, that no man or woman is able to escape its possessive grip.

No baby, either.

My eyes drift to Nina beside me as we once again continue our trek through the Labyrinth's tunnels.

I don't know what I'd do if anything happened to her and our baby. Kai… He'd have no reason to live anymore. That's fucked up, but we all know it's true. He wouldn't hesitate to put a bullet through his brain. And the twins—they'd have each other, but they'd never be right in the head again. Cain would lose himself to the darkness, and this time, he'd take Abel with him. And without Nina, Damien is a kindling doused in gasoline, just waiting for the flame to hit it. Heaven only knows what'd he do, who he'd kill, before death eventually claimed him. And he'd embrace it eagerly, with a wide smile on his face. Rion would destroy the entire fucking world…or himself. I can't tell you for sure which one. I truly believe that the last strand of his sanity would sever like a cord being cut in two.

And me…

Could I go on without her? Knowing that I'd never see her face again or hear her laugh? Knowing that she'd never smile up at me with those beautiful white eyes? I know I'd never be able to fall in love again, but could I survive it? Could I survive her death?

No. I don't think I could.

I can't let her out of my fucking sight.

"When we were down here before," I begin gruffly, startling her. From the owlish look on her face, I take it she's been lost in her own head, just as I've been. Clearing my throat, I try again. "When we were down here before, when you were kidnapped by Alyssa…well, you saw what we went through." I frown, remembering the walls of nails and the swinging machetes and all of the other horrors we faced. "What I mean is, we don't know what to expect. Not really. Since the pathway always changes, we never experienced two of the same traps."

Fuck, for some reason, I'm trying to justify myself to her. To explain why I almost fucking died and left her.

I think a part of me just needs to remind her that I'll never purposely leave her, that I'll fight tooth and nail to remain by her side. If I had fallen into that black pit, I would've quite literally clawed my way back to the top.

Nothing can keep me from her and that child.

"I know." Her smile is soft, tentative, but it illuminates her features like a giant spotlight. My breath hitches at how fucking gorgeous she looks right now. How could I have ever been with other women? They may as well be flashlights next to the brilliance of the sun. "If Logan hadn't..." She trails off, that smile disappearing from her face as quickly as it appeared.

I begrudgingly glance backwards at the cupid, his eyes trained on the walls as he searches for more hidden traps. I really need to thank the fucker for saving my life. He didn't have to—we all know that he could've let me fall and no one would've been the wiser. Yet he risked his own life to save mine. I could've just as likely pulled him in after me.

He's...what? Two hundred pounds soaking wet, if that? It's a miracle he was able to hold me up for even a split second.

"What's the plan?" Nina asks abruptly, and I blink at her, my gaze studying her angelic profile with undeterred intensity. "I mean, when we make it out of here. Where will we go?"

"We have a few options," I confess. "My family is more than willing to hide us for the time being." I lower my gaze to where my hand interlocks with hers. I love the difference in our skin tone—hers so creamy, it could be a strand of moonlight bottled up. And mine as golden as the sun.

Night and day, side by side.

The smile slips from my face, because truth be told, that story is kind of a fucking tragedy. The moon constantly chases the sun, never able to get a hold of her. It's a never-ending cycle of unreciprocated love and need. Or maybe I got it all wrong. Maybe the sun and moon actually despise each other and are desperately attempting to escape one another.

Either way, a fucking tragedy.

Kai pauses up ahead, holding up a single fist to instruct us to stop as well. I drop Nina's hand and wrap my arm around her waist, holding her tightly against me as I survey what's captured the group's attention.

Up ahead, the pathway forks in two. One hallway is significantly smaller than the other, appearing as if it'll barely fit my body through.

It's also covered in nails. Tiny nails, long ones, rusty ones…but all sharp.

A hallway of sharp fucking nails we'll need to cross to get through.

The other one is significantly larger, easily able to fit two people shoulder to shoulder, but a green goo is dripping from the walls. I can't quite tell what the substance is, but even more covers the flooring. The entire air is contaminated with a lime-green mist that takes up every inch of airspace.

"Well this is like my fifth family reunion all over again," the crazy shifter exclaims, clapping his hands together.

Cain's eyes narrow as he steps in front of Kai, surveying first the hallway of nails and then the one of green goo.

"Which one are we going through, boss man?" Abel tries to smile, but it wobbles when his gaze flickers to Nina. He's scared, but the asshole will never show it. No, he'll remain the flippant, debonair flirt until his last fucking moment. But at the same time, I can tell his lighthearted tone has a calming effect on Nina. The iron grip she has on my hand loosens slightly as her shoulders relax with her next exhale.

Over her head, I give Abel a pointed look and nod almost imperceptibly. Easily reading my unspoken message, Abel sidles up to Nina and rests his elbow on her shoulder.

"Would you like to be *nailed*, Bambi?" he questions, his voice oozing sexual innuendo. She scoffs, but there's a tiny glimmer in her eyes that wasn't there prior.

"You're ridiculous." She giggles, and I swear all six of us—seven, if you include that fucker Logan—breathe easier at the sound.

"Don't you mean ri-*dick*-ulous," Abel stresses, grinning. "And I'm talking about my dick, if you didn't gather that already. Once we get out of this place, I'm gonna dick you real hard on an actual comfy bed. You hear me?"

"Oh my god!" Her cheeks flame, but I know we have her distracted. For now, at least.

As Abel describes to Nina in explicit, R-rated detail all the things he plans to do to her to celebrate our escape, Kai nods at Cain.

The sex demon takes a shuddering breath, his shoulders so taut they reach his ears, and moves towards the hallway lathered in the disgusting green goo. He squeezes his eyes shut, reaches towards the nearest glob hanging from the ceiling like a demented icicle, and touches the tip of his bare fingers against it.

And immediately screams in utter agony, his face creasing with pain.

"Fuck! Oh shit! Fuck! Fuck! Fuck!"

"Cain!"

Nina starts running towards him, but he holds up the hand that isn't covered in the green go and shouts, "Stay back!"

I band my arm around her waist and hold her against me, even as she struggles.

"What the fuck happened?" Abel's face is pale as he hurries towards his brother, eyeing the green goo like you would a rabid dog, one that's foaming at the mouth in its attempt to get to you.

"It feels like it's eating away my skin!" Cain bellows through gritted teeth.

"Oh God." Nina finally stops struggling and rests against

me, her breathing uneven. "We should just go back. We should just—"

"We can't." Damien strolls towards Cain with that ineffably calm stare of his, flipping a dagger over and over again in his hand. But even with his feigned nonchalance, I can see how stressed he is. There's a tightness around both of his eyes that belies his easygoing disposition. "There's no way we'll be able to find our way back now." He physically forces Abel aside, removes his suit coat, and then rips off the sleeve of his white dress shirt. With slow, careful movements, he begins to wipe away the goo on Cain's hand, ignoring the way the sex demon hisses and grunts in pain.

"Can't you, like, sense other people?" Nina demands, turning to focus on Logan. The cupid has been uncharacteristically quiet since we first entered the tunnels, almost subdued. Violet shadows line both of his eyes as he lifts his head to stare at her.

"Normally, I can. But for some reason, the power of the Labyrinth is—" He hesitates, glancing warily from Nina's face to mine. "It's fucking with my cupid magic."

"You gotta be fucking kidding me!" Rion sneers, for once sounding completely coherent...and pissed as fuck. He unleashes the hurricane force of his stare on Logan. "Wasn't that the whole reason we took you with us? To use your powers? To sense other inmates and guards?"

"How was I supposed to know that my powers wouldn't work?" Logan's hands ball into fists, and I can't help but grin. Apparently, the little church boy has more fight in him than I initially expected.

Kai's voice is curt when he speaks next, his nostrils flaring. "Logan's right. I'm even having trouble accessing my dragon."

"My magic is...weak at the moment," Damien declares,

though reluctantly, as if it pains him to confess that he isn't almighty at the moment.

We all turn towards Nina, who, up to now, has been silent. As if she can feel the combined weight of our stares, she shifts in my arms.

"I feel perfectly fine," she confesses, shrugging her tiny shoulders. "But I haven't tried to do anything too extreme."

"It's the power of the Labyrinth," Damien explains coldly, finally removing the ripped cloth from Cain's hand. I make a face when I see the condition of his skin—dark red interspersed with light pink and white, all of it appearing sticky and bloody.

The goo burnt his skin away.

"At least, that's my theory," Damien continues as he waits for Abel to grab gauze from his backpack, and I can tell he's struggling to keep his expression placid. "Probably another way to keep us contained down here. The farther we get into the Labyrinth, the weaker we become. Some of us, like me, Kai, and Nina, are stronger than others. Our powers will take longer to dissipate entirely." He says that all impassively, not an ounce of inflection in his tone. He could've been talking about the weather instead of something as fucking terrifying as losing our powers.

"It's a pretty shitty theory," Abel murmurs, his green eyes wide with fear.

Fear that he quickly tries to mask, however, when he turns to face Nina.

"So I suppose we're going through the hall of nails," Rion interjects, beaming. Crazy fucking psycho. "Did I ever tell you the story about my twelfth birthday party? My momma decided to organize a birthday party with the theme of pain. Did you ever attend a party with that theme? God, I remember it like it was yesterday. We put a bullseye on my younger cousin and made him run around the backyard while the rest of us lined up with crossbows—"

"I will push you into the nails if you don't stop talking," Damien deadpans.

Rion's grin simply widens. "Are you trying to top me, my sexy bitch mage? Because I'll have you know...I am so fucking down for that."

I swear, Damien's eye twitches as if he's imagining all of the things he could do to Rion with the blade in his hand.

Kai's voice breaks through the bickering like a bomb detonating. It's not that he speaks the loudest of us all—that would definitely be Rion or Abel—but more that we turn towards him for leadership. Even Damien, though he'll never admit it. Since Kai first arrived in the prison many, many years ago, he innately commanded the respect and attention of every inmate in the Labyrinth. He became the king through bloodshed, but he kept hold of the crown through loyalty.

"We need to discuss options," Kai continues, staring intently at Nina in my arms. "How we're—"

"I have an idea," I interrupt, smoothing my hand over her stomach. I swear I feel a baby bump. My heart swells at the thought, even as I brace myself for what I'm about to do.

Before anyone can stop me or protest—not that anyone would when it comes to Nina's safety—I have her nestled in my arms and I'm running as fast as I fucking can through the hall of nails.

They dig into my skin, eliciting gasp after gasp of pain, and I feel blood trickle from the various wounds.

But I don't stop.

I keep my body hunched over Nina's, protecting her from any of the wayward nails.

What feels like hours later, but I know is only a minute or

so, we reach the other side of the hall, and I collapse on the ground, bringing Nina with me.

She's as white as a sheet, her hand shaking as it travels across my body, coming away red with blood. One glance down my nose confirms that I'm riddled with tiny marks. They're fucking everywhere.

"Oh, Bron." She places a hand to her mouth in horror, blinking away tears, before she seems to gather herself.

She continues to shake as she unzips my backpack, grabs a medical kit we put together, and begins to dab at my bloody cuts with rubbing alcohol.

"You shouldn't have done that," she snaps, her patience finally wearing thin. "Why do you guys always feel the need to—"

"Because you're the most important thing that matters to us," I say, cutting her off, meeting her fierce stare with one of my own. I'm not gonna lie—despite the pain I'm in, my cock hardens in my pants. There's something so fucking sexy about my girl standing up for herself and putting us in our place.

Are we overprotective assholes?

Most definitely.

Are we going to change anytime soon?

No way in hell.

No one should be surprised at this point.

She lifts her hands to explore the masculine planes of my face, using both of her thumbs to trace the curve of my lower lip. My tongue follows the motion, and I swear her body gives an involuntary shudder.

Damien and Rion are the only two *not* yelping in pain as they run through the hall, bleeding from the wounds scattered all over their bodies. The former keeps an apathetic mask plastered on his face, while the latter cackles maniacally. Nina tends to everyone's injures, and though her face is pale and her hands shake, she scolds each and every one of us for taking stupid risks.

But hey. We never claimed not to coddle her, and we sure as fuck aren't going to stop now.

CHAPTER 40

NINA

We decide to rest for the night, using our packs as pillows.

All of my men are gradually healing, though it's been slow going due to their dwindling powers and strength. Still, when I pull the bandages away from Bronson's arms, I'm relieved to see the diminutive cuts have become nothing but pink, puckered skin.

I sit next to Kai on one of the few sections of cement that isn't covered in puddles. His arm is positioned behind my back, providing me with a makeshift backrest.

Less than an hour ago, Damien pushed back his sleeves, revealing his impressive forearms, and squeezed his eyelids shut, his hands drifting over the kindling we collected. But instead of a roaring heat, the fire fizzled once, twice, three times as his blue magic sparked from his fingertips. Even now, the fire is nothing but embers gradually sputtering out.

I can tell how much it's bothering my mage, who sits opposite us around the fire. Through Kai's eyes, I can see how hard he's attempting to school his expression, to keep it placid and ineffably calm. But does anyone notice the way his right eye twitches as he stares at the diminishing flames? The way he obsessively brushes at his suit coat with haughty indifference? The way his eyes flicker from the fire to my face?

"I wonder how long it's going to be before you start showing," Kai muses conversationally, looking pointedly at my stomach. I instinctively cover it with my hands, a slow smile spreading across my face. It's a lazy sort of smile, one brimming with contentment and joy for what the future will hold for me. Kai's eyes flicker across my face, and my smile widens, a delicate blush erupting on both of my cheeks.

"I wonder if it's going to be a girl or a boy," I whisper, attempting to keep my voice down so I won't disturb the others as they sleep. Cain and Abel are cuddled together against the far wall, while Rion is quite literally hanging upside down from a pipeline, his face serene with sleep. Bronson is standing guard a short distance away, while Logan lies beside Damien. I can't tell if the cupid is sleeping, but his breathing appears even.

"We better hope it's a boy," Damien cuts in from across the fire. The blue flames flicker across his face, making his strong features appear even more arresting and prominent.

"Why?" I ask, feeling slightly indignant. I level him with a frosty eyed glare, though I can no longer see his expression since Kai turns his gaze back towards me. "You don't want a daughter?"

"I would kill anyone who so much as looks at my daughter," Damien deadpans, and I honestly can't tell if he's joking or not.

"I definitely think it's going to be a boy," Kai interjects, placing his hand over mine on my belly. There's no mistaking the male smugness radiating from his voice. "A proud, fierce dragon."

Damien snorts. "You fucking wish. No, our little man is

going to be a mage. A powerful one, for that matter. Maybe he'll even be able to surpass his daddy."

Rion's kinkiness must be rubbing off on me. I totally get flustered hearing Damien refer to himself as "daddy."

"I think it's a little girl," I throw in, smiling softly. "I don't know what species, but I definitely think this little nugget is a girl."

"A girl," Kai breathes, wonderment lacing his tone. "What would we name her?"

"We can't pick out names already," Damien says with a scoff. "Especially if we don't know the gender or species."

"A girl…" I tap a finger against my chin. "Juliet? Holly?"

"No." Kai's vision wavers as he shakes his head. "Brittney?"

This time, it's Damien who vehemently declares, "No."

"I still think it's a boy," Kai says, and he almost sounds petulant. I visualize the scary dragon stomping his foot on the ground as he throws a tantrum, and my smile broadens.

"Do you want to make a bet, Malakai?" I taunt, resting my head on his shoulder.

"Hmmm. I could get behind that." His voice is a rumbly purr that reverberates through me.

"A wager? I would like to join in on that as well," Damien says, forcing Kai's gaze back to him. The tall mage stands, straightening out his suit coat, and regards us stoically. "What, exactly, are we betting on? The mere gender of the baby or which one of us fathered it?"

"Does it matter?" I'm suddenly nervous. Terrified, even, as I await their answers with bated breath. My heart hammers a daunting tune in my chest as I chew on my thumbnail. "I mean, would you guys think less of—"

"No." Kai cups my cheeks with both of his hands, his callouses a rough contrast against my smooth skin. "It doesn't matter to any of us who the biological father is. That baby is ours."

"Agreed," Damien says curtly, though there's something soft in his tone that wasn't there prior. Something vulnerable. "That baby will be the most protected offspring of all time."

"Now, about the bet—" Kai's words cut off abruptly when a low growl rumbles from directly behind us. My muscles tense as my men jump to their feet, calling out to my other mates and jerking them awake.

In less than a second, I'm surrounded by seven warm, masculine bodies.

"What's going on?" I whisper as the first growl is joined by a second, and those are joined by a third and fourth. Soon, there are over a dozen low hisses, growls, and roars that fill the tiny halls of the Labyrinth.

"Another one of the prison's traps," Cain bites out bitterly, just as the first monster ventures around the corner.

And yes, it's a monster. There's no other word that's even close to encapsulating the creature crawling towards us. Bile fills my throat as I use Kai's eyes to stare into its sunken face, his head canted precariously to the side.

It appears to be a male—or at least it was a male at one point in time. His body is thin and wiry, the torso longer than both his arms and legs combined. His limbs appear to be miniscule extensions of his rectangular shape, jutting out at odd, ninety-degree angles. Coarse brown fur covers his face and neck, disappearing down his nude back and to his legs. The underside of him is nothing but mottled, red and pink skin that's peeling away. And his face...

He has no eyes. Nothing but empty sockets remain in his distorted face. His bloody lips pull away, revealing three rows of razor-sharp teeth.

He crawls forward. Not walks. Not runs. Just crawls, like some sort of human-centipede monster.

No, it's not a he. It's an *it*.

"Oh, wow," Rion muses as he twirls a blade in his hand. "He looks just like my mom."

And then the creature pounces.

Well, *creatures*.

They materialize from every corner, every hallway, every nook and cranny that they could've been hiding in. Dozens of them, some male and some female, but all with disproportionate bodies, hideously disfigured faces, and dark fur.

My guys immediately split off, fighting with weapons and claws and magic.

Damien—and Logan, surprisingly—remain in front of me, shielding me from any monster who dares to get too close. I watch through Kai's eyes as he expertly rips the head off of one of the gruesome creatures with his bare hands and then tosses it to the side. When a second one arrives, crawling out of a hole in the wall, he bares down on it with a low, threatening growl.

I pull out of his eyes to check in on my twins, currently standing back-to-back. Cain raises his dagger and stabs it through the heart of one of the monsters pouncing on him. When a second one arrives, he ducks just in time for Abel to send a clawed hand across its neck, causing black blood to spurt.

Bronson is in his shadow wolf form, fighting far away from the flickering, subdued blue flames of the fire. He jumps on a creature and pulls out its neck with his sharp, canine teeth. He bucks suddenly, a low, pained whine escaping his throat, and turns rapidly, attempting to dispel the creature clinging to his back, its nails digging into his flesh.

But then Rion is there, a cheerful grin on his face as he stabs at the creature with a sword of his own.

"Damien!" Logan screams, and I drop into Damien's head just in time to see him throw up his dagger, fending off two of the creatures. Two more arrive, circling him until he's surrounded. But Damien isn't perturbed. He simply steps farther away from me, slicing at one creature and then stomping on another's head when it gets in range.

I feel someone's hand wrap around my wrist, and I startle, attempting to free myself.

"Shh! It's just me! Nina, it's me!" Logan cajoles, pulling me behind him and protecting me from the fight.

"We need to get her out of here!" That's Kai, and though he sounds out of breath, he doesn't appear to be in any pain. I easily slide out of Damien's mind and into Kai's, allowing him to lead me farther and farther away from the others. I want to protest and scream, but I know I'll only be a liability. I'll endanger my men instead of protect them. I've been training to fight every day with Damien, but my skills are subpar at best. And my men are too protective of me to allow me to fight. No, if I stay, they'll get sloppy by focusing on me.

The shouts and grunts and growls begin to fade as we hurry through the tunnel. I worry that we'll lose sight of my mates, that they won't be able to find their way back to us, that the Labyrinth will change its pathways before they can catch up to us, but I don't voice this out loud. Internally, however, my panic ricochets through me like a pinball.

"We need to—Gah!" Kai falls to the ground with a pained noise, spinning onto his back just in time to see a monster fall on top of him.

"Shit!" Logan releases my hand, prepared to go to him, but Kai lets out a strangled noise.

"No! Get her out of here! Logan, get her out—" A second

creature appears, opening its huge jaw and clamping down on his arm. He bucks, his skin taking on a reptilian-quality…

Before his power sputters out.

"Shit. Shit. Shit," he curses, and I detect something in his voice I've never heard from him before. Panic.

"Kai!" I lunge forward blindly, only knowing that I need to get to him. That I need to save him. But before I can make it more than a step, Logan bands his arms around me, holding me close.

A third monster slithers towards Kai and takes his other arm, pulling it between its teeth and shaking its head back and forth like the limb is a chew toy for a dog. And then another monster arrives. And another. And another—

"Don't let her look!" Kai screams. "Logan, don't let her—" He roars in agony as a monster tears at the skin of his chest, slicing through his shirt and skin and causing blood to bubble.

"Kai!" My voice breaks, even as Logan continues to pull me backwards, continues to pull me *away* from my fallen lover. "Logan, we need to—"

Logan places both hands on my cheeks and presses his forehead to mine. And then I can feel his presence inside of me, cocooning me in warmth, and I'm yanked abruptly out of Kai's head. Logan's hands turn sweaty on my skin as he uses the last bit of his power to pull me out of Kai's mind and forces me into darkness.

"Logan, please—" I sob, struggling to free myself.

He keeps his forehead against mine, his own tears mingling with mine on my face. "You can't look. God, Nina, you can't look."

Kai's screams reach me. Muffled, at first, as if he's trying to be quiet for my benefit. And then louder.

I don't even realize that my screams have joined his until

Logan continues moving us away, his head still connected to mine.

"Kai!" I sob, another scream catching in my throat. "Oh my god. Kai!" I wail, pounding my fists against Logan's chest. The growls from the monsters get louder and louder, accompanied by the sound of flesh being ripped apart. Kai's screams of anguish gurgle with blood.

And despite how hard I struggle, despite my attempts to call on my powers, Logan forces his will into my mind, making it impossible for me to see through my dragon's eyes. So I scream. I cry. I plead with whoever is listening.

When Kai's screams finally go silent and all I hear is the sound of monsters eating his corpse, I realize that there's no one listening.

"No!" I sob hysterically, snot and tears cascading down my face. "No!"

"Nina…" Logan's voice is choked, nearly inarticulate, as he cries too.

But whatever he's about to say is interrupted by a low, creaking noise. Logan curses, pulling me closer towards him, just as the growls of the monsters, the screams of my other men…

It all goes silent.

CHAPTER 41

NINA

The pain devours me. Drowns me.

It's unlike anything I've ever experienced before, something so consuming and demanding that I lose a piece of myself. A piece that I know I'll never be able to get back no matter how much time passes. Even breathing seems like a chore, as if my lungs don't want to take in air. What's the point? To any of this?

So I sob.

I sob as my heart breaks into thousands and thousands of pieces. No, it doesn't just break. It *shatters*. Crumples into particles finer than dust. They lay at my feet like an offering. An offering that no god or goddess will accept.

Kai…

Even saying his name in my mind causes my entire body to spasm. I can barely breathe around my ragged, gasping sobs.

And my other mates…

The Labyrinth's pathways changed once more, separating me from my other men. I have no idea if they're still alive or if they're—

I fall to my knees, dimly aware of Logan saying my name. Everything hurts. Aches.

Can't breathe.

Can't think.

Pain.

I press my forehead against the cool ground as Kai's screams infiltrate my mind. His pleas for me not to look, for Logan to block my power. The agony emanating from his voice.

No. No. No.

He can't be dead. He just can't be.

No. No. No. No.

My mate's dead.

He's dead.

Dead.

Dead.

I throw my head back and scream. Just scream. It's a broken, brittle sound, though it's nothing compared to the sensation of my heart splitting in two. An angry, virulent storm wages inside of me as my scream reverberates off the stone walls, embedding itself in my very soul. I'm sure for years to come, this scream is going to haunt me. It's a part of me, this brutal, broken, savage sound. A part of my genetic makeup.

I wrap my arms around my stomach and twist my body, like burning paper curling in on itself.

Pain.

Pain.

Pain.

Pain.

And something inside of me...snaps. I can't say for sure what it is, but one second, I'm broken and bleeding, wishing for death, and the next, ice encapsulates my heart. A translucent veil bathed in blood and sin shrouds my mind as all at once, the agonizing sounds pouring from my lips stop.

Everything freezes.

"You…" I barely recognize my voice as I stagger to my feet, jabbing an accusatory finger where I suspect Logan to be. My searching finger touches something hard—his arm, more than likely, or maybe his stomach—and I feel him flinch. "You kept me from my mates!"

I'm broken.

I'm nothing.

Just a candle burnt all the way down until only a sliver of wick remains.

And this wick is ready to burn the entire world to the ground.

"Nina," he pleads, but his voice is like a razor blade being forced down my throat.

"I could've saved them! I could've saved Kai!" Tears and snot cascade down my face, but I don't lift a hand to rub them away. My arm is too heavy, too numb. "How did you do it? How did you stop me from seeing through Kai's eyes?"

"It's a power I always suspected I had, given my lineage as an angel, but I never tested it out on you. I wanted you to trust me, and hindering your powers was not a way to bolster the trust that was slowly forming," he answers softly.

Numb.

I'm numb.

Kai…

The pain threatens to drown me again, but I transform my pain into anger, hurling dagger after dagger into Logan's chest with my eyes.

And he takes it.

"I could've saved him like I saved myself from Alyssa!" I scream. "Like I saved Bronson! Why did you stop me?!"

Emotions hover over us both like the blade of a guillotine waiting to drop. I know my mates want to protect me, but what about *me* protecting *them*?

"The Labyrinth dampens our powers, Nina," Logan begins tiredly. There's no hint of the friendly, flirty guy I've come to know. He sounds…dead. Remorseful. "Even you would not be strong enough. And I'd be damned if I didn't honor Kai's wishes and protect you."

"Who even are you?" I cry, wanting him to hurt, to bleed. Just as I am. "You're not my mate, Logan! You don't get to have any say in my life. Just go away. Go—" My legs tremble, my knees caving in on themselves, and I fall forward, the strength finally waning from my bone-weary body.

"I'm sorry," I sob into his shirt as his arms lock around me. "I'm sorry. I didn't mean that. I'm sorry. I'm sorry." My words become incoherent, laced with agony and a loss so pronounced that my body feels leaden. "Why did my powers fail me? Why? Why did… How could…?"

And in Logan's arms, I fall apart a second time.

Kai.

Damien.

Rion.

Abel.

Cain.

Bronson.

My mates. My loves.

One dead. Five separated.

Alone.

So, so alone.

"You're not alone," Logan cuts in vehemently, sounding choked up as he smooths a hand down my hair. "I'll get you out of this, Nina. I promise."

I'm already shaking my head before he even finishes speaking. "I can't. I can't. I can't."

"You can." He holds my chin in a firm grip, forcing my head up. "You can, and you will. Kai—" He breaks off, swallowing heavily. "He wouldn't want you to fall apart like this. He would want you to fight, dammit. You know that just as well as I do."

More and more tears create bitter tracks down my face. "It hurts…" I moan.

"I know, sweetheart. I know. But I'm not going to let you die down here. I refuse to. So I'm going to give you ten more minutes. Ten more minutes to fall apart and rage at the world. But don't lose yourself to the grief. Not yet. Because once those ten minutes are over, we're going to begin moving once more. We're going to find that door, sweetheart, and get out of here. You know as well as I do that your mates will be heading in that direction too. And when you're all free of this hellhole, you can fall apart. But not now. Not yet. You're not just fighting for yourself anymore. You're fighting for your unborn daughter or son."

"Logan…" I sob, shaking my head. "I—"

"You can," he interrupts, knowing what I'm going to say. "You can. I'll be with you every step of the way. So take your ten minutes. Fall apart. Know that I'll be watching over you, that I won't let you shatter. And then pick yourself up, remember your baby and what Kai would want, and start fighting." He brushes his lips against my forehead, the chaste gesture shattering something inside of me, before taking a step back. "Ten minutes."

I scream.

I cry.

I rage at the world. Rage at the beast inside of me who protected Bronson and myself…but who failed to protect Kai.

And then I place a hand over my stomach where my baby rests and bolster my resolve. Brick by brick, piece by piece.

My baby.

Kai's baby.

Our baby.

It doesn't matter who the father is. This baby belongs to all of us.

So when the ten minutes are over and Logan takes my hand in his, gently leading me down the hall, I've shoved all of my emotions in a steel-enforced box and wrapped it in coils of barbed wire. When we're finally free of this maze, free of the dangers that lurk inside of it, I'll unlock it and embrace my pain and agony. Embrace the wound that will never heal properly, that will constantly flay me open.

All I can pray is that it doesn't consume me.

THE HOUR WE WALK FEELS LIKE A LIFETIME.

Logan and I don't speak...

But I also don't release his hand. It's like he's my anchor and I'm adrift at sea. I'm afraid that if I let go of him, I'll lose myself to the merciless and ruthless waves of the ocean.

He pauses suddenly, hissing out a breath of air, and I freeze beside him.

"What is it?" My voice is strange to my own ears. Detached. It sorta reminds me of how Damien speaks to most people.

"Can you look through my eyes?" Logan asks, and with a heavy sigh, I do as he requests.

My power fizzles around me, sparking hotly and reaching towards Logan...

Before immediately retracting back inside of me.

Furrowing my brows, I try again, pushing my awareness into the bright ball of energy and light I've come to associate with Logan. It takes me a few tries, my pulse racing, but when I'm finally able to use his eyes for myself, I feel physically and mentally tired.

Logan's gaze is fixed on me, his eyes sweeping over my haggard appearance. My face is red and blotchy with dark, crescent moon shapes beneath both of my eyes. And my eyes themselves...

They're dead.

"You're getting weaker," Logan whispers in horror. "How long do you think you can hold the connection between us?"

Through his eyes, I watch my shoulders lift in a small shrug. My face is still devoid of any expression. Lifeless.

"If I only use your sight, I could probably hold on to the connection for an hour or two," I say in that monotone, impassive voice of mine.

I hear him swallow before he tears his gaze away from me, focusing on the hall we must need to travel through. "Good."

Colorful square stones create the flooring. Red, green, orange, yellow, blue, and purple. There doesn't seem to be a rhyme or reason for the placement of the colors, four in each row and about nine or ten creating a column.

"What are we waiting for?" I ask, taking a step forward. Logan immediately bands an arm around my waist, pulling me back.

"Wait." He fumbles through his backpack and procures an apple. Crouching down, he rolls the apple until it lands on a green square.

For a moment, nothing happens.

And then a green mist erupts from every single crevice in large fumes.

I recognize it immediately as the green substance that burned Cain. Logan, his arm still wrapped around my waist, releases a low curse as his eyes narrow, distorting my vision.

"Fuck. We're going to need to turn around," he hisses, already pulling me back.

Continue moving forward. I jump ten feet in the air at the silky voice inside my head. It almost seems familiar. Low, masculine, and sultry. Confusion wages a battle inside of me as I turn desperately in a circle, searching for the source of the voice.

"Nina?" Logan stares at me intently. "What's wrong?" Instantly, he's on alert, moving until his body is standing protectively in front of me, his knife extended. "What did you hear?"

Continue moving forward, the voice repeats. *Green. Orange. Orange. Yellow. Red. Blue. Red. Yellow. Orange.*

"What?" My voice shakes.

Green. Orange. Orange. Yellow. Red. Blue. Red. Yellow. Orange.

"Nina, we need to go." Logan tries to tug me after him, back in the direction we just came from, but my feet remain rooted to the spot as I process the mysterious voice's words.

And then I picture the hallway in my mind's eye.

Is this voice…? Is this voice giving us the pattern we need to follow to safely cross it?

The more I think about it, the more sure I become. There's something about the voice that I trust innately. I have no words for why, only that I do. I trust that voice the same way I trusted my mates when I first arrived at the prison, confused and alone and scared out of my mind.

"Logan," I tug on his arm until his gaze dips to me, "I think I know how to cross the hallway."

"No," he says immediately, shaking his head slowly. "We're not risking it. And how would you even…?"

There's no way in heck I'm going to tell him about the voice in my head. He'd think I'm insane. Or worse—he'd believe me…and then freak out.

"The combination. Green. Orange. Orange. Yellow. Red. Blue. Red. Yellow. Orange."

Yes, that's right. You know it's right, Nina, my own mental voice coaches as the surety of my words cascade over me. My intuition knows without a shadow of doubt that this is the right combination.

Now all I need to do is get Logan to trust me.

"Logan, please," I beg. "I'll go first if you don't—"

"Don't be fucking ridiculous," he snaps, already turning back towards the hallway. "There's no way I'm allowing you to go first."

Before I can stop myself, my mouth drops open. "Just like that? You trust me just like that?" He didn't demand to know why I knew what I did. He didn't scoff at me and tell me that I was being stupid. He believed me irrevocably and unconditionally.

He pauses, spearing me in place with his gaze. "I trust you with my life, Nina Doe."

Cracking his neck from side to side, he dances on the balls of his feet, preparing himself. And then he gracefully jumps from stone to stone. First green, then orange, and then the second orange in front of the first one. Then yellow, red, blue, red again, yellow and finally orange. When he reaches the end of the hallway and not one trap has been detonated, we both release heavy breaths.

Who was that voice in my head?

Why did he warn me?

And why did I trust him so…implicitly?

It almost sounded like…Nick. The man from my dreams.

But that's impossible, right?

"Come on, Nina!" Logan calls, focusing his attention on the floorboards so I'll be able to see where I'm going. "And don't you dare fucking stumble and unleash a trap."

I place both hands over my belly, drawing strength and

comfort from my unborn child, before taking a deep breath and stepping into the hall.

CHAPTER 42

NINA

After a few more hours of aimless wandering, we choose to rest for the night.

Logan hands me a wrapped sandwich from his backpack and an apple, but I barely taste the food as it goes down my throat. I could be eating dirt for all I care.

The pain from before is beginning to seep into my bloodstream, permeating my very soul. I'm afraid to even speak, as if one word will be the catalyst that sends me careening over the ravine.

When I bring a water bottle up to my lips to take a sip, my hand shakes wildly, the water sloshing over the sides. And though it's cold from a spell Damien placed on it before we entered the Labyrinth, it burns my throat. I don't even argue when Logan places something tiny and square in my hand. A prenatal vitamin. Bronson must've packed them for me, my overprotective, growly wolf shifter.

I begin to smile when I think of him, envisioning the fierce glint always present in his eyes, but the smile wavers when another flood of pain bombards me. My entire body begins to shake, and all I want to do is curl into a ball on the ground, cry my eyes out, and never get back up.

But I can't.

My mates need me.

My baby needs me.

And…

Another shuddering breath leaves my parted lips.

And Kai needs me to be strong.

That revelation settles like a huge block of coal in my stomach, and I rub a hand absently at my chest, almost as if I can stop my heart from leaping out from beneath my rib cage and splattering on the ground.

Logan clears his throat from where he sits on the other side of the cackling fire. Absently, I turn my gaze in his general direction. It's something I always do, strangely enough. It's almost as if I fear the person I'm talking to will feel uncomfortable if I don't maintain direct eye contact. On the contrary, I have a feeling I unnerve people more when I *do* maintain eye contact, because my eyes aren't exactly the most pleasant to stare into.

"I thought I was in love once," Logan begins, his tone almost conversational. But there's an edge to it that wasn't there prior. The glint of a blade seconds before it plunges into your heart.

"Oh?" I can tell what he's trying to do—distract me—but my heart gives a painful tug at the thought of Logan in love. There's a certain wistfulness to his voice, and I can't help but wonder whom he's thinking about.

"Amanda," he begins with a hoarse laugh, answering my unspoken question. There's a brief pause, followed by the crunch of an apple. "Met her in…high school? I think?" His voice rises in pitch as he considers before he finally concludes, "Yes, high school. Senior year. She was beautiful—

flowing blonde hair, big green eyes, perfect smile. Cheerleader."

"And let me guess," I begin, remembering some of the romantic comedies I watched with Abel. "You were the quarterback?"

He chuckles. "Nah. Not athletic enough. I was just the pretty boy in all of her classes." Self-deprecation enters his tone, but before I can comment on it, he forges ahead. "Anyway, I asked her out at the beginning of the year, she said yes, and we began dating shortly after."

"And you loved her," I point out, trying to ignore the slithering snakes of jealousy taking up residence in my stomach. Why does the thought of Logan being in love with another woman bother me immensely, even though that woman is a part of his past?

"*Thought* I loved her," Logan corrects immediately. Another chuckle. Another snort of self-loathing. Another heavy, loaded sigh. "You're missing the point of the story, sweetheart."

"I'm sorry. Go on."

"We continued dating into college, and I remember thinking, 'Wow, this girl is perfect. She's the one for me.'"

I shift uncomfortably, trying to ignore the burning stab of pain twisting up my insides. I know Logan is trying to distract me, but I'm only falling deeper and deeper into a dark pit I'm not certain I can escape from. A pit where my monsters crawl up the walls with gaping maws and glowing red eyes, just waiting to devour me whole.

"Once, we were in the school's cafeteria, and I noticed my girl smiling. Like, a huge fucking smile, unlike anything I've ever seen before. It made her eyes fucking sparkle, as cliché as that sounds," he continues. "But then I realized...she wasn't looking at me. She was looking over my shoulder at Ross Vandergoosh, the college football star."

"Oh no." I place both of my hands over my mouth in horror as Logan chuckles humorlessly.

"Oh yeah. And the kicker? No pun intended. He was staring back at her." He pauses, and I hear the sound of him chewing his apple, seemingly deep in thought. For a moment, I don't think he's going to continue, but when he speaks next, his voice is subdued, weary. "I had the grand epiphany of grand epiphanies that day. Amanda? She never smiled at me like that. And I never smiled at her like that either. I thought I loved her, because in my mind, she was beautiful and perfect. But perfect is this abstract construct that we're not entirely capable of grasping. At least…not until you come face to face with it. I confronted Amanda, and she promised that she never cheated on me, and I believed her. But I also knew that it wasn't me she was thinking about when I took her to bed. We broke up that day, and only a few weeks later, Amanda and Ross were together. Happier than ever." He scoffs, and another long stretch of silence ensues. I wonder what he's thinking about. Or *whom* he's thinking about. Is his mind focused on the girl who broke his heart? Who smiled at a man who wasn't him?

"Have you…?" I tentatively bring my water bottle back to my lips, struggling to articulate my thoughts. "Have you found someone to smile at?"

"What do you mean?"

"You know…the way Amanda smiled at Ross. Have you found someone?"

His silky voice is low and uncharacteristically serious. "Yes, I believe I have."

I want to ask him more questions about this mysterious man or woman who's captured his heart, but my body takes that moment to give in to my fatigue. A loud yawn cracks my jaw as I arch my back like a house cat. Like…Rion.

Another pang of yearning and sadness ricochets through

me. All of the walls I constructed around myself shatter into dust, lying at my feet while all I can do is stare despondently at the remains.

"I think it's about time to go to bed," Logan murmurs. "Sleep, Nina. I'll stand guard. I won't let anything happen to you."

I want to protest, to tell him that if I fall asleep now, I'll be plagued by vicious nightmares. That I can already feel my soul shaking in the beginning stages of an earthquake, just waiting to crack entirely in two.

But I'm exhausted. And broken. And so, so empty.

I curl into a ball on the ground, using his backpack as a pillow, and wait for sleep to claim me.

If Logan hears the desperate sounds I make as the pain consumes me, he doesn't comment.

If he's aware that I'm sobbing my heart out, he doesn't say anything.

He simply allows me to fall apart under the safety of his gaze as I mourn my mate, my first friend, the first man I ever truly loved.

Kai...

I'm distantly aware of Logan covering me with a blanket from his bag, but even the warmth from it doesn't stop the desperate shivers from taking over my body.

Kai. Kai. Kai. Kai.

I'm so sorry.

I love you.

Kai.

His smiling face—I wonder if he smiled at me the way Amanda smiled at Ross—is the last thing I see before unconsciousness mercifully consumes me.

～

Surprisingly enough, my nightmares don't include Kai's face.

Instead, I'm faced with the endless, relentless darkness I've grown to associate with Nick, the enigma I can't quite figure out.

There's no pain here, no grief, only a tranquility that takes my breath away. A sigh escapes me as I stand suspended in nothingness, my bare feet seemingly floating above the ground. Or maybe they're touching the ground, but it's made of soft, wispy clouds.

I release another breath of air, tilting my face up as if the darkness contains a sun that beats down on my skin. But there's no heat here. No cold, either. The weather can best be described as tepid, comfortable enough to endure in only a thin, white dress.

"I do not like it when you cry," a soft, melodic voice says, seemingly coming from directly behind me. No, wait. In front of me. No…to the side of me.

Everywhere.

It comes from every direction, bouncing off the walls and creating a nest around my body.

"Where am I?" I ask in a detached, emotionless voice. There's no pain in this other place, no anger or hurt or fear.

But there's also no joy.

"Everywhere." The barest of breaths caresses my ear, and I swivel in his direction.

"I'm no longer sad," I continue, absently bringing my hand up to rub at my chest. I know that the second I wake up, the second this illusion dissipates, I'll be bombarded by my feelings again. By the stomach-churning pain that makes vomit crawl up my throat. By the shaking of my legs that threatens to send me toppling over. By the erratic *thump-thump-thump* of my heart as the organ breaks through my chest, splattering on the ground.

Because pain? There's no expiration date. It doesn't go away when you desire it to. It's like the gentle splatter of rain on the roiling, turbulent ocean. Each individual raindrop is so tiny, so insignificant, when looked at separately. When combined, they have the capacity to completely transform the ocean, to create ripples in its tranquil depths. To call upon the fiercest of waves capable of devouring shorelines. Sometimes, it pours for days, while other times, there's an endless drought with clear skies and no clouds in sight. But the rain will always come back. It's inevitable, just like grief. Just like pain.

And my pain…

It continues to pile up. Never stopping.

Always falling like rain on the ocean.

And though I should be relieved that I have a break from it, a momentary pause from the relentless torture, a part of me wants to mourn Kai. Wants to remember the way he loved me, how he died for me. Wants to hold his memory as tightly as I can, refusing to release it.

"You are in my world," Nick explains, and I feel the gentle swipe of his finger down my cheek. "My creation. I do not want you to feel sad. I am…I am sorry about your dragon, but I am certain he will find his way to you again."

Scratch. Scratch. Scratch.

There's a presence scratching at my chest, demanding to claw its way free.

Is it my pain trying to escape? My anger? My fear? A combination of all three of them? And when they finally escape, finally break free of the shackles Nick has imposed on them, will they rip me open to the point of no return?

Scratch. Scratch. Scratch.

"The door is near, little one," Nick continues in that soothing, silky voice of his. It reminds me of the butterscotch candies Kai used to—

Scratch. Scratch. Scratch.

"Just keep moving straight. I will do what I can to lead you there."

Scratch. Scratch. Scratch.

"Just...just leave me alone." I don't raise my voice, but then again, I don't have to. It's so silent in this suspended nothingness that I could've been screaming. My words shoot through the air like a gun being fired.

I can feel Nick's body behind me, the heat he emits almost palpable, as his hands land on my shoulders and his mouth touches my ear. "I am afraid I cannot, little one."

"Why?" Still monotone. Still impassive.

Scratch. Scratch. Scratch.

"Because you are my mate," Nick responds candidly. And then, "Wake up, little one."

Wake up.

CHAPTER 43

NINA

"Nina, wake up." Logan gently shakes my shoulder. "We should start moving again."

Cloudiness still fogs my mind, but I force my eyes open, stretching my taut muscles. A memory clings to me, scratching at my skin incessantly. Something I need to remember…

"I had a dream," I whisper, turning my head in the direction I sense Logan to be. I hear the sound of his backpack being zipped up before he stills, granting me his full attention. The majority of my dream remains just out of reach, evading my hands like wispy strands of smoke. But one part remains clear. "I think we're on the right track. I think…I think we have to go straight."

How do I know that?

I have a vague recollection of Nick telling me that. But why do I trust him? Who even is he?

Questions continue to bombard me as I stagger to my feet.

"Straight?" Logan's voice sounds cautious. Wary.

"Do you trust me?" I ask him, and when he hesitates,

another piece of my heart shatters into particles finer than dust.

"Yes," he decides on at last. "But, Nina, you need to explain things to me. How do you know where we need to go? I trust you, I honestly do, but this prison…it's designed to play tricks on you."

I nibble on my lower lip as I debate what to tell him. Do I confess the truth, that I'm being visited by a man I've never met before? That he declared I'm his—

I'm his what?

The memory falls through my fingers like water dripping from a faucet.

Logan takes a deep breath, and before I realize what I'm doing, I'm standing directly in front of him and capturing his hands in both of mine. His breath hitches, and I swear I can hear his heart skip a beat.

"I know I can't ask for your trust. Not yet, at least. But I've been having these strange dreams of this man named Nick, and he told me to go straight. For some reason, I trust him. I know we don't know each other that well—"

"I trust you, Nina," Logan interrupts with a shaky laugh. "Fuck, I trust you more than I ever trusted anyone in my life. It terrifies me. If you say we need to go straight, then we'll go fucking straight. I'm sorry I made you question my trust in you." His words send me staggering back a step, each one a knife to the heart, as warmth blossoms in my stomach. It's nothing but an ember, a flicker of heat, but it sends a tentative smile to my face, one that immediately vanishes when the phantom tentacles of pain wrap around my throat, squeezing tight.

"Come," I say, not even bothering to force a smile this time. It's too much work to lift my lips the way a smile requires.

Pain.

So much pain.

And we walk.

We don't run into any other traps or monsters, and I have to wonder if Nick had a hand in that. But how would he?

Who the heck is he?

Still, I don't allow myself to feel any relief until Logan hisses out a breath of air.

"Nina," he says, tugging my arm until I stop and turn towards him. "Use my eyes."

I cock an eyebrow curiously but do as instructed. Like before, it takes me a few tries to enter his mind, to use his eyes as my own. My power sparks and fizzles before it eventually relents to my needs.

And there, directly in front of us, is the door Rion described. Just a plain wooden door with multiple padlocks. And also like Rion described, something is pounding against the wood, demanding to be released. I can hear the monster howling, growling, shouting. The sound of claws being dragged against wood. The thump of a body hitting the door.

"Is this…?" I whisper, dumbstruck.

"I believe so," Logan replies. He sounds just as enchanted as I am, his gaze never wavering from the door that can either lead to our escape…or our doom.

It's so…insignificant. I don't know what I expected, but this definitely wasn't it. Maybe something golden and shiny? Or a large sign in neon lights blazing, "Exit!"

"This must've been what Nick wanted me to find," I muse breathlessly.

Logan's gaze whips to my face. "Do you think…?" With an urgency belying his still calm voice, he grips my shoulders and continues, "You don't think this is a trap, do you?"

I can feel my brows furrow. "What do you mean?"

"A trap," he repeats. "You said you've been having dreams of a strange man. What if…" He swallows heavily before starting again. "What if the man you've been having dreams of is the monster on the other side of that door? What if this is just a trap to get you to release him…or *it?*"

As if on cue, the monster behind the door releases another ear-shattering roar, pounding against the wood. It's as if the monster hears us. Senses us.

Knew we were coming.

"What?" My voice quivers slightly, even as I shake my head. The voice in my mind, the man from my dreams…I trust him, don't I?

"What if this isn't the way out?" Logan continues, his voice verging on a desperate plea. "Nina, how can you know that you can trust the man from your dreams?"

"I…" I rub at my chest once more, where that scratching sensation has begun again.

Scratch. Scratch. Scratch.

"I don't know," I confess at last, my voice barely audible. "I don't know if I can trust anyone."

"You can trust me," Logan declares vehemently, adamantly, not a shred of doubt in his voice. His grip on my shoulders tightens slightly. "I'll never hurt you, Nina Doe."

My hands begin to shake, and I have the sudden urge to lean into Logan's embrace, to place my forehead on his chest and allow him to wrap his arms around me. Comfort me. Soothe me.

But then that familiar wave of pain crashes through me, this time accompanied by a sliver of doubt, and I turn away from Logan with a choked sob.

Why does everything have to hurt so much?

Pain.

So. Much. Pain.

Instead of Logan's chest, I place my forehead against the wall of the Labyrinth, opposite the doorway still creaking against the weight of the monster. And then the strangest thing happens. It almost feels like heat erupts from where I touch the tunnel wall, shooting through my bloodstream like an errant star falling from the sky. The blistering pain has me gasping, pulling away from the Labyrinth as if I've been shocked. The second my bare skin is no longer in contact with the stone, the heat lessens, coiling into a tightly curled ball in my stomach before disappearing completely as if it was never there to begin with.

"Nina?" Logan asks tentatively, taking a step closer to me from behind.

And then…

I hear it.

The singularly most beautiful sound in the entire world—the meow of a cat.

Forcing myself into Logan's head once more—I didn't even realize I left in the first place—we turn in the direction of the noise just as a cat comes sprinting around the corner.

A very, very familiar cat.

"Mr. Scruffles!" I cry as the cat throws itself at me, licking every inch of my face with his scratchy tongue. As I sob and hold him to me, the cat transforms into a very real, very solid, very naked man.

"Buttercup," Rion says as he continues to lick my face. "Don't." Lick. "Ever." Lick. "Leave." Lick. "Me." Lick. Lick. Lick. "Again." He punctuates the last word with his tongue moving from the base of my chin to my forehead.

"Rion!" I sob, holding him even tighter, wishing I could disappear in his body.

He's here. He's safe. He's alive.

He's here. He's safe. He's alive.

I repeat that in my head like a mantra.

"Where are the others?" I ask, consumed by a desperate, restless energy.

"Nina!" Bronson. I would recognize his guttural growl

anywhere, more wolf than man. I pull away from Rion with another cry, throwing myself at my wolf shifter just as he materializes at the end of the hallway. I take a second to note that he's covered in hundreds and hundreds of tiny scratches, almost as if he lost a fight with a piece of paper, before my worry over his health is overtaken by the relief that he's alive and in front of me.

"Bronson! Oh my god." His arms feel amazing wrapped around my waist, as if we can survive any storm the world throws our way.

"Goddess." He nuzzles my cheek, the move decidedly wolf-like, before twisting his face towards my neck. His teeth graze the sensitive skin there as he breathes me in deeply, ensuring with his own senses that I'm alive and well.

"Let me at her," Damien growls out. I'm spun out of Bronson's arms and immediately wrapped in Damien's. My stoic mage…he's trembling. Anxiety pours from his body in tangible waves as he holds me to him, stroking my hair repeatedly as he whispers softly to himself. At first, I can't make out his words, but when I focus, I can distantly hear him muttering, "She's here. She's here. She's here." Again and again and again.

"Damien, I was so scared," I confess. And through Logan's eyes, I watch his eyes shutter closed as if he's overcome by a strong emotion.

"Me too, Angel. Me too."

"Is it time for a group hug yet?" Abel asks with forced cheer. And when I finally, reluctantly, pull away from Damien, it's to turn towards my last two lovers. My sunshine and moonlight twins. But this time, not one of them is smiling, their faces grave as their eyes lock on me.

We move as one, as if we're opposite magnets attracting. As if there's a rope connecting my soul to theirs and theirs to each other. One second, we're simply standing in front of each other, and the next, I'm in their arms. Cain and Abel box me in from both sides as they touch everywhere on my body they can reach, every bare inch of skin my small dress reveals. Their hands caress my arms, my throat, my cheeks, my lips, even my thighs.

"Never letting you out of our sight again," Cain murmurs.

"We're gonna have to handcuff you to us," Abel agrees, peppering kisses to my head. "Forever and ever."

"This is it?" Damien interrupts, his curt tone at odds with the way his body still trembles. "The door?"

"It could lead us out of this shithole," Rion says, and when Logan's gaze swings his way, I can see a slightly deranged and manic smile on his face. It's almost as if…

It's almost as if our separation broke something inside of the already eccentric shifter. As if it made him even more unhinged. He's always been a grenade, only now, it feels as if he's missing his pin as well, just waiting to unleash himself on the world.

"Where's Kai?" Damien demands, removing a dagger from his jacket sleeve. "We need to decide on a plan."

The world stops.

Freezes.

Or maybe I stop.

Freeze.

Everything stops.

Freezes.

Hurts.

Pain.

My breath comes out in shallow, gasping sounds as Damien's head whirls in my direction, shock splayed onto his face, and Logan curses.

"What the devil…?"

"Don't," Logan admonishes with a brisk shake of his head.

Rion is abruptly standing in front of Logan, his eyes

glinting with madness and his head cocked to the side. "Where is my precious Dragon Breath?" he asks in a deceptively low and calm voice. "Where is my motherfucking BROTHER HUSBAND!" The last words are a roar, and I can finally see why Rion is feared and revered by everyone in the prison. Sure, I knew he had a few screws loose, but he's always kept such a tight leash on his anger around me.

For the first time ever, I'm seeing Rion completely unrestrained.

Rion embracing his madness.

His hand snaps out, wrapping around Logan's throat and pushing him against the wall.

"Rion!" I scream in alarm, my fear for Logan momentarily outweighing my pain. "Stop!"

"Where. Is. My. Dragon?" Rion grits out. "Did you do something to him?"

"Rion." This comes from Abel, who takes a tentative step forward. "Rion, drop him." When Rion doesn't remove his hand from Logan's throat, Abel adds, "You're scaring Nina."

At that, Rion whips his head in my direction. I can't see the expression in my eyes, or his for that matter, but whatever he sees has him releasing Logan, the cupid falling unceremoniously to the ground and gasping for air.

"Buttercup…" Rion moans, moving towards me. He takes me in his arms, placing his nose in the swell of my neck and breathing, just breathing me in.

"Nina, what happened?" Abel's voice is solemn, devoid of its usual mirth.

"Kai…" I pause. Gasp. Swallow. Choke on a sob. "He didn't…" Gasp. Swallow. Sob. "He didn't…" Gasp. Swallow. Sob.

The guys release muffled curses. Bronson throws his head back and emits a mournful howl, one I feel in my very soul.

"The monsters…" I continue around my sobs, tightening my arms around Rion's waist.

"Shhh. It's okay, my precious buttercup. No one will hurt you. I'll protect you. I'm never leaving your side again. Ever. Ever. Ever. Ever. Ever. Ever. Ever." He continues to repeat "ever," his voice a soft rasp against my neck.

"Thank you," Cain says, directing his words at a still gasping Logan, "for protecting our girl."

Logan rubs at his neck before using the wall to climb to his feet. "Always," he says, his voice raspy. Clearing his throat, he repeats, "Always."

"What the fuck do we do?" Abel interrupts, forking his fingers through his shaggy blond hair. "Do we—"

Before he can finish his thought, the door releases an ominous creak. Wood splinters, flying in all directions, as another roar echoes through the tiny room we've found ourselves in.

And then, to all of our horror, a fist appears in the cracked wood. And then an eye. And then the monster uses its head to break it open the rest of the way.

We're defenseless, powerless…

And an eight-foot-tall minotaur is currently running straight at us.

CHAPTER 44

CAIN

Kai's dead.

The knowledge settles like a weight on my chest as I stare into Nina's wide, white eyes. Her lower lip trembles as she struggles to regain control of her tumultuous emotions.

No. No. No.

This wasn't the way it was supposed to happen. We were supposed to leave the prison together, dammit, and worship Nina the way she deserves. Just willing servants at the altar of their goddess. Kai's our brother, and he was supposed to be there with us.

A life without him in it…

It's impossible to wrap my head around. There's a tightness in my throat that threatens to choke me, devour me, consume me.

How could we have let this happen? How could *Kai* have let this happen? He was supposed to be fighting for her until the very last moment. The Kai I know and respect would never willingly give himself over to the Grim Reaper.

A surge of self-loathing and guilt floods me.

I should've been there to protect him and our girl.

Now, Kai's dead, and Nina is a shell of her normal self. Even her eyes seem duller than usual, milky white orbs wide in an expressionless face.

I yearn to comfort her, soothe her, barely aware of anything else over the sudden roaring in my ears. It deafens me.

"What the fuck do we do?" I hear my brother say, his tone laced with something I rarely hear from him—fear. So much fear. He says something else, but my attention is suddenly focused on the mysterious doorway.

Just as it caves in and a monster steps into the hallway with us.

Ohhh...shit on a stick.

Minotaurs exist, I know that, but I've never seen one up close and personal. And I've never seen one that is...feral. More beast than human.

His head is that of a bull, coarse, reddish-brown fur covering a broad forehead and elongated snout. Pitch-black eyes peer back at me, rimmed with madness that puts even Rion to shame. White horns erupt from either side of his head, curling upwards and ending in sharp points. And while his face is completely animal, his upper torso is that of a man. A strong chest, wide, bulky arms, and human hands that are currently curled into fists. At his waist, his legs once more transition into those befitting a beast. His furry, broad legs end in two cloven feet. A fuzzy tail flicks against the floor irritably, the puff of fur at the end resembling that of a lion.

My entire inspection of the beast lasts only a second, ending when the fucker charges at us, his head lowered and horns extended.

Rion twists Nina in his arms until his back is to his beast and his body is folded protectively over hers. Knowing that my brother is looking after her gives me the strength and courage to do what I have to do.

Fight for my damn life.

No, I correct myself. *Fight for my girl's and baby's lives.*

Without my powers, I feel naked. Stripped and vulnerable and just waiting for the scary monster to devour me whole.

But I'm not entirely useless, and as Damien charges forward, his dagger raised and slicing at the beast's torso, I fumble for my own weapon. We lost the majority of our bags after one of the hallways we were in exploded, but I was able to secure a tiny steak knife. It might not be the scariest weapon known to man, but it's better than nothing.

"For her, brother?" Abel asks, and I see him holding a hammer out of the corner of my eye, his knees bent as he prepares for battle.

"For her," I agree, and with a roar, we lunge.

The minotaur, who is fending off attacks from Damien like a beast possessed, doesn't notice us as we descend on him from both sides. Abel throws his hammer against the monster's wrist just as I stab the knife into his unguarded side.

The beast roars, throwing back his head in agony as Bronson launches at him from behind. He's unable to shift completely into his wolf form in here, but his movements are decidedly more wolf than human as he tears at the mino-taur's throat with his bare teeth.

Batting at the gigantic man on his back, the minotaur spins in a circle, prepared to throw Bronson off. Before he can take a step, Logan is there, his baby-blue eyes darkened in anger, and slashes with his dagger at the minotaur's throat.

The creature throws his head back, the movement dislodging Bronson, and roars.

It's like a seismic wave. An earthquake. The entire Labyrinth begins to shake as the minotaur roars and roars and roars. The force of it throws all of us back, and my head careens off the stone wall. Bright lights explode behind my eyelids as pain cascades through me, white-hot and blistering.

"Fucking hell," Abel gripes from beside me, struggling to his feet. I turn desperate eyes towards Nina, but she's still where we left her, huddled in Rion's embrace as he shields her from the beast.

Before I can even get completely to my feet, Damien is stalking forward, his suit rumpled and black hair disarrayed. His blue eyes glint manically as he brandishes his weapon, slicing, cutting, slashing…and then nimbly moving out of the creature's way before he can swipe the mage's head off. It's times like these when I remember that Damien is one of the scariest men in the entire prison. The best assassin to have ever graced the earth. He fights like it's a dance, one that only he knows the choreography to. And though the minotaur is larger, taller, stronger—obviously not hindered by the no powers rule that the Labyrinth has—Damien is smarter and quicker.

Cut after cut mars the beast's chest as he roars his agony towards the ceiling. And even when another seismic wave knocks us all off our feet, Damien remains upright, a lock of dark hair falling in front of his face.

And then the minotaur makes another fatal mistake.

He turns towards Nina in Rion's arms and takes a step towards her.

Damien releases an enraged battle cry, unlike anything I've ever heard before, and renews his attack with a relentless vigor. We don't even bother to join in on the fight. This is Damien's kill.

"Stop this madness!" a voice bellows, and the entire Labyrinth shakes with the force of it.

And shakes, and shakes, and shakes.

The floor seems to fall out from underneath me, and I collapse on my ass, blinking stars from my vision. Once again, only Damien remains upright as he ducks a blow from the minotaur, though his glacial blue eyes are trained on the figure approaching us from the hallway we just came from.

The man appears to be in his mid-to-late twenties with dark brown skin and pitch-black hair. His brown eyes almost look amber as they glare heatedly at the minotaur. His muscular body is clothed in a brown trench coat that flows around him as he walks. In his hand is a silver spear, the tip seeming to radiate a bright green color. It almost reminds me...

Well, it almost reminds me of the green mist from the Labyrinth. The one that burned my hand.

Nina releases a breath of surprise, her blind gaze fixed in his general direction, as he offers her a fleeting stare. For a moment, I swear his features soften when he gazes upon her before he instantly hardens them. Turning back towards the beast, still engaged in a fierce battle with Damien, he lifts the spear and flings it at the creature's unprotected back.

It penetrates his skin and organs, slicing cleanly through his torso, and the monster releases another pained roar, falling to his knees.

"I did not want to do that, my old friend, but you left me no choice," the newcomer says with a sad shake of his head.

The minotaur lets out a keening cry, his dark eyes wide in his face, before collapsing into a puddle of dark blood, directly at Damien's feet.

"Well, that was not how I expected to introduce myself," the trench coat wearing man says with a sneer, wiping his hands together. He doesn't have a second to catch his breath before Damien is jumping over the minotaur's body and pinning him to the wall, his eyes flaring dangerously. Most men would shit their pants from being at the receiving end of such an expression, but this guy—this strange, unfamiliar man—just seems curious.

"Who the fuck are you? Why were you following us?" he demands, punctuating each statement with a swipe of his dagger against the man's neck. A tiny cut appears on his dark skin, and blood wells. No, not blood.

Green acid.

"What the fuck are you?" I demand, once more glancing towards Nina to ensure she's all right. Her eyes are wild, dark hair tousled, as she blinks in the guy's direction. Bronson has his arms around her waist, while Rion nibbles on her fingers like the crazy psycho he is.

"I was not following *you*," the man states with a decisive eye roll, ignoring my question. "I was following *her*." He turns pointedly towards Nina, and we all stiffen, even Logan, who moves to stand in front of her to obscure her from view.

"Why?" he demands, bunching his hands into fists.

"The same reason you guys are," he replies evasively, and as I watch, transfixed, the green spear disappears back into his hand—literally. It seems to melt before my very eyes, becoming one with his body, as if it never existed in the first place.

"Let's just kill him and continue on," Damien suggests icily, and the man blinks again in confusion.

"Why would you do that?" he asks, genuinely perplexed.

Before any of us can respond, there's another sound from the hallway we emerged from.

Fucking hell. Is there a parade going on that I didn't know about?

Seeing as I'm not currently occupied with Nina or the asshole, I step forward, Abel on one side of me and Logan on the other. I can't help but think that this is the way it should be—all of us fighting to protect our girl from harm.

But then all thoughts flee as the figure staggers forward.

Blood coats his shredded shirt to his chest, and his face is a myriad of bruises and gashes that he hasn't been able to heal due to the Labyrinth dampening his powers. But his dark eyes are familiar, as is the dragon tattoo on his upper arm, visible where his shirt has been torn.

He dismisses the minotaur, the newcomer, all of us, as if we're barely a blip on his radar. His eyes focus on the only person in the room who matters, our reason for fucking breathing.

She releases a strangled sound as Rion and Bronson both release her, and his lips twitch in the beginnings of a smile, though it's laced with pain.

"Did you miss me, baby girl?" Kai rasps out.

CHAPTER 45

NINA

There's always a moment in your life that defines you. The one moment that is imprinted on your mind for years to come. For centuries to come. It's that memory you'll treasure above all else, the one you'll cherish when you're on your deathbed.

And my moment is coming face to face with the man I love.

The man I thought I lost.

"Kai..." My voice trembles, breaks, and then I'm running towards him, trusting that he'll catch me.

His arms wrap around me as he sweeps me off my feet, burying his face in my hair as he whispers words meant to soothe and calm.

"I'm sorry."

"I'm okay."

"I'll never leave you."

"I'm sorry."

I don't know why he's apologizing, but as his words penetrate my head, infusing me in a layer of warmth, I fall apart. I cry and cry and cry, wrapping my legs around his waist as my hands tangle in the hair at the base of his neck.

"Never. Leave me. Again!" I sob as his grip tightens.

"Never," he vows with a finality that could lead nations to war. My dark, devilish king.

"I thought you were dead," I continue as I cry my heart out. Relief is a palpable entity, one that coils around me like barbed wire, digging into my skin until I'm weeping blood.

"I would've been," Kai admits on a shaky breath as he rubs a hand down my back. "If he hadn't saved me." He nods his head in the direction I know Damien and the newcomer to be.

The newcomer who's silky, baritone voice reminds me eerily of Nick's.

"As you can see, I am not the villain you accuse me of being," the man in question states softly, as if admonishing a disobedient child. "Would you please remove the knife from my throat?"

"What do you want?" Damien hisses, his cold, cruel voice at odds with the gentle way he spoke to me only minutes ago. I'm too tired and weary to enter anyone's mind and use their eyes as guidance. Instead, I rely on my other senses, listening to the new man's huff of indignation.

"I thought I was doing the right thing by protecting my... What do we call each other? Brother?"

Kai tenses in my arms, and I just know he's glaring at the man over my head.

"I appreciate you saving my life, but I am not your brother."

"No?" Genuine confusion, and maybe a little bit of hurt, seeps into his voice. "Then what would you call the mate to your mate?"

Silence reigns, so intense and potent that I'm practically choking on it.

And then all at once, like a pebble being thrown into a tranquil puddle of water, chaos erupts.

"What?"

"No fucking way."

"I vote we just kill him."

"Oh! Idea!" Rion pipes in eagerly, his loud voice carrying over the others'. "I packed nipple clamps in my bag—"

"I thought I said to only pack the essentials," Kai growls out, and I can't help but laugh giddily. No reason, except for the fact that he's alive. He's okay.

He's here.

He never gave up on me, on us, on our baby. He fought the Grim Reaper and emerged victorious, bearing down on the Labyrinth with the fires of hell in his eyes.

"Nipple clamps are essential," Rion protests. "Now, if you'll stop interrupting me like a meanie butt…" He waits, as if ensuring everyone is listening to him, before he steps up behind me. I can feel his warm breath on my neck as he wraps his arms around both Kai and me, holding us tightly and rocking us back and forth. He nuzzles my back as he speaks. "So, what I'm proposing is called the Waterfall."

"The Waterfall?" Cain repeats in a half delirious voice, barking out a laugh.

"No. Inter. Rupting," Rion snaps, pausing between "inter" and "rupting." "So we'll take the nipple clamps to Trench here—"

"Trench?" Abel interrupts, and I just know that my trickster demon is doing this to rile Rion up.

"Trench Coat Man," Rion elaborates with a hiss—a literal hiss, like he's a cat preparing to claw at someone's face. "Now shut the fuck up and let me discuss torture options, dammit!"

"Sorry. Continue."

"Anyway, so we'll take Trench's balls—after we remove

them from his body of course—and connect the nipple clamps—"

"Oh, enough of this!" Bronson growls, and I hear the sound of flesh hitting flesh.

"Brother!" the newcomer says, sounding aghast. "Why would you hit me?"

"I am not your brother!" Bronson seethes. "Tell us who the fuck you are and what you want!"

"Bronson!" I warn, my voice wobbling ever so slightly. "Stop it. Don't hurt him." I don't know why I'm defending this man, this stranger, but the thought of harm coming to him leaves a sour, acidic taste in my mouth. I tell myself that it's because he saved Kai and brought my dragon back to me, but I know that's not entirely the truth.

"Buttercup…" Rion whines, still nuzzling my back. "Can't we just do an itty-bitty little maiming?"

"No!" I snap, and Kai shifts us so Rion is dislodged from my back. Keeping my voice low and soothing, I plead to the man, "Just tell us what we want to know."

There's a pause before he finally speaks, almost as if he's considering his words. "I assumed you remembered me from your dreams, but perhaps I was mistaken."

"Dreams?" Bronson roars.

"Trouble," Cain asks, "what the fuck is he going on about?"

I shift in Kai's arms, but when he tries to let me down, I cling to him like a spider monkey. There's no way in heck I'm leaving his arms anytime soon, not after I thought I lost him. Not when the wound is still so raw, so bloody.

"I told Kai," I confess. "I just assumed he told you."

"I didn't think it was anything serious," Kai admits, placing his cheek on top of my head. His voice grows darker, nothing but a growl dripping in malice. "But perhaps I should've reconsidered."

"I've just been having weird dreams," I admit, trying to shrug. It's hard with my body wrapped so tightly around Kai's massive one. "I didn't really remember them when I woke up, but they always left me feeling…strange."

"Strange?" Damien asks curtly. "What do you mean?"

"I don't know how to explain it. I wasn't unsettled afterwards, per se, but I felt like there was something important I had to remember. Sometimes I recalled the dreams in vivid detail, but other times, they slipped through my fingers."

"That would be my fault," the man confesses. "I am still learning how to control these new powers I have developed. I have been asleep for so long…" He trails off, his breath hitching. "I never intended to remain anonymous. I assumed our dear mate remembered me when she woke up after our encounters."

"Don't call her that," Rion snaps.

The man makes a noise of bemusement. "Don't call her what?"

"Mate." This comes from Bronson, his voice nothing more than a hoarse growl. He sounds as if he's seconds away from closing the distance between the two of them, digging his teeth in the other man's neck, and pulling until blood colors the walls of the tunnels.

"But she *is* my mate," the newcomer protests. "I recognized her as mine when she first entered the Labyrinth. I just did not have the power to visit and claim her."

A chorus of growls erupt from my guys. Apparently, they don't like the thought of someone other than them claiming me for himself.

"Who are you?" Logan interrupts, and the man releases a heavy, tired sigh.

"I apologize. I am still learning, and I am afraid my manners leave much to be desired. You may call me Nick."

I knew it was him, I did, but hearing it confirmed dispels the breath from my lungs, leaving my head spinning.

"Nick." Kai spits his name as if it leaves a foul taste in his mouth. "*What* are you?"

Without missing a beat, Nick answers, "I am the Labyrinth."

The silence this time is heavy. So freaking heavy, I swear I can feel it clogging my airways like barrels of maple syrup. My hands shake where they rest on Kai's neck, digging into his tender flesh.

"What… That's… How… Impossible!" I've never heard Damien sound so out of sorts before.

But the truth of Nick's statement permeates my very soul.

The Labyrinth.

In the flesh.

"It is true," Nick declares candidly, seemingly oblivious to the shock rippling through us all. Or if he does notice, he chooses to ignore it. "When the mages and wizards created the Labyrinth beneath the prison hundreds and hundreds of years ago, the amount of magic wielded was enough to create a sentient being. A being so powerful and strong, his presence kept the Labyrinth afloat, despite the fact he was not tangible."

"And you're saying that *you're* that being?" Abel interrupts with a choked laugh. "That's fucking insane."

"Is it?" Nick asks, and the question isn't rhetorical. It almost sounds as if he's curious about their thoughts and reactions, as if he wants to know if his existence is legit insane. When the silence stretches, not one of us daring to break it, Nick continues, "I have been asleep for hundreds of years, a sentient being able to see and hear through the walls of the maze, when I awoke a little over a year ago."

"When I arrived," I breathe, my nails digging into Kai's

neck. If it hurts him, he doesn't show it, simply tightening his arms around me as if he wishes to protect me from Nick's candid words.

"Yes," he replies without preamble. "You awoke me, little one. I knew the second I set eyes upon you that you were my fated mate, the woman capable of freeing me from this prison. Because rest assured, I was in prison just like you all were. I may not have been a criminal, I may have been an innocent party, but I was still trapped in a cage with no hope of escaping.

"Over time," Nick continues, "I was able to fine-tune my skills. My powers. I discovered that while I couldn't quite hold on to a physical form, I could enter Nina's dreams. I manipulated the tunnels to show Rion the exit when he was in here earlier. But it was only recently that I was able to take this human form and walk the halls I once controlled."

"Hol-y fuck," Abel breathes.

"I tried to do what I could to help you maneuver these dangerous paths," Nick continues, "but I was weak. It was nearly impossible for me to hold my physical form and still manipulate the Labyrinth to get you to where you needed to go. I tried to help when the monsters attacked, but then you all got separated. I did what I could for my dragon brother and tried to lead all of you to the doorway."

"Why the fuck would you do all of this for us?" Bronson interjects, but I already know. Before he even says the words, I know.

"It is as I told you. Nina Doe is my mate."

The breath leaves my lungs in a whooshing exhale as the rest of my guys hurl insult after insult at him, disbelieving scoffs reverberating through the stone room.

But I can't deny the rightness that embeds itself in my soul. The truth of his words.

It's scary to know that this man, this stranger, is my fated mate, but I can't deny the surety of it either. I don't know him and I don't love him, but there's a part of me that wants to learn everything there is to know about him. It's the same way I feel about my men. The same way I feel about…Logan.

Nick is my mate.

Of that, I have no doubt.

The question is—what am I going to do with that knowledge?

"When we leave, my powers will leave with me," Nick continues, his tone holding a note of warning.

"Leave?" Damien asks with a huff of laughter. "Why would you think you're coming with us?"

"Because Nina is my mate and I love her," Nick responds in confusion, and his words send a flood of heat through my body, followed immediately by a surge of ice.

Love?

No.

He can't love me. Not yet.

Blood rushes to my ears, and I feel faint.

Continuing on as if Damien hadn't interrupted, Nick says, "There is a chance that the entire Labyrinth will fall if I leave. That the magic prohibiting the inmates from leaving will fail."

"Are you saying that the others could potentially escape?" Rion asks, and I can't quite tell if he sounds aghast by the prospect or excited. With my crazy shifter, it's hard to know for certain.

"It is a very real possibility," Nick admits, sounding as if he doesn't care either way. "But I am not leaving my little one." For the first time since we met him, since he made himself known to our group, something dark creeps into his tone. "You will have to kill me first."

"Nina," Kai whispers, placing his mouth near my ear so only I can hear his words, "what do you want to do? This decision is yours, baby, and we'll support you however you see fit."

"I…" Biting on my lower lip, I think through my choices. We could escape, just the seven us, and leave Nick behind. He's a stranger to me, an enigma, and I don't know for sure if I can even trust him

At the same time, he saved all of our butts more times than I care to count. He saved *Kai*. He could be a psycho serial killer for all I care, but that fact alone puts him in my good graces.

And I know without a shadow of doubt that he's my mate. The second he said those words, I sensed it in my very soul, almost as if my heart was screaming at me to listen and believe him. At the same time, my head was warning me against trusting him, trusting anyone who wasn't one of the six guys I've grown to love.

"I don't want to decide anything right now," I confess, keeping my voice just as low as his. Despite that, everyone hears me, their entire attention fixed on me as if I'm the only thing that matters. "So we'll bring him with us, and I'll decide what to do with him later."

Decide what to do with him…

As if he's a stray dog that I'll either let into my house or kick out onto the street.

Guilt fills me, but I push that emotion aside, tightening my arms around Kai's neck.

"As you wish, Angel," Damien murmurs, and from his tone, I can't quite tell how he feels about my decision. Does he resent it? Resent *me*?

I don't know what to do about any of this. In a span of minutes, I discovered one of my mates was still alive and that I potentially had a new one—one who didn't exist until mere seconds ago. One who I thought was nothing but a figment of my imagination.

One who has been stalking me long before I knew of his existence.

"Come then," Damien continues curtly. "If this door is the way out of here—"

"It is," Nick interrupts.

"—then we need to get moving."

"Kai," I whisper into his ear. "I don't know what to do about any of this. I didn't know—"

"Shhh." He rubs at my back soothingly. "It's okay, baby girl. None of us expected this. But we'll figure it out when we're clear of this place once and for all. But no one, absolutely no one, will resent you, no matter what you decide. You got that?" I'm overcome by the enormity of my emotions for this man. Instead of answering, I kiss the side of his neck, grateful all over again that he's alive and well. If I'd truly lost him...

"I love you," I say into his skin.

"I love you more," he responds gruffly. "But are you sure you want to bring him with us? If his magic fails, the other inmates might be able to escape the prison. Are you sure—"

"Yes," I interrupt. "I truly believe he's one of my mates. I may not know him, but I'm not leaving him behind. Not until I can figure everything out."

"Okay, baby. Okay." There's no judgement or malice in his tone, and I realize with a start that he's telling me the truth. All of my men will support me no matter what I choose to do with Nick...or Logan for that matter, though I refuse to spend more than a second focusing on that thought. My men love me, love this family, and they'll never begrudge me a mate because of jealousy or rivalry. It's why Rion and Kai were able to put aside their differences when we first met. It's why even now, my men rely on each other like brothers.

Like family.

"Let's do this," I say determinedly, taking a deep, calming breath to bolster my resolve.

Still in Kai's arms, his lips brushing repeatedly against my temple, we step through the doorway.

CHAPTER 46

LOGAN

Freedom.

So close, I can taste it.

The flavor is surprisingly pleasant, resting on the tip of my tongue like a sugar cube. It overpowers everything else, including the crippling jealousy that continuously threatens to send me spiraling into a red-hot rage.

I never understood why green was always associated with jealousy.

As I watch Nick smile at Nina, a translucent veil bathed in blood shrouds my vision, darkening everything until it feels like I'm watching the events unfold through macabre sunglasses.

Mate.

The fucking Labyrinth in the flesh is her mate.

While I…

I'm just a man hopelessly in love with a woman who will never love him back.

She doesn't smile at me the way she does the others. Her features don't soften when she stares up into my face. I removed my flirty mask so she could see the real me—the broken, unlovable cupid.

And she still rejected me.

Maybe not with words, but she never acted as if she wanted more. As if she wanted *me*.

My pain sours each breath until even the air tastes like poison.

There's no describing the relief I felt when we discovered that Kai was still alive. I don't necessarily like the man, but I can't stand to see Nina in pain. When she cried, acting as if her heart had been forcibly removed from her chest, I cried with her. Silent tears that traveled down my face and caught on my lower lip. It was only then that I realized…

I'm in love with her.

She can never know.

The thought springs to me unbidden as I force my gaze away from her sincere face, still in Kai's arms as he turns towards the broken doorway.

The last thing I want is for her to pity me. Or worse, feel obligated or uncomfortable. I'll never do anything to mess up this tentative friendship we're forming, so if I have to love her from afar, then so be it.

I'm not used to feeling like this.

Jealous…

Heartbroken…

I'm a cupid, for fuck's sake. I've gone through more men and women than I'm willing to admit. No attachments. No strings. No feelings. Those were the rules I lived by, the rules I held close to my heart as I flirted like a fucking champ and fucked like it was a sport.

Now, my heart's at the feet of a goddess, and she can either claim it as her own or stomp on it. Either way, it's hers forever. I don't want it back.

What need do I have for a lump of black coal that only beats for her?

I lick my upper lip, my eyes locking on Nick.

The Labyrinth.

It still blows my mind when I think about it. I half expect him to break into laughter and tell us it's nothing but a joke. How can one man be responsible for the entire Labyrinth? The power he must exude...

He smiles when he catches me looking, not a trace of mocking in the upwards tilt of his lips. He seems genuinely excited to see me.

I'm not gonna lie. He's a good-looking guy, with obsidian skin, buzzed black hair, and perfectly white teeth that shine in his face. The opened brown trench coat reveals a skin-tight black T-shirt and similarly colored jeans. I half wonder where he got the outfit—did he steal it? Or did he magic it on himself?

A snort of amusement escapes me when I picture a poor inmate running around in his underwear because the fucking prison itself stole his clothes.

"Hello." The man lifts his hand and waves it. "My name is Nick."

"I know that," I grunt out, bringing my fingers to the bridge of my nose and squeezing. I can feel a headache rapidly approaching.

"It is a pleasure to meet you, brother," Nick continues, flashing me another disarming grin.

I'm sure my answering smile is more of a grimace.

And why the hell is calling me his brother? I'm not like the other men. I'm not Nina's mate.

Though a piece of my heart begs to differ.

"Same."

Even though I want to pound your face in for stealing a girl who never belonged to me.

"Shall we go?" Nick gestures towards the doorway, and with a start, I realize that we're the only two people left inside the Labyrinth. Everyone else already exited.

Trepidation rushes down my back like an ice cube being dropped down my shirt, the feeling enticing goosebumps to break out along my body.

The broken doorway…leads to nothing.

When I stare through the shattered remains, I see nothing but a pitch-black abyss that threatens to lure me in and claim me forever.

"Where did they go?"

Nick tilts his head curiously to the side, regarding me with wide, guileless eyes. They're eyes that hold not a hint of deception. Is he that good of an actor? Or is he truly as innocent as he appears to be?

"They left the Labyrinth," Nick answers simply, seeming confused by my question. "Is that not what you wanted yourself?"

My pulse quickens as I flick my eyes back towards the doorway. Back towards the nothingness.

Where Nina is.

Loving her is like jumping out of a plane with no parachute, trusting that you'll survive the crash.

But some people are worth the risk.

Without answering Nick's question, I steel my spine and hurry through the doorway.

The darkness presses in on me from all sides, stealing the oxygen from the room.

Is this what Nina experiences daily?

This…darkness? This oppressive, restricting, nauseating darkness?

It clogs my airways like barrels of sticky tar, and I can feel panic overwhelming my senses. My breathing comes out in ragged, stuttered gasps as I force my feet forward.

And forward.

And forward.

The first thing I'm aware of is the sun beating down on my face.

A hysterical laugh escapes me, the noise joining in with that of my brethren. My friends, if I'm even allowed to call them that. I can hear Nina's giggle as Kai releases another whoop of pleasure.

When was the last time I felt sunlight like this? Felt its warm rays caress my skin, the touch lighter than a moth's wings?

It's a bittersweet sensation. Security doesn't instantly flood my system. The warmth from the sun doesn't completely chase away the ice permeating my body.

The sun actually blinds me, forcing me to squint against the harsh glare. It feels too hot on my pasty skin, too demanding, and I find myself scratching absently at my arms, almost as if I'm trying to peel away the raw, abused skin.

It takes me a moment to orient myself to my surroundings. I squeeze my eyelids shut before forcing them open.

"We did it! We fucking did it, Bambi!" I hear Abel exclaim as I focus in their direction. He takes her from Kai and spins her in a circle as she giggles madly.

"Where the fuck are we?" The cold, disdainful voice belongs to Damien. He stands near the edge of the group, the only one not smiling. His arrogant face is drawn tight as he peers into the distance.

I follow the direction of his gaze towards a large, foreboding building.

Nightmare Penitentiary.

It's nothing but a speck in the distance, the orangish sun casting strange shadows around the ominous structure. It's just as creepy as I remember it being when I first arrived.

Have we really walked that far? This entire time, has a

cavern of tunnels and monsters been lurking just beneath the red sand, accessible to anyone who dares ventures this far out? The door we came out of is nowhere to be seen—almost as if the Labyrinth spit us out and then burrowed back beneath the sand like a worm. I don't know if I should be grateful or terrified.

Like, if I piss my pants right now, would it be a happy piss or a scared one?

That is the real question.

I resist the urge to flip off the prison, which has been my home for far too long—not as long as the others, of course, but long enough to give me a healthy appreciation for walking the straight and narrow path. A life of crime? Not worth this shit.

Peeling my gaze away from the prison, I study our surroundings.

In every direction, I see nothing but a canvas of bright blue sky and red, compacted dirt.

From my research before I entered the prison, I know that the main exit has a dirt road you're forced to follow for miles and miles until you finally find some semblance of civilization.

But apparently, the Labyrinth—I glare in Nick's direction —has a twisted sense of humor and dropped us off on the wrong side of the fucking prison.

"We're out, man!" Abel squeals, jumping up and down and shaking his ass. "I feel *sunlight.*"

"It fucking hurts," Cain grumbles, folding his arms over his chest as he glares at nothing in particular.

"Where do we go?" Bronson turns towards Kai, all of them falling back into their usual roles now that their leader is back. Despite no longer being in prison, I can see that the guys will still defer to the hierarchy from before.

Kai scratches at his chin as he twists his head from side to side—towards the prison in the distance and then straight forward, where miles and miles of red sand spread as far as the eye can see.

"We can't risk getting caught," Kai states. "Right now, we have no reason to believe the guards even know that we escaped, but we can't hope for that anonymity to last. There's no way we can cross by the prison without being seen." He reaches absently for Nina's hand and twines their fingers together. She smiles softly up at him, and my heart gives a painful squeeze. I force myself to look away, catching Nick's gaze, who once again, smiles and waves at me.

Fucker.

"He's right," Damien announces curtly. "We need to keep moving forward. Hopefully, we'll run into something that can help us get farther away from this fucking place."

"Is that really the best idea?" I interject for the first time. When all of their eyes swivel my way, I find myself struggling to keep my head held high. These men? They're scary as fuck. *I'll just find a nice little hidey-hole and live there the rest of my life, thank you very much. No reason to stare at the cupid.* But my stupid voice keeps spitting out words, despite my better judgment. "That way," I jab my finger over my shoulder, in the direction of the prison, "has trees we can use for cover. Over here, we're sitting ducks."

Kai considers my words carefully as his gaze once again flickers towards Nina. "You make a good point."

"But we can't risk going near the prison," Damien argues. "We can't—"

As the two of them argue, I allow my eyes to drift towards Nina, as they always seem to do nowadays. A smile tugs at my lip as her cute nose wrinkles, her head tilted curiously to the side as she listens to Kai speak.

Almost as if she feels my eyes on her, she twists her head in my direction.

Time stops.

My heart rate picks up speed, thrumming erratically in my rib cage, as her beautiful white eyes lock with mine. I know she can't see me, but I swear she's staring into my very soul, tearing through layers and layers of bravado until the vulnerable man beneath is stripped naked before her. Watching. Waiting. Begging.

She takes a step towards me, and her presence siphons all of the oxygen from my lungs.

"I can feel your eyes on me," she says with a teasing grin.

"Well…" I fork my fingers through my messy blond hair. "Your head is in my line of sight."

She gasps in mock horror. "Are you saying my head is big, Logan?"

"Err." I shrug, a wry grin playing on my lips. "Above average for sure."

"Shut up!" She giggles, the sound traveling through my body and ending at my cock. I wish I could make that sound my ringtone. You know, once I get a phone again. And if I don't die.

I pantomime zipping my lips shut and tossing her the key. Smiling, she captures the "key" from the air and places it in her dress pocket.

The smile on her face fades as suddenly as it arrived, and she shifts from foot to foot. "Logan, there's actually something I wanted to talk to you about."

Warmth blazes through me as she unleashes the hurricane force of her stare on me.

What does she have to talk to me about?

Oh my god. I'm quivering like a schoolgirl giving her crush a card that says, "Do you like me? Yes or no."

Fucking hell.

Instead of immediately responding, I quirk a finger at her. Her brows dip in confusion.

"What?"

Sighing, I move closer to her and reach into her dress pocket, ignoring her sharp intake of breath as her eyelashes flutter, and grab the "key" she stashed in there. I pantomime unzipping my lips and then gasp dramatically.

"I thought I was going to die of suffocation," I confess, panting. "I'm not much of a nose breather."

She chortles, bringing both hands to her mouth to stifle the adorable sound, and my grin widens. I suppose being a renowned, debonair flirt has its advantages. If I'm able to make my girl laugh even for a second, then it's worth it.

A noise pulls me from my thoughts.

My brows scrunch together in confusion as I turn towards the strange sound. The rest of the men are completely oblivious, still arguing with each other over the best course of action. My breath leaves me when I realize it's the distinct sound of tires on sand.

A black SUV with dark tinted windows drives forward, rapidly approaching us. And then three more crest the hill behind the first, seemingly materializing out of thin air. And then three more. And then three more.

And then three more…

"Guys!" I bellow, but they're already watching with wide eyes.

Kai grabs Nina the same time Bronson does, both of them shielding her with their considerable builds. Rion shifts down to his tiger form…before his power fizzles and he's forced to be human once again. It's a miracle he was able to hold his cat form as long as he did in the Labyrinth.

Even though we're outside of the prison, our powers are still weak. My own sparks and fizzles before instantly depleting like a fire being soaked in water. It'll return in time—I can already feel it growing inside of me—but not soon enough.

"Do we run?" Abel demands, turning frightened eyes onto Nina.

"Nowhere to fucking run," Damien snaps as he removes his suit jacket and tosses it on the ground. He rolls up his dress sleeves as he waits for the SUVs to arrive.

"I am *so* going to stick my fist up their asses," Rion singsongs, a familiar, dangerous glint in his eyes as he swaggers forward, cock swinging. It's the same one he wore when we first reconnected, when he pinned me against the wall and threatened to kill me.

It's a look ravaged by anger and madness.

My heart stutters and gets caught in my throat as the SUVs slow to a stop in front of us.

Are they from the prison? Have they come to take us back?

I don't want to go back, dammit. I'm too pretty to "drop the soap."

One by one, men in black exit the vehicles, each one holding a machine gun.

Fuck. Fuck. Fuck. Fuck.

We're getting anal fucked so bad right now...and not in the way I normally like.

"You here to take us back?" Kai asks darkly, his skin rippling as ruby-red scales slash across his skin. I can see his dragon struggling to break free.

"I'll have you know that I have a mighty craving for testicles today," Rion says casually, whistling as he stalks forward. He doesn't have any weapons on him, but then again, Rion doesn't need weapons to be a formidable opponent. He may not be as skilled at fighting as Damien, but he's crazy enough to kill a man with his bare hands.

"You always have a craving for testicles," Damien murmurs, and Rion swoons.

"Awww. Bitch Mage! You understand me. Are you," he flutters his eyelashes, "offering me a taste of yours?"

If looks could kill, Rion would be dead faster than a bullet from one of the guns pointed our way.

"We don't want a fight," one of the largest men declares, slowly removing his hands from his weapon so it swings against his chest, the strap over his shoulder keeping it in place. He places both hands up in surrender. "We just want the girl."

Every one of us goes perfectly still. Not a single breath can be heard as we stare at the army surrounding us. Because that's what this is—a fucking army.

Come to take our girl.

Dammit. Their girl. Not yours.

Is this really necessary right now, mental me?

"What the fuck do you want with her?" Bronson growls, his eyes flashing amber. I can see his wolf struggling to break free, to destroy these men who threaten the woman we all love, but he's still too weak to do more than growl threateningly.

"We can be friends," the man continues in that same condescending tone. It makes my teeth ache.

"How can we possibly be friends with you when you are threatening our Nina?" Nick asks in bewilderment as he steps forward, his brown coat swinging around him. He tilts his head to the side, resembling an animal hiding beneath abnormally tall grass, just waiting for the sweet gazelle to take a sip from the stream so he can pounce. His strange, yellow-brown eyes dance with an indecipherable emotion. "If I am not mistaken, that would make you our enemy." He glances towards Kai for confirmation, but the dragon shifter only has eyes for our enemy.

"Leave if you want to live," he threatens, and even I get

goosebumps from his low, threatening voice. My manly bits tingle a little too.

Hot damn.

The man from the SUV sighs heavily, though he doesn't seem surprised by our answer. He turns towards a tinted window in the closest SUV, and the door opens, an unfamiliar man stepping out.

Or...

A *familiar* man.

As I watch, horrified, his face flickers from male to female. Old to young. Young to old.

Once again, my surroundings blur as I try to stare directly at him, try to see past the illusion spell concealing his true features from view.

"Smith," I breathe as horror engulfs me.

"Smith?" Abel whips his head to glare at me, an accusation in his verdant green eyes.

But how is this possible? I didn't tell Smith anything about Nina. How did he—

"Good job, Logan." Though it's still impossible for me to see his face clearly, I swear he's smiling. I detect a hint of amusement in his low, baritone voice. "You did good bringing her to me."

"I didn't..." I struggle to defend myself as all eyes turn to stare at me. But I don't focus on them. My attention is fixed on Nina.

Her white, guileless eyes are wide with unshed tears. Betrayal is etched onto her face, morphing her beautiful features into something unrecognizable.

"Logan, is this true?" Her voice wobbles.

"Of course it is," Smith declares with a haughty laugh. This time, his voice is high-pitched and decidedly feminine. I wonder if he'd still be laughing if I stick my fist down his throat and rip his vocal cords out. "I know what he told you. It was exactly what we *wanted* him to tell you. He said he came into the prison to kill you, am I correct?" Another laugh. Another vivid daydream of throat punching the fucker. "We wanted him to build trust with you, Ms. Nina Doe. And once he did that, he would get you out and bring you to *us*."

"Us?" Rion hisses, baring his teeth. "Who the fuck is *us*?"

Nina's voice is the barest breath of sound. A whisper that carries in the stale, stagnant air. "The Compound."

"You're not as dumb as you look," Smith taunts. He lifts a hand, beckoning Nina forward. "Now come with me, and your men don't have to die."

"Logan," Nina's face twists, a tiny crease appearing between her brows, "is what he's saying true?"

"Yes," I confess as desperation courses through me. I lunge forward, ignoring the threatening growls from Nina's mates, though they remain focused on the larger threat, and take both of her hands in mine. "But I swear to you, I never intended to go through with it. Maybe at first...but then I got to know you. I fell in love with you, Nina. I will *never* hurt you."

"He is telling the truth," Nick interjects. "I have never sensed any deception from him in his interactions with her."

"Nina, please." I'm not above begging. Even if I were to die today, die fighting for her, I'd die a happy man if I knew she didn't despise me. "I think..." A shaky laugh escapes me. "I never felt this way about anyone before. I think...I think you're my mate. You already know that I used to work for a man named Narian...and you also know how evil that bastard is. When I was offered a job to break a beautiful girl out of prison, I agreed. I thought it was the only way to free myself from him. To make a better life for myself, one where I'm not an assassin or a killer. So I stole a stupid feather from Lionel Green and was sent here. God, I was so stupid. So naïve. I thought I was doing what I had to do to survive. I know you don't trust me right now, I know you hate me—"

"I don't hate you," she interrupts vehemently. She gently places her hand on my cheek, her thumb inching dangerously close to my lips, before she lowers it and turns a fierce glare onto the Compound members. "How did you find us? And don't you dare say Logan told you. I know that's not true."

Her trust in me is humbling. I'm once again struck by my feelings for her—feelings unlike anything I've ever experienced before.

Smith sighs heavily, as if this entire conversation is beneath him. As if he doesn't like the fact Nina addressed him directly.

"You're right—Logan *didn't* tell us. But we still figured it out from him."

I break away from Nina and lunge forward. I probably would've gotten myself shot from one of the men pointing guns at me if Cain didn't grab the back of my shirt, pulling me to an abrupt halt.

"You lying piece of—"

Smith points to his arm, and I whip my head in the direction of my own limb.

"What...?"

Damien releases a fierce growl and stalks towards me. When he lifts his dagger, I legit think he's going to murder me. I'm man enough to admit I shit myself a bit.

But instead of slicing my throat, he digs his blade into my skin, ignoring my hiss of pain, and rips out a tiny black device.

A tracker.

"I swear I didn't know that was in there," I declare immediately.

"Of course you didn't," Kai grunts. "They probably put it in you when you were unconscious."

Smith's smug silence is answer enough.

"Enough of this," he barks out at last. He lifts a hand, dark red magic sparking on his fingers, and a second later, his illusion fades.

My breath leaves me, and I stagger back a step. Horror squeezes my heart in an iron vise as I stare at the familiar man standing before me.

Beside me, Damien rasps out, "I killed you."

Narian Teres, the leader of the assassins' guild who hired both me and him, smiles. He looks exactly as I remember him, with pitch-black hair peppered with gray and a thin, muscular build. He has a bald spot on the top of his head that he desperately tries to hide with a few wispy strands of hair.

"You killed a man wearing my face," Narian corrects with a laugh. "I'm the best assassin in the fucking world and a master of illusions. Did you really think I would be that easy to kill?"

"*You're* Narian," Nina says on a gasp.

He bends his waist in a dramatic bow as I struggle to refortify my defenses.

My tormentor, my abuser, my *rapist* is standing in front of me.

Staring at the woman I love.

The woman I believe is my *mate*.

That's the only logical explanation for all of this. For the way my heart pounds unsteadily when she stares at me, the way I was drawn to her from the very first moment, the way my hands sweat and my body shakes. I didn't want to look at it too closely, because if it wasn't true, a piece of my heart would cease to exist, but I'm surer than ever that Nina Doe is meant to be mine.

Or maybe…

That I am meant to be hers.

The helplessness dissipates, and anger rushes to the surface in its place. My pulse races, the sloshing of blood in my head so loud and deafening, I can't think straight.

"You're part of the Compound," I say in realization.

"I'm not just a part of the Compound," Narian says with a huff. "I *am* the Compound."

"You worked with Alyssa and Raphael," Kai deduces with a snarl. "To…what? Create mutant super assassins?"

Nina's face has drained of all color, her spine ramrod straight.

"You're not going back, Bambi," Abel whispers to her. "I swear to you, we won't allow that to happen."

"But—"

"You're not going back," Cain agrees earnestly. He gives her a hand a squeeze.

"It's simple, really," Narian continues, waving his men forward. A few of them branch out in either direction until we're completely surrounded, all guns aimed on us. "Alyssa and Raphael were determined to create and experiment on rare supernaturals. I saw it as a business opportunity— purchase their prisoners and train them for myself. But when Alyssa and Raphael were killed," his upper lip curls, "the operation fell apart. We lost most of our assets. Except for one." His smile rests on Nina, and she shrinks away.

"We'll fight you," Damien promises, vengeance in his eyes. "And I'm betting on us winning."

"Or maybe," Narian continues on, acting as if Damien never spoke. "We can end this once and for all. Kill all of you and eliminate the last trace of the Compound." He shrugs his broad shoulders before flicking his gaze between me and the stone-cold mage. "My disgraced sons." His eyes drop to Nina. "My failed experiment."

"Narian…" Damien warns.

"Or maybe I'll just kill you guys and keep the girl for myself," he states, cocking his head to the side. I can see the moment he comes to a decision, his eyes hardening until they resemble granite. He lifts a hand in the air. "Kill them. But spare the girl."

Everything seems to happen in slow motion.

The guards' fingers tighten on their triggers, and I stare at the gun nearest to me.

I'm going to die.

We're all going to die.

And Nina will be at the mercy of this sadistic asshole.

That realization bolsters my resolve.

If I'm going to die, I'll be damned if I don't go out kicking and screaming and blowing so much lust into my enemies' faces, they come in their pants.

And then I hear a strange noise from beside me. I want to call it a scream, but that seems too tame for what it truly is. Too…simple.

It's a sound ripped from a person's soul. Shredded and bruised and bleeding, contaminating the air like the acid inside the Labyrinth.

It's also coming from Nina.

Her mouth is open, an anguished scream emanating from her tiny body, as she lifts her hands.

As I watch, unsure if I should be entranced or horrified, her face distorts until there's not a trace of softness left. Her eyes turn blood-red as horns curl on either side of her face. Wings erupt from her back, splitting open her white dress.

Demon. Angel. Human.

She raises her hands in Narian's direction, and all of the men in the immediate vicinity go flying head over heels. They land in undignified heaps on the ground, releasing pained groans. The SUVs shake, almost as if the ground beneath them is breaking open, before flying backwards, tumbling chaotically like tumbleweeds.

"Kill them!" Narian roars, staggering to his feet.

Nina twists her attention towards the guards to the right of us and lifts her hands once more.

"Oh my god," Abel breathes in horror as the men begin to convulse on the ground. Terrified screams leave their parted lips as blood cascades down their chins from their eyes, mouths, and ears. One by one, they explode, guts and blood flying in all directions.

Nina lifts another hand, and screams and grunts fill the air as the machine guns begin to smoke, flames eating away at them.

All hell breaks loose.

The remaining guards rush towards us, some attempting to fire off their rapidly melting weapons while others use their bare hands. A man lunges at us, shifting into a big ass bear when he's mere feet away.

But then Nick's there, not a trace of his customary smile in place, as he swings his cane like a fucking pro. He jabs it into the bear's side, and the shifter roars in agony as green goo erupts from the tip, penetrating his flesh.

I turn away, just as the toe-curling smell of burnt flesh permeates the air.

Desperate to do what I can to help, I reach towards one of the fallen guards and grab a dagger from out of his sheath.

And then I fight for my damn life.

I cut, slice, duck, and gift the guards illusions of all of their sickest sexual fantasies until my power sputters out.

Damien and Rion are fighting back-to-back, the differences in their fighting styles plain to see as they tear down their enemies.

Damien fights with a lethal grace, while Rion is all brawn. The two of them together are nearly unstoppable.

"Does this mean you want my babies, sugar daddy?" Rion calls as he flips a guard over his shoulder and snaps his neck.

Damien stabs his dagger into the stomach of one of the men before twisting and slicing open the neck of another.

"Shut up before I kill you," he threatens, completely serious.

Rion pouts. "Buttercup! He's threatening to murder me again! Spank him for me and call him daddy!"

But Nina doesn't hear him—or if she does hear him, she doesn't respond.

She stands surrounded by the twins, Bronson, and Kai as she absolutely obliterates her enemies. A group of around twenty men runs towards her—most of them vampires, if their speed is any indication—and she flicks her wrists, sending them flying backwards. The ground opens up beneath them and swallows their bodies whole.

Holy shit.

I'm sooo going to masturbate over that for years to come.

Movement out of my peripheral captures my attention.

Narian stands behind his men, using them as human shields, and has a handgun gun, which must've been hidden when Nina destroyed their weapons, raised.

At an oblivious Nina.

I don't think, just react.

As the gunshot ricochets through the air, I race forward and throw myself in front of Nina.

The bullet hits my chest.

I'm sorry, Nina. For everything.

Darkness.

CHAPTER 47

Through Bronson's eyes, I watch Logan drop.

There's nothing graceful or agile about it. He lurches forward, blood forming at the edges of his lips, and twists his head in my direction. His wide, baby-blue eyes are stamped with pain before his lashes flutter shut, concealing them.

He slumps forward, still.

"No," I scream, my voice nothing but a rasp of air. "No!"

Denial thrums through me.

Logan can't be dead. He just can't be. Not now. Not after we just found each other. A part of my heart breaks into cruel, jagged shards that stab repeatedly at my chest, drawing blood.

He's my mate.

The realization doesn't take me by surprise. Not truly. And the second I think that, I can sense a silver cord linking my soul to his, just as it does with the other men who have captured my heart.

Logan is my mate.

No. No. No.

Rion releases a roar of pain somewhere in the distance as five shifters pounce on him, holding him down. Damien turns to help him, but two vampires leap at him from either direction. He slashes with his knife, but his arms are physically yanked behind his back, holding him still.

I'm consumed by ineffable energy. It's almost as if all of the magic I've used before now has been nothing but water dripping from the faucet. Now, it surges out of me, so potent that it tickles my skin. Rage blazes a red-hot trail as I turn my attention in the direction I know Narian to be.

After a moment, Bronson twists his head in Narian's direction as well, and I'm able to see the coward for myself, hiding behind his men.

Anger like I never felt before erupts out of me like a detonating bomb. I raise my hands in his general direction and scream my rage and heartbreak for the world to hear.

"You're all going to die!" I scream...or I think I scream, but the voice isn't mine. It's superimposed with something infinitely darker, ten times more malicious than I can ever remember hearing it.

My magic curls around me, whispering to me.

Hurt. Kill. Destroy.

Yes... I agree as I tilt my head back and let my power free.

It disregards all of my mates, searching only for our attackers.

And then, the screams start.

Agonizing, horrified screams erupt as their bodies are ripped apart, their limbs tossed in opposite directions. Blood splatters in all directions, staining my skin and dress, as more and more power flows through me. My body convulses with the force of it. This much power...

It shouldn't exist in one person.

Narian releases a scream of terror as my magic wraps

around him, tightening. His eyes flicker past Bronson and towards me, the fear in them plain to see.

"You don't get to hurt my mates," I rage. "You don't get to hurt Logan and Damien. You don't get to hurt *anyone!*" The last word is a roar as the tendrils of magic turn into keen blades that slice at his skin. Blood wells as he struggles to free himself, struggles to overwhelm the power containing him, but for the first time in his life, he's the prisoner.

And I'm his captor.

He screams and screams and screams as I skin him alive. Nothing but pink muscle remains, and even then, I don't kill him.

Not yet.

My magic actually keeps him alive, forcing him to remain conscious for every second of this torment.

First one arm is removed. And then the next. And then his left leg. And then his right.

When only his torso and head remain, I step forward, pushing past my mates and stopping beside Logan's fallen body. I'm distantly aware of some of my magic splintering away from Narian and entering Logan, but I don't pay attention to that. Not yet. I know my magic won't hurt him. Instead, it seems almost…tender as it caresses his fallen body.

"You will pay for all of the things you have done, Narian." I speak each word slowly, succinctly, allowing him to stare into my eyes and see the face of the Grim Reaper herself. Because I'm going to kill him.

For the things he did to the men I love.

For the things he did to me.

For the things he did to countless other "experiments" in the Compound.

And maybe, just maybe, this will finally be over.

I lift my hand, relishing the way his face creases in agony and fear, and snap his neck.

He falls to the ground in a heap of dismembered limbs.

My magic snaps back into me like a rubber band being pulled too taut. I stagger back a few steps, my fisted hand resting on my chest and rubbing at my heart. I'm forced out of Bronson's head and back into the darkness as I tilt precariously to the side.

Strong arms catch me, holding me against his body. The pine scent indicates him as Bronson.

"I got you, Goddess. I got you," he whispers into my ear.

"Logan...?" I moan as I struggle to maintain consciousness.

The last thing I hear before I surrender to the encroaching oblivion is Logan's weak voice whispering, "Nina?"

I black out.

~

"She's going to be okay..." Bronson's soft voice pulls me to the land of the living. "You checked her out yourself, man. She and the baby are fine."

"I would feel better if she just woke the hell up," Damien snaps as I wearily feel for my power. It does my bidding slowly, sluggishly, searching for a familiar mind and plunging inside.

The height shows me that I'm in Bronson's head once more, though I don't recognize our surroundings.

We appear to be in a...vehicle? I haven't been in many, but my guess is that this is one of the Compound's. Bronson is currently staring out the window, and I marvel at the sights and sounds.

Lights. So many lights. They adorn every building and

tree, giving the town a festive look. Darkness blankets the surroundings, and a moon is bright overhead. Midnight, perhaps?

I don't know for sure where we are, but the storefronts resemble the set of a romantic movie I watched with Abel and Rion the other week. They're so close together that it almost appears to be one long continuous building instead of numerous tiny ones.

My mind is fuzzy as I try to remember all that has happened. A mental inventory confirms that I've been cleaned since I was last awake, though I can't remember why I would need to be washed. And then it hits me with the force of a wrecking ball.

The escape.

Narian.

The Compound.

My powers.

Logan.

Logan!

I sit upright in the car, my pulse skittering and my head pounding.

"Nina," Damien says in alarm, nearly swerving the car into oncoming traffic. Bronson curses and catches the steering wheel from the passenger seat, righting the car.

"Careful!" my growly wolf shifter snaps. "We have precious cargo."

"Logan," I whisper desperately.

"I'm here," a soft voice coos from behind me. "It's okay, Nina. Everything's okay." A gentle hand guides my head back to his lap where I must've been lying. His hand leisurely strokes my hair as my body shakes and shakes and shakes. "You overexerted yourself after…after the showdown," Logan continues. "But you're safe now. The baby's safe. We're all safe."

"Where are the others?" I won't believe it until I see with someone's eyes that they're alive and well. The escape combined with the fight afterwards have left me lightheaded and reeling.

Could we have done it?

Have we really escaped Nightmare Penitentiary?

Are we free?

"They're in the car behind us," Damien explains in that curt way of his. "They're safe."

Logan's hand continues to stroke my hair until it pauses, one of his fingers touching my cheek tenderly. Reverently, almost.

"Nina..."

"I forgive you," I say quickly. "I don't even think I need to forgive you for anything, but I know you were just about to apologize. I forgive you, Logan, but you don't need my forgiveness. I can't blame you for something you never did."

"But I almost did," Logan protests softly. "If I hadn't met you, if I hadn't fallen in love with you," my breath hitches, my heart pounding a racing tune, but he continues on, "if you had just been a normal girl...I would've turned you over to them." Self-loathing thickens his tone.

"I don't believe you would've," I reply automatically, pulling out of Bronson's head so I can focus on Logan. "You see yourself as the villain. As someone who isn't deserving of...anything."

"I'm not deserving of *you*," he states scathingly.

"I don't believe that."

"Nina—"

"I know you're my mate," I interrupt again, attempting to sit up. He pushes me back down. "I can feel the connection between us. Have you...have you known?"

He's a cupid and was able to sense the mate bonds

between me and the others. How long has he known? Why hasn't he said anything?

Logan swallows audibly. "I didn't know."

"Because you weren't looking, man," Bronson says from the front seat. "You didn't even think it was a possibility, so you didn't bother to look."

"Yeah, well..." Logan trails off, the silence stretching between us until it feels fragile.

"I thought you almost died, Logan," I press on. "And I realized..." I pause, suddenly uncomfortable. What do I say to him? I know Kai assured me that the others would be okay with me claiming my mates, but are they really? My hesitation extends a moment too long, and Logan releases a defeated sigh, removing his hand from my face.

"Goddess?" Bronson's voice is a rumble that travels through me.

"Yes?"

"Claim your fucking mate." Heat laces his tone, shooting fire straight to my core.

Logan's breath hitches as I sit up in his lap, straddling him.

"Well...maybe claim your mate with a seatbelt on," Bronson grumbles, and Damien makes a noise in his throat.

"Let the kids be, Bronson," he chastises.

"Drive carefully," Bronson retorts.

"Like a grandma on Sunday," Damien reassures him.

I giggle at their banter before focusing on the man before me. The man with the gentle heart, flirty demeanor, and tattered soul.

Slowly, giving him ample opportunity to pull away, I press my lips to his.

It's the first kiss to end all kisses. Gentle and chaste and achingly sweet. Each brush of his lips feels like fireworks are exploding in my stomach.

I moan into his mouth, and he takes it as permission to deepen the kiss. His hands move to my ass, groping the tender flesh, as he tilts his head to the side. His tongue tangles with mine as I arch into his touch.

We're both gasping for breath when I pull away, though his lips don't leave my skin. He places tender kisses to my jawbone, my throat, the swell of my breast…

He pauses, his warm breath on my skin eliciting goosebumps, and whispers, "We did it." There's a note of wonderment in his voice.

A giddy laugh escapes me when I comprehend what he means. "We did it."

We escaped.

We're free.

"Unless we get caught," Bronson murmurs, and Damien hushes him.

Logan reclaims my lips fervently as I rock against his rapidly hardening dick. I can feel it straining against his pants.

Consumed by desperation, I dig my nails into his shirt and *rip*. He hisses out a breath as my palm touches bare, hot skin.

"Fuck, I want you. I want you so bad," he moans.

"You have me," I promise as I clumsily remove the rest of his shirt.

I know that this isn't the time or place, that we're not truly safe yet, but I can't stop myself. And apparently, neither can he.

He pushes my dress down until my breasts spring free and then takes one of my nipples into his mouth. I gasp, throwing my head back as he licks and sucks on the aching nub. My fingers tangle in his blond hair, my nails scratching at his scalp, but if he's bothered by my rough treatment, he doesn't show it.

I reach between our bodies for his zipper, but his hand on my wrist stops me.

"Sweetheart, are you sure?" He removes his lips from my breasts and presses a chaste kiss to the corner of my lips. "We can stop if you don't—"

"I want you, Logan. I told you that already." I roll my hips against his cock a second time. "You're my mate, and I want you. Every. Last. Part." I punctuate the words with kisses to his jawline, cheek, and lips, respectively. "I want your pain. Your fear. Your happiness. I want the tears you try to hide and the genuine smile you haven't found anyone to be worthy of. I want *you*."

He makes a strangled noise in the back of his throat before claiming my lips with his own and tilting our bodies so I'm sprawled on the seat with him over me. He pushes my dress down the rest of the way, rips away my panties, and then spears me with one of his fingers. I gasp at the sensation, my hips bucking, and Logan kisses away the noise.

"For fuck's sake, drive slower," Bronson snarls.

"I am driving well under the speed limit," Damien responds stiffly. "And for all that is holy, quit touching your cock in front of me! I'm already traumatized from the time I saw Rion's. We are *not* masturbating together."

"Fuck off. You can't even touch yourself, asswipe. Not while you're driving," snaps Bronson.

Logan lifts his weight off of me, and I hear the sound of him removing the remainder of his clothes. When he's on top of me again, I feel nothing but bare skin.

"Are you sure?" He waits until I nod my approval before adding, "You don't know how long I've been imagining this." He slowly slides inside of me, inch by inch, until he's seated to the hilt.

I gasp at the sensation, pleasure flooding me, and I lift my hips to get him to move.

"Logan…"

It's feral and primitive and rough.

Desperate.

Wanton.

Hungry.

He pounds me into the seat with the force of his thrusts, his lips capturing one of my bouncing breasts in his mouth. His other hand tangles in my hair, baring my throat, and when his teeth leave my nipple, it's to graze over the sensitive skin there.

"I'm going to—"

"Come for me," he demands, his free hand playing with my clit. I explode, stars dancing in my vision, but he doesn't stop. He can't.

He's a man possessed.

He flips me so I'm on my hands and knees before plunging his cock back into me. My body is awkwardly bent, but the uncomfortableness is overshadowed by the angle he's hitting with his thick cock. This new position also causes my breasts to dangle, and I lift one hand to fondle them as Logan squeezes my hips.

"Fuck this," Bronson growls.

"What the devil are you doing?" Damien demands, but Bronson doesn't answer. I hear the sound of his seatbelt being removed and then his huge body joins us in the back-seat. "Oh, for fuck's sake! You're not going to fit back there! This isn't a fucking clown car, though I'm beginning to believe you guys think it is."

"Is this okay, Goddess?" Bronson whispers, nibbling my ear.

"Yes," I moan as Logan continues to thrust in and out of me.

I don't know where Bronson fits his huge body, but the next thing I'm aware of is his lips on my nipple. I gasp at the dual sensations as Logan brings his finger back down to my clit and expertly begins to circle it. And then he pushes a little bit of his power into the touch...

I scream like I've never screamed before, my voice turning hoarse.

Damien curses, swerving the car to the sound of many angry honks.

"Can you take me, Goddess?" Bronson growls, and in answer, I twist my head in his direction and open my mouth. A second later, his thick cock brushes my lips as I swallow him.

"Fucking hell, I'm getting passed left and right for going too damn slow," Damien grumbles. "Shall I put my hazards on for you three? Did you forget that we're on the run from the paranormal police?"

His words penetrate my head, but I'm too lost in the tidal wave of pleasure to answer him.

Bronson slides in and out of my mouth as I hollow my cheeks. I try to lift one hand to wrap around the part of his base my mouth can't quite reach, but the car takes that moment to jerk, and I nearly lose my balance. Only Logan's hands on my hips keep me upright.

My cupid's grip turns bruising on my skin as he throws his head back, roaring his release.

Pulling my lips away from Bronson's cock, I tilt my head back. "Logan..."

He grips my hair, forcing me to arch my neck, and then kisses me senseless. I'm sure he can taste Bronson on my mouth, but that only makes me hotter.

"I love you so goddamn much," he murmurs against my mouth before releasing my hair and spanking my ass. "Now go please your other mate."

I whimper but do as instructed, feeling with my hands for Bronson's muscular thighs. He must be uncomfortable the way he's positioned, squished against the door, but he doesn't complain as I crawl onto his lap and line myself up with his hard, thick cock.

He might not be the longest of all of my guys, but he's definitely the thickest. His cock brushes against my walls in a way that's almost uncomfortable as I begin to ride him, my breasts bouncing in front of his face.

"Fuck, I'm gonna come again," Logan warns, and I wonder if he's touching himself. The thought spurs me on, and I quicken my pace, my breaths coming out in shallow pants.

"Can you come for me again?" Bronson's voice is more of a demand than an actual question.

"Yes!" I cry as he presses down on my clit.

"Now!"

We come together, his hips jerking erratically underneath mine before slowing. My orgasm courses through me, liquifying my veins and turning me into a puddle of lust and need and desire.

And love.

So much love.

"I love you," I whisper as I kiss Bronson's lips, sweaty and sated and so incredibly happy.

"I love you with everything that I am," he declares.

"And I love you." I direct that at Damien, who grunts in response, muttering something about 'proving my love in the next vehicle,' before turning towards the last man in the car. My newest mate. "I know that this isn't the most romantic setting." I giggle. "I mean, another man's cock is still inside of me. But I—"

"Not yet," Logan says, placing a finger to my lips and cutting me off. "I want you to be sure."

"But I am—"

"And I want to be worthy of you before you say it," he

continues. "I know what you're going to say, but this is for me as much as for you. I don't think I'll truly believe it until I can prove myself to you. And to your other mates. My...brothers."

My heart swells with love.

"Okay," I reply softly, resting my cheek on Bronson's sweaty chest. I understand where Logan's coming from.

For so long, he's been without love. And when he thought he had it, he discovered it was nothing but an illusion. His past is tainted by shadows and darkness, and I can't even begin to understand all that he went through. But I do love him. The sweet, flirty cupid who makes me laugh and protected me in the Labyrinth. The man who deems himself unworthy of any true happiness.

The past doesn't matter. I want to hear every sordid detail of it, know everything he endured, but it doesn't change my feelings for him.

And we'll get there in time. Soon, he'll know everything there is to know about me, and I, him.

But for now...

I slip into Bronson's head to see him glancing at Logan out of the corner of his eyes.

My cupid's baby-blue eyes are fixed on me, a gorgeous smile lighting up his face.

A smile that will only ever be directed at me.

CHAPTER 48

"What is this strange contraption?" I ask in wonder as I watch the glass slide back up. My finger hovers over the tiny button that seems to be controlling the new and exciting invention I discovered.

"That," Abel reaches over me and places a hand on my wrist, stopping my movements, "is an automated window."

"Wow! Do all vehicular transporters have these?" I query as I rip my hand free of Abel's and press a finger down on the button again. The automated window lowers, and a cold breeze caresses my face. I stick my head farther out the window as I marvel at the lights and sounds of the city we have found ourselves in.

"No fair!" Rion pouts. "He's allowed to stick his head out the window like a dog, but when I try to do that, you threaten to swerve off the road until my head is crushed by a street lamp." He folds his arms over his chest and levels all of us with a fierce glare. "Not. Fucking. Fair."

"The wind feels amazing on my face," I explain, not wanting to upset my eccentric shifter brother.

Abel, sitting on the opposite side of Rion, grins. "You know what would make it feel even better? If you stick your tongue out and pant."

"For fuck's sake..." Cain gripes as I eagerly do what Abel requested of me. My tongue lolls to the side as I release exaggerated panting noises.

"Like this?" I question, my words garbled from how my mouth is opened.

"You can shake your butt too, like it's a tail," Abel suggests. *Weird request...*

I shift until I am crouched down, my head still hanging out the window, and begin to shake my butt back and forth. I have no idea how the butt shaking aspect will add to the pleasure of the wind on my face, but I do not dare question the demon.

Loud guffaws erupt around me, and I awkwardly join in, my head still hanging out the window and my butt shaking.

The outside world...

It is so different from what I imagined. Not even my wildest fantasies could prepare me for this. I do not know where to rest my eyes, as everything demands my complete attention. There are numerous buildings, each one colored in shades of dark brown, black, and red, as well as trees interspersed throughout.

I breathe deeply, my eyes fluttering shut, as I listen to the hearty laughs of drunken men wandering down the street, the giggles of females, and the music blaring from one of the buildings.

It overwhelms and excites me simultaneously.

"Nick," Kai snaps, "get your head back inside the SUV. Now."

"Yes. I will do that." I smile brightly at him as I reclaim my seat, reluctantly rolling the automated window back up. "Where are we going?"

The burly dragon shifter runs his hand through his shoulder-length dark hair as his fingers tap against the steering wheel.

"For now, we're going to get a hotel. We're far enough away from the prison to not raise any red flags. And according to Cain, the prison guards have not been made aware of our escape yet. I imagine Braelyn has played a part in keeping that a secret."

The sex demon, who has a stolen computer balanced on his knees, nods curtly. "Nothing that I can find online, at least. So unless the prison is being hush-hush about our escape, they don't know we left yet."

"That is good." I nod my head seriously. "I do not wish for those men to find my little one." As an afterthought, I add, "Or you guys."

"That makes two of us," Cain murmurs.

"We confirmed that these vehicles have no trackers on them, but we need to lose them now rather than later," Kai continues. "Damien will use one of his illusion spells and the fake ID he made in the last town to get us a few rooms. Hopefully, he'll be able to extend the illusion spell to us when we leave the SUV. I don't want anyone seeing our faces. We'll steal a van capable of holding all of us early tomorrow morning before we leave. But for now, we need to shower, change our clothes, and solidify our plan."

"The Labyrinth made Damien weak," I agree with a nod. "But he should be strong enough for the spell."

A wrinkle appears between Abel's brows. "Aren't *you* the Labyrinth?"

"I was." I shrug my shoulders nonchalantly. "But not anymore."

Abel immediately whips his head around to address Cain and Rion. "Can we just beat the shit out of him already? He talks like a douche."

I talk like…a shit?

Is that not the meaning of the word? Or is deuce the correct synonym for shit? Why is it impossible for me to remember?

Do I talk like a deuce? Is that the correct terminology?

Though I did hear prisoners daily refer to each other as douches and pieces of shits. Do those mean the same thing? I make a mental note to ask Abel about it when I have the chance.

For now, I will go under the assumption that 'douche' is another meaning for 'piece of shit.'

Bringing a finger to my chin, I think of the best way to explain my existence. "I have come from the Labyrinth. I *am* the Labyrinth. A manifestation of its magic, if you would like to be specific. Just like the monsters who attacked Kai. Just like the green mist. Now that I am gone, I believe that the magic of the Labyrinth will eventually fail as well. Think of me…" I consider my words carefully before turning to Rion. "Do you remember that vibrator you used on Nina and your balls a few months ago?"

His eyes widen comically. "For fuck's sake, how did you—"

"Think of me as the batteries that operate the vibrator," I continue, pleased that I have come up with an analogy that they can all relate to. Rion is still staring at me with his mouth popped open. "Without the batteries, the vibrator fails to work. It still exists, but it cannot do what it was meant to. You can still use it to pleasure yourself—or your balls, as Rion did—but it is no longer as effective for stimulation."

I rest back in the seat, satisfied with myself.

Silence descends as all of the men stare at me. Even Kai, who is driving. That is dreadfully unsafe. He really should pay attention to the other vehicular transporters on the road.

"You…" Rion tilts his head to the side. "You watched me stick a vibrator into my girl? And on my balls?"

"And in your asshole," I say with another bright smile. Is this male bonding time? "And in your mouth…though I don't understand why you would put it in your mouth *after* you put it in your asshole. Does the…does the douche make it taste better?"

Does Nina like douches? I would have to ask my little mate as soon as we stop for the night.

"Don't encourage him," Abel whispers out of the corner of his mouth, and the car is basked in silence.

I smile broadly as I finger the button to the automated window once more. "Maybe once Nina and I get into the stage of our relationship where we are sexually intimate, I can take a douche on her. Would she like that?"

Kai almost causes a vehicular transporter accident.

THE "HOTEL" WE ARRIVE AT IS NOT ACTUALLY A HOTEL. THE sign declares it as a motel, whatever that means. When I question Abel about it—he seems the most likely to answer my questions—he tells me "hotel" is a blanket statement. I ask him why statements need blankets, and he tells me, "To keep them warm, of course."

Strange, strange world.

Damien places an illusion spell on himself and uses his fake ID to procure us three rooms side by side.

Despite that, all of the men pile into the one Nina chooses for herself, hovering around her like besotted puppies.

"You're such a sweet little cherry sprinkled in sugar and ready for daddy's mouth, aren't you?" Rion purrs as he drops a sweet little cherry sprinkled in sugar into his mouth.

The men have all picked up food from a gas station—

according to Abel, it is where men go when they have to "let one rip." Very peculiar—and the beds are now cluttered with a collection of candy, wrapped sandwiches, drinks, and more.

Nina sits at a seat near the window, seemingly far away in thought as she gazes blindly at the drawn curtains. Anxiously licking my upper lip, I move to join her.

"Are you okay, little one?" I question as she whips her head in my direction. My heartbeat picks up speed at being the sole focus of her white gaze. Has there ever been a time where I have captured her complete attention? I cannot recall.

A strange, fluttery sensation swirls the meager contents of my stomach around. I think I might vomit.

Having a physical body is very, very strange. For the first time ever, I have to eat. And drink. And go to the restroom.

A lot.

What else will change now that I am free? Will I lose my powers? Will I grow old and eventually die?

I shove those thoughts to a dark corner of my mind, one that consists of nothing but memories of loneliness, and focus on the girl in front of me.

The girl who has altered my entire life.

"Everything has just happened so...suddenly," she confesses at last, her long lashes fluttering against her cheekbones. My pulse skitters. "One second, I'm sentenced to a life in prison, and the next, I'm freed." A huff of dry laughter escapes her. "I'm so grateful to be out of there, but at the same time..." She fiddles with a strand of her long, inky hair and shifts her gaze so it's on my shoulder. "I accepted my position in that life, the Queen of the Labyrinth, but now I need to find a new future for myself. A new role for me and my baby. And I have this constant fear that we're going to get captured, that I'm going to be separated from all of you."

Both her hands come to rest on her stomach. "I don't know if I'm making any sense—"

"You are making complete sense," I interrupt, tentatively claiming the seat opposite her. The other guys have stopped their conversations and are listening intently, though they are trying to be nonchalant about it.

Except for Rion. He has silently moved onto the table during the course of our conversation and is now perched like an eagle directly in front of an oblivious Nina.

"But is it wrong to think that your place...is with us?" I continue. "We can figure out everything as long as we are together." I blow out a breath and run my hand over my buzzed head. "And that is another thing I have been meaning to talk to you about..."

"Guys?" She twists her head to stare in the direction of her other mates. "Can you give us a second?"

Warning growls and rumbles echo throughout the room, and her shoulders sag in annoyance.

"Seriously? You all know he'd never hurt me. Stop being ridiculous and wait in one of the other rooms," she snaps fiercely, and Abel whistles.

"Damn, girl," he purrs, crawling off the bed and sauntering towards her. He presses his lips to her forehead, a twinkle in his eyes. "I love it when you get all feisty. Really makes my cock hard."

"Come on, Casanova," Cain grumbles as he pulls on Abel's shirt collar, tugging him out of the room. "We'll be right outside," he assures Nina.

The rest of the guys slowly, reluctantly, follow after him.

Logan stops directly in front of Nina, and in a move that surprises me, claims her lips in a fiery, passionate kiss.

Joy blooms inside of me, and I smile widely. I am proud of my brother for claiming his mate.

Finally.

He has been so lonely, so despondent, that I am grateful he found a light in the darkness.

Soon, it is just me and Nina…and Rion.

"Babe?" Nina quirks an eyebrow in the shifter's general direction. "You do realize that I know you're there, right?"

Rion, for his part, simply grabs a grocery bag and holds it in front of his face in an attempt to hide from us.

Ridiculous.

He should know that I am able to still see his legs with how he is crouched on the table. He should really practice hide-and-seek in his spare time.

"Rion…" Nina's voice holds a note of warning.

His face wrinkles with his displeasure, and with a heavy sigh, he does a backflip off the table and army crawls out of the room, muttering under his breath, "I'm a ninja."

I make a mental note to whisper *I am a ninja* whenever I leave a room.

Rion is probably a good subject to study for societal norms.

Once the door closes behind him, I turn my attention back to Nina. Her pouty lips are pursed slightly, the color more red than pink, and are so plush and kissable that I have to physically restrain myself from leaning in.

It would be my first kiss.

"I understand your trepidation—" I begin, but she interrupts.

"I don't know you. Not truly." Her long, slender fingers tap against the wooden table. "All I know is that you're the man of my dreams."

My brows furrow in confusion. "Is that not what most females wish for? The man of their dreams to be real?"

Her own face creases. "Well, yes…"

"I am afraid I am confused." I mimic her posture, tapping my fingers against the table in tandem to hers.

A giggle escapes her, seemingly unbidden if her shocked face is any indication. "I think that makes two of us."

"We can…what is the word…*date* if you so desire? Get to know each other." A hint of vulnerability creeps into my voice. "But I have no past, really, to speak of. My days were spent asleep, my magic fueling the powers of the Labyrinth. And even when I was awake, I spent my time watching you."

"You said that before, and I don't—"

"You are my mate," I state simply. "Do you want to hear the exact moment I knew I was in love with you?" I wait for her tiny nod of acquisition before continuing. "When you were fighting that female in the ring. You were bruised and broken and bloody…and I cannot remember ever seeing anyone more beautiful. You fought for what you believed in, what you thought was just, and you emerged stronger because of it. How could I not love you?" My throat closes as I recall that day.

All I could do was observe, my powers not yet strong enough to reach her. Helplessness like I had never felt before coursed through me before that quickly transitioned into blinding anger.

One of the prison guards got lost in the Labyrinth that day and was killed by the monsters, though I cannot find it within me to have any remorse.

"Nick…"

"My past is a blank slate, but my future? My future can be yours, if you want it. Perhaps we can learn this strange new world together."

What if she rejects me?

Then you will continue to do what you have always done.

Watch her from the shadows.

"Nick…" she repeats, seemingly at a loss for words. I can deal with that. I can deal with anything besides an outright rejection. My entire existence revolves around her—quite literally. I would still be lying dormant inside of the maze if she had not awakened me.

"We could go on romantic walks through the park like they do in the movies you like to watch," I press on, my knee bouncing. "Or we could…" My eyes snag on a strange device I recognize from the Labyrinth's kitchen. "Go on a coffee date."

I practically trip over my own two feet in my haste towards it.

How the devil do you work this thing?

I press a button at random before remembering that I need to put the brown drug powder inside of the slot thingy. Where is the brown drug powder?

Nina giggles, the sound instantly calming my frayed nerves.

"Do you even know how to make coffee?" she questions in amusement, and I glance at her over my shoulder.

"I am just looking for the brown drug powder," I explain, grabbing a squishy cup and turning it over and over in my hands.

"You mean ground coffee?" Another laugh escapes her as she moves to join me.

"Yes," I say, flustered. "My apologies."

Ground coffee.

Not brown drug powder.

Noted.

"Don't apologize," Nina says, taking the cup from my hand. "And I don't need any coffee." Her nose wrinkles adorably, and I have to fight the urge to press a quick kiss to it. "Honestly, I don't like the taste. It's sharp and bitter. But," a smile dances on her pretty face, "if you add a bunch of cream and sugar, it tastes super sweet."

"Are you talking about my cum again, Buttercup?"

We both jump at the sound, turning in the direction of the voice.

Perched on the ceiling fan—one that is precariously close to collapsing from the ceiling—is Rion. He gives a two-fingered salute.

"Rion," Nina admonishes with a huff.

"Don't mind me. I'm just a *fan* of this conversation." In the next second, a tiny cat takes the place of a man. He walks in a circle, his whiskered face twitching, before curling into a ball and staring down at us with wide, yellow eyes.

"You're such a stalker," Nina says with an amused shake of her head.

Rion simply lifts his little paws before piercing me with an indecipherable stare. And then one of his paws lifts as if he's mimicking cutting his own throat.

I feel like he is threatening me. But I do not understand why. Or maybe he is asking me to cut his throat for him? That seems strange, but what do I know?

"Ignore him," Nina says, claiming my attention once more. "I do."

An irritated hiss echoes from above us.

But not even Rion can alleviate the tension coursing through me. What I am about to ask her…

It is the most important question a man like me could ever ask.

"Nina," I begin softly, "you were right when you said we do not know each other that well yet." *Though I have been watching you for over a year and have heard all of your deepest, darkest secrets.* "But I want to. I want to know everything there is to know about you. I want to wake up with you beside me and fall asleep with you in my arms. I will be the best mate possible, if you give me the chance."

I don't breathe as I await her answer. I have to curl my hands into fists to keep them from shaking.

If she says no…

If she turns me away…

I will respect her wishes, though a piece of my soul will perish.

"Yes," Nina answers at last, a sheepish smile materializing on her face. And I know then that my life has truly begun. It will be riddled with tumultuous storms and deadly traps, but Nina is worth all of that and more. Nothing else matters from this point on. "Nick, you're my mate. I don't know what the future will hold, but I want you by my side. I want *all* of you by my side. Forever."

A delicate blush stains her cheeks, almost as if she is embarrassed by her candid words, but my heart swells with love for this incredible woman.

We do not kiss as I take her into my arms and hold her tight. I know that this is not an appropriate time and our relationship is not there yet. But soon.

Soon, I will be able to kiss her without fear of her reaction. Without worry of my own worth.

For now, I will prove to her every second of every day that she made the right choice accepting me as her mate.

I will love her until the day I die, and if there is a life after that, I will love her then too.

All of us—me, her, my brothers—are so inextricably tied together that there is no escaping. No running or hiding or leaving.

It is all of us against the world.

Forever.

CHAPTER 49

NINA

We drive nonstop for the next two days, the guys switching out who's driving and who's… offering me comfort in the backseat in the form of naked, sweaty bodies. Of course, they've been making me keep my seatbelt on, so we're forced to get creative.

Not that I mind.

When we finally stop at our destination, I gasp in wonderment, using Cain's eyes to see our surroundings.

It appears to be a camp nestled deep in the woods of a sprawling mountain. In the distance, I can see rocky peaks cresting the clouds, highlighted by the golden-orange sun. Trees spread as far as the eye can see, their tapestries a shade of verdant green in the summer season. Interspersed throughout are log cabins. Some are small, appearing to be only a single room, while others are towering high above the tree line. Sandy pathways connect all of the cabins to each other before leading to another cluster of buildings. One restaurant and a few stores sit in a circle around a stone fountain of a wolf.

And speaking of wolves…

They're *everywhere.*

Russet fur, black fur, white fur. Some look to reach only my knees, while others appear as if they'll tower above my head. Their furry heads twist in our direction as we drive past in the van we stole.

Bronson, in the passenger seat, beams back at me.

"Welcome to my pack, Goddess."

An older woman bearing a striking resemblance to Bronson stands in front of the fountain, a young girl on either side of her.

She's beautiful. I notice that instantly. Her blonde hair, now peppered with silver from age, hangs in two loose braids over both of her shoulders. Her unbuttoned red flannel shirt reveals a black tank top underneath, and her jeans are covered in stylish holes. She looks younger than what I know her actual age to be, emanating an innocence at odds with the fierceness in her stare.

"Bronson," I whisper, stunned. They've told me the plan numerous times since we left the motel two days ago, but I still can't wrap my head around it. "Are you sure this is safe?" The last thing I want is for our presence to put his family at risk. I would never forgive myself if anything happened to them. He already lost his younger sister, Ali, and I know it will break him to lose anyone else in his family or pack.

"This is the safest place we can be," Damien interjects from beside me. "Pack laws are different from those imposed on us by the Council. Nightmare Penitentiary would be required to procure a special warrant if they wish to search the premises."

"And by then, we will have enough warning to hide," Kai adds. A smile graces his handsome face as he stares out the windshield. It's fleeting, there and gone in under a second, but my heart skips a beat at the sight. Because that smile…

It was laced with *relief.*

For the first time ever, we don't have to constantly fight. Hide. Run.

Maybe, just maybe, we can settle down and *live.*

"There's a system of caves in the mountains that no one but our pack members know about," Bronson adds, pointing towards the mountain range in the distance. "If for some reason the pack gets searched by the supernatural police, we can hide there and no one will be the wiser."

"There are also numerous spells surrounding the property that prohibit most people from entering." Damien purses his lips as he stares disdainfully out the window. He looks out of place in his crisp black suit and tie when compared to the lumberjack type men ambling about, staring curiously at our vehicle.

"This community...they'll die before they give us up," Bronson whispers, reaching back to squeeze my hand. "I'd never ask them to do that, but I can't deny the comfort and relief I feel to know that they'll do everything within their power to protect you and our child. And speaking of our baby...he or she will be the happiest little bugger in the world. She'll want for nothing."

"So you think it's a girl," I tell him, shooting a smug smirk in Kai's direction. He rolls his eyes good-naturedly.

"If it is a girl," Bronson begins, his voice a growl, "she'll never be allowed to date."

"Never?" I cock an eyebrow.

"Well, maybe when she's thirty."

"Forty," Cain interjects.

"Fifty," Rion argues.

"Not even then," Abel says solemnly. "She'll be single for life. No guys will even be able to look at her."

"What if she likes girls?" I counter. "Can she date then?"

"Well," Rion pretends to think about it for a second, "girls aren't as stinky as boys are."

"Oh my god!" I laugh, swatting at his chest. "Is that how you're going to decide who dates our daughter? If the person is stinky or not?"

"It's a logical solution!" Rion protests, raising his hands in mock surrender.

"I still think it's a boy. My little man," Kai says as he slides out of the van and breathes in deeply. A few of the wolves growl at his presence, a dragon amongst wolves, but Kai stretches his taut muscles, seemingly unperturbed.

Bronson exits the vehicle next, opens up the back door, and all but yanks me into his arms. I slide out of Cain's head and into his. Still holding me, Bronson hurries towards the woman gaping at us.

"Momma." Bronson finally places me on my feet. "I—"

"My boy!" The woman throws herself into Bronson's arms as she sobs. He pats her back soothingly as she clings to him. "When you said you made it out of there, I didn't think... I mean, no one ever makes it out of Nightmare Penitentiary... I just..."

"What she means to say is that she's happy you're here, doofus," one of the girls I noticed earlier interprets. This one has a pretty, oval face and unnaturally bright red hair.

"You dyed your hair." Bronson's voice is muffled from where he rests his lips against his mother's head. "Again."

"And she *still* has a boyfriend," the younger one pipes in. Her light brown hair cascades around a cherubic, square face and draws attention to her bright green eyes—the exact same shade as Bronson's.

Bronson stiffens at the girl's words, pulling away from his mom and casting a fierce glare in the red-headed girl's direction.

"Is that true?"

"Momma! Tell him to stop being a caveman," she protests, stomping her foot.

"Bronson." The beautiful woman captures his face between both of her palms. "Aren't you going to introduce me to…" She trails off with a pointed look in my direction. Bronson's face flushes red with shame and embarrassment. Both girls turn to stare at me eagerly, tiny smirks erupting on their faces.

"Is that…?"

"She's gorgeous!"

"Why didn't you tell us?!"

"Momma." Bronson's voice is heady with pride and warmth as he wraps an arm around my waist and pulls me into his side. "This is my mate, Nina. Nina, this is my mom, Gemma."

"Hello." I duck my head, suddenly unbearably shy. Through Bron's eyes, I watch the woman's face soften instantly.

"Hello, Nina." She captures both of my hands in hers, and a startled squeal escapes me, one she graciously ignores. I've been doing much better with touch now that I have my men, but sometimes, I still feel antsy when strangers touch me without warning.

"Mom!" Bronson snaps, but she simply gives my hands a comforting squeeze, ignoring him.

"Thank you, Nina, for protecting and loving my son. He's told me so much about you."

"Almost too much," the red-haired girl murmurs, and her sister giggles.

"It's a pleasure to meet you too," I reply earnestly. And it is. To see the woman who gave life to one of the men I love above all else…

No words can express how much she means to me. I already love her just because of how much she loves her son.

"These are my girls, Bronson's sisters. Marbella—"

"Bella," the redhead corrects.

"—and Lola."

The youngest lifts her hand in an eager wave.

"You're *so* much prettier than Bronson's last girlfriend. I like you already. And what happened to your eyes? I've never seen white eyes before. Are they contacts or real? Bella tried contacts before and—"

"Spitfire!" Bronson bellows, and she smiles sheepishly, suddenly looking embarrassed.

"We can talk once we settle in," I assure her. "I really need to have some girl time." Her face brightens instantly as she bounces from foot to foot. "And we can talk *all* about Bronson's ex-girlfriends…as long as they don't live here as well."

Bronson groans as both Lola and Bella giggle.

"I hate you both."

"You loveeee us," Lola singsongs. "But not as much as you love her." She points towards me, and this time, it's *my* turn to blush crimson.

"Lola, don't embarrass your sister-in-law," Gemma chastises, and I swear my face turns into a sauna.

It takes me a moment to smother the flames of embarrassment and speak coherently.

"I can't even begin to describe how grateful I am that you took us in," I manage to say to the kind-eyed woman. "I don't want to put you and your family at risk—"

"You guys *are* my family," she says automatically, squeezing my hands once more. "And the entire pack will agree."

Almost as if they've been eavesdropping, a chorus of howls reverberate through the evening sky. It's a beautiful, haunting sound, one that entices goosebumps to break out on my skin.

"Let me introduce you to the rest of Nina's mates,

Momma," Bronson suggests, gesturing behind him towards where the other men stand. Bella narrows her eyes at them distastefully, while Lola blushes crimson, especially when her gaze lands on Damien. It seems as if the small girl finds my mage attractive.

I snicker thinking about Bronson's reaction to that.

"Damien, Kai, Logan, Cain, Abel, Rion, and Nick," Bronson introduces, pointing down the line.

"Thank you for opening up your home," Kai says sincerely, moving to step forward and shake her hand.

"You're our family now," Gemma replies without preamble. "And we protect our family. We already have a cabin ready for all of you—the biggest one available."

"You didn't have to do that," I protest meekly, but she waves my words away.

"Nonsense! We'll never separate a family, and that's what you guys are now. A family."

My hands drop to my stomach as something rushes through me. An emotion I can't quite remember experiencing before.

Hope.

"Especially with this little one on the way," I say softly.

And…

And I allow myself to picture a future. One where we're not prisoners. One where we're not leaders of a vicious, deadly gang. One where we don't have assassins gunning for us and evil Compounds lurking over our heads.

One where we're all…happy. Or as happy as we can be.

Where we're safe and protected, surrounded by family and the people we love. Where our baby can not only survive, but flourish.

A wistful smile tugs at my lips.

"A baby!" Gemma's mouth pops open comically as Lola and Bella both squeal. "Why didn't you…?" She begins whacking Bronson on the arm. "Why didn't you tell me that *I was going to be a grandma?*"

"Because our phone call last night had to be quick so it didn't get traced," Bronson protests. "And I didn't know Nina was pregnant when you last visited me in pris—"

"That's no excuse!" Her voice turns shrill as she pierces her daughters with desperate, wild eyes. "Tell Tom down at the hardware store to start putting things together for a nursery. And inform Doctor Everett that we're taking Nina in for an appointment as soon as they're settled. And…"

I tune them out as I leave Bronson's eyes and go into Rion's. As expected, my eccentric shifter is whipping his head from side to side, attempting to stare at everything at once. When I focus on him, I can hear him mumble, "That tree is good for climbing. And that one will make a nice sleeping tree. And that one is good for fucking my buttercup. And that one—" His eyes move to a lone figure standing beside the van, his brown trench coat flapping around him in the evening breeze.

Nick.

My heart aches at the lonely look in his amber eyes, the way he glances in our direction before immediately looking away. I thought our conversation two days ago would've alleviated some of the tension in his shoulders, but I guessed wrong.

Using Rion's eyes as guidance, I move away from my men and towards Nick.

He glances up when I'm directly in front of him, a soft smile playing on his thick, pouty lips.

"Hello, little one." His deep, baritone voice rumbles through me, and I shiver. I've never been one to get turned on by voices, but maybe I just haven't found the right one. I definitely feel something I've never felt before when he speaks to me.

His body hovering over mine, his husky voice curling around me as he screams my name...

I blush at the direction of my thoughts and ask, "What are you doing all the way over here by yourself?"

He hesitates, a wrinkle appearing between his brows, before confessing, "I was not sure if I would be welcomed."

My mouth drops open. "Why would you think that?"

"Because I have not known you and the others that long. At least, you all have not known me. Even Logan is better suited for this family than I am." There's no reproach in his voice, no anger. Just grim acceptance that steals the breath from my lungs.

"Nick, you know that's not true. We talked about it."

His face creases. "Yes, you said you would be willing to give me a try as a mate. But I believe we are still in the—how do I say this—trial period? Yes, we are still in the trial period. I do not know if that constitutes me being a member of this family."

A bark of laughter escapes me as I grip both of his hands and squeeze them. "Nick, there is no trial period. I want to date you, yes, but you're still my mate. That's never going to change. You're a part of this family, a part of *me*, and I'm sorry I didn't make that clearer to you."

He swallows heavily, his hands shaking when he brings them up to cup my face. "Can I...? Can I kiss you?"

In answer, I push up onto my tiptoes and press my lips to his. It's a chaste kiss, softer than what I'm used to.

Fireworks explode behind my eyelids as I lose myself in Nick, in my final mate. A giddy part of me relishes being his first kiss. His first *everything*.

And hopefully, his last as well.

I don't know what the future will hold for me and my men, but I know that with them by my side, I can face anything.

CHAPTER 50

NINA

THREE YEARS LATER

"Mommy!" My three-year-old daughter tugs incessantly at my skirt, demanding my attention. "I want juice box." I turn my attention away from her twin brother to smile down at her.

"Did you already ask Daddy Kai?"

"I want juice box," she insists, tugging again. I smirk at her indulgently.

"But did you already ask Daddy Kai?" I press, reaching blindly for her tiny shoulder.

"Yes…" I can tell from her wobbly voice that her lower lip is trembling.

"And what did he say?"

"Daddy Kai meany! He say no!" She stomps a foot as I bite down on my lip to hold in my laughter.

"And why did he say no, baby?"

"Cuz I have one," she whines, and I finally give in and giggle, leaning down to press a kiss to her forehead.

"You know you're only allowed to have one open at a time. Where did you put the juice box we already gave you?"

"Daddy Rion took it to space!" she declares immediately, and my smile broadens.

"Oh, did he?"

"I'm innocent!" The man in question screams from directly behind me. I slide into his eyes just in time to see him pick up Carter, our devious son. We can't be certain—we decided not to do a paternity test—but we think Carter is Abel's biological child. He has his father's mischievous streak. No doubt, the three-year-old is thinking of ways to steal a new juice box for his sister. He's already fiercely protective of her. I can't even imagine how he'll be when they're older.

"So you didn't send Callie's juice box to outer space?" I ask my crazy shifter husband, cocking an eyebrow.

He steps towards me and plants a tender, mind-numbing kiss on my lips. I immediately try to deepen it...before remembering we have two toddlers staring up at us with wide, innocent eyes.

But every day I fall even more in love with my mates until it feels like I'm bursting from it. And every day I desire them even more. I didn't think it was even possible to love them as much as I do, but I desire them with a ferocity capable of pulling the moon from the sky.

"That would involve me building a rocket," Rion murmurs as he pulls away from me. "And the last time I tried to build a rocket ship..."

"You blew up the entire garage," I finish with a laugh.

"Abel dared me," Rion defends immediately. "And you know I can't say no to dares involving rocket ships."

"How many dares involving rocket ships have you—"

Rion interrupts me with a kiss I can feel in my very soul.

My toes curl up in my shoes, and I half expect my wings to burst from my back and fly me towards the sun.

The last three years…

They've been heaven.

The cabin Gemma gifted us is as far back into the forest as possible. It's a spacious, three-story manor with over fifteen bedrooms and ten and a half bathrooms. It has everything I never knew I needed.

Even a torture room for Rion and Damien, though the two like to pretend I don't know it exists.

The walls and floors are constructed of unpainted wood, but instead of giving the cabin a rustic aesthetic, it looks surprisingly modern. The black leather couches immediately to the left of the main entrance are arranged in a semicircle around a flatscreen TV and provide a hint of color to the brown room. All of the appliances are sparkling new and either white or black. At first, I thought the monotonous colors gave the room a masculine flare, but the hint of beige and pink throughout softens it. Windows take up the entire back wall of the cabin. Bulletproof, of course. They let in so much sunlight that most days, we don't bother turning on any lamps.

Bronson was right. The three times the officials came to look for us, we knew two days in advance and were able to hide in the surprisingly cozy caves. But we haven't had anyone search for us in years. Not after…

Not after the Labyrinth failed and hundreds of prisoners escaped, most of them significantly more dangerous than me and my men. I always feel a stab of guilt in my chest when I think of all of those criminals free in the world, but Kai assures me time and time again that it's not my fault. It's not Nick's fault either. Still, his soothing words do very little to assuage my guilt.

Only a few weeks after I heard on the news that the prisoners escaped, I received a phone call from Braelyn. She's living in Spain now with Jenny and is happier than ever. They told me Haley escaped as well, though they don't know where she's hiding, only that she hasn't been caught.

Rebecca was killed during the escape. Shot down by guards.

I cried for days when I heard the news, though I couldn't help but notice the strange look on Kai's face when he thought no one was looking.

Still, I count my blessings every day that Braelyn and Jenny are alive and flourishing. They may not have been the best people in the world, but they're my friends. Hopefully, I'll be able to see them again.

My stomach chooses that moment to twist uncomfortably, and I release a groan of pain.

"Mommy!" Callie screams in alarm, and Rion spins to face me. I hear the pound of footsteps, and a moment later, the room is full of testosterone.

"I'm fine!" I assure my mates, waving them away. "The baby just kicked."

"Because he's fierce like his daddy," Bronson says smugly, placing a hand on my lower back and rubbing gently.

"Um…he's a hugger, not a fighter," Logan protests. "I'm sure of it."

"He's already thinking of ways to stab all of you in the neck," deadpans Damien. Abel and Cain both cackle.

"Did he just make a joke?" Abel asks, wiping an imaginary tear from his eye. "I think we're growing on him." When Damien swivels his gaze in Abel's direction, my trickiest demon pales and attempts to hide behind Cain. "I'm just kidding. He's still scary as fuck."

"And don't you forget it," Damien snaps, but the second he turns away, I can see his lips tugging into a grin. And when our little girl throws herself at his legs, that grin trans-

cially since Nick seems to like it when I pull on the strands during sex.

"Nina." He chuckles against my boob as he lifts his head and claims my lips once more. He's very, very careful not to place his body on top of mine. Instead, he rests all of his weight on his elbows as he hovers over me.

Protecting me and my unborn baby.

Like always.

He presses his lips to my neck and creates a blazing trail down my breasts, then over my stomach, and finally to my wet core. He shifts to his knees and rips my dress down the middle, baring my flesh to him.

When he doesn't immediately touch me, I wiggle uncomfortably.

"You are not wearing any panties," he muses in wonder, placing one finger into my tight channel and swirling it through my juices.

I blush when I think about the way Rion and Damien tag-teamed me only a few hours earlier. Damien pocketed my underwear, and I forgot to put on a new pair.

"That is…so sexy." He lowers himself between my legs and tentatively rests his tongue against my flesh. He doesn't lick me right away. Instead, he simply sits there, as if he's memorizing my flavor.

"Nick!" I beg, thrusting my hips into his mouth.

He chuckles, the dark, delicious sound flooding my system until I'm consumed by him and only him. "So eager, little one."

He places his dark hands beneath both of my thighs and lifts them up until they're resting on his shoulders.

And then, he feasts.

Unlike my other lovers, who have *way* more experience than I care to admit, Nick learned my body and my body alone. Through trial and error, he figured out exactly what I liked and how I liked it. Which spots make me gasp and have my hips bucking.

So when his tongue circles my sensitive bundle of nerves, I just about jump out of my skin. And when his teeth graze my clit and his fingers scissor inside my channel, I begin to cry, begging for release.

"Nick!" I beg tearfully, but instead of giving me what I want, he pulls away and stands. I hear the sound of fabric hitting the ground and spread my legs even wider. He settles his huge body on top of me, kissing the corner of my lips.

I don't need vision to know that Nick is a chiseled work of art. Dark skin, sinewy muscles, a face capable of making angels weep...

And mine.

He's all mine.

His thick cock teases my entrance, wetting itself on my arousal.

"Are you ready for me?" he whispers as he kisses me once more.

"Always, my love," I reply as he thrusts himself inside of me. We both groan at the contact, and he pauses, allowing me a second to adjust to his considerable girth, before he begins to rock his hips.

He makes love to me slowly, languidly, both of us knowing we have all the time in the world.

There are no prison guards threatening us.

No Compound coming for my blood.

No assassins.

Just us, our family, and our future.

Nick thrums my clit as if it's a string on the guitar he's been learning to play. Damien has been a great teacher.

In more ways than one, if the way Nick controls my body and pleasure is any indication.

"Come for me, Nina," Nick whispers, and we reach the

precipice together. It's slow and beautiful and earth-shatter-ing. It's that sensation you get when you climb the highest mountain and look down at the landscape below. When you feel so inconsequential and insignificant in comparison to the world as a whole.

And my family?

They *are* my world.

Ecstasy rips me apart and then stitches me back together. Or maybe that's just him and his talented cock. Either way, I'm ruined.

"You didn't tell us you were going to have an orgy!" Rion says, bursting into the room. I don't bother to cover myself as I turn my blind gaze in his general direction.

"It's not an orgy with two people, Mr. Scruffles," I tease. "But you're more than welcome to join in."

"Don't mind if I do..." Before he can shut the door completely, I hear more footsteps entering. I slip into Nick's eyes to see that all of my mates are surrounding the bed, half of their clothes discarded on the floor.

"Wait!" I protest around a laugh as I greedily drink up all of my men on display. Damien's shirt is half unbuttoned, showing off the sculpted planes of his chest. The twins are entirely naked and are already stroking their erect cocks. Kai has his shirt off, and Bronson is removing his clothes as we talk. Logan is simply standing beside me, staring down at my flushed and naked body with his baby-blue eyes blanketed in heat and desire.

And Rion? He's already climbing onto the bed and dangling his cock above my head.

"Open sesame!" he declares, poking my cheek with his dick. I laugh and twist my head away—only to have Abel do the exact same thing on the other side. I'm suddenly surrounded by naked men and cocks. Lots and lots of cocks.

"Wait!" I protest, giggling. "What about the—"

"Mom took them for the night," Bronson explains, placing a hand on my pregnant belly. "So tonight, you're ours."

I suddenly find myself on the receiving end of eight lustful stares. Heat blazes through my body, and I tighten my thighs around Nick's waist, hoping to alleviate some of the pressure in my core. I'm afraid to admit that I actually whimper, so consumed by the love I feel for all of them.

I love them all. And I'll make sure to tell them every day for the rest of my life.

Our story is not a traditional fairy tale. How can it be when my men baptized themselves in blood and became knights of darkness and sin?

But it's *our story.*

A story full of pain and heartache. Of betrayal and regrets. Of fear and happiness. It's a story of first love and old love, of friends and enemies.

And just like with all romances, my story ends in a happily ever after.

"Maybe," I begin slowly, flashing them a smile. "Maybe, you guys are *mine.*"

Through Nick's eyes, I watch all of my men grin hungrily down at me.

"Yours," they agree at once, their voices blending together.

Mine. Yours.

Ours.

Forever and always.

The way it was always meant to be.

I was blindly indicted, imprisoned for a crime I didn't commit, but I fell in love. I fell in love eight separate times with eight incredible men.

And that love freed me, both metaphorically and literally.

It *acquitted* me.

And I've never been happier.

AFTERWORD

Wow! I honestly have no words to say. This is one of my favorite series I've ever written. I absolutely adore Nina and her men.

Thank you all so, so much for sticking with me. This second book wouldn't have come about if it hadn't been for the support and encouragement from my readers. Thank you guys for convincing me to revisit this world and these characters. I'm so happy I was able to give Nina and her mates the ending they deserve.

And I'm sorry if I ripped your heart out during the process. We're all good now, yeah?

ACKNOWLEDGMENTS

I would like to thank my readers first and foremost for convincing me to revisit this world. I'm so happy I listened to you guys!!!

Thank you to my alphas for helping me make this book worthy of publication. I was so nervous to release a sequel, and you guys talked me off the ledge more times than I can count.

Finally, a big thank you to my editor for squeezing me in and polishing my manuscript for me. You're the best!

ABOUT THE AUTHOR

Katie May is a reverse harem author, a KDP All-Star winner, and an USA Today Bestselling Author. She lives in West Michigan with her family and cat. When not writing, she could be found reading a good book, listening to broadway musicals, or playing games. Join Katie's Gang to stay updated on all her releases! And did you know she has a TikTok? Yeah, me either. Follow her here! But be warned...she's an awkward noodle.

2. First Dates

3. Group Outing

4. Game Night

5. Exes

Kingdom of Wolves (Shifter Reverse Harem Duet)

1. Torn to Bits

2. Ripped to Shreds

CO-WRITES

Afterworld Academy with Loxley Savage (Academy Fantasy Reverse Harem)

1. Dearly Departed

2. Darkness Deceives

3. Defying Destiny

Darkest Flames with Ann Denton (Paranormal Reverse Harem)

1. Demon Kissed

1.5. Demon Stalked

2. Demon Loved

3. Demon Sworn

STAND-ALONES

Toxicity (Contemporary Reverse Harem)

Blindly Indicted (Prison Reverse Harem)

Not All Heroes Wear Capes (Just Dresses) (Short Comedic Reverse Harem)

Charming Devils (Bully/Revenge Reverse Harem)

Goddess of Pain (Fantasy Reverse Harem)

Demon's Joy (Holiday Reverse Harem)

www.ingramcontent.com/pod-product-compliance
Lightning Source LLC
Chambersburg PA
CBHW031238310726
48971CB00004B/1080